THE FORTUNATE ORPHANS

# THE FORTUNATE ORPHANS

A NOVEL BY CRAIG MACINTOSH

FOR JOAN—
REVENGE IS SWEET!
NOT SWEET!
MAC

ISBN 10: 1-59298-271-9
ISBN 13: 978-1-59298-271-4

Library of Congress Catalog Number: 2008942583
Printed in the United States of America
First Printing: 2009
12  11  10  09  08    5  4  3  2  1

Cover design by Kent Mackintosh
Interior design by Ryan Scheife, Mayfly Design

BEAVER'S POND
PRESS

Beaver's Pond Press, Inc.
7104 Ohms Lane, Suite 101
Edina, MN 55439-2129
(952) 829-8818
www.BeaversPondPress.com

To order, visit www.BookHouseFulfillment.com
or call 1 (800) 901-3480. Reseller discounts available.

For my father, and his fellow veterans of World War II,
who answered the call and saved the world.

*"Vengence is mine; I will repay, saith the Lord."*

(ROMANS 12: 19)

# ACKNOWLEDGEMENTS

No book is a solitary effort, and I am indebted to many people for helping shape this story. Thank you to best-selling author John Camp for his initial encouragement and introductions to friends in the publishing world.

Two individuals in particular were responsible for shaping the story. I am grateful to Mademoiselle LaRae Ellingson, a teacher with an inexhaustible knowledge of all things French. Her input was critical, particularly for the European scenes.

For the realism of the forensics and ballistic details, I owe special thanks to a friend in the FBI who wishes to remain anonymous. I'm also grateful to Karen Little and Bob Cristofono.

Several persons read my manuscript and gave me wise advice. Foremost was Cynthia Rogers, an editor who possesses a keen eye for clarity and grammar. Her work was crucial. WWII veteran Ray Christensen, and his wife Ramona, weighed in with valuable comments about the early scenes. John Vessey and John M. O'Connell, both retired Army generals, graciously read my book and furnished valued quotes of endorsement. Howard Lyon, a good friend, and also a WWII veteran, added his approval. Bob Mathis read chapters on Normandy and Bastogne for accuracy, and Ron and Mary Bosrock, seasoned European travelers, were kind enough to read the London sections. Chief Mike Scott of the Eagan Fire Department added his expertise.

The staff of Beaver's Pond Press is due a thank you for shepherding this manuscript. Milt Adams, Joe Moses, Amy Cutler and Dara Moore watched over the book's progress. Michele Bassett used her considerable skills to proofread the text. My brother, Kent, contributed his design talents as did Ryan Scheife.

My wife Linda supported my writing throughout the process.

# PROLOGUE

On December 16, 1944, more than 200,000 German soldiers in five armored divisions and twelve infantry divisions smashed into American lines in the Ardennes. A majority of the nearly 90,000 U.S. casualties occurred in the first three days of battle as the Germans poured through the shattered defenses. What became known as the Battle of the Bulge was the single bloodiest combat the American Army fought during WWII.

Soldiers and civilians alike suffered grievously at the hands of the infamous Waffen SS during their murderous thrust into Belgium and Luxembourg. In the end the Americans prevailed and the Germans were forced to retreat, leaving behind nearly 85,000 casualties of their own.

The war in Europe would continue for another five months.

# CHAPTER ONE

## ARDENNES, DECEMBER 16, 1944, 8:30 A.M.

He was alone now.

Struggling uphill, every yard a tortured step in deep snow, he barely glimpsed his trail marked by tiny drops of red. He was a drab brown, ragged bundled shape. A target, silhouetted against the white carpet. Somewhere to his front he knew there was a road.

His helmet bobbed as he lurched ahead, left arm held close to his chest. He groaned as he leaned into the wind, an M1 rifle serving as a staff. Staggering more than walking, he willed himself to reach the road, and when he finally found it he paused at the edge of the snow-packed track and listened. Though he had wrapped a heavy overcoat over a wool sweater, he was certain his heart would betray him. Its rapid pounding seemed to echo in the woods.

He stabbed stiffening legs into the snow and pushed his reluctant body the last few yards onto a narrow slushy path. Suddenly, Private First Class William Noble was standing like a sentinel at the side of a one-track roadway. Gradually his heartbeat slowed and his breath slackened from ragged clouds of steam to measured breathing. He looked down at his left sleeve, slick with blood beginning to freeze against his coat, his limb immobile.

Unless he moved, they would find him like this. Frozen solid. A roadside statue of carved ice.

Noble squinted left and right to make sure the road was empty.

It was clear. Safe for now. *God, watch over me*, he prayed.

He stood there, head back in the cold air, scanning skeletal treetops, smiling at his accomplishment. Far behind him, more to his right now, loud rumblings of artillery. *Ours or theirs?* he wondered. Most likely the enemy's. He looked down at frozen tire tracks carved like furrows in the snow and set off in the opposite direction from the growing thunder.

He walked for what he thought an eternity along the deserted road, empty rifle slung over his right shoulder. To slake his thirst he bent to scoop fresh snow with his free hand, savoring the taste. Occasionally he stopped to listen to the woods around him. Only distant booming from artillery broke the silence.

Noble walked for another hour, the road gradually descending into a narrow ravine lined with towering pines. He thought about taking to the woods to avoid the road altogether, but he was tired and wet and decided to continue following the trail.

As he crested the hill, he spotted coiling smoke ahead. Cautiously, he approached an intersection in the forest.

A burning jeep. American.

Judging from the splintered trees and twisted metal, it had taken a shell burst. Small flames still licked at the smashed vehicle. He stopped to warm himself, ignoring a grotesque charred shape with blackened claw hands still clutching the wheel. He drew strength from the warmth, but when the flames sputtered and died he began walking again. Up the road were two more American bodies, one headless, probably hurled into the road during the shelling.

For the next twenty yards he found equipment strewn across the road, and he helped himself to two bandoliers of ammo and a partially burned blanket with shrapnel holes. Cannon fire was louder now and he hurried from the targeted crossroad. The woods thinned at the edge of a small clearing and he weighed the danger of crossing two hundred yards of open meadow. His road ran straight toward hills with thick stands of dark trees on the far side.

Before crossing, he paused to pull one clip from a bandolier and tried to push the ammo into his rifle. The bolt was frozen. Welded shut by the cold.

He cursed himself for not having freed the weapon over the jeep's flames when he had the chance. Noble shouldered the useless M1 and tucked the blanket around his shoulders before stepping into the clearing.

Without knowing he was there, artillery followed him, tossing a series of shells into woods behind him. Noble tried to guess the origin and size. German 88s, maybe bigger. There had been rumors along the front of monstrous railway guns the size of battleships, but no one had seen them. He hurried along, mouthing another silent prayer. *Please God, don't let me be caught in the open. It would be cruel to let me get this far only to end it here.*

Noble pushed himself as fast as he dared, the left arm causing him constant pain. He finally gained the dark woods and breathed easier. He knelt in a ditch to gather more snow and heard metallic clicking sounds.

"Don't move, you sonofabitch!" Brooklyn English, a good sign.

He rose slowly with his right hand high in the air.

Two silhouettes appeared at his front, rifles pointed at him.

"Private William Noble. American!" he volunteered.

Two men halted, shapes with weapons trained on him. A voice from behind barked, "Who you with?" The silhouettes separated to cover him from both sides, weapons ready.

"What division?" someone behind him asked.

"Hundred and Sixth," he answered.

"All right, check him out, boys."

He was hustled into the woods and a short, filthy, bearded soldier took the M1 from him and opened Noble's greatcoat to frisk him. The GI's partner stepped back and kept his rifle ready. The smaller man checked his dog tags and then fished in Noble's pockets for personal items. The wounded private looked down at the interrogator examining his belongings.

"He's okay, sir. Checks out. Name really is Noble."

They handed back his M1 and for the first time since he began his odyssey, Noble felt relief. His eyes filled with tears and he choked back his emotions.

"Need some chow?" a voice asked from the thicket.

"Yeah, I haven't eaten in two days," he said gratefully.

"Soleski, get Mister Noble some grub, then hustle him over to me."

"Right, Lieutenant."

The two scruffy riflemen beckoned for Noble to follow. They led him between thick pines to a large dugout under an upturned hay cart. A small two-burner stove was heating a large can of soup. A metal coffee pot sat on the other burner, its delicious aroma wafting through the bunker's opening. Two litters took up the far end of the sheltered trench, their occupants wrapped in blankets. One of them, a round-faced, blonde-haired youth, propped himself on an elbow and welcomed Noble.

"Bet you think you've died and gone to heaven, huh?"

"Yeah. God, am I glad to see you fellas."

Another soldier, barrel-chested, with scraggly whiskers and thick, unruly black hair was squatting by the stove. He dipped a mess cup into the soup and poured it into a small can for their visitor.

He offered a hand. "Ole Johnson."

"William Noble." He shook the man's hand and took the tin of soup.

He sat in the straw, back against the hard dirt wall, cupping the warm container in his right hand, inhaling the fragrance. He couldn't stop smiling.

"Ain't you gonna try it?" Johnson laughed. "It ain't poison, you know."

The men in the dugout chuckled. Noble nodded and slurped the brew noisily, licking the edges of the container carefully. After devouring the contents, he ran two fingers along the inside of the cup and licked them clean.

They offered him a second helping and then took him to the lieutenant.

## CHAPTER TWO

### DECEMBER 16, 1944, 11:30 A.M.

Noble followed the small, wiry, bearded sentinel named Soleski. They passed several shallow trenches filled with pairs of shivering, sullen GIs. A jeep, draped in a torn white bed sheet, was parked next to a shallow square that had been excavated from the pine needle carpet. Frozen shards of earth were piled like field stone in a farmer's wall to give shelter from the wind. Two brown tarps had been stretched as a low tent over thin poles, creating a makeshift command post. Pine branches scattered over the material provided scant camouflage.

Noble drew himself up and saluted. The officer nodded at him, ignoring the formality of the salute and told him to sit on an ammo box across from him. Noble's escort took advantage of the moment to hover over a glowing lantern. His chapped hands caressed the warm globe.

Lieutenant Lyle Pressman, a haggard, worn twenty-four year-old who appeared to be twice his age, seemed anything but a leader in his grimy field jacket. Tufts of sandy hair poked from under a wool cap and his unshaven face gave him a menacing look. His gray eyes were bloodshot with dark-lined pouches beneath. The officer glanced down at Noble's left arm and blood-stained sleeve.

"Soleski!" he barked at the other man. "Get Doc over here to look at this kid's arm."

The GI rose to his feet and went out into the wind. The Lieutenant shook out a cigarette from a crumpled pack of Lucky Strikes and offered one. Noble took off his helmet and ran his good hand through auburn hair.

"Thanks, but I don't smoke, sir."

The officer chuckled. "Neither did I a month ago."

Noble shifted his weight to regain feeling in his feet. The Lieutenant studied him through a cloud of cigarette smoke.

"How old are you, Noble?"

"Eighteen, sir."

"Where's home?"

"Minnesota, sir."

"Nice state. I went through Minneapolis once on a troop train."

Noble beamed. "It's beautiful, sir. God's country." He turned to look beyond the tent flap at the pines. "Actually, parts of it kinda look like this, to tell the truth."

"I'm from Pennsylvania myself," volunteered the officer wearily.

Footsteps sounded outside the tent. A short, swarthy GI carrying two bulging bags, one over each shoulder, stepped down into the shelter. He waited for the officer to speak.

The Lieutenant pointed his smoldering cigarette stub at Noble's left sleeve. "See what you can do for his arm, Doc."

The medic set to work wordlessly, gingerly freeing the wool overcoat from Noble's limb. He peeled back the sweater and cut a bloodstained shirt cuff to expose the flesh. He began cleaning the wound as the officer talked.

"Where's the rest of your outfit?"

"Most of 'em killed. Probably scattered or prisoners, sir." Noble felt detached, watching the medic work.

"Tell me what happened," said the officer.

Noble looked at the Lieutenant. "It was about zero five-thirty. Three of us were on firewood detail, trying to find enough dry branches to get a fire going so we could get warm, when the Krauts started firing artillery, sir." The officer's cigarette smoke drifted between them.

"You take casualties?"

"Yes sir, right away. They must have had us zeroed in pretty tight. Seemed like every round fired killed someone."

The officer asked, "How'd you get hurt?"

"Me and some of the guys were trying to get back to our squad when an air burst hit the trees." Noble looked down at his wound which had begun to bleed again under the medic's prodding.

"I guess I got lucky, sir. All the others were killed."

"Yeah, I'd say you were lucky, kid."

The officer pulled out a map and unfolded it, studying it for a minute before spreading it for Noble to read. "Can you point out your position?"

Noble shook his head. "No, sir. All I know is we were north and west of a town called St.-Vith."

The Lieutenant stared at the map, tracing a line with his finger.

"Does that help any, sir?"

"Hmmm, yeah. You must have walked about nine or ten miles, son."

Noble grimaced as the medic tugged at splinters in his forearm.

"It wasn't all a straight line, sir," he said. "I had to go cross country to get here."

"Sure, but your sector was about here." Lieutenant Pressman tapped a penciled line. "Were you tied in with outfits on both sides?"

Noble looked down at the map, then back at the officer, helpless. "I'm a clerk with headquarters company. We were spread pretty thin in front of our battalion CP, sir."

The medic spoke as he dusted Noble's arm with sulfa powder.

"You had a nasty splinter in there, pal. Probably from that tree burst. But it don't look bad now. Just bled a lot, huh?" Noble nodded and tried to smile. The medic wrapped a gauze pad with scraps of tape and then carefully wound a bandage around the arm. He unrolled Noble's sleeve, minus the cuff, and put away his kit.

"Anything else, sir?"

The Lieutenant looked up. "No. Thanks, Doc. Good job as always."

"Yeah, thanks," said Noble as he slipped his sweater over the arm. He shrugged into his field jacket as the officer finished his smoke and shredded the cigarette butt.

"Soleski!" The Lieutenant yelled again and the grubby soldier stuck his face into the tent. "Tell Sergeant Swanson to report to me on the double." The man disappeared.

Noble stood and saluted. "I sure appreciate you taking me in, sir."

The officer laughed ruefully. "You're my newest orphan, Noble. You're in for a wild ride, Private. But we can always use another man."

He pointed at Noble's M1. "You any good with that?"

"Qualified marksman, sir."

"Do any hunting back home in Minnesota?"

"Yes, sir. I could put dinner on the table when I had to."

"Well, let's just see if you can score some Kraut meat when the time comes. Stay alert, Noble. We'll all get through this if we take care of each other."

Footsteps pounded outside and Soleski pushed through the tent flaps, followed by a grim-looking staff sergeant with an M1 carbine slung over his shoulder. Shock finally gripped Noble's body and he began shivering as the sergeant brushed by him. Soleski threw a blanket across Noble's shoulders and hunkered down beside him in a corner of the canvas shelter.

Brief salutes were exchanged. "You wanna see me, sir?"

"Yeah, Sergeant Swanson, sit down. We need to talk." The noncom blew on his hands and sank onto the ammo crate opposite the officer. Pressman arranged the map in front of them. "Here's the situation." The officer eyed the dog-eared sheet.

"The Krauts must have blasted a pretty big hole in the front this morning.

"We only have eight men left from our original platoon. Hell, most of these guys we have now are pick-me-ups from a half-dozen outfits. Some of them were bugging out and some were just beat up and had no where else to go. We've been picking up people all morning and Noble, here, is our latest."

To Noble, it seemed the officer was talking to himself.

"Clerks, cooks, some red leg radio guys, one medic and a handful of riflemen." He paused. "How many of us now, Swanson?"

"We've got a grand total of twenty-five, sir. Two litter cases." He glanced at Noble, saw the bloodied jacket. "Five, including this new kid, are walking wounded, the others, okay."

The Sergeant rattled off statistics. "We got no radio, one jeep, a thirty-caliber with one hundred rounds and no idea of what the hell the Krauts are doing."

On cue a series of thunderous booms rippled in the east, shaking snow from the tree tops. A salvo screamed, ripping the sky, whistling to the west. Noble flinched as shards of ice drifted down in a shower on the tarp. He counted the number of shells overhead, all west-bound.

The Lieutenant cocked his head to one side. "There's your answer, Sergeant. We can't stay here. They're going to use this road sooner or later."

"Sooner, rather than later, sir," interrupted the noncom.

Lieutenant Pressman stabbed a finger at a spot on the map. "We'll pull back here. I know it. It's a small village on higher ground. Just short of ten miles west along this road. Maybe we can find some of our own people. Get a better position for a stand. But we've got to put some distance between us and the Krauts."

Swanson nodded.

"Okay, Sergeant, let the men know we're going to move out in ten minutes. Burn anything we can't carry. Put the litters on the jeep and see if Corporal Parker's in any shape to drive. I'll walk point. You bring up the rear."

The Sergeant ducked back through the tent's opening to organize his men. He motioned for Noble and Soleski to follow him.

Noble trailed Soleski to a shallow trench where a GI warmed himself over a small fire at his feet. The GI barely glanced up as Soleski introduced him.

"Noble, this is O'Reilly." The short, bundled soldier, reluctant to leave the flames, offered a muffled hello and moved over to share what little warmth the flames provided. All around them GIs began throwing surplus gear into a pile for burning.

Noble kicked his boots at the iron-hard earth to get his blood moving and held his rifle close to the fire. "Bolt's frozen," he explained.

O'Reilly saw Noble's bandaged left arm and held out a gloved hand for the M1. "Here, lemme do that for you." He held the weapon over the glowing coals until he was able to work the bolt loose. He handed it back to Noble. "Musta' got wet and froze," he mumbled through his scarf. Noble thanked O'Reilly, jammed a clip into his M1 and then rose to help scatter the dying embers.

Off to the east, down the snow-covered road, small arms fire popped in the dark forest. Noble looked at the far wood line, as if expecting German infantry to emerge from the pines.

Instead he heard the faint sound of machines moving in his direction.

# CHAPTER THREE

## DECEMBER 16, 1944, 3:30 P.M.

Four riflemen, a pair on each side of the road, scouted fifty yards ahead as the small company headed west. Behind the point men the jeep rolled slowly in low gear, two stretchers with casualties across the back seat. The windshield was folded down, the light machine gun propped on the hood, ready for action. Behind the vehicle walked the rest of the retreating group. Lieutenant Pressman led the column from his position in the middle of the road while his sergeant handled the rear guard. The NCO constantly scolded his men in hoarse whispers to maintain proper intervals. They moved for hours without stopping. Occasionally, artillery lighted the gloom like lightning, shells splitting the sky as big guns dropped rounds beyond them to the west. Cold gnawed at them; the litter cases, unable to move, suffered more than most.

Private William Noble was paired with Corporal Dawson O'Reilly, and the two walked single file along the right side of the road, Noble leading. When Soleski had introduced them, Noble had been pleased to find another Minnesotan among this small band of refugees. The two had shared brief family histories before the word came to move from the little grove of pines. O'Reilly had helped Noble free his M1's frozen bolt over the fire and had offered the newcomer a spare, half-full canteen.

Noble had also met Ken Wolf from Wisconsin and a Chicago Jew named Sam Cohen. Their Midwest reunion had been cut short by the orders to move west. Now they walked in silence, glancing into the woods on their flanks, expecting an ambush at any moment.

They had left their flimsy roadblock just in time. According to the Lieutenant, the machine noises were probably tanks and their tiny band would have lost the fight against armor. To press the attack German tanks needed roads, even narrow second-rate avenues like the one Noble and his fellow soldiers were now using for their escape route. A message was whispered down the line. "Village in sight. Hold up while the Lieutenant checks it out."

Noble and O'Reilly closed ranks and knelt, huddling with their backs to the wind. Twenty yards behind them another pair of GIs trained their weapons on the empty road to the rear. "How's the arm?" asked O'Reilly, glancing down at Noble's coat.

"Not bad. Doc did a good job fixing me up."

"Yeah, we're lucky to have him with us."

Noble asked the obvious. "You think we're gonna make it out of here?"

His fellow Minnesotan shrugged. "We're probably in the same fix as a lot of outfits right now. Just got to keep going till we can find some of our own people."

In the distance, east, faint clanking sounds again.

"Geez, O'Reilly, that sounds like armor."

"That's why we've got to get off this road."

Sergeant Swanson approached and knelt. "The Lieutenant says the village is clear," he whispered. "There's friendlies there, so we're going in real quiet like. Keep your intervals. Don't bunch up." He wagged a gloved hand at them. "Remember, two single files on each side of the road like we been doing."

The two nodded and stood, moving off along the road.

The jeep in front lurched forward with its tortured cargo.

The deserted village was really just a small ruined manor house and four other shells of homes surrounded by a shredded orchard. The buildings nestled against a hillside where the road climbed a slight rise and then fell away west, swallowed by more forest.

A half-dozen jeeps and an M10 tank destroyer idled in the center of the village. A knot of officers and NCOs huddled near a barn, comparing maps with flashlights. Lieutenant Pressman was in the middle of the impromptu war council.

"I hope to hell they know what they're doing," said O'Reilly.

The men drifted together and stood against walls, out of the wind. Cigarettes were shared and most of the men took the welcome break to relieve themselves in nearby snowbanks. Booming artillery sounds began again and shells fell in the forest beyond the little hamlet. Noble and O'Reilly watched the impromptu war council break up and heard orders barked to the column of jeeps. The M10 tank destroyer revved its engine, bucking and snorting clouds of exhaust before moving back down the road Noble's ragtag outfit had just traveled.

"Boy, I sure don't envy them guys," said O'Reilly as they watched the machine clank by them. "Might as well have a giant bullseye painted on them."

Noble agreed and watched the tracked gun go a short distance beyond the village's outskirts before leaving the road and hiding in a thick grove of pine. The machine's driver backed into the trees and jockeyed his treads in the snow to give his gunner a field of fire from a concealed position along the route into the village. Several crewman dismounted and lazily dragged tree branches across telltale tracks, a cursory attempt to hide evidence of its presence. After ten minutes of sweeping the snow, the men tossed their brush against the machine's hull and climbed aboard.

Lieutenant Pressman appeared again, his NCO in tow. The men gathered.

"Noble, O'Reilly," rasped the officer, indicating a low, barn-like hovel across the road, "Go with Sergeant Swanson and the others and set up the thirty-caliber in that building." The Lieutenant put his hand on Noble's shoulder.

"We've picked up another three hundred rounds of ammo and we're going to cover the road with the gun. There's bound to be infantry with the tanks and your team will need to put down suppressing fire to keep their troops back. That way they'll bring their armor forward and the tank destroyer can go to work. Don't worry, you'll have Johnson, Cohen and Wolf with you."

The cook, Ole Johnson, his frame draped with belted machine gun rounds, was headed their way.

Pressman looked hard at the ragtag outfit. "Got it? Any questions?" They could think of none, though neither man was thrilled with the prospect of facing tanks. The officer patted Noble's back. "Okay, kid, let's see how good you are with that." He nodded at the M1 slung over the private's right shoulder.

"Yes, sir," mumbled Noble.

The squad hustled into a crumbling building by the road.

In the center of the village, several jeeps loaded with wounded began winding up the road behind the hamlet, taking their cargo out of immediate danger. Suddenly the little collection of buildings became a ghost town. From the hillside, a small knot of observers and their radiomen began calling for artillery. Targets were plotted and soon a series of sharp explosions erupted in the wood line east of the village as spotters worked over suspected targets.

They were answered in kind by hidden enemy batteries that sent shells back toward the ridge and woods near town. Forward observers scrambled down from the hill and took refuge in the pock-marked manor house. In the midst of the escalating artillery duel, two of Noble's hastily assembled squad chipped away at a wall, punching a firing hole in the side facing the route the Germans would have to take.

Corporal Dawson O'Reilly moved among them, arranging boxes of belted ammunition and piling field packs out of the way. Two others joined them. Soleski and a quiet Californian youth named Lopez helped set the machine gun on its tripod.

Noble cradled boxes of ammo in the crook of his bandaged left arm and began loading M1 clips for the squad. He passed the ammunition to the others, then stuffed his overcoat's pockets with ammo and took up a position in the southeast corner. He nestled behind a perfect vantage point, a ragged oval-shaped shell hole left from previous fighting. The opening gave him a wide view of the road and woods. He poked his M1 through the slot, checked his sights and settled himself. Though trembling, he breathed slowly, hoping others wouldn't notice.

Sergeant Swanson crabbed across the road and entered the barn. He stood like a coach in the building's doorway, encouraging his hastily assembled machine gun crew. He addressed each man by name and sprinkled profanity along with crude jokes about their fighting abilities. Like a good NCO he worked to defuse their fears about the upcoming fight.

"Now Private Noble here is the newest fish we have. He's a clerk but claims to be a crack shot and says he'll guarantee the Krauts won't get within a hundred yards of this here deer stand." William started to protest but the sergeant held up his hand. "It's true. And O'Reilly says he and Johnson are gonna keep the Krauts from using this road."

"Clerks and cooks. If the Germans only knew."

Laughter echoed in the barn.

Two more men scrambled in behind the sergeant.

"Cohen, Wolf!" barked Swanson, wheeling on them. "Goddamnit, where you two been? We almost started the fight without you!"

Both latecomers grinned broadly. Corporal Samuel Cohen indicated the hillside dwelling with a nod of his head and held up two bottles of wine in each hand. "In the manor house, Sarge, a whole basement full. Untouched."

The other soldier, Wolf, dropped to his knees by the machine gun and passed a bottle to Ole Johnson. Noble watched from his corner perch, fascinated. He had tasted wine at a church communion service in England a lifetime ago.

"Lemme see that, Cohen," demanded Swanson. He took a bottle from the GI, lifted it to his lips and tilted his head for a long swallow. He smacked his lips loudly. "Gotta hand it to the locals, they do like their wine."

He handed the bottle back to Cohen and bellowed to the squad. "Don't let me catch you fighting drunk! Remember, no infantry gets closer than two hundred yards! Got it?" Murmurs of agreement. Bottles clinked in toasts.

"The Lieutenant and I are gonna be right across the road with the others."

"What if they got tanks, Sarge?"

"Oh, they'll have tanks, O'Reilly," Swanson warned. "Keep in mind the Krauts will probably send their infantry out first to see what they're up against before they risk their tanks. That's where you come in." He waved at the road beyond. "Stop 'em here on the outskirts."

"Do not . . . I repeat . . . do not let them flank you. They flank us and we're history."

He pointed over his shoulder with his thumb. "We got some One-O-Fives working over the woods right now but they're rationing shells. Everybody's calling for artillery and we'll have to wait our turn."

Another flight of incoming shells screamed overhead to underscore his words. A series of explosions rippled left to right in the distant woods, throwing up frozen clumps of earth in ugly geysers of fire and snow.

On the hill behind the village, an observer team had gone back into position and was calling in shots that were shattering the tree line and bracketing the road a thousand yards from the village. Somewhere beyond the shell flashes in the woods, Germans were preparing to attack and American forward observers were determined to break up their advance. With each tremor the little farm building dusted Noble and his fellow soldiers with thatch and dirt.

"All right, boys. Keep 'em away. They want this road. Make 'em pay for it!" The sergeant sprinted out the doorway and took up his position across the road in the other building.

## CHAPTER FOUR

DECEMBER 17, 1944, 5:30 A.M.

Noble heard it first.

Unmistakable sounds of clanking treads on an icy road. Like chains being dragged across corrugated metal. An engine grinding. He shook himself awake and peered out his firing hole.

Metal beasts were snorting and huffing in the dawn mist. Fog hugged the ground, enveloping the little collection of buildings where other GIs were hiding.

Noble tossed a clod of dirt in O'Reilly's direction.

The Midwesterner stirred, irritated. He squinted at Noble. "What?" he uttered before he, too, sat upright at the sound of machines.

O'Reilly's gun crew, Privates Wolf and Lopez, were jostled awake. The three men scrambled behind the light machine gun and pried open ammo cans. Cohen and Soleski crept into a corner and peered from cracks in the wall.

"See anything?" O'Reilly whispered hoarsely to Noble.

The young rifleman nodded yes without taking his eyes from the firing hole.

In the distance, on either side of the approach to the village, figures emerged from milky haze. Gray mottled shapes moved slowly into the open, flanking the route leading to the village.

William Noble's tremors began again. His pulse raced.

He watched transfixed as German infantry fanned out, heading for woods to his right. He released his weapon's safety and pushed the M1's muzzle slowly through the opening. Training took over and he picked a target on the very end.

Noble squinted in the poor light and drew a bead on a figure struggling through a field, ankle-deep in icy mud. He let the man drift into his line of fire and centered his sights on the soldier's chest. Noble squeezed the trigger as he had been taught and the M1 exploded, barking loudly, throwing his shoulder back in a powerful recoil. Four hundred yards to his front, his target raised his arms and fell back in a clump of gray.

*That was much too easy,* thought Noble. *I've just shot my first human being and it was effortless.* Acrid cordite fumes stung his eyes. He moved his rifle several inches to the left and watched another figure stop briefly at his fallen comrade and then quicken his pace in the field, shouting a warning, pushing quickly now beyond the crumpled body, trying to clear the killing zone. Noble let this new quarry work into his sights and squeezed off another shot with the same result; the enemy threw up his hands and fell backwards in a shower of snow and mud.

Running on instinct now, Private William Noble spaced his shots and took out an additional three enemy. Now, no one challenged that side of the road. They shifted, concentrating their approach to the buildings on the other side of the road. The .30 caliber opened up, a sweeping scythe of fire. A half-dozen Panzergrenadiers went down on the outskirts of the nameless little town and the Germans began to fire back, most of the shots high or harmless hits that cracked against the buildings.

A SdKfz 251 half-track roared up the middle in support, wildly firing its MG34 machine gun, spraying the sides of the buildings with fire. Noble ducked, hugging the plastered wall below his firing port. He felt the bullets chipping away, thudding into the stone and plaster just above his head.

When the fire shifted from his portion of the wall, he raised his head, thrust his rifle back out the hole and picked off two more infantry cowering beside the half-track. *Amazing*, he thought again to himself. His tremors had disappeared, replaced by complete calm. To his left, O'Reilly, Lopez and Wolf hammered away at the enemy with their light machine gun. Soleski and Johnson joined the fire fight, mechanically pumping out rounds from their M1s. Corporal Sam Cohen fired at a huddle of soldiers who were dragging a wounded comrade to safety. He cut down two of the enemy. Out front, the half-track began timidly backing away, trying to shield the infantry's withdrawal with short bursts of machine gun fire.

The Americans watched the armored wagon slowly pull back down the road toward the woods when suddenly the hidden M10 tank destroyer fired a three-inch shell into the half-track. With a burst of flame and smoke, the ambushed half-track shuddered to a grinding stop. The M10's first round had split the steel plates and men on fire leaped from the armored track. O'Reilly's machine gun went into action, knocking down the blazing targets as they rolled in the snow trying to smother the flames. Noble heard screaming as he watched enemy soldiers flail and twitch, mowed down by machine gun rounds tearing into smoking bodies.

A second round from the concealed tank destroyer killed the half-track, lifting it from the roadway in a ball of fire, sending the driverless machine aimlessly toward a ditch where it halted at a grotesque angle, burning front wheels spinning slowly.

Louder clanking sounds echoed from the woods and a Mark IV tank suddenly rumbled from the trees, firing its main gun at the hidden M10. The panzer's gunner was good. His first shell burst against the M10's open turret in a terrific explosion. The second shot tore into the base of the wrecked turret and split the steel body in an explosion that touched off ammo.

A huge arc of flame and fireworks of white phosphorous shattered the dawn, raining down burning shrapnel.

On came the German tank, an avenging wraith driving up the middle of the road, its coaxial machine gun spitting a steady stream of bullets into American positions. Another round from the tank's 75mm gun destroyed the building across the road from Noble in a thunderous explosion. Roof tiles and timber showered down in the smoke and GIs ran from the ruined building only to be cut down by the tank's machine gunner.

Panzergrenadiers suddenly appeared from behind the Mark IV and Noble knew his position was the tank's next target. He didn't wait. Yelling a warning to the others, he bolted from the building and cleared a pile of firewood in one leap, running for the safety of the manor house, bullets chewing up the muddy ground around him.

Behind in the shed, Soleski and Johnson abandoned their sniper's corner and followed Noble. Cohen fired his last rounds at the advancing infantry and then fled. The remaining three, O'Reilly, Wolf and Lopez, dragged the machine gun to a new point and began firing at a line of Germans. It was a defiant gesture that drew the attention of the tank's commander.

The big machine ground to a halt, the turret swiveling ominously in the barn's direction.

Lopez took over the gun and fed the last belt into the gun. He ordered the others to run. To cover their escape he fired at viewing ports, trying to blind the tank. Rather than wasting ammo the machine simply lurched forward, crushing the flimsy structure in raw power, treads mounting up against the stones and then slamming down as the machine rolled over Lopez who continued firing as the tank crushed him.

O'Reilly and Wolf raced into the village square where they joined other GIs heading for the manor house at the base of the hill. Noble had already reached the manor and was dragging wounded survivors over a low stone wall that formed the house's courtyard. Americans who sprinted into the woods were being cut down by Germans sweeping through the orchard.

The tank backed up and leveled what remained of the barn. Behind the armored hulk streamed more infantry, firing bursts into the rubble, putting an end to the contest. The panzer rotated its turret and put a shell through the second story of the manor house, setting it on fire.

It was over. Someone inside the mansion found a scrap of bed sheet and tied it to a tree limb to signal a surrender. Further resistance was useless and a GI raised the banner, waving it from a shattered window.

# CHAPTER FIVE

## DECEMBER 17, 1944, 8:00 A.M.

The tank kept its main gun leveled at the manor house where the Americans huddled. The machine sat there, belching exhaust. A hatch opened and a man wearing headphones appeared against the dawn sky. He waved Panzergrenadiers forward and they approached surviving GIs with their weapons ready. Another lieutenant, not Pressman, limped forward, hands raised, flag bearer beside him. A single German in a camouflage parka and armed with an MP40 submachine gun came forward.

Noble and O'Reilly watched from the low wall.

Behind them, GIs were already stripping their rifles and pistols and smashing receivers against masonry. Others tossed bullets, scattering precious rounds about the ruins. William Noble unloaded his M1, broke it down quickly and smashed stock and trigger housing, rendering his rifle useless. Like the others, he would not let the enemy use his weapon against fellow GIs. Men stood, hands above their heads. Lieutenant Pressman and a captain with a bloody scalp held in place by a field dressing emerged from the doorway of the smoking manor house and walked slowly toward the negotiators. This small group of

Germans and Americans began talking under the tank's menacing guns, while enemy troops surrounded the manor house. Another half-track emerged from behind the tank and parked nearby. The Germans gestured and shouted while the Americans listened stoically.

Into this mix, a mud-covered Kubelwagen command car arrived, skidding to a halt.

The riders were dressed in similar camouflage-patterned jackets that were thrown open, revealing black uniform blouses with runic slashes on collar tabs.

Next to Noble, a grizzled looking corporal measured the unfolding situation. "This don't look good. Them boys is SS."

The small car parked in the square alongside the tank. A youthful looking blonde officer grabbed a map from inside his fur-lined parka and mounted the tank to shake hands with the soldier in the turret. The two engaged in animated gestures and studied the map for several minutes. Climbing down from the tank, the officer carried the map to the small group of prisoners. He shouted at the Americans and jabbed at the map.

"Hell, that old boy's lost," said the corporal standing close to Noble.

"How do you know? You understand German?" asked O'Reilly.

"Don't have to. Look at 'em. They sure act like they're lost."

Noble and O'Reilly were joined by Ole Johnson and Wolf. Until now, neither side had moved from their positions, but German Grenadiers continued straggling into town. A third half-track, pulling an anti-tank gun, parted the formation and took up position on the far edge of the square, its machine gunner covering the courtyard with his weapon.

The impromptu conference broke up and Lieutenant Pressman rejoined the watching Americans.

Noble studied his leader's face. "What's happening, sir?"

"They've agreed to a cease-fire. We've been allowed to collect our wounded and gather them here in the courtyard of the manor house."

Sergeant Swanson appeared from behind a ruined stone pillar, his intact carbine discreetly at his side.

"You won't be needing that, Swanson. We've surrendered."

The sergeant looked down in disgust. "Then I'm going to bury it for later."

"I know," sighed Pressman. "I don't like it any better than you, but we've got no choice now." He pointed to the smoking hulk of the M10 tank destroyer in the nearby woods. "That was our only hope. Those guys bought us some time . . . but in the end" His voice trailed off.          ·

"Still, you men can be proud of yourselves." He looked around at them. "You held them off for an hour. Most likely screwed up their timetable and took down a lot of their troops."

The lieutenant smiled at William Noble and put a hand on his shoulder. "Damn if you didn't shoot down those Krauts just like you said, son. When I get back I'm putting you all in for some decorations."

It felt awkward to talk like this with the victorious enemy standing around them. Their enemy began moving in pairs among the Americans, frisking prisoners for weapons. Germans began confiscating wallets and personal belongings they found to their liking. Noble lost his watch and wallet to a beaming captor who trumpeted his good fortune to comrades. Around him, men were ordered to strip off their jackets and turn pockets inside out. When the looting ended, the Germans returned to their formation and loaded captured weapons into the half-track. In the village square, the young German commander's mood was growing foul, and he pounded his vehicle's hood several times as he and others studied the map.

"Didn't I tell you?" The older corporal pushed back his helmet and watched the lively conversation at the command car. "They're lost and they can't agree on where to go next. That old boy sure ain't happy." He nodded at the blond officer who paced, map in hand, before a semicircle of subordinates. The other Germans stood respectfully, waiting for orders.

By now, all wounded Americans had been moved into ·the safety of the walled area and a harried medic was bending over each man, checking on those most seriously hurt. Lieutenant Pressman leaned back against the wall and plucked a last cigarette from his field jacket. He lighted a smoke and inhaled, watching the shouting match in the village square. A glowering German trooper confiscated the lieutenant's lighter and Pressman regretted his mistake. All around them enemy soldiers stood casually, displaying their prizes, weapons lowered but ready.

The bloodied American captain and his flag bearer were approached by the young German commander and six soldiers armed with MP40 machine guns and MP44 assault rifles. The two ranking enemy commanders talked for a few minutes and then the American captain called for Pressman to join them. There were no smiles as introductions were made.

Noble and others crowded behind the two officers to eavesdrop.

The captain nodded at the SS officer.

"Lieutenant, this is Captain Von Wurtz. He wants to know what's up ahead on the road." Pressman studied the young commander's face. The enemy before him was almost adolescent looking, eyes pale blue and his hair, white blonde, shaved high along the sides. He wore a black wool campaign hat with a silver death's head. Pressman was unsure if the man before him spoke English. He turned to his fellow officer. "Well, how would we know, Captain?" he answered, ignoring the German officer. "And even if we did know, we sure as hell wouldn't tell him." Pressman stared at the SS officer. "Let him find out for himself."

The German smiled slightly and replied in excellent English. "Very correct, Lieutenant. I would certainly say the same thing were I in your place."

The American officers wore slight smiles, as though they had won a debating point.

"However," cautioned the German, grim now, his voice suddenly loud enough for Noble and the wounded Americans to hear, "I am not in your place! And you have annoyed me with a doomed defense of a worthless little village!"

Noble was within earshot of the American captain's confident answer. "This worthless little village, as you call it, has cost you a good number of your men, sir. We both know it was a credible defense that has cost you time."

Noble was suddenly, instinctively, wary of the conversation's direction.

The SS man raised a gloved hand. "Of course. You are right, Captain." The German stepped back to address his prisoners. "But you should have accepted that the outcome was inevitable." He flashed a tight smile. "I ask, yet again, for the sake of your men here, what are we to expect further down this road?"

The American officers did not answer.

"Very well," said the German. He left his guards and returned to his vehicle where he gave a series of rapid orders to his entourage.

Pressman and the captain returned to their waiting men and stood by the wall.

"What do you think he'll do?" asked the captain.

Pressman rubbed his jaw. "Well, from the arguing going on, they seem lost. Maybe he doesn't want to admit it. Probably separated from his main group. I doubt he'll turn around. I wouldn't if I was in his shoes."

The captain shrugged. "So he's got to keep going until he links up with them. I just hope he runs into one of our outfits first."

The Germans formed two columns behind the Mark IV tank. The big machine revved its engine and the tank commander sat in the open hatch listening to his headset, nodding. The young German captain had settled back in the scout car and again studied his map, pouting. Irritated.

"Only now he's got a bunch of us prisoners, sir," volunteered Sergeant Swanson.

Pressman nodded.

Noble spoke up. "What'll happen to us, sir?"

The lieutenant surveyed the two dozen surviving Americans in the courtyard. "They'll have to detail some men to send us behind their lines."

"What a lousy turn of events," Swanson snorted. "I buried my weapon in the woods behind the manor house, Lieutenant."

"That was risky, Sergeant."

"Well, sir, it ain't over yet."

The corporal beside Noble volunteered his opinion. "They're SS, Lieutenant, and that old boy is pissed 'cause we didn't let him go waltzing down this here road like he wanted." The enlisted man stood and propped a boot on top of the low stone wall. He frowned at the waiting German infantry.

"I say we make a break for it as soon as we can, sir. I sure as heck don't want to spend the rest of this war in no POW cage."

# CHAPTER SIX

## DECEMBER 17, 1944, 9:00 A.M.

A line of Germans approached the wall and a senior NCO stepped forward.

"Our commander wishes to speak to you once more, Captain."

The Kubelwagen pulled even with the idling tank and the German sat there studying his map, waiting.

"Pressman, keep an eye on the men," said the captain. He eyed the corporal next to Noble. "Don't let anyone try anything foolish."

The lieutenant nodded.

The German sergeant and the American captain approached Von Wurtz's vehicle. The NCO and his prisoner halted beside the scout car. Von Wurtz raised a Walther P38 pistol and shot the American in the forehead. The captain, his face fixed in surprise, crumpled in a heap by the vehicle, blood spreading in a pool under the right front tire, staining the snow.

Shocked, Pressman and the others started forward but were halted by the circle of Germans who leveled their weapons at their prisoners.

Noble looked past the lieutenant, incredulous, as he watched the German officer holster his pistol and resume reading the map spread across his knees, not bothering to look at the body of the American. Instantly Noble knew what was about to happen, yet he was powerless.

The German captain looked up from his map and nodded to his senior NCO who barked a single order to the line of waiting troopers.

"FIRE!"

Immediately the semicircle of German soldiers began firing at the mass of American prisoners in the courtyard. When each German emptied his weapon he reloaded and poured more fire into scrambling GIs.

Noble saw O'Reilly go down. All around him men screamed and cursed as they fell on one another. The flag bearer waved his scrap of white cloth wildly and was torn in half by a full burst from an MP40. Soleski was hit in the side and then Johnson fell to the ground. A bullet caught the side of Sam Cohen's head and a second round punched his shoulder, spinning him, dropping him to the earth. Bullets ricocheted off masonry, causing second and third wounds.

Still the Germans fired.

A gunner on the parked half-track tucked the butt of his weapon against his shoulder and began hitting GIs with five-round bursts from his MG34, firing an entire belt of ammo into panicked, unarmed men. Noble threw himself down behind the wall and saw Lieutenant Pressman catch a burst of bullets in the chest and throat. The officer fell, pitching forward, and was shot in the head by an advancing SS sergeant armed with a pistol. Noble caught ricochets in his right calf and shoulder blade as he hugged the wall. His breath was knocked from him and he cried out in pain as someone fell on top of him, blood and intestines splattering his back.

He blacked out.

When he regained consciousness he lay still, eyes closed, listening to guttural voices as the enemy walked among bodies, further looting watches, wallets, boots and gloves they had missed the first time. There was more shooting.

Someone tugged at his wrist, looking for a watch. Laughter above him. Another voice. Behind. Kicking at him. Noble kept his face to the frozen earth, bearing the searing pain. He heard moans and then single shots or occasional three-round bursts as executioners looked for survivors among the bodies piled in the courtyard.


Noble forced himself to think of home. Solitary nights camping in the dark forests. He dreamed of family. Drifting in and out of consciousness, he heard muffled roars of armor moving off somewhere. The voices faded. He slept. Awakened.

He relieved himself without moving, enjoying the all-too-brief rush of warmth.

A light snow drifted down, delicate crystals melting on his bloodied hands. He willed himself not to move. His soaked trousers froze to the ground, pinning him to the earth. The corpse on top of him seemed to increase in weight and he listened for signs of life.

Machines rattled in woods far away. Miles away, artillery thundered.

*I have to move*, he told himself. *I will die here if I stay like this. Must move. Will move.*

He tried to push himself from the frozen ground but the weight above him would not give. He rolled to one side and found that he could push himself free by rocking back and forth, freeing his burden. Finally he was able to lift his head and looked around.

Worn boots and bare feet and brass casings. Everywhere, blood. Arms crooked in macabre poses, legs twisted in impossible ways. Sightless pairs of eyes stared at him.

A shattered mouth yawned in silent agony. Rigor mortis, allied with cruel cold, had worked its will on the surrounding flesh, and stiffened limbs were fixed in odd postures in the crimson-soaked courtyard. Helmets lay scattered about among ribbons of used bandages. Bloodied uniform jackets lay discarded in the open air charnel house.

Noble propped himself on his right elbow and caught his breath in short gasps.

He wriggled free of his corpse shield and sat up, back against the stone wall, his right calf throbbing in pain. His upper back burned in agony.

The village was deserted. Fresh tank tracks trailed west on the narrow road.

*Lost or not, they had gone ahead as the lieutenant had predicted,* he thought. *God, let them walk into a trap. Make them pay for this.*

He reached into his jacket, under his arms, and found the pair of wool gloves he had hidden there. With difficulty he pulled them on and drew his knees up towards his chest. His coat was stiff with blood from the wound on his back and his left forearm now throbbed with new pain. He checked his calf and thanked God that the round had been a clean shot through muscle. His pants leg was now blackened scarlet and looked as though he had bled out.

He pulled a used handkerchief from his breast pocket and pulled up his trouser leg to tie the cloth like a bandana around the wound. He pushed the cloth down, rolled to his right and got on all fours.

That was when he heard the sound. A soft crying.

He crawled toward the sound, dragging himself over a dozen bodies before he found the source. Noble reached out and grasped the survivor's outstretched hand. The two GIs tightened their grip on each other. A weak voice.

"It's me. O'Reilly."

The wounded man dragged himself close to Noble and tried to smile. His head had been creased, a shallow furrow had plowed across his scalp and had bathed his entire head in blood. His teeth gleamed ivory in a red-painted face.

"I played dead. Some poor bastard fell on me. Saved me. How about you?"

Noble wheezed an answer. "Same here."

"We gotta get out of here, Noble."

O'Reilly looked over the courtyard and raised his head to the ruins of the town. "What if they come back?"

Another voice. This one stronger. "Hey, buddy. Give me a hand." One more survivor. It was Ken Wolf. He held a bloody arm aloft for the others to see. "My writing hand. The lousy sons of bitches." He pulled his right arm to his chest and grimaced at the effort.

The three helped each other stand and looked around them, bewildered at the carnage.

"Hey! O'Reilly!" Another voice from the far end of the tangled courtyard.

The three hobbled over to find Ole Johnson, dazed, sitting upright against the wall, a corpse across his knees. He was nonchalantly smoking a crushed cigarette.

"Geez, I shit my pants," he lamented.

The other three did not laugh. "You ain't the only one."

Wolf leaned over the cook. "Where you hurt, Ole?"

"Shot in the foot. I think I lost a toe. Hurts like hell. The bastards." He tugged at his boot.

"Can you walk?" asked Wolf.

"Yeah, but I might need help." He rose, leaning on Wolf.

"What'll we do?" asked Noble. "We're probably behind German lines now."

In silence, they thought about their chances. The sound of cursing made them turn as one. Two pairs of hands waved at them.

"Cohen! Soleski!" yelled O'Reilly.

Noble and O'Reilly left the hobbled Johnson leaning against Wolf and worked their way to a cluster of bodies where Corporal Samuel Cohen cradled Soleski. Nearby Noble recognized the body of the medic who had patched him up the previous day. The man's head was a bloody pulp.

"Aw, geez, they killed Doc," wailed O'Reilly.

"Hey! Give us a hand, you guys!" The surviving pair tried to rise, using the manor house wall in support. Their field jackets were riddled with holes. Cohen's left shoulder was dirty crimson, his dark hair wild, matted with dried blood. They faltered, then stood unsteadily. Noble and O'Reilly supported them with some difficulty. Cohen was breathing heavily and Soleski was dazed with pain.

"Got hit in the shoulder and nicked above my ear." Cohen ran a grimy finger along his right temple to indicate his wound. "Lucky, I guess," he said. "Soleski's hurt worse than me."

The little man held a hand to his right side. "I took a round," he said, removing his hand to reveal a large clotted wound just above his hip. He held a wool sock rolled into a ball which served as a dressing.

They grinned, arms around each other. Wolf and Johnson limped to join them.

"There's another one over there!" cried O'Reilly, pointing to a GI on all fours. The man stood swaying, unaided, staring at them. He grasped his throat where a jagged wound bubbled scarlet with each short breath. O'Reilly led him by the hand to the small group. "You'll be okay, pal. We'll get you out of here." The man tried to smile. Someone produced a scrap of bandage and they created a dressing for his neck. He nodded his thanks and produced his dog tags with the name "Mitchell, Theodore."

For a long time the men stared at the bodies surrounding them. Gusts of wind dusted the survivors with swirling snow and rattled naked branches in the treetops.

Cohen broke the silence. "We gotta get all the dog tags. We have to let our guys know what happened here."

They stared at him, not comprehending what he was saying.

"Dog tags!" he snapped. "Collect one from each guy. We'll take them with us. Headquarters has to know about this."

It finally dawned on them what he was asking and they staggered from body to body, plucking one of the shiny metal tags, inserting its twin into the mouth of each corpse. The last body they reached was Lieutenant Pressman's. His chest had been ripped apart in the first salvo and a second burst had torn open his jaw. Noble knelt down and began to weep beside the officer's body.

"Can it, Noble," scolded Wolf. "Ain't going to do any good now."

Cohen rebuked him. "Leave the kid alone, Ken."

Wolf shrugged and finished threading his collected tags onto a single chain.

When they were done, Cohen lifted three strings of dog tags over his head. "If anything happens to me, you make sure these get to the higher ups, right?"

It was then they heard their sergeant's voice from the doorway. "You guys waiting for the sons-of-bitches to come back?"

The men stumbled to the shattered doorway and gathered around Staff Sergeant Burt Swanson in a grim reunion.

"How did you escape this?" asked O'Reilly, sweeping his hand around the corpse-strewn courtyard.

The NCO sat down wearily on the threshold and stretched out his right leg wrapped in a filthy, bloodied scrap of shirt. He kneaded his thigh. "Got hit going over the wall when the shooting started. Crawled off into the woods behind the house and waited until the Jerries left."

He looked up at the survivors and tried to smile but failed. "I should have seen that coming. You guys deserved better."

O'Reilly spoke for the men, trying to console him. "Nobody saw it coming, Sarge."

"Thanks, O'Reilly. But it ain't true. They were SS. We should have known." He waved a hand at the pile of bodies. "That corporal . . . never got his name . . . he knew."

"What could we have done, Sarge?" offered Wolf. "They had us."

Swanson looked disconsolate. "Yeah, they had us all right."

They stood clustered by the doorway quietly for several minutes, their mood one of confusion, despair. The sergeant suddenly changed his expression to a look of determination. He struggled to his feet and leaned against the door frame. "We can't stay here. There may be more of them coming. Or they may come back this way. We've got to get to our own lines. You men in any shape to walk out?"

"Do we have a choice?" lamented Soleski.

"Yeah, we can manage, Sarge," said Wolf, answering for everyone.

"Okay. We need to look for food and water," said Swanson. He began issuing orders. Their sergeant again. "Pick up any dressings you can find and look around for any usable weapons and ammo. I buried my carbine behind the house. I'll get it."

"We already collected dog tags from these guys." Cohen displayed his silver necklaces.

"Good job, Sam. All right," said Swanson. "Soon as you guys get the stuff we need we're moving out."

It took them thirty minutes to rifle the corpses for supplies. Noble found two serviceable M1s, one with a shattered stock, and twelve rounds of ammo. Wolf and O'Reilly scrounged among the dead in the outlying woods and returned carrying a pistol with three rounds and an MP40 submachine gun with a half-full magazine. With Sergeant Swanson's carbine and the salvaged weapons, they at least felt armed.

Food and water were a problem: only three packs of sugar and a half-pound of coffee. They collected field dressings the Germans had missed and used them to patch each other's wounds. Soleski and Mitchell with his throat wound were the most serious.

The most coveted find was a compass Noble discovered in the pocket of the American captain.

Sergeant Swanson tousled the youngster's auburn hair and held his prize aloft. "This will get us home, boys!" He pulled a well-worn map from his jacket pocket and unfolded it. Soleski and the others crowded around.

"Take us anywhere them Jerries ain't, Sarge," requested O'Reilly.

Before they began moving, Soleski suggested they pray. None could kneel.

Even Samuel Cohen, a Chicago Jew and self-proclaimed agnostic, moved his lips as the tiny group mumbled the Twenty-third Psalm.

Their minimal spiritual cover in place, Sergeant Swanson looked hard at his ragtag squad of survivors. "I want you each to remember what happened here. You got that?" He circled solemnly, looking each man in the eyes, poking his finger in their chests. "Don't ever forget what they did here."

"If we make it back . . ." he corrected himself, ". . . when we make it back, we are going to tell our people what they did and we will . . . see . . . justice done. Never, ever forget." He gestured at the shattered bodies in the mud and snow. "You owe it to them to tell what happened."

He had given them their mission. To survive and to tell the story for the dead.

The sergeant handed Noble the only intact M1 and put him at point to take advantage of the private's proven marksmanship. The NCO took a rough bearing on the road with the tank tracks and said they would pursue that route as long as it went west. If they sighted Germans, said Swanson, they were to move immediately off the road and continue through the forest. He figured they had a day, maybe two, to reach an American unit.

Like the others, Swanson really had no idea just how far away their own lines had moved in these first two days of battle. Five hours of daylight travel now lay in front of them and Noble waited for the sergeant's sign to move. When the NCO waved to him, the young soldier stepped off at a moderate pace in order to spare the wounded struggling behind him. West of them a huge battle raged, judging from the sound of guns.

A light snow covered the bodies left behind with gentle, white shrouds.

Noble eyed the dark woods and prepared himself for the worst.

# CHAPTER SEVEN

## VA HOSPITAL, MINNEAPOLIS, JANUARY 19

Life for William Noble now depended on a slim green metal cylinder and eight feet of flexible plastic hose feeding compressed air to his failing lungs and heart.

The old man spent most of his day in a stiff red leather chair attached to this hated tank, its plastic necklace looped around his neck and ears. Every half hour, a nurse checked a dial measuring remaining air. When he slept, a bulky gray box near his hospital bed pumped air into his plastic tubing through the night. William Noble detested these devices that kept him alive. He sat in a square of sunshine pouring in his window at the Veteran's Hospital and remembered life before his doctor's diagnosis of congestive heart failure.

Back when Ellen was still alive. Prior to her cancer. Before the doctors and nurses and the endless parade of home healthcare aides from somewhere in West Africa, who spoke only broken English. They bathed and fed his Ellen like the fragile doll she had become. That was before the gentle, smiling nuns arrived to stay with his wife during her last two months of life. She had insisted on dying in her own home and those hospice volunteers had honored that request with compassion.

Now, five years after her death, he was certain it was his turn.

Listless, bored, in his blue wool bathrobe, he wished for death. When his melancholia lifted, he read the local papers and used precious oxygen to rail against the decline of the country, politics and the courts. No one listened to his lonely tirades and he eventually sputtered and mumbled incoherent sentences before falling silent. His body was failing him. Imprisoning him in his eighty-first year.

Yet William Noble had unfinished business, and he pinned his hopes on his only living relative, a grandson. The young man's visits were the only thing that could brighten his day, put a temporary end to his morose pouting.

At twenty-six, Peter Noble resembled his grandfather at that same age.

The younger man was taller at six feet, but his features mirrored the same square-jawed, determined look of photos from 1944. Thick, dark brown hair, hazel eyes and heavy eyebrows that bounced when he talked excitedly. The signature Noble smile was there as well, a toothy grin spread wide in raucous laughter when sharing a ribald joke or some hilarious family story told at a distant relative's expense.

Every gesture reminded Noble of his youth.

The old man loved this mirror image and rejoiced in his grandson's twice-weekly visits. William's own son, dead now for ten years, had never bonded like this grandson, and Noble regretted his awkward parenting, having never really understood the role of a father. His own parent had been equally distant, something in the dark brooding Scandinavian character that was locked in the family's men.

Not so his grandson. Peter Noble was light against the dark. Open instead of closed. Given to a spontaneity that baffled but delighted the old man. A year ago Peter had sold his downtown loft on the Mississippi River for a scandalous profit and had moved into the basement apartment at his grandparent's Minnehaha Avenue bungalow to care for the patriarch. The face-saving reason was to economize, but they both knew the real purpose was to prolong the old man's life.

With Peter's clerical job at the County Government Center, the nearby train to downtown made the move practical. Peter Noble paid no rent, his only obligations being maintenance, meals and shopping. William loved the arrangement.

He buzzed again for the ward's elusive male nurse who was about to go off duty. When the tardy man finally arrived, Noble demanded to be taken to the large waiting room at the end of the hall. There he could look east and watch the light rail train station for his grandson. The nurse made a noisy show of helping Noble to his feet. They shuffled as a pair, down past the nursing station and out to the open area where cushioned chairs were drawn up in soldierly rows against a bank of windows. Noble dismissed the man with a cursory nod and stood leaning against the windowsill, the wheeled tank sitting beside him like a watchdog tethered by its plastic leash.

The Hiawatha line ran in front of the main gate of the Minneapolis VA Hospital and the station was visible just beyond a sea of cars covering every foot of open space. Snow had fallen steadily since early morning, creating drifts, blanketing sidewalks and streets. The old man wondered if his grandson would decide against coming.

*He will come*, he thought. *He must come. We have to talk. Settle things. He has to know*, he told himself.

All these years without speaking of it and now it had come down to this. These last few precious years. Maybe only months, if his doctors were to be believed. Once he had thought his son, an only child, would have been the one to tell. But then, at age forty, his namesake and daughter-in-law had perished in a car crash, killed outside Duluth by a drunken driver. In the wake of that event, Noble suffered the first of his two heart attacks and had put away the secret.

Only his grandson was left now.

It was his grandson Peter who now gave the old man hope. *I will tell him*, he thought. *We will sit down and he will listen to me without interruption.*

"Are we all right, Mr. Noble?"

He knew the swing shift nurse's voice and did not turn from the window.

"I'm fine, thank you, Francis."

He kept his eyes on the transit platform, ignoring her shadowing presence behind him, knowing she was sneaking up to check the tank's remaining air.

"Well, let me know when we're ready to go back to our room."

He snorted, barely acknowledging her. He heard her footsteps fade.

*Why do medical staff always refer to "we"?* he wondered. *"We" are not suffering. I am suffering. "We" wish to be left alone.* He smiled at his sarcasm.

Beyond the hospital parking lot, out past the Crosstown Highway, beyond the hidden banks of the Minnesota River, a single airliner approached the airport, its landing lights piercing a sudden snow squall. He watched it float down and disappear behind the terminal and hangers. Another plane was already in its wake, coming in low across the river. And beyond that one, another was lining up.

Noble touched a window and quickly drew his hand back from the frigid glass. Snow swirled against the panes and the sun yielded to twilight.

Minnesota winters depressed him. Though he had lived here all his life, the older he got, the less he embraced this season. He mourned when colors bled from the landscape and lakes were locked in ice until April. Each succeeding winter affected him more and he longed to be home, settled in his high-backed wing chair, watching flames devour logs he had cut at his lake cabin.

Not this year.

A train pulled into the station and he scanned the exiting crowd filing across the pavement. He spotted his grandson, clad in a familiar yellow down vest and jeans, striding across the parking lot, working his way through rows of cars toward the main entrance. The old man turned and sank into the padded chair, facing the bank of elevators. He rehearsed his appeal and waited for the doors to open. Minutes crept by.

When the elevator stopped on Noble's floor, a volunteer rolled out a wheelchair with a pale elderly veteran. The old soldier was shrunken, hidden in a too-large robe and tied to an IV on a pole. A young black couple followed the chair and then Peter Noble stepped out and crossed the reception area to his grandfather.

"Hey, Gramps." A handshake and a hug for Noble as he tried to rise.

"Wasn't sure you'd come in this weather."

His grandson pulled up a chair next to the patriarch. The signature eyebrows rose and fell. "This storm? You kidding? It's nothing. We might get a foot before morning." He stretched in the chair. "Don't worry, I've already got the Peterson kid shoveling the walk and driveway for us." The younger man sat back and undid his vest, shaking off melting snow. "How's your day been?"

Noble shrugged, palms up. "No change. How about you. Your job okay?"

"What can I say? It was the same as yesterday. It'll be the same tomorrow."

"And how's Jean what's-her-name?" Noble asked, more out of courtesy than real interest.

This latest girl was someone at work who Peter had dated for several months. Noble did not approve, thinking the young lady shallow and sour, but held his tongue or steered the conversation elsewhere whenever her name was mentioned. An angry lady with too many rough edges, he thought.

Peter sighed. "Aw, I don't know. I'm not sure it's working out. She seems so needy lately. Kinda bossy, too." He threw up his hands. "Nothing seems to please her like when we first starting seeing each other."

His grandfather let him talk.

"What's your opinion of Jean, Gramps?"

Noble rubbed his chin and toyed with the oxygen tub under his nose. "Women." He shrugged and cleared his throat, attempted a deflecting smile. "Sorry . . . I don't really know. Guess it's really your problem to solve, Peter." Noble wanted to avoid the subject. Talk about more important things.

Peter leaned in to catch his grandfather's eyes. "Your opinion is important, Gramps."

"Want me to be blunt?"

"Of course. Grandma always said you had good intuition. So, what do you think?" said Peter, "Should I wait it out?"

He shifted in the chair. "Don't take this the wrong way." He paused. The junior Noble waited. "Seems to me she's kinda . . . pardon my French . . . bitchy . . . most of the time."

Peter let out his breath slowly and produced an embarrassed smile.

"Sorry, kiddo, but you asked," said the old man apologetically.

"No, no. You're right. I've felt it for weeks, you know."

Silence. The moment passed.

Noble leaned forward and gripped his grandson's knee with a gnarled hand. "Glad you came. We need to talk, Peter."

"Sure, don't we always?"

Noble stared at Peter. "Not our usual banter, kiddo. I mean, I need to tell you things. Get you up to speed on certain . . . arrangements."

His grandson put a hand on Noble's arm and smiled gently. "If you mean all that funeral stuff again, I don't want to hear it."

The old man waved aside the comment. "Naw, that stuff is not that important. I've got that all written out. No, what we need to talk about is something I've wanted to tell you for a long time. Wanted to talk to your dad about it when the time came, but . . ." His voice trailed off and he turned to avoid his grandson's stare.

He cleared his throat and the awkwardness of the moment passed. "You know, I'm being discharged. After Wednesday I'll officially be on out-patient status again. It's good timing. I've got things to show you."

Peter straightened in his chair. "Are you really ready to come home? Your doctors must be pretty confident to let you leave."

Even though Noble had made this trip to the VA hospital twice before he had never expressed an urgency about returning home and he sensed his grandson's concern.

Noble waved. "Ah, they've probably written me off and they just don't want to tell me outright. I don't care about the reason. I'm ready to go home."

"If I need to," said Peter, "I can probably get the rest of the week off from work if you need me to stay with you during the day." He leaned forward, closer to his grandfather's face. "You know, just to make sure you don't push yourself too hard."

The old man patted his air tank.

"As long as I take along a couple of these babies I should be okay."

"What's so important about leaving now?" asked Peter, curious.

The old man folded his hands in his lap. "I have papers I need to explain to you. Lay some things out for you. You have to know about these things. Certain events. Things that happened. Things that have to happen. Will happen. Plans."

Peter reasoned with him. "If it's just some estate papers or family stuff, couldn't I just bring what you need to the hospital?" He tried to sell the idea to Noble. "You know, write down what you want. I could go down a list or something."

Noble shook his head. "No, Peter. We've got to have some uninterrupted time together. It has to be this way. See if you can get those days off, will ya?" He picked at the lapels of his robe. "I didn't think I'd be in here this long. Didn't think I was that sick. But now it can't wait. Has to be done right."

"Okay, okay," conceded Peter, "we'll talk to your doctors before you leave."

Noble took his grandson's hand in his and for the first time in their relationship he felt as if the guard were changing in some unspoken way. The moment was ruined by his nurse.

"Dinnertime, Mr. Noble," Francis sang at him from the hallway.

"Peter, let's talk tomorrow. I'll keep the pressure on my doctors on this end to make sure they don't change their minds. You could call them. Finalize things, okay?"

"Sure, Gramps," he smiled at the old man. "Your keepers are going to miss you."

They both laughed. The mirror image of the Noble grin on both faces.

# CHAPTER EIGHT

## MINNEAPOLIS, JANUARY 21

The mid-week discharge from the VA went ahead as scheduled. William Noble had badgered his doctors through the week to honor their promise to release him. He spent his last day gleefully reminding staff that he would soon be beyond their grasp. His grandson had already stocked a half-dozen extra bottles of air and the compressor sat silent at his home's bedside, ready for use.

Noble drafted one of the hospital's volunteers, a skinny Korean War veteran wearing a bright red baseball cap and black silk American Legion jacket with an embroided red dragon on the back. He got the man to wheel him to the elevators and stay with him until Peter picked him up in the loading zone. Handicap vans were lined up nose to tail and it took his grandson two passes before they spotted each other

"I'm surprised you're not wearing an ankle bracelet," kidded his grandson as he tucked a quilt around the old man.

"There's probably a tracking device hidden in one of my oxygen tanks," joked Noble.

They thanked the volunteer for his assistance and pulled out from a line of vans. Several women passed them in the cold, pushing wheelchairs with slouching elderly men riding in them. A three-chair caravan negotiated the crosswalk in front of them and William Noble stared as the wheelchairs passed.

"Thank God your grandmother didn't live long enough to end up doing that."

Peter chided him. "She would have been happy to do it, Gramps."

"Yeah, I know. She was a blessing, kiddo."

They left the VA and drove in silence along Hiawatha Avenue, past gas stations, fast-food restaurants, grain elevators and ugly warehouses turned into rental storage. The city's skyline loomed ahead of them. Noble had insisted they follow a roundabout route along the parkway that paralleled the Mississippi River. He wanted to see the city before heading home.

As instructed, Peter took the Lake Street exit and doubled back onto the parkway, heading south past beautiful, large homes fronting the curving road.

Noble felt captivated by the scenery. He turned to his driver. "Do you know how good this feels?"

His grandson grinned, pleased. "Must get pretty boring in the hospital, huh?"

"You betcha."

They followed the winding boulevard and Noble asked to see Minnehaha Falls. The parking lot was empty, dusted with snow. They pulled up to the curb and Peter came around to the passenger side and steadied the old man.

"Leave the damned oxygen tank behind for now," Noble ordered.

He walked arm in arm with his grandson and they stood against the wall to watch a meager icy flow trickling over a rocky ledge. William Noble breathed deep, intoxicated with the freedom of his excursion. A mother and child, faces wrapped in matching scarves, were the only other people in the park. The winter sky was swept clean of clouds and the sun's warmth masked the temperature.

"All right, I've seen enough. Let's go home," wheezed Noble.

They retraced their route to the car and when he had settled his grandfather, Peter drove along Minnehaha Avenue. He followed the ruts down their alley and parked next to Noble's garage. Peter helped the old man up the short flight of steps into the house. William Noble claimed his favorite chair facing the fireplace and accepted the oxygen hose without objection. Peter raced outside to put the car in the garage and when he returned, Noble asked him to light a fire.

"Won't we go up in a fireball?" Peter asked, nodding at the tank.

"Peter, chance it for your grandfather's sake, okay? Besides, it's only compressed air."

The young man shrugged and lit the kindling. He closed the brass doors, twisted the damper handle and watched the wood catch, the glow filling the room.

His grandfather was delighted. Peter pulled an ottoman next to the old man.

Noble spoke. "You know that wooden footlocker in my den?"

"The old green one with the lock?" asked Peter.

"That's it. I want you to get the key. Look under my bowling trophy." He continued. "Open the chest and lift the tray. You'll find a red leather box at the bottom. I want you to bring that to me, please."

Peter rose and left the room.

Noble watched flames lick logs of oak and maple and rehearsed his speech.

When his grandson returned with the box, William set it on his lap and reverently opened the lid. For a long time, he stared at the contents. Then he removed three manila envelopes and a small, bulky, gray felt bag and set the box aside.

"This one," he lifted the top envelope, "has instructions for my funeral. Who to contact, funeral home, prepaid cremation, safety deposit box inventory, forms for the VA, burial plot and even a music list. Make sure you don't play any of that modern stuff, kiddo." They laughed, breaking the seriousness of the moment.

The old man continued. "My will is included in here. Home, the cabin in Wisconsin, car, everything. It's a complete package, Peter. You shouldn't have any problems." He set the envelope aside and lifted a second one, staring at it for a long time before speaking.

"Did you ever hear me mention something called the 'Fortunate Orphans'?"

Noble detected a faint smile on his grandson's lips and he furrowed his brow to underscore the seriousness of his question. Peter shook his head, no.

Noble took several deep breaths, the tank giving him needed strength. "You know I was in the war, don't you?"

Noble's stories about his Army days in World War II had been rare, and even when told, seemed vague on details. His Ellen would always stop whatever she was doing and summon him to listen when certain forties tunes played on the radio, those particular songs from the war's era an intimate secret between the two of them. Noble's avoidance of war movies was the only other evidence of things unsaid. He knew his grandson had only a meager idea of what role he had played in the big war.

"You never talked about it, Gramps. Mom said you avoided it for the most part."

"Not entirely true, Peter." He passed a hand over his face, rubbing his eyelids.

"Your grandmother never approved of the name of my . . ." he corrected himself, "our . . . little group. 'The Fortunate Orphans.'"

Peter finally smiled in spite of himself.

"Catchy title, don't you think?" said Noble. "Ever hear of Bastogne, Peter?"

His grandson sat up. "Yeah, sure. Everybody knows the story, Gramps." He nodded at the envelope. "Is that what this is about? Were you there?" He paused, waiting for an affirmation.

"No, not actually at Bastogne. But it was all part of what's known as the . . ."

"Battle of the Bulge," his grandson interrupted. "I've seen some movies."

The old man snorted. "Ha, movies. Hollywood never got it right. Never will."

Peter protested. "*Band of Brothers* and *Saving Private Ryan* were pretty good though, Gramps."

Noble stared down again at the papers in his lap. "I wouldn't know," he said. "But I'm going to tell you a story, Peter. It's true. Every word of it. What I can remember, that is." His grandson got up to poke at the wood and added more logs.

Peter resumed his seat. "Did Dad know all this stuff, Gramps?"

He shook his head slowly. "No, I never had the chance. It wasn't time yet and then . . . the accident." He sighed. "Maybe it's just as well he never knew. He had his own life, and you were about to go to college. I meant to tell him when the time was right, but . . ." He left the thought hanging there, unfinished. How to return to the moment? How to set the mood? "Why don't we have lunch and then take some time here by the fire, Peter?"

"Sure, Gramps, you gather your thoughts while I fix us something."

Noble was grateful for the respite. He leaned back against the chair and closed his eyes. How to explain this? Would Peter listen? He scolded himself for waiting all these years. But it couldn't be helped. There was no urgency until late last year when the doctors got into the act. And now, there's so little time. *God help me*, he pleaded. *I must get every word right.* He ran the story in his head once more, waiting to start again.

Noble relaxed and shared a platter of fresh fruit, cheese and bread with his grandson. They ate in near silence, the only sounds coming from the fireplace, where birch logs popped as flames devoured them.

Noble finished eating and lifted the envelopes from his lap. He gave them to Peter. "Why don't you put these on the dining room table. We can go through them in a bit, okay? I'm going to rest my eyes for a bit."

Noble pulled a quilt tight around his frail body and yawned.

Peter gathered the envelopes and tiptoed into the dining room. He dropped them on the table and sat down to read through the first folder.

Noble opened his eyes and gazed across the room at his grandson hunched over the contents of the envelopes. He knew Peter was making a mental inventory of the paper spread out in front on him. *You will find every possible contingency has been covered in the event of my death*, Noble thought. *No surprises there for you, kiddo. So precise, so thorough. So prepared.*

Behind the glass doors, the fire dropped glowing embers softly to the hearth.

Peter put the paperwork aside and stared at the remaining two envelopes but did not open them. Instead, he reached for the small, gray felt bag.

Across the room, Noble closed his eyes, then opened them in time to observe his grandson loosen the drawstring and empty the bag's contents onto the tablecloth. Sunlight glinted off the metal stars and rainbow ribbons. A polished, wreathed badge with a silver musket on a field of blue enamel tumbled out on top of the other medals. He picked up a gold star hanging from a red, white and blue ribbon and held it delicately in his palm. Peter found two Purple Hearts among several other medals. There were several bronze medallions with faded striped ribbons attached to them. He slipped them back into the soft bag and pulled the string tight.

"They're only part of the story, Peter."

He was startled by his grandfather's voice. The old man had been watching him.

"I was just curious, Gramps," Peter said apologetically.

"No need to excuse yourself, kiddo. I'll get to those medals in due time."

He stretched in the chair and yawned again. "I needed that nap," he said. Peter, embarrassed, put the bag back with the funeral envelope and got up from the table.

Noble shrugged off the blanket. "You know, kiddo, I really don't feel much like dinner if that's okay with you." Peter shrugged. "No problem. I'm not that hungry either."

"Say, Gramps, how would your doctor view your sharing a bottle of wine?"

"He'd vote no, but I'd love it. Pour us some."

Peter returned with two large goblets of blush wine and handed one to his grandfather.

The light was beginning to fade, shadows lengthening on the small living room floor. The fire needed tending. The young man set his glass down and stoked the flames, adding more fuel. He returned to his position beside Noble.

"When I was younger than you . . . hell, Peter, I was just barely eighteen. A lifetime ago. Didn't even know your grandmother then. Thought I was a real patriot. Had to get my parents' permission to enlist. That was tough on them . . . Ended up in Europe. Thank God I missed Normandy. Oh, those poor guys . . . Had friends who came through it, but I didn't go over until fall in forty-four. I ended up with a front seat for one of the biggest battles in the war."

The old man took a long swallow and began his recitation about the Ardennes.

## CHAPTER NINE

Yellow-white embers formed a glowing mound on the brick hearth.

The living room filled with silence. An antique brass clock broke the mood, its soft gonging sounds announcing the hour from the oak mantel. Outside, the wind had dropped to an occasional breeze, twisting wind chimes on the bungalow's front porch. Peter Noble poured the remaining wine into his grandfather's goblet and studied the old man's face in the firelight. The tale had taken hours to reach this point.

"Did you make it back to the American lines?"

William Noble looked down into his wine and sighed. "Yeah, we made it back after two days of hide-and-seek with the Germans." He drained his glass. "We eventually had to leave the road and head southwest to avoid their armor. They were everywhere. None of us had ever seen so many tanks before."

His grandson rose and placed a small log on the fire to keep the flames alive. He abandoned the ottoman and pulled an armchair next to him.

"We mixed leftover sugar with coffee and divided it between us." He chuckled. "It tasted awful but it was all we had. Ted Mitchell died just before we finally found our lines. Lungs gave out. Died without complaining. Must have drowned in his own blood." His voice was emotionless. "You know, Sport, I'm suddenly very tired." He looked at his grandson. "You think we could continue this in the morning?"

The younger man nodded and helped Noble to his feet. He escorted him to the back bedroom with its adjoining bathroom. They embraced and Noble sank heavily onto the thick quilts. "I'll be all right, Peter, thanks."

His grandson switched on the oxygen box beside the bed and offered the tubing.

"At least I won't be alone," laughed William.

His grandson retreated. "If you need me for anything, Gramps . . ."

Noble picked up a ceramic bell on the nightstand and shook it.

"I know," he responded, "just ring." Peter laughed and said goodnight.

Noble sat on his bed and undressed. He heard his grandson in the living room, poking at the dying fire, scattering glowing coals to kill the flames.

Peter closed the glass doors and left a hall light burning. As his grandson descended to his basement apartment, Noble was humming happily in the bathroom.


The old man was up first.

He flipped off his air pump and shaved and dressed before his grandson stirred. Noble shuffled into his kitchen and made coffee in the microwave.

He cupped the steaming mug as he stared through frosted windows at drifts along the sidewalks. A city plow worked its way up Minnehaha Avenue, throwing an arc of gritty snow against the curb. The big orange truck wove its way around parked cars that snow had turned into immovable white mounds. He imagined the driver cursing the obstacles.

Street lights winked off in the dawn.

The retired Honeywell engineer next door was up early, chopping perfect pathways through snowbanks with customary precision. With his neighbor's rhythmic shoveling, Noble drank his good strong coffee. A tardy newspaper carrier battled drifts to the porch and stuffed the *Star Tribune* through the mail slot. He heard his grandson moving in the basement apartment. Hot water clicked in plastic pipes and radiators hissed in chorus, comforting Noble as he sank into a favorite chair.

*Thank you, Lord, for bringing me back home,* he thought, smiling.

Peter emerged from the basement stairs and waved good morning. He poured a glass of orange juice and passed through the living room on his way to the front door where he plucked the paper from the porch below the mail slot. A shot of sub-zero air followed him indoors.

"Whoa, it's really cold this morning, Gramps."

He shouldered the door shut and padded back into the kitchen to start breakfast. Noble sipped from his mug and enjoyed the sounds of home.

Peter was an excellent cook and in thirty minutes he ushered his grandfather into the kitchen for breakfast. The two sat across from each other on hard white benches flanking a formica top dating to the late fifties. The men ate in silence, each with his part of the morning paper. They traded sections and lingered over plates of scrambled eggs, bacon, biscuits and fruit. "More coffee?" asked Peter.

Noble held out his mug without looking as his grandson re-filled it.

"I've probably maxed you out on sodium for the week," chuckled the youth.

"And bless you for it. That was a terrific breakfast, Sport."

They laughed and finished reading. Peter Noble cleared the dishes and cleaned up the kitchen. He made a pot of tea for himself and freshened the old man's coffee.

Noble spoke. "Let's sit at the dining room table, if you don't mind."

While his grandfather shuffled toward the long oak table, Peter brought a slim green tank and breathing tube from the bedroom and sat it beside the old man. When the nose tube was in place, Peter twisted the dial to the proper setting and sat next to Noble. William pointed to the largest manila envelope and wagged a finger, indicating he wanted it. Peter set it in front of him and Noble stacked the contents neatly in three parallel piles. Noble took several deep, slow breaths that relaxed him and plucked up two sheets of paper stapled together.

"Remember yesterday when I asked you if you had ever heard of Bastogne?"

Peter nodded. Waited.

"Ever heard of Malmédy, Peter?"

His grandson did not recognize the name.

"Well," said Noble, "it's pretty well known to GIs who fought in the Battle of the Bulge. The SS captured a bunch of GIs from an artillery battalion and opened fire on them after they had sur-rendered." Noble looked down, grim. "They murdered eighty-six of our guys. Lined them up and shot 'em down."

"Like what happened to your outfit, Gramps?"

"Exactly, Peter." Noble took more deep breaths.

"Our group was only two dozen guys. From different outfits."

He put a hand on the young man's shoulder. "We weren't the only ones. Stuff like this was going on all over the front. GIs, civilians, whoever got caught up in that fight." Noble sat back, staring at the piles of paper. "But history remembers the Malmédy Massacre. That's what it was, really."

"Was it the same group of Germans that captured your outfit?"

"They were all related in a way. Malmédy was the work of Kampfgruppe Peiper. That means Battle Group. It was an SS outfit led by a Lieutenant Colonel named Joachim Peiper. He was a tough Nazi bastard and he took no prisoners during the Bulge."

The old man straightened the stack of papers in front of him and continued. "Our own version of Peiper was a guy named Von Wurtz and he was as much an evil sonofabitch as any of them. Same division. Only difference was numbers."

Noble read Peter's solemn expression and knew the tale had deeply affected him.

The old man was pale, as though the re-telling had drained the life from him.

Noble paused, asked for water. Peter returned with a filled glass and his grandfather emptied the tumbler. He fussed with the papers, gathering his thoughts.

"What happened to these guys? Were they ever caught?"

Noble flashed a tight smile. "Oh, yeah, Peiper was put on trial after the war. He and some of his men were sentenced to death but it got commuted and he served about twelve years in prison."

The younger Noble was taken aback. "He got out of jail after all that?"

"Story doesn't end there, Peter. He moved around. Couldn't go back to Germany because of his past." Noble snorted. "He eventually settled in France of all places. Near the German border somewhere. There were other SS around. All of them close enough to the Fatherland but out of the public eye."

"They still there?"

Noble seemed to grimace. "Who knows? Not Peiper, though. Someone leaked his whereabouts and he had to send his family back to Germany. One night in the late seventies, some locals, probably some communists, set fire to his house and killed him. End of story."

His grandson sat there, a stunned look in his eyes. "Justice, huh, Gramps?"

Noble nodded, flashing a tight grin as he shook his head slowly. "Now, to business at hand. I want to tell you about Sam Cohen and the others."

William Noble plucked a piece of paper from the top of the pile and read slowly through a list of names. He heard his voice but his mind remained focused on the image of bloodied fields and American bodies crumpled in snow and mud.

# CHAPTER TEN

## CHICAGO, LAW OFFICES OF COHEN,
## GREEN AND SHOWALTER, JANUARY 22

As Noble read names to his grandson in Minneapolis, the first man on that list was sitting at a long table in a Chicago law firm's conference room.

Attorney Samuel Cohen was studying a report prepared by four of his law firm's junior partners. The anxious quartet faced Samuel Cohen across the polished mahogany surface. Four months of their work was arranged in a smooth, red leather folder in front of the senior partner of Cohen, Green and Showalter, one of Chicago's most prestigious firms.

Unlike the Ivy Leaguers facing him, Samuel Cohen was a GI Bill product of the city's John Marshall Law School. In 1947, he and fellow serviceman Stanley Green had joined lawyer David Showalter, a Navy veteran with an encyclopedic grasp of Chicago politics and a rising star in the city's legal circles. The trio were soon running circles around their WASP contemporaries and the firm prospered.

Those two original partners were long dead, honored with somber oil portraits in the firm's quiet, paneled hallways. Cohen had always looked to the future and, as sole senior partner, had been drafting carefully since the seventies, attracting quick talent—like the latest crop of hungry young men facing him across the conference table.

Cohen's heavy-lidded blue eyes drifted over his acolytes, past the heavy silk draperies and rich paneling, to a panorama of Lake Michigan filling a bank of floor-to-ceiling windows.

He was legendary for ordering his thoughts this way, using the shimmering body of water as a focus while his mind cataloged and arranged words, so that when he spoke it was with finality.

Cohen's Zen, the staff called it behind his back.

His gaunt tanned face broke into a paternal smile as he turned back to the eager foursome and pushed the portfolio toward the middle of the table.

"I think . . ." he said quietly as the men leaned slightly forward. Cohen paused, detecting the shifts in their postures, and tried to let them down gently. No reason to throw away several months' work, he told himself. "I think, gentlemen," he continued, "that your presentation is basically sound."

The foursome relaxed a bit. They were not home free but they had passed the first hurdle.

"However, you might want to think a little more conservatively about the settlement you suggest here." He tapped the folder twice and watched for signs of disappointment. No response. No arguments. Nothing. *Good*, he thought. "Jeremy, would you agree?"

Cohen waited for a reaction from the team leader, a dark-haired, athletic-looking Harvard Law alum who favored serious brooding looks when challenged, as the senior partner was doing now. On cue, the man's handsome face darkened, thick eyebrows dropping into a gloomy furrow. "Well, sir, we thought the case pretty weak given the way the first two plaintiffs settled so quickly."

"Rolled over, or maybe bent over, would be a better description," said Cohen, defusing the tension. The young men chuckled nervously as one.

"My words, of course," offered Cohen. "I suggest you talk over that last piece amongst yourselves and give us a new option, okay?" He glanced at his watch. "Let's meet at four and agree on new numbers."

"We'll be here," said the quartet's leader, rising, the four nodding to each other.

Samuel Cohen stood and threw a verbal bouquet after them. "All in all, good work all around, Jeremy. Solid on your details, gentlemen."

They smiled politely as they filed past the massive table in their matching blue shirts and striped Robert Talbot ties. "Thank you, sir," each mumbled in turn.

"See you at four then," beamed Cohen paternally.

He turned back to his view of Lake Michigan and studied wintertime joggers as they pounded along the cleared lakeshore promenade far below. Pushing away from the table, he smoothed his thinning silver hair, touching a faded scar along his right temple out of habit. Cohen strolled back to his corner office, his hatchet-faced profile reflected in the glass panels of the conference room.

His secretary, a pale, narrow-faced blonde in her sixties with too much makeup, wide hips and large, out-of-date eyeglasses, was waiting for him. She had a phone tucked against her shoulder and waved an orange phone slip at him.

Orange was for urgent personal calls.

Cohen plucked the note from her hand without stopping and pulled a pair of reading spectacles from his breast pocket as he entered his large corner office. He scanned the handwriting and sank down into a high backed leather chair.

Long distance. Washington. Name and number unfamiliar. He dialed it himself.

The line rang twice and Cohen swiveled in his chair to gaze at the wedding cake architecture of the Wrigley Building framed in his window.

A woman's voice answered on the third ring. "Office of Special Investigations. Mr. Banner's office. How may I help you?"

The office's title made him pause. Perhaps something concerning a client? "Samuel Cohen in Chicago. Returning Mr. Banner's call."

"One moment, please." There was a pause and then a male voice. "Richard Banner here, Mr. Cohen."

"Yes. You called earlier?" Samuel Cohen waited.

"Of course. I need to tell you this is an unofficial communication, Mr. Cohen."

"Well, all right, go on," said Cohen, puzzled.

Banner's voice deepened. "We have a mutual friend, I believe. Carl Goldman from Senator Proctor Johnson's office?"

Cohen was momentarily stumped. Proctor Johnson had been the state's senior senator until a crushing loss in the last election. He was now turning out critical books on foreign policy with the regularity of a Bob Woodward. The former senator was also a high profile evangelical who lobbied for Israel as well as an assortment of wealthy business clients who paid him handsomely for his Washington connections.

Part of the reference jogged Cohen's memory.

"Yes. Carl Goldman." He remembered the name. The two had crossed paths at several Council of Foreign Relations dinners in the last three years.

"What's your connection to Carl Goldman, Mr. Banner?"

"I have what might be interesting news, Mr. Cohen. It's a confirmation of sorts, concerning information Carl brought to your attention this fall."

Samuel Cohen tried hard to order his thoughts. "Perhaps you could refresh my memory, Mr. Banner."

"I don't mean to be obtuse but Carl said you had asked his help for a veterans group called the 'Fortunate Orphans.' Does any of this make sense, Mr. Cohen?"

The attorney drummed his long elegant fingers on his desk. "Ah, yes, I vaguely recall that conversation." Cohen was still slightly perplexed but did not admit it. He grasped for details. "And what exactly is your role in all this, Mr. Banner?"

"Are you familiar with our office, sir? Do you know our mission?"

"Would I be right to assume you are with the federal government?"

"That is correct, sir."

"Sorry, Mr. Banner, but even as an upper-bracket taxpayer I'm ashamed to say I haven't the foggiest idea what your agency does." Cohen leaned back and waited.

"Not surprising, sir. We may well be the only federal office that's actually trying to work itself out of a job."

Cohen was growing impatient with the veiled talk. "I don't mean to be blunt, Mr. Banner, but perhaps if you got to the point."

"Fair enough, sir. Our office is a division of the Justice Department, and our mandate is to hunt a dying breed . . . Nazis."

Cohen sat upright, suddenly intrigued. "Go on."

His caller continued. "Primarily we investigate people who managed to slip into America after World War II. People who lied about their role in the war. Those who served in the camps, the Nazi party, killing squads . . . the SS. War criminals, sir."

The connection was starting to register with the senior partner of Cohen, Green and Showalter.

"Mr. Cohen, your long-term interest in the whereabouts of one particular party is the subject of my call. Am I making myself fairly clear?"

Now both men understood the need for code. Samuel Cohen sat back, blood beginning to pound in his ears. "Yes, I'm gratified to know you've been able to confirm my inquiry to Carl."

Banner again. "One glitch in this scenario, sir. Your party of interest is no longer presently within our department's jurisdiction."

"You're saying the party is still alive and was once within your jurisdiction?"

"Yes to the first part. But the answer to the second part of your question is bit more complicated."

"I don't understand," said the lawyer.

"We thought we had probable cause to look into this party but apparently he had not entered the country in search of residency. We think it was a business visit, possibly as recent as eight months ago. No contacts since."

"Then why the call?" asked Cohen, aroused.

"Strictly a favor to Carl. He asked me to contact you once our sources could confirm his inquiry on your behalf. He put out a lot of feelers and our office was one of the positive hits, I guess. My obligation was to verify his information. Think of this phone call as a good faith effort from our office, sir. A courtesy to you and your friends for your past service, Mr. Cohen."

Was this a classic bureaucratic disclaimer? Samuel wasn't sure. Didn't care. Here was proof. He had to talk to Carl Goldman, and quickly. Contact the others if what he was hearing was true.

Banner ended the conversation. "We won't talk again, Mr. Cohen, but I hope this helps. Godspeed."

The line went dead. The attorney stared at the phone and then leaped nimbly to his feet and poked his head out the door. "Anne, see if you can find the number for a Carl Goldman in Senator Proctor Johnson's Chicago office. Try to get him on the phone. If I'm in a meeting, call me out, okay?"

His secretary looked up, reading his urgency.

"Will do. Oh, and remember your lunch with the Mathis group at noon."

"Try to reschedule it," ordered the attorney. "If that doesn't work, ask Hank to take it for me. He can brief me later. I'm going down the hall again. If you reach Goldman, transfer the call, please."

Samuel Cohen headed back to his firm's conference room. He had to process his caller's startling news. He felt apprehensive but also ecstatic. It had been sixty-plus years since the war and each year pushed the memory of the men in the Ardennes further back in his mind.

Fortunate Orphans. The name had been his idea. He and his old friend William Noble were the twin driving forces, the conscience of the group. Cohen and Noble were the ones who kept the little band together with reunion dinners. The years between gatherings had increased as they aged but they always answered when he called the others with plans for the next get-together.

It was past time, he knew. He would call Noble and then the others.

But first Samuel Cohen needed to gaze at Lake Michigan. To think. Maybe grieve, perhaps rejoice.

## CHAPTER ELEVEN

Cohen sat in contemplation for twenty minutes before his solitude was broken twice.

His first interruption was law partner Hank Moser, poking his bulky, disheveled body halfway into the conference room doorway. He coughed discreetly and Cohen turned away from the lake. Moser nodded. "Samuel."

"Hello, Hank."

"You want me to take the Mathis meeting? Something else come up?"

"Yes, I've got to meet with someone from Senator Johnson's office today and the Mathis thing gets in the way. I'd appreciate it if you'd handle it for me."

The other lawyer tugged at his bright red suspenders. "Any complications I should be aware of, Sam?"

They had both shepherded the contract with the Mathis Utilities board from day one but it had been Cohen's idea.

"There shouldn't be any surprises. Anne has the file. She'll fill you in on the last two calls I had with them."

"Okay, that should be routine then." He turned to go but paused. "Everything okay, Samuel?"

"Yes, Hank. Everything is fine. Just fine. And thanks for doing this for me. I'll owe you . . . again."

Moser's pink jowls jiggled in a chuckle. "That's what I like to hear. The senior partner owes me one."

When Hank Moser left, Cohen turned again to the lake, but within minutes his secretary's voice derailed his thoughts.

"Carl Goldman from Senator Johnson's office on line one, Mr. Cohen."

"Thanks, Anne, I'll take it. Oh, and Hank will be coming by for the Mathis file."

"Very good, sir."

She rang off, and Cohen leaned forward and punched a button on a console on the polished table. Goldman's voice boomed through the machine.

"Samuel, it's good to hear from you."

"Likewise, Carl." Pleasantries aside, Cohen launched into the reason for his call. "Had an interesting chat earlier, Carl. With one Richard Banner of the Office of Special Investigations, Washington."

Goldman's voice dropped lower. "Good. I wanted him to confirm some information I turned up on your behalf."

"Well, it was very intriguing," Cohen replied. "Question is, what do I do with it now?"

Goldman answered immediately. "Could we talk more about this, Sam? Say, over lunch?"

Cohen had hoped for the offer. "I'd like that. I've canceled the one big meeting I had scheduled and I don't have to be back here until four to wrap up some details on a contract. Lunch would be good. How about Nick's Fishmarket on Clark and Monroe. Do you know it, Carl?"

"Like a second home, Sam. We'll have to try their lobster bisque."

"All right, let's make it for eleven-thirty. I'll call ahead. It's usually crowded."

"Done," agreed Goldman.

Samuel Cohen rang off and focused on his lake.

# CHAPTER TWELVE

## CHICAGO, CLARK AND MONROE

Carl Goldman reached the restaurant first and followed the host to a table in the back of the main dining room, a table that promised a reasonable amount of privacy. In his early forties, with thinning black hair combed over a large pale dome, Goldman reminded people of Richard Nixon's hatchet man, John Ehrlichmann. Like the Nixonian aide he resembled, Goldman took no pains to conceal his superiority around those he considered intellectually inferior. Goldman was a human remora, owing his existence to men more powerful than himself. He had cultivated a habit of attaching himself to the right man at the right time.

As Senator Proctor Johnson's chief of staff, Carl Goldman had gained footholds in both Washington and Illinois politics and, for a while, it seemed that all things were possible for a man many considered Johnson's alter ego. But after two elections and a flirtation with presidential politics, something had gone awry for the senior senator from Illinois. Goldman had tumbled with him, his Senate talisman shattered in pieces. Proctor Johnson lost his last election in a humiliating reversal, blindsided by personal indiscretions and a fickle electorate.

As a result, Carl Goldman had seen his own influence wane. For now, he was surviving, content to wait until the next sure thing, sniffing out new opportunities as the former senator's public liaison to publishers, lobbyists and evangelicals. Something would break Carl Goldman's way and soon. He knew he was not destined to serve as a glorified fixer or errand boy. Carl Goldman spent his energy carefully now, touching people throughout the system, dispensing favors and arranging things for powerful men with long memories. He was accumulating IOUs, filing them away, always calculating.

And so he sat in this restaurant, waiting to meet with one of Chicago's most powerful lawyers, hoping that he had turned another seemingly trivial piece of information into gold, something important to his lunch guest.

Goldman ordered two glasses of house wine and dismissed the waiter just as he spotted Samuel Cohen's lanky frame threading his way between tables near the entrance. He signaled the lawyer and the older man turned his way. Goldman rose and leaned in a subtle bow. They shook hands.

"Counselor, nice to see you again."

"You too, Carl. Good of you to meet on such short notice."

"When one of Chicago's most illustrious members of the bar calls for a meeting, I make the time, Sam." Goldman at his obsequious best.

Cohen winced. "You sound just like one of our junior partners, Carl."

Goldman laughed. "Seriously, Sam. I'm here on behalf of Proctor Johnson to do what I can for you. You know that."

He spread his napkin across his lap as the lawyer sat down.

"And I appreciate the gesture," said Cohen.

"I took the liberty of ordering," said Goldman. "Lobster bisque, a small house salad and a glass of the house wine."

Cohen set aside the menu. "I approve of your choice, Carl." A waiter approached with two filled glasses. When their server left, Cohen laced bony fingers together and leaned forward. "Your man Banner had some very interesting things to say, Carl."

The other man smiled. "I thought you'd find his information quite useful."

Cohen continued. "He corroborated your initial report to me, and if I understand what Banner was telling me, the man I've been searching for actually stepped foot in this country eight months ago. Could that be right?"

Goldman nodded. " Correct. He was here looking for some deep pockets in our own American Midwest. It's not a done deal but a couple of Franco-German companies are putting together financing for a development in Germany. The thing's rumored to be in the billions. Some sort of huge business park venture for folks with lots of venture capital to burn. Even the Saudis might be interested."

Cohen snorted. "Part of the globalization thing, I suppose."

"Something like that. But that's not the important part, is it? I mean, that's not the real point of interest, is it?"

The server arrived with their salads. Cohen waited for him to leave and then looked down as he toyed with his silverware. "No. The gentleman is the point. Are you sure it's him?"

"Without question, Samuel. It's him." He pulled a manila envelope from a dark case beside his chair and placed it on the table, teasing Cohen, letting him stare at it.

"What's that?"

Goldman purred, "It's everything you need to know about your man." He stroked the package. "The senator insisted that you be given all the pertinent information. It's very current."

Cohen eyed the envelope, obviously fascinated. "Convey my gratitude to him. Perhaps I can return the favor someday."

Carl Goldman allowed himself a patronizing smile, filing away the offer. "I'll be sure to pass your thanks on to him." Goldman pushed the envelope at Cohen, who seemed reluctant to take it.

The lawyer picked up the package and placed it to his right.

Goldman launched into an outline of Proctor Johnson's latest book, a lengthy scolding of the Palestinians and their inability to govern themselves. Cohen nodded approvingly and politely, asking several questions as they ate.

After a pair of waiters arrived with the lobster bisque and the men began to eat, Goldman broke the spell again. "What are you going to do with it?" He pointed a fork at the package.

The lawyer appeared distracted. "I don't know." Cohen moved his spoon slowly back and forth in his porcelain bowl. "I never thought anything would ever come of this. That I'd actually live to see this day." Goldman sipped his wine and ate his bisque, averting his eyes, sensing that he should let the lawyer do the talking. "All these years . . ." Samuel Cohen's gaze drifted around the dining room. "I've wondered about a moment like this but never thought about what I'd actually do if the time ever came."

Goldman brought the lawyer back to the present. "Once you have a chance to look over the contents, might I suggest that you call me? I know people who may prove useful to you in the future."

Cohen arched an eyebrow at his luncheon partner. "Oh, who? In what way?"

Goldman turned conspiratorial. "Just those who have some expertise in . . . um, matters similar to this." He put a reassuring hand on the lawyer's arm. "I think they might be able to help make some sense of this for you. Will you call me?"

"Of course," promised Cohen. They finished their lunch and declined dessert. Cohen insisted on paying for the meal.

"What's next, Samuel?"

The older man stood and tucked the envelope under his arm. He patted the parcel. "I'm going back to the office to sort through this. Then I'll make some calls to friends who have a right to know." He extended his hand to Goldman. "Some of us might get together and talk." He waved the manila envelope. "I'm grateful, Carl."

"My pleasure, Samuel. I'll tell the senator you were pleased."

"Do that."

Goldman sank back down and lifted his wine glass. "Sam, remember what I said about putting you in touch with people who can help you with this . . . venture of yours."

"I'll do that."

Goldman watched the lawyer disappear in the crowd.

Carl Goldman lingered at the table, finished his wine and then flipped open his cell phone. "It's Carl, put me through to the senator."

Proctor Johnson's voice boomed through the cell phone. "Did he accept the package?"

"Yes, sir, he did. All went according to plan. He seemed very pleased."

"Good job, Carl. Score one for our side. You think he'll accept the other offer?"

Goldman reflected on the last part of his lunch conversation. "He's thinking about it. He'll be open to it once he processes the package."

Goldman watched the lunch crew changing around him as Johnson asked another question.

"Right now he's going to make some calls, sir. Contact the others. Yes, Senator, I'll keep you posted. I'm heading back to the office now."

Carl Goldman snapped the cell phone shut and pushed away from the table.

He was elated at how the lunch with Samuel Cohen had gone. On the way out of the restaurant he spotted a high-level executive with the Tribune Company and stopped to press the flesh, keeping his profile alive, selling Carl Goldman.

# CHAPTER THIRTEEN

## MINNEAPOLIS, JANUARY 23

"We're going to Chicago, Sport!"

In south Minneapolis, William Noble hung up the phone and turned to his grandson, smiling.

"We?" asked Peter Noble.

"Affirmative," replied the old man. "That is, if you can get a long weekend next month." Noble sank down into his recliner and clapped his hands.

"What's this all about?"

"That was Samuel Cohen, Peter." He looked up and grinned. "Corporal Samuel Cohen, to be exact."

"One of the Fortunate Orphans, right?"

"That's him, Peter. He's sending us round-trip airline tickets to Chicago for a reunion at the end of next month."

The young man pulled up an armchair next to his grandfather.

"And you want me to go along?"

"Absolutely, Sport. I'll need your help. Plus, you'll get to meet all the guys."

Peter sat back, hands laced under his chin, thinking. It would be no problem taking an extra day or two from his vacation hours and it would obviously please the old man. Chicago in February. The weather could be brutal. He glanced across the room at the pile of yellowed papers still sitting on the dining room table. The two of them had been sorting through the stack prior to Samuel Cohen's phone call. Peter rose, strolled to the dining room table and picked up the top sheet of paper with its list of names.

"All these guys coming to Chicago?"

His grandfather nodded, and pointed at him. "We'll be flying first class, kiddo!"

Peter didn't bother to look up. "This Cohen guy must be loaded."

Noble smiled. "Peter, Chicago has a lot of wealthy lawyers, but Sam's one of the best. Been on top of the pile a long time. Very generous with his dough when it comes to the Fortunate Orphans." The old man mused. "Oh, yeah, he's rich, but he's a helluva guy. You'll see. Sam and I are of one mind, really. We've kept the Fortunate Orphans alive."

He turned serious again. "Sam once told me I was the conscience of the group and maybe that's so. But I told him, 'What good's a conscience if you don't have someone to tell you where to go?' Yeah, Sam Cohen, he's been point man for us."

Peter watched his grandfather contemplate the thought of Chicago and what the trip would mean.

Noble's eyes brightened. "It's important to me, Peter. Will you come along?"

"I don't see why not, Gramps, but are you sure you're up to it?"

Noble snorted at the question. "You just watch." He nodded at the oxygen tank nearby.

"I plan to wean myself off that by the time we go."

The young man smiled at his grandfather's bravado and placed the sheet of names on top of the stack of paper. He shuffled the papers into some semblance of order and placed them back in the box. There were chores to be done. The following Monday he planned to return to work and leave his grandfather on his own during the day, but he had reservations about the elder man's goal. *We'll see*, he thought. If it were simply a case of determination, he knew his grandfather could do it, but he had serious doubts about the old man's level of endurance.

He decided then to go to Chicago out of love for his grandfather and a sense of family duty. Peter Noble also admitted to himself he was curious about the full story of the Fortunate Orphans and the wartime bonds that still existed after sixty-plus years.

## CHAPTER FOURTEEN

### SUPERIOR, WISCONSIN, JANUARY 23

At Ole Johnson's Cafe on Broadway, regulars were bellied up to the polished mahogany bar, pulling on beers alongside long-haired youths in letter jackets, gnawing on thick cheeseburgers. People drifted in, seeking shelter from a blizzard roaring ashore in Superior, Wisconsin. Three flat-panel TV monitors, each tuned to a different Duluth station, were tracking the storm.

The tantalizing aroma of frying burgers mingled with the greasy scent from a vat of bubbling fries. Somewhere in the back, Roy Orbison's falsetto crooned from a vintage, rainbow neon juke box. Under a twelve-foot ceiling of pressed tin, plastered red walls were hung with glowing beer lights. A dozen booths were lined up single-file opposite the long bar. Spotlights wearing green shades hovered ten feet above ancient maple flooring.

A huge picture window etched with Ole Johnson's name framed the snowy afternoon. A row of liquor bottles on glass shelves was reflected in a gilded mirror running the length of the bar. Tap handles stood at attention and snack bowls overflowed with popcorn and peanuts at intervals along the dark wood surface. Back by the bathrooms, coin-operated pool tables and pinball machines beckoned.

Ole Johnson favored old fashioned, glass-topped games with hair-trigger flippers, heavy silver balls and bright lights and bells, not their phony high-tech video versions. Johnson also loved hockey players, and those who wielded sticks were always welcomed by name. Pictures of local teams dating to the forties hung on all the walls along with a framed copy of a *Duluth Herald Tribune* article celebrating the bar's fifty-year anniversary. Patrons learned to negotiate tipsy dart game players and posturing locals who swarmed the pool tables, carrying their cues like spears. Despite the edge this odd mix of customers created, Superior Police Department calls to the bar were among the lowest in the port city. The reason was owner Ole Johnson, a tough octogenarian who had presided with an iron fist as patriarch, barkeep and owner since 1953.

Short and barrel-chested, Johnson was a ruddy, red-nosed, blue-eyed Swede with thinning silver hair and thick eyebrows. His face was a map of wrinkles and he had a loud, engaging laugh that made newcomers feel like old friends.

Johnson loved working the crowd, moving along the booths, shaking hands, slapping hockey players on their backs, flirting with single women, kissing his regular ladies and singing along with jukebox ballads.

Things were good for Ole Johnson, but it had been a blue collar struggle.

When he came home from the war, Johnson found steady work in Superior's Fraser shipyards building ore boats. His welding skills spared him from the call-up of veterans feeding the Korean maw. Johnson saved his money until he had enough to buy a failing bar he'd had his eye on since moving to Superior. The bar cost him his first marriage ten years after the purchase. Five years later Ole Johnson met Frances, an attractive Irish redheaded divorcee from Duluth who, with friends, became a weekend regular. To keep her close by, he hired her and she went to work tending bar while a romance grew, eventually blossoming into marriage. A good partnership and success followed. Fran kept the books and did the hiring; Ole did the cooking, bartending and schmoozing.

They remodeled the upstairs apartment and furnished it with restored antiques, creating themselves an oasis with a roof garden for sultry summer evenings when breezes from Lake Superior cooled them. On warm nights they gazed at Duluth's lights scattered like candles on steep dark bluffs across the harbor. A third generation had discovered the pleasures of what Ole Johnson had created and tonight was no different.

A group of college kids roared through the bar's frosted doors, winter's wind chasing them, causing nearby barflies to scowl at the frigid intrusion.

Ole Johnson sized them up and ambled from behind the bar to head them off before they seized one of his booths.

"How ya doing, gentlemen?" He clamped a big hand on the shoulder of the one he read as the leader. "You boys from UMD?"

The pack's alpha male stared down at Ole's wizened face. "Just finished finals," he said, grinning happily.

"Congratulations," said Johnson. "Your first round is on the house then." The little group whooped in chorus. "Lemme see your IDs," he challenged, "then you can grab a seat."

Johnson held out his hand. The young men dug in their pockets and produced licenses for him to read. He scanned birth dates. Satisfied, he handed them back and ushered the men to an open spot. Once he had them installed, he bellowed to a passing barmaid.

"Hey, Kerrie, a pitcher and four glasses."

A tough-looking blonde with a tray smiled and nodded and Johnson turned his attention to the eager young men settling into the booth. He pointed at the shaggy-haired kid in the corner, matching the face with the ID he had just seen.

"You Soderlund?" The man shucked his jacket and nodded yes. "Any relation to Butch Soderlund who used to play for the Bulldogs?"

"He's Butch's kid brother," volunteered one of the group.

Ole Johnson beamed down on the youngster. "Butch was one helluva hockey player. Nobody played the boards better than him. Saw him score a hat trick against the Gophers in his very last game a couple of years ago. They could use him now."

His buddies razzed the younger Soderlund.

"Where's he now?" asked Johnson, leaning into the booth.

"Joined the Guard," answered the student. "Iraq."

The group folded into awkward silence. Ole planted his big hands on the table and flashed a wide smile at them.

"A patriot, huh? Well, God bless him then."

Their waitress arrived with a brimming pitcher of draft beer and a tray of glasses.

"It's on me, boys. And don't forget to raise a glass for Butch in Iraq."

He turned to go. "Remember, after one round, you buy."

They all laughed and Ole Johnson waded back into the crowd. "Thanks, Ole!" the group cheered him as he walked away. He waved over his shoulder. Calls for burgers and fries were beginning to pile up and Ole slipped behind the bar to grab an apron.

"Order up!" Someone working the grill yelled at a server as the old man picked up a spatula and began turning patties. The storm was filling his bar and he was busy, oblivious to the surrounding din.

"Ole!" Someone was at his elbow, yelling in his good right ear. "Ole! Fran wants you!"

"What?" he bellowed at the interruption.

The cook next to him pointed past him to Fran at the end of the bar. She was waving a cell phone aloft, trying to get his attention.

He brushed his hands against his apron and pointed down at the crowded grill. "Watch them burgers, Pete! Don't let 'em burn!"

His short order cook smiled and slapped Johnson on the back.

"Long distance, Ole." Fran was shouting now. "Chicago calling!"

He snatched the phone from her and cupped a hand over his left ear, pressing the cell phone against his head.

Samuel Cohen was on the other end.

# CHAPTER FIFTEEN

## MARQUETTE, MICHIGAN, JANUARY 23

Same lake, different man.

Myron Soleski emerged from the engine hold of his nephew's beached trawler, his hands and arms blackened with grease. He reached for the least filthy rag on the crowded deck. His sister's son, Manny, a stocky, dark-haired man in his early forties who knew nothing about Cummins marine diesels, looked down at him as he wiped his grimy hands. The younger man's face was a broad pale melon with a broken nose pushed to one side. His mouth, too small for his teeth, was fixed in a permanent pout.

"So, how's it look?"

Soleski shrugged. "I'll have to go over to the shed and cannibalize one of them other engines."

The young man squatted at the hatch. "Okay, but how soon will she be ready?"

"Hard to say. I'll have to . . ."

"Yeah, I know," interrupted his nephew, "ya got to pick up a piece at the shed."

Soleski ignored him and took one last look around the cramped engine space for tools. "Hell, Manny, what do you care? You ain't going nowhere till the ice goes out anyway. Gimme a hand," he said, reaching for the other man.

The younger man easily hauled Soleski from the open hatch.

Soleski, forty years older than his nephew, was slight, bow-legged and bald. His brown eyes sparkled under shaggy brows and his thin, lined face had lost its Great Lakes summer tan, leached out by the Michigan winter. His three-days' growth of beard was flecked with silver and a slight frown indicated ill-fitting dentures.

Soleski twisted his torso into a checkered red wool shirt and pulled a dark wool watch cap over his bald head. Even inside the trawler, the cold was brutal and his breath came in short bursts of steam. He hauled up a glowing trouble light from the hatch and flicked off the switch, plunging the cabin into semi-darkness.

Manny yanked open a sliding door and stepped into a snow squall.

Outside, at the harbor's edge, huge slabs of ice had broken and piled against the pier in greenish chunks. An abandoned iron ore dock towered over them, its quarter-mile long dark shape above the harbor and marina. Soleski followed his nephew from the trawler's cabin and inhaled. Gusts of wind drove snow across the deck.

The frigid air of Marquette, Michigan, felt like tiny shards of cold glass stabbing his lungs and he broke into a hacking cough. Thirty years of a pack a day still affected him even though he no longer smoked. He kicked at the accumulated snow and ice on the quarterdeck and turned, backing carefully down the ladder into the marina yard. The trawler was held in a large wooden cradle for winter storage and Soleski had been working on the diesel's guts for the past two days. He had a way with engines, anything mechanical, but Manny was getting on his nerves and the older man needed a break.

*Maybe a couple of days more on this engine*, he thought, *after I look through the shed for usable parts.* Manny followed him like an overweight puppy, down the ladder and across the yard, shuffling in the snow to keep up. Soleski, despite his eighty-plus years, scuttled crab-like across the yard between stored boats.

Soleski unlocked the shed and began rummaging through a pile of parts stacked on a sturdy workbench. After twenty minutes, with Manny hovering over his shoulder, Soleski found what he wanted and carefully wrapped it in an oily rag. He'd send Manny back to the trawler with the part to get rid of him.

"Here, take this back to the boat and put it in the corner of the cabin over by the engine hatch." His nephew hefted the piece obediently and turned to go. Soleski followed him and locked the shed behind him.

"Ain't you coming back?"

"No," said Soleski, "I'm done for today. Too damn cold to work anymore." He rubbed his hands together and tried to grin. "I'm going home to warm up. If I know your aunt, she's got stew and popovers for lunch." Manny halted by the shed, obviously displeased at the interruption in work. "You can come if you'd like," said Soleski, hoping Manny would decline.

"Naw, I'm going to clean up the cabin a bit before it gets too cold."

Soleski laughed. "It is cold! Maybe if you didn't have so much fat on your bones you'd feel it like I do."

His nephew dismissed him with a wave and headed for the ladder.

Myron Soleski blew on his chapped hands and headed up the street, away from the harbor. He walked briskly in the snow, warming himself with the effort. He spotted the twin stone bell towers of St. Peter's Cathedral silhouetted against the winter sky and continued up Fourth Street, heading for the small, two-story, gray house leaning against a hillside in the shadow of the church.

Soleski pried open a frosted storm door and kicked against the worn threshold to dislodge the snow from his boots. He stomped into the addition that served as a mud room and shucked his footwear before stripping off his wool shirt.

His wife's husky voice boomed from the front room.

"Lunch is waiting, Sollie!"

Marjorie Soleski had one volume, loud. Her voice had taken ten years off her husband's hearing during more than fifty years of marriage. He had courted and married her five years after the war when he returned home to Escanaba. She'd been more soft spoken then, an attractive Finn, short and green-eyed with a nice figure. Not a knockout, but cute enough to attract the ex-GI who impressed her with his cocky certainty. Soleski always seemed to land on his feet no matter what came at him. After they married, they had lived with her parents until he found work in Marquette.

Commercial fishing was finishing its golden years and Soleski crewed several boats until overfishing and the vampire lamprey finished the good runs on Superior. It had dwindled down to stingy hauls of whitefish, chubs and alewife, not enough to support a family. By the time he came off the lake for good, two children—a boy and a girl—filled their modest home and Soleski had gone to work on Marquette's docks, working the trains bringing ore to the long boats. For a while, paychecks were steady but when layoffs became more frequent, he quit the docks for good and, in 1970, took a job at Northern Michigan University. There Soleski worked his magic with machines and tended the boilers in the heating plant until his retirement.

His children had long since left home for jobs in lower Michigan. To keep his hands busy, Soleski occasionally filled in for vacation absences at the university or picked up a few bucks when someone was baffled by a problem with a boat motor.

Like his nephew and his Cummins 380 diesel. Manny was a moron when it came to engines.

"Did you hear me?" Marjorie barked at him from the living room where she had sunk into the couch watching *General Hospital*. Smoke from a cigarette curled up toward the ceiling from an overflowing ashtray beside the sagging sofa.

He shuffled into the small kitchen and lifted a pot's lid.

A delicious meaty aroma filled his nostrils and he scooped thick stew into a bowl. He replaced the lid and carried his lunch to a tiny two-person table set against the room's only window, which was taped with frosted plastic to keep the cold out six months of the year. The woman could really cook, and he was amazed that he didn't weigh three hundred pounds after fifty years of her culinary wizardry. The weight that should have piled on him had ended up on Marjorie's five-foot frame instead. Soleski had remained whippet thin, while his wife had slowly morphed into a doughy apple-shaped lump. At her stage of life, women were either rotund creatures with blue hair or wispy feminine shadows of the girls they had once been. Marjorie Soleski was definitely the apple type.

He ate in greedy silence, sopping his stew with one of Marge's signature popovers. Soleski rose and plucked a long necked bottle of beer from the refrigerator. It was only when he had finished eating and was rinsing the dishes that Marjorie remembered the phone call.

"Sollie, you had a long-distance call. From Chicago."

He stood at the foot of the couch as she tried to remember the details. Focused on some weeping blonde on a hospital bed, she finally pointed in the general direction of the phone by the stairs.

"I wrote it down, over there somewhere."

He finished his beer and wandered over to the cheap antique table at the bottom of the stairs. Marjorie was sniffling now, the

TV blonde apparently slipping into a dramatic coma just before a commercial break.

Soleski strained to read her handwriting. He didn't recognize the scribbled number.

"They give a name?" She didn't hear him. "A name. You get a name, Marge?"

She teared up and waved him away as the soap opera blonde expired. The TV volume jumped suddenly with a detergent commercial, and she turned to him.

"Cohen. Something Cohen." She screwed fleshy jowls into a thoughtful frown. "Maybe that guy from Chicago. Yeah, I think it was him, Sollie." She kept one eye on the screen. "You know, your lawyer buddy."

Soleski looked down at the note, studying the numbers. *Samuel Cohen? It had been, what, four or five years? Must be important.* He would clean up first and then call when the soaps were done at three. Before Marge assumed the position again. Before she arranged the cushions and propped her bulk to watch *Jeopardy* and then the local news. Always best to use the phone before Alex Trebek began inane banter with his contestants. By then Marjorie would have the volume way up so she could bark answers at Trebek and his players.

He shoved the message into his pocket and limped up the stairs.

*Maybe Samuel Cohen was organizing another one of his reunions.*

# CHAPTER SIXTEEN

## HOT SPRINGS VILLAGE, ARKANSAS, JANUARY 26

Hints of twilight were chasing a foursome down the final fairway.

"Last hole. Par five. Four hundred and eighty-nine yards, gentlemen," said Burt Swanson as he stood behind his ball and eyed the center of the green carpet stretching before him. He lined up and took a slow graceful practice swing. Satisfied, he stepped closer and shot one last glance down the corridor of pines. He focused on the ball and drew back his driver in a high arc and, with a powerful twist of his torso, cracked the tiny white sphere perfectly. His shot sailed high and straight, bounced twice and rolled into the middle of the fairway as his watching companions whistled in appreciation.

The next hitter, a burly, retired Chrysler executive in loud plaid pants and yellow pullover, shook his head admiringly as he readied his tee shot. "Nice hit, Burt. You're really playing well today."

"Thanks, Howard." Swanson was pleased with his drive. Some days he felt every one of his years but not today. To-day he was nearly perfect. The men were playing the final hole on DeSoto, their home course in Hot Springs Village, Arkansas. Every Tuesday, Burt Swanson and three companions played eighteen holes. This round had gone fast. A slow-moving women's foursome had let them play through on the tenth hole.

Tall, still lean in his eighth decade, his lined face tanned from years as a river pilot, Swanson was the strongest of his group. His arms had lost little of their former strength but he had mellowed in retirement, exchanging the stress of running barges on the Ohio and Mississippi Rivers for the comfort of a home in the Village.

He made exercise a priority and was often mistaken for someone ten years younger. His spouse Mary, fifteen years his junior, was Swanson's second wife. His first wife had died ten years ago, and their two sons lived on opposite coasts.

Burt Swanson had stayed in the Army after the war, thinking he would make it a career, but Korea had cured the former first sergeant. In the snow-covered hills of that ugly little country he vowed that if he survived, he would quit the service. From there he had drifted to Texas oil fields and then to the Mississippi where he obtained his riverboat pilot's license. For the next twenty years, he herded barges of cement, grain and corn through the heart of America.

One day, he simply announced that he was done, coming off the river without ever looking back. He and his first wife had seen Hot Springs Village during a trip through Arkansas and they had stayed to build a home on DeSoto's sixteenth fairway. Golf, his cronies and evening happy hour became his new routine.

Swanson picked up his tee and stuffed his driver in the bag on the back of his cart. He sat in the driver's seat, waiting for the last man to hit. The final golfer, a retired naval officer, looked up at the last second and dribbled a weak hit toward the cart path. He cursed loudly and the other three players roared at his poor shot and sailor's language. They had seen this before.

"You want a mulligan, Neil?" said Swanson smiling.

"Hell no," grumbled his partner, stomping off the tee. "I'll shoot from there."

He rammed his driver into the other bag and hopped into the cart beside Swanson. They drove off in silence and stopped for the man's second shot with a three-wood. This one was good, flying low and straight: redemption for his tee shot.

"Nice recovery," offered Swanson. His passenger shrugged, allowing a grin.

The two carts crisscrossed the fairway as the foursome hit approach shots to the green. Swanson's fourth shot was a soft arc that put him ten feet from the pin. The others hit safely across a water hazard and joined him on the eighteenth green, which was flanked by tall pines near the pro shop. Swanson winced as he lipped the cup and then tapped in, settling for a bogey.

But overall, he was pleased with his playing.

The men drove to their cars in the parking lot, unloaded their clubs and changed into street shoes. While the high scorers returned the carts, Swanson and his partner strolled into the clubhouse cafe. Several groups of card players were holding forth at corner tables and greeted them. The two men got cold beers for their quartet and went outside to sit under the patio's awning. Their playing partners joined them to verbally replay the last four holes. Swanson nursed his beer and listened to the lies.

A chubby middle-aged woman manning the pro shop's register poked her head out the patio door and beckoned to Swanson. He rose and went over to her.

"Your wife called, Burt. Said to come home as soon as possible."

"Anything wrong?"

"No, just that I was to tell you to come home when I saw you." She smiled and retreated.

Swanson returned to his group and excused himself until next week's round.

Ten minutes later he was home. His wife was reading on the enclosed porch.

"They said you called for me at the clubhouse. What's up?"

The tiny silver-haired woman looked up from the couch, a thick, large print novel balanced on her lap. "Oh, he said it was important. From your friend in Chicago." She waved at him. "You know, the lawyer fellow."

Swanson searched for a name. "Sam Cohen?"

Her face brightened. "Yes, that's it. Samuel Cohen. You're to call him back as soon as you can. The number's on the message board." She resumed reading.

He wandered into the kitchen and read the scribbled digits.

Her voice followed him. "How was your game today?"

He memorized the number. "I was pleased. Didn't make a fool of myself."

"That's good," she replied automatically.

He started to dial, thought better of it and went into his den to make the call.

# CHAPTER SEVENTEEN

### RICHFIELD, MINNESOTA, JANUARY 26

A 747 came in low over the Minneapolis suburb of Richfield, ruining every conversation in its path. Retired Minneapolis Police Sergeant Dawson O'Reilly was lecturing his in-laws about the Minneapolis crime rate when the big plane passed overhead, drowning his words in a rushing, ear-splitting roar. Even indoors his guests held hands to ears, muting the sound until the jet passed.

"How can you stand that?" his wife's sister asked with a pained expression.

"Didn't hear a thing," laughed O'Reilly. The heavyset, balding ex-cop fixed his watery blue eyes on his wife's sister and straightened his stooped frame, picking up the threads of his conversation, warming to his subject. The family gathering was in the final stages of dessert, and the eighty-two-year-old retired cop was buzzed, alcohol fueling his pugnacious nature. His jaw jutted defiantly from his round face.

"I tell you, Lois, you can't believe how niggers have changed Minneapolis."

O'Reilly's wife rolled her eyes. "Dawson, don't talk like that."

He ignored her and continued. "Time was, cops commanded respect on the street. Respect! Not any more." He waved his half-full glass at the small group.

"They don't care if you wear a uniform nowadays. No regard. They'd just as soon shoot you as look at you. Now I remember when I first came home from the war . . ."

The audience knew where this was going. They had heard his litany a thousand times. The old cop continued his recitation. "When I got home from Europe I was proud to be a veteran and I wanted to be a cop. To serve my city. Was good at it, too."

His wife's sister looked down, embarrassed for the old man.

He droned on, oblivious to their bored looks. "I loved working the beat. To Protect and To Serve, yessir. Served thirty years. We had respect back then. Things went to hell in the seventies, I'll tell you. That's why we moved out here. A blind man could see what was happening."

They knew what was coming next. The lecture about blacks moving north.

He didn't disappoint them. "Bad element started coming up from Gary and Chicago. Gangsters right outa those projects. Nigger sonsofbitches couldn't wait to come up to the Promised Land for welfare handouts." He sneered when he said it.

O'Reilly's brother-in-law was clearly irritated at the direction of this escalating conversation and tried to steer the talk toward neutral ground one last time.

"Well, the city is changing, I agree. But crime is up regardless of whatever group you want to blame, Dawson. It's just the price of living in the city."

The retired cop smirked and gulped his drink. "Hell, Win, you never want to face facts. It's niggers and immigrants. Somalis, Jamaicans, Ethiopians. Ask any cop. These foreigners are busting the cops' balls and nobody wants to face facts."

His in-laws exchanged wary glances and rose to leave. Their strategy was one of retreat. Just surrender what was left of the evening and avoid further confrontation. O'Reilly rose with them and waved his nearly empty tumbler.

"Hell, just look at the phone scams for example. Who do you think is behind all that shit?" They began to make their way from the patio, leaving the belligerent cop behind. He was yelling after them now. "Nigerians, that's who!"

"You left out the Vietnamese, Dawson," taunted his brother-in-law.

O'Reilly hurled one last burst at them as they retreated into the kitchen. "Hey, don't even get me started about them or the Mexicans and their gangs!"

His wife's relatives were picking up their Tupperware and mumbling hurried goodbyes in the crowded kitchen. O'Reilly let them go as another jet shrieked overhead, drowning out his ranting. He drained his glass and staggered outside in the frigid air to shut off the grill's propane tank. His wife began picking up stray dishes and silverware. She glared at him when he came indoors, cocking a painted eyebrow as she scolded him.

"Dawson, why ruin a perfectly good evening with Ginny and Winston?"

He held out his hands in supplication. "Ah, Patty, you know how it is. Win started it with that same old sanctimonious crap about politics and poverty and people's environment . . ."

She cut him off in mid-sentence. "At least he can hold his liquor and tongue at the same time." He shrugged off the familiar sting. "Besides," she continued, "he's entitled to his opinion even if it differs from yours." She gathered the last of the dishes and hurried toward the kitchen where the phone was ringing.

He mumbled to himself and after a few minutes followed her. She was on the phone, holding one hand over her ear as another jet rumbled over their modest rambler. She held out the receiver, shaking it at him. He plucked a hearing aid from his good ear and pressed the phone against his head to guard against inbound planes. He heard a familiar voice.

"Dawson, it's Sam Cohen . . ."

# CHAPTER EIGHTEEN

### ROSEMOUNT, MINNESOTA, JANUARY 26

The next call the Chicago lawyer made was to Ken Wolf. He reached the retired engineer on the first ring. Wolf was hovering over a jigsaw puzzle's unfinished border of Van Gogh's "Sunflowers." Two thousand pieces of the Dutchman's bright yellow blossoms were proving a challenge. A fresh Manhattan sweated watery rings on a glass coffee table as Wolf turned an orphaned piece between thumb and forefinger.

He picked up the portable phone on the couch beside him and stared at two wide gaps in the puzzle's border. "Ken Wolf," he said.

"Samuel Cohen here, Ken. It's been a while."

Wolf dropped the puzzle piece back into a pile on his coffee table and broke into a smile. Five, maybe six years, had passed since the two had spoken at a reunion of fellow survivors from the Ardennes. An eternity at their ages. He rose from the couch to pace as he talked.

"My God, Sam Cohen. How are you?"

"I'm well, Ken. You and Mary?"

Wolf looked from the doorway at his wife, laboring over dinner in the kitchen. "We're both well. How's Sondra?"

"She's winding down, Ken. Doesn't really know me any-more."

Wolf suddenly felt awkward. "I'm sorry to hear that, Sam." He changed topics quickly and tried to lighten the conversation. "And to what do I owe the honor of a call from himself?"

On the other end, Cohen laughed loudly, the sound of gravel rattling in a can. "It's time the Fortunate Orphans got together again."

Wolf nodded, smiling at the thought. Cohen had orches-trated all their reunions.

"Hell yes, we're overdue, Sam. How long's it been?"

"Five years."

"What are you thinking?" asked Wolf.

"Are you sitting down, Ken?"

"Should I be?"

"What would you say to a meeting in Chicago at the end of next month?"

"I'd say you're crazy, Sam." He sat down on the couch and threw his right arm across the back of the sofa. "You'd have to scramble all the other guys and . . ."

The lawyer interrupted. "I've already talked to everybody, Ken."

"What'd they say?"

"They all agreed."

"Soleski, Ole?" asked Wolf. "What about O'Reilly?"

"They're all coming. Even Swanson." Cohen's voice took on a pleading tone.

"You're last on my list, Ken. Can you make it on such short notice?"

Wolf thought for a minute before he answered. "Why not? Say the word and I'll be there, Sam!" His wife was signaling him from the kitchen. "I'd have to talk it over with Mary, but I'm sure she'll say okay."

"This is just the guys this time, Ken. Think she'll understand?"

He thought for a second or two and replied. "We could visit friends in Evanston for a couple of days, Sam. Course I'd have to let Mary loose on Michigan Avenue to get her to agree." Cohen's ragged laugh echoed in Wolf's ear.

"Good. It's done then."

"I assume you talked to Bill Noble."

"Of course. He was the first one I called."

"You know, I haven't seen him in a while, but I hear he's not in very good shape these days."

"We talked about that," said Cohen, "but he's willing to give it a try. Look, I'll get details to everyone by the end of the week."

They exchanged email addresses and said goodbye. Wolf sat back, dazed by the startling conversation. So unexpected. He felt energized at the thought of seeing his wartime friends. They had been through hell together and he had assumed each previous reunion had been their last. Leave it to Samuel Cohen.

After the war, Wolf had gone to St. Thomas University on the GI Bill, excelling in mathematics, eventually ending up in a new industry that gave birth to mainframe computers. During that time he married, raised a family and rose in his profession. He spent time in Canada with a new technology company called Control Data and stayed on as the software industry exploded. Eventually Wolf left the company, striking out on his own as a consultant. It made sense. The money was good and venture capitalist clients everywhere were giving away suitcases of money to those in his profession.

He took an abrupt turn along the way and served on his local city council, eventually being groomed to run for the State Legislature where his reputation as a moderate Republican who thought outside the partisan box endeared him to his constituents. But his temperate approach to politics earned him the enmity of party apparatchiks who ran the show, and when campaigns embraced the negative attack mode in the eighties, Wolf quit his House seat abruptly and went to work for the state as a consultant. He had just celebrated his eighty-second birthday, surrounded by his three children and six granddaughters, and was content. His health was excellent, the result of rigorous swimming during the summer and indoor tennis in the winter. He had remained slim, just a few pounds over his wartime weight, with a full head of silver hair and a creased handsome face that readily broke into a wide smile at ribald jokes. He and his wife Mary sold their large home and settled into a townhome community in Rosemount, a sleepy third-ring Twin Cities suburb. Finally retired, Wolf felt life entering a steady phase. Not boring, not drifting, but predictable. Serene.

Sam Cohen's phone call had altered that.

His wife called to him again and he rose obediently to join her in the kitchen. As he sat down, he smiled at her across the table, Cohen's summons a secret for now. He had a selling job to do, but Michigan Avenue's shops would help.

# CHAPTER NINETEEN

## CHICAGO, JANUARY 26

One by one the offices at Cohen, Green and Showalter went dark, leaving the firm's senior partner alone in his office. Fifteen floors below, Chicago's Loop blazed with light as Samuel Cohen finished his phone calls to the Fortunate Orphans.

Cohen's last call with Ken Wolf had touched on the subject of William Noble's health, but the lawyer reminded Wolf that their old friend had nonetheless promised to come to the Chicago reunion, chaperoned by his grandson as a precaution.

Cohen and William Noble were the guardians for the group's memory. They had nursed the remembrance of their ordeal in the Ardennes. Kept the flame alive.

And now it was their moment.

The lawyer was feeling the effects of his long day. Time to go home. He tucked the envelope from Carl Goldman under his arm, turned out his lights and dropped a scribbled note on his secretary's desk asking her to research flights and hotel reservations for the Fortunate Orphans. Over the coming weekend Cohen would put together a presentation for the reunion, but first he would spend his evenings digesting the contents of the package he carried.

He passed the usual night cleaning crew coming off the elevator, exchanging pleasantries in Spanish with their leader, a tired-looking woman who was probably half her apparent age. Cohen rode to the street in silence and waved goodnight to two security guards who were telling each other jokes at the lobby desk. The winter air braced him, and he pulled his wool coat tighter, heading for a trio of cabs idling at the curb. He hailed the lead one, got in and gave his address. When he arrived at his apartment building, Cohen added a ten-dollar tip to the fare, delighting the driver, a small West African with a round face and scraggly goatee. Samuel Cohen entered the building, pausing for the uniformed doorman to buzz him into the lobby. They chatted about the weather until the elevator doors opened and swallowed him up.

He rode to the eighteenth floor, head down, chin tucked into his chest. Melting snowflakes formed beads of water on his expensive wool coat. Cohen shook them off as he exited the elevator. Soft lights on the landing glowed warmly in contrast to the inky night outside the floor-to-ceiling windows at the end of the hallway.

Inside the condo, he dropped the parcel on a narrow marble topped table in the foyer. A tiny dark-eyed woman with a flat brown face crossed the parquet foyer and stood before him, her long black hair tied back, a pair of hands folded in front like a respectful schoolgirl.

"Good evening, Señor Cohen."

"Buenos noches, Gabriella. How is Señora Sondra?" said Cohen.

"She is the same. No change. Same like yesterday."

Cohen patted the little woman on the shoulder and smiled as she took his coat. He moved past her down a wide hall to a bedroom door, stepped inside and walked to a king-sized bed where a sleeping woman was propped against a small mountain of satin pillows. He bent down and kissed her forehead.

"Hello, sweetheart. It's Sam."

He thought she stirred. But then, he always thought that.

His beloved wife of sixty years was slipping away, one day at a time. Sondra Cohen was in the last stages of Alzheimer's, robbed of her mobility and memory, a large porcelain doll with no sign of recognition for those around her. The entire year had been this way and he knew there was no change. No happy ending to what had been a childless, but perfect union. He sat on the edge of the bed for a few moments, stroking her hand.

The housekeeper coughed discreetly from the doorway. He looked up.

"You wish something to eat, Señor Cohen?"

He shook his head. "I'll grab some fruit. Thanks, Gabriella."

"I fix for you, no problem."

He smiled, nodding agreement, and she was gone.

Cohen looked down at his wife and smiled. Her long hair was spread against the pillows like strands of fine gray silk, eyes unmoving behind pale lids. He squeezed her hand, rose and backed from the room.

A small plate of melon, grapes and pineapple waited for him in the kitchen, and he ate slowly, standing at the granite island, sipping a tall orange juice, nibbling slices of buttered bread. The doorbell's muted tones rang out, signaling the night nurse's arrival. He heard the women greet each other in the entry and finished eating. He rinsed the dishes and strolled to a large picture window overlooking Lake Shore Drive. An unending flow of lights curved along the margins of a vast blackness that was Lake Michigan.

The luxury high-rise, sheathed in dark tinted glass, held million-dollar views of the lake. As a silent partner in the development company that owned the building, he had been assured that his investment would give him the option for whatever floor he wanted.

His condominium covered one half of the eighteenth floor. Three bedrooms, three large baths, a cavernous book-lined study and a spacious living room with marble fireplace took up most of the floor plan. A formal dining room adjacent to an open kitchen provided an oasis most Chicagoans could only read about in decorator magazines. Discreetly tucked in one corner of the condominium was a comfortable guest suite with its own entrance to the outside hallway. The space consisted of a bath, bedroom and sitting room which Cohen had converted to maid's quarters. The remaining third of the eighteenth floor was owned by a retired suburban school superintendent who made no noise at all. The man sensibly fled Chicago's winters for Florida sunshine from October until April, leaving Samuel and Sondra Cohen as the floor's only occupants.

Cohen peeked inside at his wife one last time. The night nurse was making herself comfortable in a large recliner and nodded politely at him in the dim light.

He dismissed the housekeeper for the night and changed into pajamas and a favorite tattered bathrobe and slippers. In the study, Cohen snapped on the desk lamp and sat behind a polished dark oak desk with the envelope Goldman had given him at lunch four days earlier. He picked up a silver letter opener and ran the blade across one end of the envelope, removed a sheaf of papers and photos and stacked them in a neat pile. Cohen picked up the first item, three stapled sheets summarizing the Battle of the Bulge, and studied the text. Glancing at a gilded heirloom wall clock that showed nine o'clock, he allowed himself one hour before bed.

He read until one o'clock the next morning.

By the end of the week Samuel Cohen was still "herding cats." He had reserved seven rooms on the same floor at the Hyatt Regency for the Fortunate Orphans reunion, drafted an agenda for their meeting and had tried to arrange flights. The last bit of business proved the most frustrating. Only three of the group had accept-ed his proposal for round-trip business class tickets to Chicago.

First, Ken Wolf and his wife, Mary, elected to drive de-spite Cohen's assurances he would provide them with a rental car. They told him they would come two days early and stay with friends in Evanston before Wolf came downtown for the reunion.

Ole Johnson and Myron Soleski confirmed Samuel Cohen's prediction and declined his airline tickets, announcing they would drive to save him money. William Noble and his grand-son Peter, along with Dawson O'Reilly, planned to fly togeth-er from Minneapolis, opting to trade the uncertainty of winter highway travel for the comfort of Cohen's first class seats. For-mer sergeant Burt Swanson also agreed to accept the lawyer's offer of an airline ticket from Little Rock.

The weeks slipped by as Cohen put the finishing touches on his media presentation for the group's second day. Twenty-four hours before the reunion, he cleared his desk and told his office staff that he would be unavailable until the following Monday.

He went home to his wife and his view of the lake. He spent the next few days going over details and rehearsing his speech, leaving nothing to chance. He had to be perfect. Forceful. Persuasive.

# CHAPTER TWENTY

## MICHIGAN'S UPPER PENINSULA, FEBRUARY 19

One day before the reunion, on a clear cold Wisconsin morning, Ole Johnson departed Superior in a packed Ford Explorer, taking Highway 2 east along the lake until the road turned southeast to Michigan's border. He picked up Highway 28 and dodged light snow through tiny towns in dark pine woods that cloaked the Upper Peninsula. As he drained the last of his thermos's hot coffee, the road merged with Highway 41 coming from L'Anse to the north. Johnson stopped for gas in Ishpeming, then pushed on, racing fading winter light to Negaunee and then finally into Marquette as darkness settled on Superior's frosted shores.

After a restless night in Myron Soleski's home, the two left early the next morning, determined to make Chicago before nightfall. They followed 41 south toward Escanaba where they were forced inland to avoid an angry Lake Michigan storm building at the mouth of Green Bay. Johnson and Soleski emerged from the forested interior at Menominee, barely ahead of the worsening weather, and crossed into Wisconsin. The storm chased them down to Milwaukee before finally letting go. After another stop for fuel, Johnson pushed down Interstate 94, past Racine and Kenosha, into Chicago.

The sun was dying as they pulled under the canopy of the Hyatt Regency on Wacker Drive. Soleski sat in the idling van as Johnson went inside to confirm they were really in the right place. A senior concierge, primed by Cohen, sent two bellmen back with Johnson to hustle luggage from the Explorer while he registered his newest guests. Soleski, suspicious of everything

urban, reluctantly surrendered the luggage but tailed the uniformed men into the spacious lobby to make certain their bags
were not being stolen. Within minutes the two tired travelers
had turned the vehicle over to a valet and had been whisked
upstairs to their rooms along with their suitcases. Johnson offered two bills to the bellman, but the Hispanic youth politely
declined.

"Mister Cohen has already taken care of that, sir," he said,
retreating.

"That sounds like Sam's style," said Soleski from his doorway across the hall. "Or maybe the kid's not used to getting tips
from old guys wearing snowmobile suits." Johnson looked down
at his insulated overalls and boots and laughed.

On desks in their rooms, each man found an envelope with
his name. Inside was a printed note from Samuel Cohen wel-
coming them to Chicago and an invitation to dinner downstairs
at seven o'clock in the hotel's restaurant. Johnson called the desk
and arranged for a wake-up call for both rooms. The weary pair
showered, changed clothes and fell back on their king-sized
beds, grateful for a nap.

# CHAPTER TWENTY-ONE
## CHICAGO, FEBRUARY 20

Late that same afternoon Dawson O'Reilly and the Nobles rode
a commuter flight into O'Hare and were met by Burt Swanson
who had come up from Little Rock via Memphis a half hour before them. Five years had passed since these men had seen each

other and introductions were made amidst much laughter and backslapping.

As the foursome queued to retrieve their luggage, they were met by a driver sent by Samuel Cohen. The men piled into his long black limousine while their chauffeur bossed a pair of red-caps who followed with baggage. None had ridden in a limo before. On the drive from O'Hare, along the Kennedy Expressway, they caught the end of Chicago's rush hour but were content to relax in comfort as the big car jockeyed between lanes. O'Reilly singlehandedly emptied the courtesy bar while the others admired the Windy City's skyline en route to the city's heart.

At the Hyatt's entrance, the four men exited the limo, collected their luggage and followed a doorman's prompt into the lobby. Chicago's downtown glittered above a glassed atrium supported by an impressive gridwork of steel girders. Here and there small groups of guests sat among potted greenery, talking and laughing. They took the escalator to the second level and automatically filed into a check-in line defined by brass rails. A concierge quickly crossed the soft carpet to greet the quartet, snapping orders at staff to hustle the foursome's luggage upstairs to preassigned rooms. He ushered the four to the long, marble registration desk where he distributed keys to their rooms.

"Mr. Cohen has arranged for dinner in our restaurant at seven, gentlemen," purred the man. "Mr. Cohen said he would meet you for a drink prior to dinner." He swept his hand across the mezzanine level toward a glittering cabaret where multi-colored lights inside nylon tubes floated above an extended bar. Piano music and fragments of conversation floated in the atrium, mixing with the sound of splashing fountains on the lower level. The concierge, his job done, bowed slightly and withdrew.

The new arrivals, keys in hand, hesitated.

William Noble glanced down at his watch. "I don't know about you fellas, but I'm going to grab some shut-eye for an hour before dinner. See you down here at six-thirty." He turned slowly and headed for the elevators. His grandson smiled at the others, excused himself and shadowed the old man. Swanson and O'Reilly followed.

# CHAPTER TWENTY-TWO

At precisely six-ten, Samuel Cohen exited a taxi and swept into the Hyatt's lobby, heading directly for the escalator. At the landing, he turned and walked to the Big Bar, the hotel's signature watering hole. He draped his overcoat across a stool and took a table with a view of the lobby and ordered a soda water with a twist of lime. A call from the concierge had alerted him that all his guests had arrived and been shown to their rooms. Now he waited, tapping manicured hands on the bar table, scanning the hotel's foot traffic.

First to show was William Noble and his grandson.

Cohen raised both arms in the air and waved to the pair from the railing. Peter Noble watched his grandfather throw back his shoulders and straighten, walking briskly toward the lawyer. The men embraced, laughing. *Tears in their eyes?* Peter wasn't sure.

Next was Wolf with Swanson, Soleski and Johnson at their sides. They had met in the hallway outside their rooms on the eighth floor and had ridden down together. Noble sent his grandson to intercept them and steer them to the bar where he and Cohen waited. Each man in turn smothered Cohen with bear hugs.

Finally, Dawson O'Reilly shuffled from an elevator and made his way to the bar, unaware his friends were already there. He eyed the gathering and bellowed on approach, oblivious to the turned heads of others in the lobby who heard his roar.

"Sam, you old sonofabitch, how are you?!"

More hugs as the men greeted each other. Noble formally introduced Peter to Johnson and Soleski. The men immediately adopted Peter into their circle with hugs and handshakes.

Cued by Cohen, a cocktail waitress appeared carrying a tray of flutes filled with bubbling champagne. As the glasses were distributed, the group pulled up stools and waited for Cohen to address them. He stood up, signaled for attention and raised his glass, speaking over the sound of the fountains below.

"Boys, this is wonderful, just wonderful. You don't know how grateful I am that you all came on such short notice." His voice broke. He swallowed, cleared his throat and continued. "It's been five years. And five years at our age is a gamble. I have so much to tell you."

He lifted his glass higher. "To the Fortunate Orphans!"

Dawson O'Reilly chimed in, "I'll drink to that!" The circle of veterans laughed.

A chant in unison. "To the Fortunate Orphans!"

Bar regulars smiled at the knot of old men toasting each other. Peter Noble sipped his champagne and watched the elders laughing, talking.

At seven sharp Cohen led them to Stetson's Chop House, the hotel's premier restaurant. The maître d' greeted the lawyer by name and led the group to two tables pushed together beneath a framed mirror at the end of the long room. Half of the old warriors settled themselves on the striped banquette, facing the other four who were ushered into their chairs. A beaming Cohen took a chair at one end, opposite William Noble, Swanson to his right. He was given a wine list by the restaurant's wine steward and ordered additional champagne without looking, whispering to their server. "The Dom Perignon." The man nodded, smiling.

More staff appeared, filling water goblets, distributing menus, placing baskets of fresh rolls the length of the linen-draped tables. Everyone studied their menus in silence until the champagne arrived and then Cohen announced another toast.

"To survival, to success . . . and . . . to those we left behind."

A somber chorus of "Hear, hear!" and O'Reilly again. "I'll drink to that!"

Their waiter appeared and recited the evening specials. He had to repeat himself several times, then memorized their orders and discreetly withdrew. Another server hovered, refilling water glasses.

Superb house wines, two bottles each of a Californian merlot and sauvignon blanc, chosen by Samuel Cohen, were delivered with the food. Their meal was excellent, the service prompt. For the next two hours the eight diners traded retirement stories, family updates and war stories. Ole Johnson eyed the pressed tin ceiling and boasted to his table mates that his own bar had one just like it.

"Yeah, but it was probably a lot cheaper to install yours," laughed Soleski.

Burt Swanson regaled his listeners with brutal stories from Korea that made some of them flinch at the telling, and most forgot they had heard them before. He recited his tales dryly, as though remembering previous business trips gone awry. Peter

Noble was content to observe, amazed at the wartime bond the men had resurrected, seemingly without effort. Occasionally one of the men would halt a comrade's conversation, reach into his ear and play with a hearing aide, trying to pick up garbled words. Several times the maître d' materialized at Cohen's elbow, inquiring if the evening was fulfilling the lawyer's expectations. Toward the end, a dessert tray, groaning with delicacies, appeared, but to a man they declined. By now they were full of wine, steak, lobster or swordfish, salad and bread. Coffee was brought to their table as the restaurant emptied and filled again.

As they lingered, live piano music drifted in from the bar at the front of the restaurant while outside, the notorious lake wind scoured sidewalks and plazas, dusting the window sills with snow. Chicago's bejeweled skyscrapers sparkled in the windows, adding a magic touch to the long evening. Cohen signaled for the bill and signed for the meal, pleased enough to leave a hefty tip.

He leaned forward and released his audience with promises for tomorrow. "You each received envelopes with a copy of our itinerary. Look it over. You'll see that we gather tomorrow at nine hundred hours in the Wright Meeting Room in the hotel's West Tower. Have breakfast downstairs or use room service, but we'll have refreshments in the meeting room and I've arranged for a catered lunch. That way we can go over old business and . . ." he paused, smiled mischievously and said, ". . . new business."

Mumbles of agreement all around the table. Ole Johnson slapped his palms on the table and O'Reilly drained the last of the wine, belching several times without apology. Ken Wolf nudged Soleski to make sure he was awake.

The meal was over.

Cohen pushed back from the table and rose, shaking hands with those seated closest to him. He went down the line, men rising now to embrace him once more. The veterans filed out in pairs, chatting with each other, following Cohen to the lobby where he retrieved his overcoat and asked the doorman to signal a cab. When his ride arrived, Cohen, surrounded by the men, said goodbye. He exited into the snowy night and the veterans headed for the bank of elevators.

"What's Sam mean by 'new business'?" asked Soleski as they waited for the doors to open. No one knew. "Haven't a clue. We'll have to wait and see," someone said.

Elevator doors parted to spill a loud, giggling cluster of nubile young women in identical athletic jackets. The old men let them pass and then claimed the car for themselves. They rode quietly and after exiting the car, drifted to their rooms with waves and groggy mumbles of "Goodnight."

# CHAPTER TWENTY-THREE

## CHICAGO, FEBRUARY 21

"How much does your grandson know?"

William Noble stood beside Samuel Cohen, gazing out the window at Saturday morning traffic on slushy streets below. The two men were alone in the hotel's smaller conference room, waiting for the others to arrive. Noble put his right hand against the glass and looked at his friend. "He knows the whole story, Sam. I told him after I got out of the VA Hospital."

Cohen stroked his chin, not looking at Noble. "Question is, does he know where we're going with this?"

"Hell, Sam, you and I are the only ones who really know where you're going with this."

"How do you think the others are going to react, Bill?"

William Noble moved away from the window and looked at his host. "I'm not much help, Sam. I haven't a clue how they'll respond."

The pair ambled over to the conference table with its leather chairs. Cohen settled in the middle where a laptop computer waited in sleep mode. Carafes of coffee and water were set the length of the conference table.

"At least tell me you're still in agreement with me, Bill," he said.

Noble was about to answer when Ken Wolf and Ole Johnson sauntered through the door, followed by Myron Soleski.

Noble shelved his response and nodded to the newcomers. "Morning, fellas."

They returned his greeting. "Swanson and O'Reilly are on their way," added Wolf. "We saw them in the lobby restaurant."

"Dawson will probably be here around noon," snorted Johnson.

"Yeah, he was moving pretty danged slow," added Soleski.

The trio wandered over to a mirrored sideboard to look over the catered lunch the staff had set for later. A pair of platters piled with sandwiches covered in clear wrapping took up half the surface along with silverware rolled in napkins and baskets of fresh fruit and small dessert cakes.

Soleski chuckled. "Looks like you're gonna keep us here a while, Sam." He pulled out a chair and sank into the soft leather, rotating the seat like a delighted child.

Wolf sat opposite him and Ole Johnson wandered over to the window to survey the city.

Burt Swanson came through the door, in conversation with Peter Noble. After greeting everyone the two sat down, the younger man taking a seat next to his grandfather. A minute later Dawson O'Reilly, sporting puffy bloodshot eyes in a pained face, shuffled into the room and quietly took a chair.

Cohen glanced at his watch. Fifteen minutes after nine. His instructions had been for a nine o'clock start but he had figured it would be ten by the time everyone showed. He was pleasantly surprised.

Samuel Cohen stood and leaned forward over the table. "Good morning, gentlemen. You're on time. I have to admit, I'm impressed." There was laughter around the table. "There is coffee and water in front of you and a restroom just down the hall if you need it. Feel free to come and go as you want during our meeting. Let's start. Peter, would you dim the lights and lower the screen, please?"

As the room darkened, a large white screen dropped slowly into place against the far wall and the men swiveled in their chairs to watch. Cohen tapped his keyboard and a slide appeared, covering the screen with U.S. Army divisional and regimental patches. He hit another key and sat down as the screen faded to black.

"Just a little refresher, guys. Bear with me."

"Will there be a quiz later?" asked Johnson, playfully.

"Just for you, Ole," replied Cohen.

The group laughed and then went silent as a black and white newsreel opened, complete with scratchy background soundtrack.

"Battle of the Bulge, Hitler's last gamble," intoned a deep voice as grainy shots of GIs shoveling frozen ground appeared. Combat footage showed jeeps and half-tracks slipping on icy roads in woods and fields. Shots of high-ranking officers talking into field phones in sandbagged tents were followed by captured German newsreels showing grinning SS infantrymen walking alongside burning American trucks.

A huge gray map of the battlefield appeared, with dark creeping arrows showing German advances and then bending at the limit of the thrusts against American lines. The voice droned on, more urgent now, as images of suffering U.S. POWs shuffled across the screen, obviously in misery. The men on the screen looked unhappy, surly, scowling at the German cameraman. At the table, no one spoke as the newsreel, accompanied by stirring martial music, finished with a brief description of the successful Allied counterattack.

The screen went black.

"That's just to set the mood," said Cohen. "Stay with me."

Next up was a map of the Bulge battlefield with successive slides that zoomed in on the Ardennes, followed by a slide titled "Fortunate Orphans."

Wartime photos of the men around the table flashed on the screen one by one, each of their GI images evoking laughter, hoots or applause from those at the table.

Suddenly, a cocky looking blonde officer in a formal SS uniform appeared. The youthful German captain wore the Knight's Cross at his neck, preening for some anonymous wartime photographer.

"Von Wurtz," mouthed Noble. The others sat up and studied the face.

The portrait faded, the computer's magic replacing it with one of a much older smiling man in a well-tailored suit and silk tie. The Nazi's studio portrait reemerged, superimposed on the screen again, pushing the civilian's face behind it until the two blended as one.

Cohen left his chair and stepped toward the screen.

"This the face of our enemy. SS-Hauptsturmführer Werner von Wurtz, Waffen SS. Nazi Party member. Murderer of Lieutenant Holden Pressman and twenty-two of our fellow soldiers." His voice broke briefly and he turned to stare at the black-and-white photos on the screen. The computer kept running the two portraits in a loop, one fading behind the other and then back again.

The room was gripped by silence.

Cohen nodded discreetly at Peter Noble and the young man stepped to the lighting controls to slowly bring the room back from semi-darkness. Cohen returned to his chair and stabbed at his laptop's keyboard. The screen faded to the logo for the Fortunate Orphans: three tongues of flame behind a rifle stuck bayonet-first into the ground with a helmet atop, black lettering in a half circle at the bottom.

All chairs turned back to the center of the table. Cohen folded his hands on top of a white, legal-sized envelope identical to those in front of every man. He took several deep breaths, then spoke.

"After all these years we finally have a new face to go with the memory."

"Was that him?" barked Johnson. "You mean the bastard's alive?"

Cohen held up his hands and continued. "In the big picture, our encounter with Werner von Wurtz was a footnote. Not an aberration given the way the Waffen SS operated, but still a footnote. Yes, Von Wurtz shot down prisoners in cold blood. Yes, he murdered other GIs and civilians before he was done. But history remembers the Malmédy Massacre.

"I mean, everyone's heard of it. Lieutenant Colonel Joachim Peiper was charged with it. He was brought to trial, along with some of his lesser known lieutenants. But what happened to him?"

With the exception of the Nobles, the men around the table did not remember Peiper's story, so he reminded them.

"He was condemned to death, then reprieved. Served twelve years in prison."

"Should have been shot," said Swanson loudly. Several amens followed.

"Yeah, Burt, you're right," said Cohen, up and pacing now. "He should have been shot, but justice has a funny way of finding people in the end. In case you've forgotten the ending, Peiper was living under an assumed name until he was exposed and killed by some locals in a small French town near the German border. That was in the late seventies."

Cohen could see them responding now, hanging on his words. "But no one ever caught up with Von Wurtz, did they?" Several of the men shook their heads in disgust.

"Bigger fish to fry," yelled Soleski.

"That's right, Sollie." Cohen moved over to the Michigan veteran. "They had bigger things to deal with right then. Like the Battle of the Bulge."

"We told the brass," Wolf reminded the men at the table. "What else could we do? There was a war on. The whole Army was trying to save its ass at that point."

Cohen moved toward Wolf. "Exactly, Ken. We . . . the Fortunate Orphans . . . got lost in the shuffle. What happened to us was not that significant in light of what was going on for those three weeks. Things were pretty dicey all around."

"Tell the boys what you're getting at, Sam." It was Noble, opening the way for Cohen.

"I'm telling you that Von Wurtz is alive and we now have proof!"

Johnson stood up and pointed at the screen. "That old man is Von Wurtz!"

Cohen stood in the middle of the room and stretched out his arms. "Yes, that is Werner Von Wurtz as he looks today. The man is still alive!"

"Goddamn, Sam. What are you saying?" Swanson seemed confused.

"The two faces you showed us . . . that's Von Wurtz, right?" asked Soleski. "You're really saying the sonofabitch is still alive?" The little man was on his feet challenging Cohen.

"How long have you known this?!" It was O'Reilly, shocked from his stupor.

Several of the group were clearly agitated, gesturing in the screen's direction. Noble remained composed, a faint smile across his face.

The meeting was on the edge of chaos but Cohen asked for calm, waving everyone down into their seats.

"A little over a month ago I was given certain information, credible facts, that point to Von Wurtz being very much alive and, like Peiper before him, living in France close to the German border."

He picked up his envelope and dramatically dumped the contents on the table in front of him. He plucked two black-and-white photos, the same ones that had floated on the screen.

"This is Von Wurtz, then and now." He gestured to the mailers at each man's place. "Go ahead, open your packets and see for yourselves."

The men tore into the envelopes, spilling photos and stapled sheets on the table. Noble caught Cohen's eye for a split second and then turned to share the folder's contents with his grandson as Peter sifted through the materials.

Each packet had a series of candid telephoto shots of an older man alighting from a car and taking a seat at an open air cafe in the company of another elderly man who sat opposite him sipping a drink. A second set showed a château with the same two old men, one of them identified by Cohen as Von Wurtz, walking in a garden, trailed by another man who hovered at the edge of the photos.

The stapled sheets had a wartime biography of Von Wurtz and a chronology of his post-war travels and business dealings. At points in the pages, black marker had been drawn across sections of the printing.

William Noble looked up at Cohen. "How recent is this information, Sam?"

"Five or six months old, Bill. I don't know if these are classified documents but judging from the censor's heavy hand, I'd say they're probably genuine."

Ken Wolf put his papers in order, stacking them carefully. "Okay, if this is who you say it is . . ." He was scanning the pages with his right hand, the pictures in his left.

"It's him, Ken," Cohen interrupted.

Wolf finished his thought. "All right, say it's him, Von Wurtz. What are we supposed to do about it?"

Wolf's question stopped everyone's conversation and they turned as one to hear the lawyer's answer.

Cohen stepped behind his chair and rested his arms on the back. "That's why we're here, gentlemen. That's why the Fortunate Orphans exist."

He touched his keyboard and the arrogant portrait of Von Wurtz in his SS uniform formed on the screen. Even in the lighted room, the man's face registered.

"What I am now going to say must never leave this room, understood?" There was nodding, murmurs of agreement. "I want to hear each of you clearly say that you understand what I'm asking."

One by one the men spoke up, giving a clear promise of confidentiality.

Cohen looked at Peter Noble and said softly. "Peter, this is not your fight. You don't have to stay here and listen to what I'm going to say. You're free to go. No questions asked."

Cohen stood perfectly still, waiting for Noble's grandson to answer.

"I think I understand what you're asking, Mr. Cohen. I'm here to support my grandfather regardless of what happens." He sat back, seven pairs of eyes following him.

"Is that a yes, a promise, Peter?" asked Swanson.

William Noble glared at Swanson. "He said he'd abide by the promise, Burt."

"Then let him say it, Bill," said the former sergeant, his gaze on the young man.

The others waited.

"Yes, I understand what you're asking," said Peter. "And I agree to it."

"Good enough for me," said Ole Johnson.

Soleski and Wolf nodded.

"No offense, Peter," offered Swanson. "We just had to know for sure."

"No offense taken."

Cohen felt a collective sigh escape from the men at the table. He went on.

"We have an opportunity that few are given. A chance to actually see justice done. We can bring Werner von Wurtz to account even though more than sixty years have passed, and we can do this in one of several ways." He picked off the points on his fingers. "We can alert French authorities to his whereabouts."

Several groans sounded from the men around the table but Cohen continued without acknowledging them. "They did pick up Klaus Barbie, the Butcher of Lyons, remember? They put him on trial and sent him to die in prison. So don't write off the French, boys."

Cohen went down his list. "We could go to Interpol and have him arrested. He's still wanted as a war criminal in Germany and Belgium."

"They must not be looking too hard, Sam," snorted Wolf.

"You could be right, Ken." The lawyer continued. "Or we can alert our own authorities and have them work with the international war crimes tribunal folks. That's probably a longer process however."

Noble spoke up, "As a lawyer, give the pros and cons for those scenarios, Sam."

Cohen sat down and stuffed the paperwork and photos back into the mailer. "The pros are that they are all legal, workable and within international law."

"And the cons?" asked Wolf.

"They each require one thing we do not have in abundance."

"Money!" exclaimed Soleski. "It's always about money."

Cohen looked at the smaller man and smiled, shaking his head.

"Money's not a problem, Sollie. I was thinking more about time."

William Noble spoke up. "Sam's right. It's the time factor. Look around."

He swept his hand up and down the table. "Except for Peter, not one of us is under eighty years old. We're survivors. The

Fortunate Orphans. Look, I'm delighted to see this day but I have to admit it's bittersweet." Noble faltered, then continued. "I've dreamed about this since the Bulge and so have all of you. But now that we know that Von Wurtz is alive, we may have to recognize that we may be too late." He sat back, exhausted by his effort.

Cohen was grateful for the break. "Thanks, Bill, for making that point. We may, in fact, be too late to see Von Wurtz brought to justice. Hell, the man's even a year or two older than our oldest member, Burt Swanson, who is . . . what are you Burt, eighty-three?"

"Eighty-four," he answered. "But a well-preserved eighty-four, thank you."

The group broke into laughter.

"Well, goddamn it, Sam," groused O'Reilly, standing. "What the hell do you propose we do?" The retired cop was nearly apoplectic. "You drag us down here to Chicago for what may be our last reunion for all we know." He was waving his arms now. "You wine us and dine us, and don't get me wrong, I thank you for that, but you give us the shock of our lives telling us this sonofabitch Wurtz is still alive. And then you say you don't know what the hell to do about it!"

O'Reilly huffed and sat down, red-faced at his effort. He gulped a glass of water trying to regain his composure. Low murmurs began around the table.

Cohen gave them several minutes to exhaust the topic. Then he rapped a spoon against a glass. All eyes turned to their host. He had them now.

"Gentlemen, I say we travel to France, find Von Wurtz and eliminate him."

# CHAPTER TWENTY-FOUR

Cohen had not expected the deathly silence that followed his proposal.

Soleski broke the spell, leaping to his feet and standing with his hands gripping the back of his chair. His mouth worked faster than his brain, the words tumbling out. "My God, Sam, did we hear right . . . that we, you, think we can actually . . ." The little man could not finish his sentence and looked around the table, gesturing frantically for someone to rescue him, help him complete his thoughts.

Noble put a hand on his grandson's shoulder and rose, waving for attention. "We all heard what Sam just said. There's no misunderstanding what he's proposed." He looked at Cohen who nodded for him to continue. "But before we dismiss his idea out of hand . . ." His eyes moved slowly around the table, fixing each man with a stern look. "Let's hear Sam out in this. Listen to what he's thinking." Noble looked over at his friend, waiting.

Cohen began walking around the seated men.

"I would never have made such an outrageous statement if I had the slightest doubt that I could not speak candidly in this group." He nodded at Peter. "And that includes young Mr. Noble as well."

Every few steps he paused for effect, making sure his audience was with him. "I know the law very well, gentlemen. I have served it all my life. And I know that what I have just shared with you is outside the pale for most of society.

"I have drawn you into an instant conspiracy just by voicing this proposition. For that I apologize. But I did so in complete confidence that none of you would betray me." He completed his orbit of the seated men and posed behind his chair. "What I am asking is nearly impossible given our ages, but I am determined to see this thing through to the end, whatever that may cost me personally."

He stared down at the wartime portrait of the SS officer on the table. "I have an outline of a plan which I want to present for your consideration." He pulled out his chair as if to sit down but paused. "But before I do so, anyone here who does not want to be part of this . . . conversation . . . and possibly this expedition, is free to leave. There will be no hard feelings if you back out now. I'll understand, as I'm sure the others will, if you feel that this is something so reckless, so crazy that you think it impossible."

"It's a little late for that now isn't it, Sam?" asked Ken Wolf.

Cohen nodded, conceding his friend's point. He finally sat down and folded his thin hands in front of him, staring straight ahead, averting his gaze from his friends.

Again, an awkward moment descended on the room.

Johnson twirled a pen and Soleski looked at the mirrored wall behind Cohen. Swanson wore an enigmatic mask while Wolf scribbled graffiti on a notepad next to an increasingly agitated Dawson O'Reilly. The retired cop appeared desperate for a drink, or perhaps it was a case of nerves, thought Cohen. He didn't blame him. William Noble's stoic face was in contrast to his grandson's puzzled look.

"Why don't we break for lunch?" suggested Ken Wolf, deflating the tension. On cue, the leather chairs backed away from the conference table and the men stretched or began filing over to the mirrored wall where the sideboard was piled with food and drink. Small talk surfaced, some laughter, and Cohen knew they were past the hard part.

O'Reilly grabbed a can of cola and swallowed half of it before pulling a small silver flask from his hip pocket and pouring its contents into the can. He shook the concoction and took a long swallow before adding more fuel from his flask.

Johnson stacked his plate high with a sandwich and fruit while Soleski chose to eat by himself, standing at a window. Ken Wolf sat to one side, in conversation with Burt Swanson as the two ate. Noble and his grandson moved closer to Samuel Cohen and passed battlefield photos back and forth as they nibbled at their food.

Cohen could see that the lunch was a needed respite, allowing some civility after the previous hour. He suggested a thirty-minute break, confident his warning would stay with them. The room emptied.

Cohen leaned back in the leather chair and closed his eyes, trying to imagine his lake.

# CHAPTER TWENTY-FIVE

Lights dimmed and Samuel Cohen stepped to a large projected map of France. "From this point forward I will refer to plans to bring Von Wurtz to justice as simply 'The Project.'"

He attempted to move quickly to his next point but Ken Wolf interrupted him.

"Wait a minute, Sam." He turned to the rest of audience at the table. "Am I the only one who thinks this is a little bit crazy?" He continued, "I mean, we're talking here as if it's a foregone conclusion that we all agree to this entire scheme."

"I only meant to lay out a concept of how to accomplish this, Ken."

"Fair enough," said Wolf, "as long as you don't take it for granted that everyone here wants to be a part of this."

"I can accept that."

"If I may . . . ?" Cohen waited.

Wolf shrugged, yielding, and Cohen continued.

"We need to plan carefully and anticipate as many contingencies as humanly possible. This is going to resemble a military plan, gentlemen. We're going to have to reach pretty far back for some of our former skills."

A few low chuckles broke from his listeners.

Cohen ran a laser pointer across the Channel to France's ragged northwest coast. "My thought is for us to go to Europe before this coming year's D-Day celebrations at Normandy. We'd have an advantage because this next anniversary is not a special milestone year. Plus we'd be just one more group of American vets visiting the continent before the bigger crowds. We wouldn't arouse any suspicion.

"There are bound to be several thousand tourists and we'd fit right in with the rest of the tours. By our being a week or so early we could accomplish our mission and also avoid all the Europeans going on holiday in August. I've got some ideas on flights, hotels and transportation."

"Geez, Sam, that's a pretty stiff price for some of us," grumbled O'Reilly.

"I know, Dawson," answered Cohen, "I've thought of that. I intend to pick up the tab for The Project." He held up a hand to forestall any protests to his proposal. "Bill Noble and I talked this over a month ago and I told him I wanted to do this, so any objections are so noted and overruled."

More chuckles and a few whistles at the cost they knew Cohen would bear.

"Hell, Sam," said Johnson, "if you're gonna lay out that kind of money why don't you just hire out the job?"

O'Reilly and Johnson laughed.

Soleski barked across the table. "Where's the satisfaction in that, Ole?!"

Cohen smiled. "Exactly. But we'll get to that in a few minutes."

The red beam wiggled down Normandy's coastline.

"Here's an outline for this little excursion of ours. We'd use legitimate passports and fly into Paris or London. We'd either take a Channel ferry from Britain or a train from Paris to the coast. We'd stay two days and nights so we can tour the beaches and blend in with the other veterans' groups."

The red dot moved shakily across the map into Paris and then northeast.

"We'd take a train to Liège, get a car and hook up with a retired American major who runs battlefield tours from Bastogne. We'd spend a day or two at the Bulge sites. We'll even find that little village where this all began."

Eyes followed the ruby light down toward the middle right of the screen.

"Next we go east to the town of Thionville and set up for the final stage of The Project. At that point, I'll make the final decision on who goes and who stays."

"Wait a minute," said Soleski. "You mean that if we agree to go, and it's a very big IF, we won't know who's going to actually pull the trigger until a day or two ahead of time?"

Cohen nodded. "That's the way it is, Sollie. It has to be my call."

"Geez, Sam that seems kinda cold-hearted," protested Johnson. "I mean, like Sollie says, we're supposed to go all the way to France and still not know if we're going to be in on it until the last minute?"

"Has to be that way," said Cohen quietly.

Swanson got up and walked over to the map. He looked at the French and German border. "You said, Thionville. Is that where the bastard lives?"

"Not in the city itself, Burt," said Cohen. He stared at the spot where Swanson had placed his finger. "He's actually east of it, in a smaller village just short of the German border."

Cohen signaled Peter and the lights came up slowly, leaving the map's faint image on the screen. Several men went over to the wall to try to locate towns they remembered from the war. Noble propped a pair of reading glasses on his nose and waited his turn.

Cohen waved at the map. "The whole European Union situation has opened up this man's world, made his life a lot easier. He travels back and forth quite a bit, but he lives in France."

"Don't the Froggies know who this guy really is?" Johnson asked.

"He's been living under an assumed name, Ole."

"Probably greases a few palms to slip in and out like that," said Swanson.

"Undoubtedly," said Cohen, holding the report aloft. He nodded to Noble. "Bill's going to walk you through some interesting facts about Von Wurtz."

He sat down and William Noble rose to his feet as the men quieted.

"It's all covered in the packets Sam gave you," he announced, looking at his portfolio. "Here's what we do know about Von Wurtz's post-war years." He flipped a page and began reading.

"Somewhere along the way, Von Wurtz changed his name to Kurt Weismann and reinvented himself as a successful European businessman and investor."

Noble peered over the top of his reading glasses.

"This won't help anyone's blood pressure, but Von Wurtz played the Cold War card and slipped through the net with assistance from our own Intelligence services. Turned up in South America around 1947."

He was right. Low murmurs of disgust rippled through the group.

"Moved around there until '55 or so and then showed up in Austria before disappearing again." Noble glanced up to make sure the men were still with him. "Surfaced in Syria and did nasty things as an advisor in state security until he was fingered by the Israelis. The Mossad sent teams to pick him off at least twice in Damascus and failed both times."

"Not like them to miss," whistled Wolf. "This guy must lead a charmed life."

"I'd say so. Right after that, Adolf Eichmann took center stage, so Von Wurtz—or Weismann at that point—was able to slip under everyone's radar and disappear." Noble scanned the report and continued his briefing.

"Someone . . . the report doesn't say who . . . got him started in the shipping end of the oil business and he worked his way into some significant money. By then he had reinvented himself again and eventually ended up back in Europe where he got into plastics. The man most definitely has a Midas touch. He's a heavy financial hitter now and apparently quite legit in top continental business circles."

Noble took off his glasses and cocked an eyebrow. "It's ironic, but sixty-plus years later this guy ends up wealthy. From oil to plastics. Eventually he expanded into communication markets at the right time and made a bundle. Shrewd investor. Quite respected. Sits on a number of boards. Does his heavy lifting out of Swiss banks and is known as something of a venture capitalist these days."

"Still a murdering sonofabitch," snarled O'Reilly from the back of the room.

"No question about that, Dawson. That he is," agreed Noble.

"How do you plan to complete The Project?" asked Swanson, leaning forward.

Noble tapped his copy of the report with his reading glasses. "Burt, the same folks who gave Sam this report have offered introductions to people in Europe who are good at this sort of thing."

"So you're hiring it out after all," said Swanson, turning to Cohen.

He ignored the sarcasm. "Not quite. These people will only help if we decide to go for it."

That seemed to satisfy Swanson.

"Look, I'm confident," declared Cohen, on his feet again, "that if we can get close enough, we can bring justice to him. Bill and I think it's worth a try. But we need to know who's willing to go with us."

No one spoke.

Cohen stood next to Noble and looked around the room. "Bill and I want to know what you're thinking."

"You actually want a decision right now, Sam?" asked Wolf.

Cohen leaned over the table. "Ken, I didn't come here expecting you guys to sign up for this after one free dinner and a couple of nights in a king-sized bed with room service. This should not be a snap decision for any of you. I know we've given you a lot to think about. You have to consider your families, your health and your commitment to The Project."

He let his words sink in for a moment, hoping for some reaction from the group. Then he added, "What I'm looking for is your honest reaction to what we're thinking of doing."

O'Reilly groused from his chair. "Don't get me wrong, Sam, Bill. I mean, I'm as gung ho as you about Von Wurtz getting what he deserves, but Ken's right. Isn't this kinda . . . well, nuts?" The former policeman was waving his arms again. "I mean, c'mon, fellas! We're in our eighties, goddamnit! I don't know about you guys, but I can't even get up a flight of stairs without wheezing. And now we're talking about doing some kinda Rambo thing on this guy? Don't tell me it doesn't sound crazy!"

Soleski looked over at O'Reilly and nodded. "I ain't saying it can't be done, but if we got caught, would we really want to spend the rest of our lives in some God-forsaken, rat-infested European jail?"

"You saying you don't want to be part of this, Sollie?" asked Johnson.

The little man glared at his traveling companion. "Don't put words in my mouth, Ole. I just don't like the idea of possibly screwing up so far from home. One tour in Europe was enough for me."

"You have to admit, Sam," said Wolf trying to sound reasonable, "it is pretty impractical for a group of old guys to travel a couple thousand miles just to whack another senior citizen."

Johnson leaped to his feet, offended by Wolf's characterization of the target. "Oh yeah?! This senior citizen, as you call him, just happens to be the Nazi bastard who murdered our friends in cold blood and nearly killed you, Ken!"

Wolf shrugged, not arguing the point, and waited for Cohen's reply.

"That's why it has to be all volunteers," said Cohen, unruffled.

Swanson flashed a cynical grin at the men around the table. "Rule Number One. Never volunteer."

They all laughed nervously.

"Two more things," added Cohen, keeping his tone even. "None of these packets leaves this room today. Too much compromising info on these sheets of paper. And, secondly, we expect each of you to honor your agreement of silence." He pointed at the door of the conference room and lowered his voice, drawing them closer so they would give him their full attention. "If word gets out about what we've discussed here today, we'll find ourselves in serious trouble. All of us. That means no sharing with wives or family. Everything said here today, stays here."

Nods and mumbles of agreement rippled around the table.

Cohen asked Peter to collect the envelopes from each man's place. "I'll come by before you check out and talk to each one of you privately. I think twenty-four hours is enough time for you to make up your minds. What I want is a decision about your willingness to be part of The Project. If you say you need more time to think about it, I'll have to consider that a 'No' because, as Bill said, we're running out of time. Fair enough?"

Everyone nodded. He held up both hands to forestall further conversation. "Don't talk to me now. Sleep on it . . . if you can. Tell me tomorrow when I come to say goodbye. And thanks for coming." He went down the line, shaking hands, looking each man in the eye as he did. The group filed out. Cohen stopped William Noble as he was leaving and asked him to stay behind. Peter was excused by his grandfather. O'Reilly and Soleski headed for the hotel's bar while the others begged off, opting for the quiet of their rooms.

## CHAPTER TWENTY-SIX

Cohen cleaned out his laptop, deleting files he had shared at the meeting. He would take precautions by destroying the hard drive and replacing it later. He stuffed the collected envelopes into his courtroom briefcase for shredding and then sat back, to peer at William Noble across the table.

"How do you think it went, Bill?"

"You put the fear of God into them, Sam. It was quite a shock."

"Had to be. I know how they feel. When I first got this information I was completely thrown off guard like you were."

He sat back, reflecting. "Neither of us thought we'd ever see this day."

Noble nodded, frowning. "Maybe I should have excused Peter, Sam. Do you think I made a mistake?"

Cohen looked out the window and then back at Noble. "I don't know, Bill. But I sensed that Peter belonged somehow. You agree?"

"In a way," said Noble. "Like I told you, I laid it all out for him a month ago and I thought I detected some righteous anger on his part when I finished the tale." He sighed, seemed to sag into the leather chair.

Cohen put a hand on Noble's arm. "Look, you don't have to do this, Bill. You can forget today ever happened, no questions asked. Take Peter and walk away before you get too deeply involved."

"What about you, Sam? If these guys back out, are you going to walk away?"

"We're not talking about me, Bill. I've made my accommodations. Thought things out pretty clearly. I'm committed to seeing this through, regardless."

"What about Sondra?"

"I lost her a year ago, Bill. She's gone. Her body is still here, but she's gone."

"You can't just leave her, Sam. What if Soleski's right? If anything were to go wrong over there . . ." He left the rest of his thought unsaid.

"Her younger sister is all the family Sondra has left," explained Cohen. "I've already asked her to come to Chicago in a couple of months and the two of us will go over estate planning. She doesn't know about any of this of course, but everything's taken care of in a family trust. I've covered every angle. Nobody can touch Sondra if something goes wrong. She'll be taken care of regardless of how this thing ends."

Cohen smiled, slapped his hand on the polished table. "Besides, we won't fail!"

"Tell me again how good this information is, Sam."

"Solid stuff. Reliable. I trust these people. And once we get to Europe we'll meet with the gentlemen I spoke of earlier." Cohen drummed his fingers on the table, waiting for Noble's response. It wasn't long in coming.

"I wanted in on The Project from the get-go, Sam. You still know that, right?"

"I knew it from the beginning," said Cohen, looking away. "But your health is a serious concern for me, Bill. I won't jeopardize this if your health problems get in the way."

Noble bristled. "I don't expect you to. I'd never compromise the mission if I thought I was going to be a hindrance." He looked Cohen in the eyes. "I want to do this. But I've got to bring Peter with me."

The lawyer slowly shook his head. "I'm not so sure about that, Bill. Think about it. Peter's got his whole life ahead of him and we're at the end of ours. Is it right to put his future on the line?"

"Then you'd better speak to him, Sam. He'll be up-front with you. I watched him during your presentation. He wants to go. And he agreed to your promise of secrecy." Noble's voice took on an insistent tone. "Just talk to him the same way you would the rest of us. If I go, Sam, I'll need Peter with me. I can't do it without him."

Cohen tried to reassure his friend. "Okay, I'll talk to him, I promise."

He looked at his watch and then back at Noble. "Look, Bill, you heard me tell everyone that I'm going to have final say over the makeup of our team. I can't compromise on that. And not because I'm bankrolling this thing. If I don't think someone's up to this, I'm pulling them off the team."

"I told you I could live with that, Sam."

"Good. Let's get out of here, I'm bushed. Have to get home to Sondra." Cohen paused, looked back. "Do you and Peter have plans this evening?"

"No," said Noble. "Thought I'd get some rack time before we eat."

The lawyer grasped his bulging briefcase. "I'd appreciate it if the two of you would come to my place for dinner. How about six? I'll tell you how I see this shaping up and we could spend some time talking over your impressions of today. Get Peter's take on things, too."

Noble smiled as they walked from the room. "I'd like that, Sam."

"Good." Cohen plucked a card from his coat pocket and handed it to Noble. "My address. Have the hotel get you a cab around five-thirty. I'll alert my doorman you're coming."

The old men headed down the hall, arms linked. "Want me to take point for you, Old Timer?" laughed Cohen.

Noble snorted. "Hell, Sam, I was walking point before you even figured out which end of a bayonet was the sharp one."

They traded insults all the way to the elevator.

# CHAPTER TWENTY-SEVEN

Dawson O'Reilly scratched his belly and fished in his room's ice bucket. He pulled out a handful of melting cubes and dropped them in a thick tumbler. Unscrewing the top of a bottle of bourbon, he filled his glass to the brim. A service cart, parked against the room's television cabinet, was stacked with a disorderly pile of dirty dishes and cups. The old cop, shoeless and wearing an undershirt and slacks, sank down in a corner chair and leaned over his glass, lapping at the whiskey like a dog.

A knock sounded. "Come in!" he bellowed.

The door opened and Myron Soleski sauntered in, followed by Ole Johnson and Ken Wolf. Soleski's hand was wrapped around a plastic cup filled with booze, Johnson the same. Wolf cradled a bottle of wine in a towel.

Johnson pulled up chairs next to the writing desk. Wolf kicked off his shoes and lowered himself onto the bed, leaning against the headboard. The retired engineer surveyed the room with a critical eye.

"Geez, Dawson, you think you're back living in a college dorm. What a slob."

"Here," said the cop, tossing an empty glass at the figure on his bed, "try this on for size, or do you wine snobs drink right outta the bottle?"

Wolf caught the tumbler, poured it half-full of wine and set the bottle on the nightstand.

"Where's Swanson?" asked O'Reilly.

"Dunno," replied Johnson. "I told him we'd be meeting in your room to talk about The Project."

"And Noble and his grandson?" said the cop.

"Not in their room," volunteered Wolf. "And I didn't see them in the bar."

O'Reilly again. "Probably went out to dinner."

"Or over to Sam's," said Johnson. "Those two are pretty tight, you know."

"Screw 'em," mumbled O'Reilly. "Bill's made up his mind already. I can tell. He's going along with Sam and he'll take his grandson with him."

The men in the room fell silent. Then Ole Johnson raised his glass in a toast. "Well, here's to the hell of a fix we're in, boys."

The others raised their glasses.

"What fix, Ole?" asked O'Reilly.

"The fix Sam Cohen's got us in. Or didn't you catch that part, Dawson?"

The old cop took a long swig of whiskey and came up for air. "Yeah, I got it. Things don't look good from where I'm sitting but we don't have to go along with it, you know. Just look Sam in the eye tomorrow and tell him you don't want any part of it."

The others grunted and O'Reilly thrust out his jaw defiantly. "That's what I'm gonna do," he added.

"What I meant," said Johnson, "was this fix makes us co-conspirators for this whole goddamn mess. Aren't we now material witnesses or something like that?"

"Well, the way I see it," said O'Reilly, "by not going along, I'm off the hook if the shit hits the fan." He waved at the others, pointing with his glass. "And it will hit the fan, you can be sure of that." He swallowed more whiskey.

"So you're not going?" queried Wolf from the bed.

O'Reilly swiveled in the chair. "Hell no, I ain't going. You think I'm crazy? Sam's talking murder, Ken!"

Wolf sat up, slowly swinging his legs over the edge of the bed. "Yeah, I've been thinking about the plan and I have to admit that worries me."

"Worries you?!" snorted O'Reilly. "The whole goddamn thing is absolutely nuts and if you guys go along with it, you're as crazy as Sam." He emptied his glass and reached for the bottle to pour himself another drink.

"I'm thinking of going," said Soleski quietly, not looking at his companions.

O'Reilly blew out his cheeks and rolled his eyes at the ceiling. "You're out of your fucking mind, Sollie. It'll never work and you guys are gonna get your asses thrown in that stinking European jail you said you were so worried about." The old cop hovered over Soleski. "It WAS you I heard saying that, wasn't it?"

The Michigan man shifted away from the boozy fumes washing over him and the cop returned to his seat. "Yeah, you heard right. I said it. But I been thinking . . ."

"That's a novelty," snorted Johnson.

Soleski smiled, ignoring him. "I think we gotta try. We owe it to the others. The ones who didn't come back."

"Sollie, that was over sixty years ago," reasoned Wolf from the bed. "If they had caught Von Wurtz, then our guys could have hanged him as a war criminal."

Ken Wolf stood up and paced, glass in hand. "Our side had the chance, but like Sam said, they let him slip through their fingers. And now we have families, homes. Some of us even have great-grandkids." He walked over to Soleski. "You can't throw all that away on some half-cocked plan, Sollie. Think about it. A plan that's illegal, I might add," said Wolf.

The little man from Michigan defended himself. "Yeah, I know, but I have thought about it. Tomorrow, when Sam asks me if I want to go back, I'm gonna say yes."

"What about Marge, Sollie?" asked Johnson. "What'll happen to her if you get in trouble over there? You think about that?"

"She's got her TV. She wouldn't even miss me," grinned Soleski.

"Probably not true!" barked O'Reilly from his corner.

"Sam's got a wife too," added Soleski, "and she depends on him."

"She's out of it, according to Noble," snorted O'Reilly caustically.

"Aw c'mon, Sollie," said Johnson. "The only difference between you and Sam taking care of your wives is . . . oh, say about twenty or thirty million dollars."

Myron Soleski stood his ground. "Well, Dawson, you wanted to get together so we could talk about this and that's my decision."

The former cop, now working on a fresh drink, threw up his hands, surrendered. "Your funeral, buddy."

"How about you, Ole?" asked Wolf.

The café owner stretched back and drained his drink. "I figure I have too much to lose at this point in my life. I've got a great business which took me a lifetime to build and I've got a wonderful wife who means everything to me. So, no, I'm not going," he declared without apology.

He clamped a big hand on his traveling companion's shoulder and Soleski smiled back at Johnson, not a trace of resentment on the little man's weathered face.

Ken Wolf got off the bed and wandered over to the window, looking down on Chicago's lights eight floors below. "I'm thinking of my kids and grandchildren," he said without looking back at the men in the room. "I just can't . . . won't . . . risk it for them."

"What about Swanson?" asked Johnson, looking around the room as though he expected to find the former sergeant in their midst.

"I'd say Burt is probably gonna be a no-show, too," predicted O'Reilly.

"Sam could sure use him," mused Johnson.

"Maybe if they convince him there are great golf courses in the Ardennes," joked O'Reilly.

The men laughed along with him. They finished their liquor and told stories for another hour until O'Reilly dropped off in thunderous snores.

Wolf pried the glass from the dozing cop's hand and they carried him to his bed before the three men left the room. Soleski turned on the bathroom light and locked the door behind them.

# CHAPTER TWENTY-EIGHT

### CHICAGO, FEBRUARY 22

In the morning, only three agreed to accompany Cohen to the continent: the Nobles and Soleski.

Though disappointed, Cohen hid his feelings as the reunion ended privately in each man's hotel room. With the interviews finished, Noble knew the Fortunate Orphans no longer existed.

Wolf left quietly, taking a cab to Evanston where his wife waited with friends. Soleski and Johnson were the next to leave, old suitcases jammed into the bar owner's unwashed Ford Explorer.

The last four, Swanson, O'Reilly and the Nobles, said good-bye and slipped into separate cabs for O'Hare. Swanson's flight to Memphis and on to Little Rock sent him down a separate concourse, and he waved a farewell salute in the main terminal. With his grandson Peter acting as a neutral barrier, William Noble sat apart from Dawson O'Reilly as the trio waited for their Twin Cities flight. The retired cop retreated to a nearby bar until boarding was announced. On the trip home, the elder Noble sought privacy by sleeping and left it to Peter to engage O'Reilly in chatter across the aisle.

When they landed, Peter flagged an electric cart and they rode in silence to the security checkpoint. Silence followed them down the escalator to the baggage claim. William Noble stood to one side as his fellow Chicago passengers waited patiently for suitcases to spill onto the revolving carousel.

The old man could not hide his disappointment with the reunion's outcome and when the men shook hands in parting, it was Peter, the peacemaker, who kept polite talk going. The Nobles declined O'Reilly's offer of a ride with one of his wife's relatives and left to make the trek across the terminal's lower level to find a cab.

"How you holding up, Gramps?"

"Boy, I'm ready for some quality sack time, kiddo. It's been an exciting weekend, but I'm running on empty right now."

That was the extent of their conversation until they were deposited at their familiar bungalow. Their driver, a thin Somali of few words, popped the trunk and hefted their suitcases up the steps as Peter steadied his grandfather the last few yards.

Noble pushed a few bills at the driver and, uncharacteristically, told him to keep the change. The taxi driver thanked them politely and returned to his idling cab. Peter led his grandfather inside and went back to the porch to get their bags.

Noble lowered himself onto the padded bench in the small breakfast nook and sat contentedly, watching Peter brew coffee and tea. Only when the steaming liquid filled the heavy mug in his hands did William Noble feel calmer. He listened to his grandson empty suitcases in another room and was pleased to be home.

Tomorrow they would pull out maps and sketch plans based on what Samuel Cohen had shared with them at dinner in his home overlooking the dark lake. Noble would have to consult his doctors at the VA, something he dreaded, and Peter would have to return to work mid-week.

For now, it was enough that they were home.

In the living room the soft, reassuring chimes of the grandfather clock declared early evening and somewhere below him the old man heard the furnace kick into life. Radiators throughout the house began ticking, accepting heat, and the house began to warm. Noble inhaled his coffee's rich aroma and took a deep swallow, feeling his body finally begin to relax. When Peter returned, arms filled with mail from the porch, he sat across from Noble to sift the collection.

"Gramps, you're happy to be back home, aren't you?"

Noble nodded and sipped his coffee.

"That was a fantastic experience," said Peter. "Meeting those guys. Hearing the stories."

"We just scratched the surface, Peter. You're gonna have to hang onto your hat these next few months, you know." Noble looked out the kitchen window at long daggers of ice on the roof's edge and thought of the Ardennes.

"Are you sorry it ended the way it did?"

"I'm still trying to figure that out, Sport." He sipped his coffee again. "I won't lie to you. I thought we'd get more of the guys to commit."

"Pretty serious thing to go for, The Project I mean," Peter said, testing his tea.

"Yeah, it is," his grandfather mused. "I just wish we weren't going in so under strength on this thing." He took a long swallow and set the mug down. "Well, it can't be helped. We go with the cards we've been dealt. How about rustling up some dinner, Peter?"

"Sure, Gramps. And after dinner how about a fire before we turn in?"

Noble smiled. "You have a frightening ability to read my mind."

"You're an open book," laughed the younger man. He got up to go into the living room and then turned in the doorway. "We can sleep in tomorrow, you know."

"Like I said, you've got this uncanny ability . . ."

They laughed and Peter began stacking kindling in the hearth. He opened the damper and thrust a lighted taper under the wood.

Outside the sun faded quickly.

*Tomorrow*, thought the old man, *they would sit down at the big table and spread out the maps and talk about Normandy and the Ardennes.*

# CHAPTER TWENTY-NINE

## OVER THE ATLANTIC OCEAN, MAY 25

William Noble raised his window shade to block annoying sunlight and pressed his seat button, easing himself smoothly into a reclining position.

To his left Samuel Cohen stabbed at his laptop's keyboard under a cone of light from the panel above him. The Chicago lawyer was still fiddling with their European itinerary. Their flight was an hour from Heathrow Airport and riding a tail wind at thirty-five thousand feet above the North Atlantic.

Behind them Peter Noble lay back, half dozing, iPod in his right hand, head bobbing slightly to one of his five thousand songs. Beside him, Myron Soleski happily devoured a small bag of peanuts, one nut at a time, a half-empty glass of white wine on his meal tray in front of him. The quartet occupied two starboard rows of paired seats in first class. Across the aisle, a chubby CPA, his lap covered in ledger pages, busily scribbled hieroglyphic accounting notes on a legal pad. The forward compartment was full of men and women in executive attire. A pair of priests—likely Episcopalians, Soleski had whispered—were enjoying their third glass of wine and interrupting each other in a windy theological discussion. A flight attendant headed their way, balancing a tray of refills in front of her. Soleski stopped her to confiscate another wine for himself. She smiled, scolding him gently before continuing to the rear of the cabin. Behind Soleski a young mother burrowed beneath her blanket, a pink silk sleeping mask covering her eyes, her napping six-year old squirming beside her. In the cockpit the captain talked to his controller in Heathrow and executed a slow turn, beginning the Boeing 777's long, routine descent into British airspace.

Samuel Cohen had given his team a short briefing about this leg of the journey, pledging a more elaborate explanation once they got to England. To combat jet lag, he promised three full days in London where they would see the sights and also meet some people who had promised to help them. Soleski and the others were content to fly in pampered style, entrusting Cohen with the details. Peter Noble had forged a relationship with the little man from Upper Michigan and the two promised to enjoy their visit to Europe as much as time allowed. Soleski had not left the States since the war and he was curious about what he would find.

Peter, like his older seat mate, had decided to focus on the first part of the trip, determined to get as much from this stage of their expedition as he could absorb. Like Soleski, he ignored darker reasons for the trip, assigning them another category in his mind.

Cohen had deliberately scheduled more time at this stage of the journey. "We've waited sixty years for this," he reasoned, "so a few more days here and there aren't going to affect the outcome. Besides, he may not pass this way again, so let Peter enjoy as much of this as he can the first time around."

The elder Noble was grateful for his friend's indulgence, knowing his grandson well enough to predict that Peter would embrace the adventure thoroughly. They agreed to cut the younger Noble loose with Soleski in tow while William Noble and Samuel Cohen, the two driving the mission, set the final sequence in motion. The Project would begin in London where Cohen's Chicago contact, Carl Goldman, had promised to meet them and arrange introductions to persons who had, as he said diplomatically, certain skills the group might need.

Noble nodded at Cohen's laptop. "You about done with whatever changes you've been making on that thing?"

The lawyer's thin hands fluttered across the keyboard and made two final taps. He looked at his friend and flashed a quick smile. "Yes . . . for now." He snapped the lid shut on the computer and slipped it into its padded traveling case. Cohen leaned back and rubbed the scar along his temple. "It's still very much a work in progress, Bill."

He angled his seat back alongside Noble's and closed his eyes. "I'm ready for some quiet time in London. How about you?"

His seat mate grunted in agreement and the two nodded off in tandem until the flight attendants came through the cabin, collecting drink glasses and alerting passengers to raise their seats prior to arrival.

After landing, the four collected their carry-on bags and waded into the herd shuffling off the aircraft to Passport Control. Once through the checkpoint they collected their baggage on rental carts and worked their way through Customs.

Ahead of them, a wall of strangers, some with signs, waited. Peter spotted a pale, bespectacled, balding middle-aged man in a light tan raincoat holding a small white board with Cohen's name on it.

"Ah, Mr. Cohen? Samuel Cohen?" queried the man as they approached.

"I'm Samuel Cohen."

The man thrust out his hand and Cohen gripped it.

"I'm Carter, sir. Due to a prior commitment, Carl Goldman asked me to meet you and deliver you and your friends, complete with baggage, to your hotel. Am I correct that you have made your own arrangements at the Hilton London Paddington?"

"Yes, we have," answered Cohen. "I thought it convenient for our needs."

Carter beamed. "An excellent choice, sir."

A sea of passengers swirled past the little knot of men as Cohen introduced his group to Carter. The other three nodded as they were named in turn. Their greeter seemed puzzled. He pushed his glasses against the bridge of his nose and squinted at the small semicircle of new arrivals. "Ah . . . but is this really all of you, sir? I was told to expect seven gentlemen."

"This is all of us, Carter. I'll explain to Carl in due time."

The man shrugged. "Very well, sir,"

He waved to a waiting porter and the man hustled their bags onto his push cart. The bookish man set off, Cohen by his side.

"We'll take the Heathrow Express. It'll only take fifteen minutes to Paddington Station and the hotel's lobby is adjacent. You'll find it quite practical, sir." Cohen nodded in agreement as their guide chatted.

The train was, as their chaperone had said, efficient, with express runs departing every quarter hour. From Heathrow their train ran non-stop into West London's historic Paddington Station, a terminal of concrete platforms and blackened furrows of rail. Arriving and departing trains glided like colorful serpents under a huge vaulted ceiling of glass panels held in place by a spider's web of wrought iron.

As their train slowed upon entering the giant shed, Peter Noble counted almost two hundred iron ribs arching over eight sets of track. The soaring metal structure, still in service after more than a century and a half, looked deceptively delicate to his visitor's eye.

They exited their car and were instantly surrounded by a cacophony of loudspeakers, machinery and voices. Carter hailed a trolling porter and instructed that their bags were to follow them. On the way he played guide, chatting about the railway's history and pointing out the old station master's office with its triptych of arched windows. Peter Noble followed in silent awe, snapping pictures of the vintage structure. The men rode an escalator to a walkway which led to the hotel's lobby. Carter led them to the front desk across polished marble floors set in a checkerboard pattern. Their greeter tipped the porter and dismissed him as Cohen registered his entourage. While the lawyer was signing in, Soleski gawked like a rube at a chandelier centered over an elaborate inlaid compass design in the entry's floor. It was surrounded by concentric rings of diamond shapes and the little man circled the lobby's floor, studying the pattern.

"Beats Motel Eight," he whispered to Peter. "I wish Ole was here to see this." William Noble shuffled up behind the pair, chuckling. "And if O'Reilly were here, he would've found the bar by now."

The desk clerk summoned bellhops in livery and the men began loading the group's baggage onto brass carts.

"I'll take my leave now, Mr. Cohen," said Carter, holding out his hand.

Each man offered their escort a handshake and thanked him for his help.

"I'll ring Mr. Goldman and report that you're safely settled."

"Yes, do that," said Cohen. "Please tell him to call tomorrow at noon."

"Very good, sir. Goodbye."

Carter pushed his glasses back up his nose, made a slight bow and retraced his steps to Paddington Station.

# CHAPTER THIRTY

### LONDON, PADDINGTON HOTEL

Peter and his grandfather were assigned a room with one wall entirely given over to curtained windows overlooking the city. Off the main room, a small balcony furnished with a table and chairs was surrounded by a railing of decorative iron scrollwork. Skylights across the width of the room allowed light to pour over the huge bed, a round table with three chairs and a comfortable writing desk.

Noble tipped their bellboy, then headed for a couch set against one wall, where he immediately put stockinged feet on a pedestal table's glass top. His eyes were heavy.

"Get some shut-eye, Gramps," suggested Peter, unpacking.

"I don't want to miss anything," murmured the old man, fighting to stay awake.

"I'll wake you if anything important happens."

"Maybe you're right, Sport." He rose reluctantly, went to the huge bed and lay down.

Within minutes he was asleep. Peter hung some clothes and then went across the hall to Soleski's room.

"Ain't Sam something?" asked the little man. He gave Peter a tour of his room with its high ceilings, large double bed, marbled bathroom and stocked mini-bar. "This is costing him plenty."

"From what I've gathered," said Peter, "he can afford it."

"Yeah, I know, but it's still something, kid. I could never travel like this in a hundred years." He held out his arms. "Do you know how much overtime I'd have to work just to pay for one night at a place like this?" He smiled to himself.

The phone rang. Soleski answered, chatted, then replaced the receiver in its cradle. "Sam wants us to stop by his place."

They shut the door behind them and stopped to look in on Peter's grandfather. He was stretched on his back, a relaxed look on his face, chest rising and falling.

"Leave him," said Soleski. "He needs the rest."

They locked the door and went down the hall to Cohen's suite, knocked, then entered. Cohen had evidently been working at the writing desk; his laptop and a folder lay open. He welcomed his guests.

"Can you believe this place? I have to give you a tour. C'mon."

He led them past the huge bed, showed them the small dining room table in an alcove and the second bedroom with its own bathroom.

"Very Art Deco, like our room," commented Peter.

"I hope I can afford it," Cohen said laughing. The old lawyer seemed energized despite the long flight. "You gentlemen hungry?" he asked, rubbing his hands.

When Peter and Soleski nodded yes, Cohen suggested they go downstairs for an early dinner in the hotel's restaurant. Room service could be ordered for Peter's grandfather when he finally awakened. Peter went back to his room, scribbled a note for the old man and slipped it into the sleeper's hands.

In the restaurant Cohen requested a corner table. They ordered wine with crusted salmon and spinach mascarpone for dinner and ate quietly, lingering over their meal in the uncrowded room. Soleski told Cohen that he and Peter planned to explore the city the next day.

"Go to it," encouraged the lawyer. "I'm staying behind. I'm expecting a call from Carl Goldman around noon. He's in the city. Bill and I need to meet with him before we go to France."

"Is this the guy who's going to introduce you to . . ."

The lawyer held up his hand, stopping the conversation. "The less said the better, Sollie. You understand?"

Soleski backed off immediately. "Of course." He glanced around the nearly empty restaurant. "I didn't meant to compromise anything."

Cohen smiled reassuringly. "Don't worry, Sollie, you didn't." He leaned toward the pair. "It's just that from now on, we all must be very discreet about talking about The Project outside our own group. We only talk privately when this subject comes up. Agreed?"

After leaving the restaurant, the three men stepped out of the hotel's entrance to watch the sky darken. The sidewalks around the station were swarming with foot traffic and Praed Street, the avenue fronting the hotel, pulsed with cars and buses. Behind them, the Hilton's facade appeared as a lighted Victorian wedding cake carved in nineteenth-century stone.

"I'm going to call home, check on things. Then I'm turning in," announced Cohen after several minutes. He led them back into the hotel lobby and they rode the elevator to their floor.

"Good evening, gentlemen."

"Goodnight, Sam," said Soleski.

Peter waved to both and entered the darkened room where his grandfather still stretched the length of the bed. He locked the door behind him and crept across the dim room. He could not resist stepping onto the balcony where the city was aglow as far as he could see. Very few street sounds floated up to him as he stood there in the night air. Somewhere out there across the Channel was the man who was the object of their trip. *What would this man do if he knew he had only two weeks to live? How will he react when we come for him?*

Peter eased into a chair at the small table for a long time, turning a disquieting question over and over again: *How will I behave when the moment arrives?*

## CHAPTER THIRTY-ONE

### LONDON, MAY 26

Samuel Cohen slept late, a luxury he seldom allowed himself at home. He rose at ten, showered and shaved and then rang for William Noble. The lawyer ordered room service for two and they ate together in Cohen's suite. Precisely at noon the phone rang.

Carl Goldman was on the other end. "Samuel, welcome to London. Good to hear your voice. How was the flight?"

"Long and uneventful," answered the lawyer.

"That's the way I prefer them," joked Goldman. "Uneventful." Cohen grunted in agreement. "My man Carter tells me that you're down to four, Sam. Is that true?"

"Afraid so. We had some disagreement about how to pursue this thing."

"We're concerned about that, Sam."

"We?" Cohen felt some irritation at the reproach.

"I'm with the senator, Sam. He's here on business with his UK publisher."

Cohen was surprised that the politician was in London. He had met Proctor Johnson just twice previously and his memory of the Illinois congressman was of a man consumed with himself and his presidential ambitions.

"Can you come our way at two, Sam? One of the Senator's friends was kind enough to offer his flat near Regents Park while he's away. The place is an absolute gem. Let me give you the address."

Cohen paused and scribbled directions on hotel stationery. "Yes, I'll be there, Carl. Will your friends show?"

"I'd hardly call them friends, Sam. But yes, the people you're interested in will be here. Shall we say two o'clock then?"

"Yes, two. Will the senator sit in on our meeting?"

"Just in the beginning. He has an appointment at half past, but he wanted to stay long enough to say hello."

"I'm flattered," said Cohen, not really meaning it. "How much does he know about our reason for being here?"

"He has a vague idea of how things stand but I'll let it stop there."

Plausible deniability. Ever the careful politician, thought Cohen. "All right, we'll press the flesh with the Senator, Carl."

"Good. Sorry about your friends letting you down, Sam."

"I'm not happy about it myself, Carl. But when push came to shove some of my people wouldn't budge. That's the way it is with volunteers. What can I say?"

"You still think it's possible with a smaller crew?"

"Yes I do, Carl. Why else would I be here? We'll just have to adjust."

Goldman was silent, then spoke again. "All right, let's move ahead on this."

"I agree," said Cohen. " Carl, I'm bringing William Noble with me. He's one of my crew. Will that be agreeable with you . . . with your associates?"

"One moment." Cohen heard Goldman turn away from the phone and say something to another party. He came back on the line. "I don't see why not, Sam. Bring Noble with you."

"Good. We'll be there, Carl. Goodbye."

Cohen hung up the phone and smiled across the table at Noble, who was finishing his second cup of coffee. "We're on at two, Bill."

# CHAPTER THIRTY-TWO

## LONDON, REGENCY PARK

From a tall, curtained window on the third level of a richly furnished Regents Park flat, Carl Goldman watched a lorry park below the balcony.

A florist's delivery man emerged from the van carrying two long white boxes and disappeared under the ornate arches of the building across the street. Goldman let his eyes wander across the rooftops to the pond in Regents Park where small boats drifted serenely across the blue surface.

"What time is it, Carl?" Proctor Johnson's deep baritone filled the room.

Goldman glanced at his watch. "Ten minutes 'til two, Senator."

He stood at the window, enjoying the view. At the far end of the room, his chief hurriedly penned his last letter of the afternoon. Goldman glanced at the ornate antique desk, watching the former senator fold the note and seal it in an envelope.

"Everything set, Carl?"

He rocked back on his heels, a nervous habit that irritated his boss. A steely glance from the seated man made Goldman stop his rocking and the senator repeated himself as if speaking to a dull child.

"I said, is everything ready, Carl?"

"Yes, Senator, we're all set for Cohen and company."

Proctor Johnson tossed his envelope into a silver tray with other letters and capped his gold fountain pen. He rose, pushed away from the writing desk and slipped into a custom tailored dark blue blazer he had draped over the chair. The former senator stepped to an intricately carved marble fireplace and checked his appearance in a gilded mirror over the mantelpiece.

The politician was six feet tall, broad shouldered, with leonine silver hair that set off his perpetually tanned face, pale blue eyes, straight nose and perfect capped white teeth. His face was a campaign manager's dream. Johnson's strong square jaw projected determination and when he smiled he joked to intimates that it was worth a thousand female votes. He smiled often.

The man had charm, Goldman admitted, and when Proctor Johnson was "on" he was unstoppable while working a room or a crowd. First appointed to fill a vacant Senate seat when the previous occupant was tapped as a Cabinet Secretary, Johnson had served out the last eight months of his predecessor's term and then handily won two elections on his own.

He had been one of the rising stars in the party, his name often mentioned for the short list of vice-presidential hopefuls and for the long list of presidential dark horse candidates. Potomac fever.

But with his matinee-idol good looks had come a corresponding flaw of arrogance. Most of the talk about the White House originated from Johnson's office, but the friendly media sycophants who were hand-fed by the senator were blissfully unaware of his part in the manipulation. It was all heady stuff to the senior lawmaker from Illinois. With such lofty status came seeds of self-destruction, and the last contest had been Johnson's undoing.

He had been caught telling a single sophomoric joke about intelligence levels of certain voters. It was badly timed banter at the expense of immigrants and minorities. His attempt at "old boy humor" with intimates had backfired, captured on a cell phone camera belonging to one of his disgruntled campaign workers.

In the wake of the recording's release on several blogs, his lead in the polls evaporated overnight. He compounded his first lapse with a series of defiant, mangled half-apologies. Even his loyalists, the hard-core base of fellow evangelical Christians, deserted him and he tumbled to ignominious defeat.

For the past two years he had undergone a very public rehabilitation in two ways: He practiced repentance by wooing Black congregations throughout the state and, secondly, by writing cogent arguments about America's Mideast policy.

Along with his welcome back into the flock, he had rebuilt his reputation as a strong, articulate backer of Israel with two best-selling books. He had just released a third treatise to critical bipartisan acclaim.

"Ten weeks on the *Times'* bestseller list and still selling," he crowed to his inner circle. "My ticket back," is what he often said to Carl Goldman privately.

Television talk show appearances with his photogenic wife, radio interviews and crowds at book signings were good signs. A recent televised debate in which he intellectually dismembered a Muslim spokesman in prime time had sent his public stock soaring, and his privately commissioned polls were showing solid gold again.

In London for book promotions and business contacts, Johnson's secondary goal was to add Samuel Cohen to his orbit in exchange for strings the former senator had pulled for the lawyer. Another piece in the politician's Byzantine scheming to regain his standing in public life was falling into place.

"My God, Carl," the former senator had beamed back in Chicago, "it doesn't get any better than this. The man's a Jew, a millionaire, a war veteran seeking justice and we're going to see that he gets it."

Goldman remembered the jubilant crowing. "He'll owe us, Carl. There's no downside!"

# CHAPTER THIRTY-THREE

A black London cab pulled to the curb on a narrow, tree-shaded street. The avenue was crowded with ostentatious apartment buildings rising above the city's foliage. Samuel Cohen and William Noble stepped onto the sidewalk.

The lawyer paid the cabby and dismissed him. Cohen checked the address Goldman had given him and nodded across the street at the three-story Regency-style terrace commanding an entire block. The stately building's row of private entries was set behind a facade of six smooth stuccoed arches, each flanked by a pair of slender, fluted columns.

They waited for a florist's delivery lorry to pass as Cohen studied the imposing building. "I expected something like this," he said to Noble.

"Pretty palatial, Sam." Noble gazed up at the decorative cornices and iron balconies. "Proctor Johnson must cultivate some pretty well-heeled acquaintances."

Cohen snorted. "That sums up his career. I don't think the man ever befriended anyone who wasn't wealthy. You don't get to be a U.S. senator by mingling with the unwashed."

He sighed, resigned to the pending meeting. "You ready for this?"

Noble shrugged. "Sure, I'm game to hear what they have to say."

"Be careful, Bill, the Senator will probably blow a lot of smoke up your ass."

Noble laughed as they crossed the street.

The two men passed under an arch at the building's southeast corner and approached a black lacquered door hung with a large brass knocker. Heavy gold and silk brocade curtains were drawn across every window on the flat's ground floor. Cohen poked twice at the ornate buzzer as the pair waited on the narrow marble stoop.

The shiny black door opened and an unsmiling Sikh in a gray, collarless jacket and baggy tan pants filled the doorway.

"Please come in, gentlemen," welcomed the man in a clipped, sing-song accent. "Senator Johnson and Mr. Goldman are expecting you."

Cohen and Noble stepped onto the entry's shiny parquet floor and waited for their bearded, turbaned greeter to lead the way. The Sikh gestured to a small lift at the end of the hallway.

"This way, please."

He installed the two men in the elevator and indicated the button for level three. He bowed slightly and closed the etched glass door. Noble grinned at Cohen, then shrugged and tapped the button as instructed. The lift rose slowly to the flat's top floor and when it came to a gentle stop, the doors opened and the aged Sikh reappeared. He stepped aside and held out an arm to usher them across the marble floor of an anteroom with a high domed ceiling and gold chandelier.

"They're here, boss," said Goldman.

Proctor Johnson tugged at his pale blue silk tie and glanced at himself in the mirror over the fireplace as he toyed with his solid gold cufflinks. He then walked to a long sofa where he placed two signed copies of his new book on a gilded coffee table and waited for his guests.

Carl Goldman, wearing an expensive dark blue suit, came through a tall arched doorway to the left of the foyer. "Samuel, good to see you." He grasped the lawyer's hand and then switched his grip to Noble. "You must be William Noble. I'm Carl Goldman."

He led them into the large living room where Proctor Johnson rose to greet them. The Sikh followed the three at a discreet distance, hands held politely in front of him, awaiting instructions.

"Ah, at last we meet," boomed the senator as he crossed the thick Persian rug to meet his guests. "The Lord's avenging angels."

If Cohen was offended at the characterization Johnson had assigned them, he gave no sign as the man descended on them. Cohen shook the tall man's hand and then introduced him to his companion.

"Senator, this is William Noble."

The man pumped Noble's hand vigorously, clasping his elbow while looking directly into his eyes.

"Bill's an old friend from the war," added Cohen.

"Yes, so Carl told me." Johnson's voice dropped an octave, oozing sincerity. "Thank you both for your service to our nation in one of its darkest hours."

Noble blushed, disarmed at the politician's patriotic sentiment.

Their host waved at the elegant sofa and instructed his visitors to sit. He pulled up an antique armchair opposite them and Goldman sat on its twin at the end of the sofa nearest Noble.

Goldman turned to the attentive Indian. "Ranjit Singh, you may bring us coffee and tea now, please."

The Sikh bowed and turned on his heel for a small butler's pantry off a large formal dining room across the marbled hall. The former senator engaged his guests, chatting about summer weather, their flight to England and London traffic while waiting for their server to reappear. Within minutes, the taciturn Sikh was back with a large silver tray with cups and saucers and pots of steaming coffee and tea.

"That will be all, Ranjit, thank you," said Goldman.

The Indian withdrew as the senator's aide poured coffee for Cohen and Noble, tea for the senator and himself.

"I'm normally a coffee man but when in Rome . . . or London." The politician chuckled as he stirred several teaspoons of sugar into his tea. When the men had been served, Johnson sipped as he eyed Cohen thoughtfully over the brim of his cup.

"So, Carl says your party is down to four, is that right?"

Cohen set down his porcelain cup and leaned against the sofa.

"Yes, it seems that way. I had hoped for several others but . . ."

The senator interrupted. "Yes, damn shame about that. You've put yourself at a disadvantage, Sam. But you and Bill here are apparently determined to follow through with this."

Cohen paused. "Yes. But let me say that we're grateful for your help, Senator."

Johnson smiled indulgently, waving off the compliment. "My privilege . . . and my duty."

Cohen began reciting the story of his receipt of the Von Wurtz intelligence and its value in relation to the success of their mission.

"Whoa, whoa," the politician laughed nervously. "Sam, hold on now. Don't give me too much information for my own good, if you know what I mean."

"I understand, Senator. But without that information we wouldn't be here. So, we're indebted to you for putting us on the right trail after all these years."

"I'd like to add my appreciation as well," interjected Noble. "Even though I'm not a constituent like Sam, I can still add my thanks to his."

The senator seemed genuinely pleased at their words of gratitude.

The Sikh appeared at the edge of the carpet and cleared his throat. The senator sighed as he looked at his watch. "Ah, yes. Thank you for the reminder, Ranjit Singh. Duty calls, gentlemen. There is other business that needs my attention. No rest for the weary, eh?"

He set down his cup and pointed at the books on the coffee table. "I took the liberty of inscribing a copy of my latest work for each of you." He leaned over the narrow table and pushed the copies toward his guests. "A little light reading for your return flight."

"Thank you, Senator," said Cohen. "It should be an interesting read."

"My pleasure, Sam."

Everyone rose. The senator thrust out his hand.

"I hope you're able to conclude this, ah . . . endeavor of yours, Sam. May God watch over you and give you firmness in your hour of need. And if there's anything else I can do for you and your band of brothers, let Carl know and we'll see it done." He shook their hands.

"Excuse me for a moment, Sam," said Goldman. "I'll just see the senator to the door." Johnson and his aide followed the Sikh from the room.

Noble got up and wandered to a wall covered with framed pictures, while Cohen began leafing through his copy of the senator's new book.

"Hey, Sam, look at this." Noble studied a photograph of ermine-covered people with dour faces. A short unhappy-looking woman in the center had caught his eye. Cohen came up beside Noble. "That's the queen, isn't it?"

The lawyer peered closely at the formal group portrait. "That's her. A face only a mother could love."

They both laughed. The same tall, austere man in stiff evening wear was in each of the pictures on the wall. Noble scanned the collection. "Must be our invisible host, the flat's owner."

"Correct, Mr. Noble." Goldman had returned.

Cohen stared at the photo with the queen. "Who's the gentleman, Carl?"

"Sir Hugh Symthson, House of Lords, former chancellor of the Exchequer."

"Ah, the Brits," said Noble, "they do love their titles, don't they?"

"Centuries of peerage to rely on," replied the aide. "Shall we?" he prompted, pointing toward a pair of oak doors.

He ushered the visitors into the flat's library, a book-lined chamber with a spreading crystal chandelier that dominated the room. Four large, red leather armchairs were arranged around a square oak table with a single manila envelope in the middle. A man in a rumpled tan linen suit, open-necked white shirt and black loafers stood at the room's single window, studying the building across the street.

# CHAPTER THIRTY-FOUR

The stranger waved without looking at them to acknowledge their entrance.

Goldman defused the man's apparent rudeness with an attempt at humor. "What are you looking for, terrorists or bill collectors?"

"Neither," said the man in a flat voice. "I am watching a very beautiful, and very naked, woman doing impossible yoga in the second-level flat across the street."

The senator's aide stepped quickly to the window and looked past the man. "Where?" he demanded.

"She's gone," shrugged the man. "You probably frightened her, Carl."

Cohen glanced at Noble, unsure if the stranger was being truthful.

Goldman realized he had been the object of a joke and reddened. "Very funny," he huffed, moving away from the window.

The man grinned as he left the window and walked to the table.

"Back to business," said Goldman. "Ari, meet Samuel Cohen and William Noble."

They shook hands. The stranger had a powerful grip.

"Ari's a useful person to know," said Goldman, "and a wicked practical joker."

The man laughed at Goldman's discomfort, revealing flawless white teeth and flashing black eyes under thick eyebrows. Just under six feet tall with a lithe, athletic build, Cohen guessed he was in his late thirties, likely Middle-eastern or North African. He was clean-shaven with dark skin, a prominent chiseled nose and full lips above a narrow jaw. The man wore his black hair cut close to the skull and carried himself with grace.

He immediately took charge of the meeting and commanded the men to join him at the table. Without wasting time he spilled the contents of the manila envelope on the surface and spread the papers before him.

Lacing his hands together, he stared at Samuel Cohen. "Carl says you might need my help."

"We appreciate you taking the time to talk with us," Cohen replied.

"Not a problem," said the man. "However, I need to know if you are sincere." He waited for the words to sink in.

"Maybe our sincerity depends on how much you know about our reason for being here," parried Cohen.

"Yes, fair enough," said Ari. "I have been briefed by Carl about . . . your Project."

Noble leaned forward. "What exactly were you told?"

The man picked up a glossy photograph from the table and studied it.

"I know that this man is the one you seek. I know he was SS and that he was responsible for murdering your friends during the winter offensive in December of 1944, what you Americans call the Battle of the Bulge."

He slapped the photo down on the table and sifted the papers to find a picture of the man they knew as Kurt Weismann. "Now he lives as this man, correct?"

"One and the same," said Cohen glaring at the picture.

"And you want him eliminated to pay for crimes inflicted upon you and others during the war, yes?" Ari sat back studying their reaction.

"My friends and I are interested in seeing justice done," volunteered Noble.

"And in this case," said the dark man, "justice means he must die, correct?"

Cohen nodded. His silence was immediately challenged.

"I need to hear you say it. Is this man to be killed?"

"Yes." Cohen frowned. "But we are not asking you to do this for us."

The man named Ari relaxed and smiled. "Very good. That is what I needed to hear from you. Now it is possible."

He looked at Goldman. "Before, I was not sure that what you told me was true, Carl, but now that I have heard him confirm it with his own words, I am convinced."

He tapped his chest. "You have it here, Samuel Cohen. I'm confident you will have the ambition, the nerve, to carry out this . . . Project."

"Does that mean you will aid us?" asked Noble.

"It is possible, yes. I might help you. But there are certain things . . . assurances I must have to become involved." He sat back and waved a finger at them in warning. "To complete such a task as you ask is not impossible, but without guarantees I am not your man."

"What exactly do you need?"

"First, realize you contemplate a capital crime in a foreign country and you are asking me to assist you in this. There can be no half-measures. The national police in France are excellent and I assure you they have a very long reach. Secondly, if I feel that your mission has been compromised in any way, I will abandon the task immediately. Lastly, if you wish me to ensure your success, you must do exactly as I say during our entire time together or I walk away."

Thrilled, Cohen raised an eyebrow at Noble, who nodded, without hesitation. They agreed to everything.

"Then let us begin."

Ari stood up and pulled a map from the pile. He unfolded it and turned it toward his audience. He poked a finger at the continent. "Very well. Tell me your exact plans. What are you thinking?"

Cohen put his elbows on the table and traced a route from England to the French coast.

"We plan to go to Normandy and visit the beaches for two days, then on to Paris for several days before we train to Brussels." His thin fingers fluttered across the map to Belgium.

"From there we meet a battlefield guide and see Bastogne and other sites."

He looked up but Ari urged him to continue. Cohen kept talking, his finger marking a line down along the German border to Thionville in France.

"We know that Von Wurtz, Weismann, lives east of this city, near the border in the village of Bois-les-Bains. Once we're there and confirm his identity, we'll strike."

"And just how do you plan to carry out this strike?" quizzed his listener.

Cohen looked at Carl Goldman but the American avoided his eyes, his gaze remaining focused on the map. Ari leaned over the table, waiting.

Noble spoke up. "We have no firm plans but we were told that we might expect your help. We understand that you have some expertise in these things."

The man's eyes bored into Noble. "I might be of some service, yes."

Ari cradled his chin in one hand and silently drew an index finger over the routes Cohen had sketched across France and Belgium. Goldman attempted to say something but Ari waved him into silence and continued studying the chart.

"In a few days you will leave London and go to France and visit Normandy. Many Americans will still be there. That is very clever of you. And probably more Americans at Bastogne of course, also very clever. The difficult part will be here."

His finger landed on Thionville and the space to the east where the German border was outlined. "Here is the hard part," he pointed at the chart.

He sat down and crossed his arms over his chest. "Carl, I would like some bottled water, if you would, please."

Goldman jumped to his feet and asked the others if they wanted the same. They declined and the aide went out to the flat's kitchen.

Ari frowned at the map spread before him. "This will take much more discretion in such a rural setting. You see, a city, with its streets and alleys would be no problem, but this . . . this will be very touchy."

He rubbed his hands together as though divining a solution to the problem.

"We must meet in Paris to work out this part of the plan." Cohen and Noble looked at each other and then at the man opposite them.

"Why Paris?" asked the lawyer. "Why not Normandy? We'll already be there."

Ari eyes bored into Cohen's. "We must meet in Paris. There is a man there, someone I have known a long time. A person suited to this business." Ari's expression was set. "We cannot accomplish this without him."

Cohen was intrigued but his partner was wary.

"Do we really need to bring in another person at this hour?" asked Noble.

Ari looked at the American as though he had asked a stupid question. "Am I not correct to assume that once you eliminate your enemy you want to return home without incident?"

"Well, yes," answered Noble, "that was always part of our plan."

The dark featured man waved his hand at them, dismissing the earlier question. "Then we must go to Paris. We need the help of this individual. You will see. He is indispensable."

"Who is he? What's his part in this?" asked Cohen.

Ari picked up the glossy photo of the German walking in a manor garden and a half-dozen pictures of him enjoying wine in the courtyard of a small café. He thrust the pictures in front of the two Americans.

"The man we need is the one who took these photos," he snapped. "He got that close to your enemy in order to provide this evidence. I know him well and I trust him."

Ari pointed at one of the pictures. "Believe me when I say that this photographer can do more than just shoot pictures of old men sharing beers. He also has many of the tools you will need."

Cohen studied the photos, copies of those he had shared with the Fortunate Orphans back in Chicago, three months ago. "You've known about this since last fall?"

Goldman returned to the room with the water and set the bottle on the table. Ari twisted the cap free, gulping the liquid as the senator's aide spoke.

"I couldn't help overhearing your question, Sam. We asked for Ari's help in this matter. The senator wanted to make sure the intelligence given you was accurate. We didn't want to pass on information unless it was corroborated by someone who had actually seen Von Wurtz."

Cohen tried to read Ari's reaction but the man's face betrayed nothing. "You really went to some lengths, Carl."

"The stakes are much too high for Proctor Johnson . . . and for you. I'm sure you can appreciate the reasons for that degree of caution, Sam."

Cohen glanced at the surveillance photos and then at Ari. "Saying you had people who might help was an understatement."

"The senator had to be absolutely sure, Sam."

The issue was settled for Cohen but he looked to Noble for confirmation.

"Works for me."

"Done then," said Cohen softly. "Bring your man on board."

Ari seemed to come to life. "In Paris, we will meet and decide how to realize your justice." He pulled a card from his wallet and handed it to Cohen. "This is a hotel where you will stay. Carl encouraged me to make the arrangements. I know it. You will find it quiet, discreet and luxurious. Once you arrive in Paris, I will contact you."

Cohen was wary, but impressed. "Seems you've thought of everything, Carl. Including your selection of our hotel."

Goldman explained the decision with a wave of his hand. "We took a chance, Sam. Reserving hotel rooms was a gamble but I think you'll agree it makes things easier."

Ari fished in his pocket and produced a tiny cell phone which he handed to Cohen. "When you reach Paris, turn on this phone and wait for my call."

Ari began stuffing photos and documents back into the manila envelope. "About expenses."

"Carl said nothing about expenses," said Cohen.

An awkward silence passed. Then Ari laughed, his black eyes flashing.

"Let us be realistic, Mr. Cohen. There are going to be certain costs associated with this mission. It is very simple. I am not a rich man but you are."

"I suppose you have a figure in mind?"

Taking a thin white packet from his jacket's breast pocket, Ari slid the sealed envelope to Cohen who pocketed it.

"There is a list inside," Ari said. "Wire the money to that account by tomorrow afternoon and I can begin my preparations immediately."

"You must have been confident that we'd agree to all this," said Cohen.

"I was prepared, yes. But one can never be certain things will go as planned."

"Is there to be an additional fee for your involvement as well?"

Ari shrugged. "Ah, Mr. Cohen, do not think I am offended you consider me a mercenary. It was an honest mistake on your part. However, Carl assures me that you are an honorable man. So let us say that if you are satisfied with my help, you alone will determine my fee and I will accept any amount you think fair. Agreed?"

Cohen nodded.

"So then, you see, we each have an investment in your safe return. True?"

The tension dissolved and the lawyer relaxed, felt his apprehension dissolve.

Ari stood and offered his hand to the two men. "We will meet in Paris."

They went into the flat's drawing room where Cohen and Noble thanked Goldman for his help and picked up their inscribed copies of Proctor Johnson's book.

On cue, Ranjit Singh appeared and guided them to the apartment's private lift. The Sikh pushed a button, closed the glass outer door and the elevator silently descended.

On the ride down neither man spoke, and at ground level they opened the gilded doors to find the Indian once again waiting for them. He led them to the front door and bowed as they went down the steps to a car, summoned by Ranjit Singh for their return to the hotel.

# CHAPTER THIRTY-FIVE

## LONDON, MAY 29

At five o'clock, on the morning of the third day, Cohen and the others were awakened by the front desk as requested.

They left their luggage in charge of the hotel's concierge, pending their return, and carried only small shoulder bags stuffed with toiletries and two changes of clothes. Cohen had arranged their check-out the night before and now the quartet moved sleepily through the lobby to the front entrance where an idling van and driver waited for them in the dark. When their bags were stacked in the rear, the men each claimed a seat and nodded off one by one as the vehicle wound its way through southwest London, heading to Portsmouth.

Their driver raced the clock south to deliver them dockside, where a fast ferry was loading for the morning run to France. They made the trip with a twenty-minute cushion of time, and Cohen added a generous bonus to the fare. Peter Noble hustled the luggage aboard the vessel and claimed four of the ship's airline-like chairs as instructed. With room for 850 passengers and two-hundred-plus cars, the younger Noble had no trouble finding four seats together on the ferry's starboard side.

He stowed their bags and the men sank into the chairs.

Soleski and William Noble promptly fell asleep. Cohen nodded at his dozing companions. "That happens when you reach our age, Peter."

Glancing at his watch, he apologized. "Sorry we had to leave London at such an ungodly hour, but this ferry will get us to Cherbourg in three hours, one hour faster than a regular ferry."

They looked out tinted windows as the big ship eased from the pier. Beyond moored Royal Navy corvettes, the restored masts and rigging of Nelson's dry docked wooden flagship, HMS *Victory*, poked above Portsmouth's roof line. Other trains filled with tourists and commuters were arriving at the terminal as the sun rose, turning the harbor into rippled copper in morning's light. Flocks of squawking seagulls circled in the boat's wake as the modified catamaran hull passed the port's landmark Spinnaker Tower towering five hundred feet above the harbor. The ferry maneuvered through the crowded anchorage, announcing its right of way with a series of deep-throated whistle blasts. It picked up speed near the harbor mouth. Soon the vessel was slicing through the Channel, its powerful engines pounding out forty knots toward the hazy outline of the French coast.

When Soleski and Noble awoke, they joined Cohen and Peter in a long queue at the self-service café. After a breakfast of rolls, fruit and coffee, they returned to their seats and Peter wandered off to play video games in the boat's arcade. Cohen read while Noble dozed beside him. When Soleski grew bored he went above to an open deck to watch their passage across the channel. After three hours of steady cruising across a choppy sea, the ferry dropped its speed as it approached the northern tip of the Cotentin Peninsula, site of the 1864 Civil War death duel between the Union warship *Kearsarge* and the Confederate raider *Alabama*. More passengers joined Myron Soleski topside to watch the ship maneuver past the mole and enter Cherbourg-Octeville harbor.

At the base of imposing bluffs this bustling seaport was two worlds. One world was a sheltered anchorage with a forest of masts belonging to hundreds of small sailboats, yachts and fishing trawlers huddling in nearby marinas. The other half of the busy port's traffic was commercial freighters of varying size. Opposite a pair of moored French warships, huge blue cranes loomed over piers, unloading shipping containers from dockside vessels. Once past the breakwater and into the inner harbor, the ferry attracted circling seagulls hoping for handouts from the newest arrivals.

To Peter, impatient to set foot in France, the vessel seemed to take forever to unload and when they finally got ashore and worked their way through the line for non-European Union citizens, he and the others mingled with a crowd outside the ferry terminal. They stood aside as streams of travelers passed them on the quay.

A stocky individual headed their way, waving a ragged piece of cardboard.

Noble pointed. "Looks like he's expecting you, Sam."

The man stopped and lowered a placard scribbled with Cohen's name. "And you would be Monsieur Cohen." It was not a question.

He offered his hand and Samuel Cohen gripped it. He had arranged for a van and driver several months before at Carl Goldman's urging, and now their chauffeur introduced himself. "I am Georges Cabot, at your service."

Reeking of cigarettes and pomade, the man smiled, revealing tobacco-stained teeth underneath an unruly walrus mustache, a broad scarred nose and sleepy eyes. His dark curly hair was clipped short, accentuating a thick neck and knobby ears that gave him the look of a wrestler who had only recently given up the ring. Cabot wore a striped, open-collared shirt and a pair of baggy corduroy trousers. The man spoke passable English and boasted that he knew the Normandy coast well.

As Cabot began loading his white Peugeot van with their luggage, Cohen told the others that, despite his appearance, the chauffeur had come highly recommended. The Frenchman offered to take them wherever they wanted to go in the next seventy-two hours for a basic fee plus fuel costs.

Cohen reminded him of their prior contract and a short, awkward silence followed. The two stepped away to bargain over finer points of their pact until a compromise was reached, allowing them to leave the port city and head southeast toward the landing beaches.

# CHAPTER THIRTY-SIX

Cabot left Cherbourg behind and drove at a furious pace down the main road, N-13, slowing only when he reached the outskirts of Ste.-Mère-Eglise, their first scheduled stop. The van weaved toward the center of the city and parked near the town square next to a dark blue Mercedes with dark windows.

His charges emerged from the van. Soleski spotted a dummy parachutist dangling from the town's church tower in the middle of town.

"I know this story," he said. "The guy was Private John Steele of the Eighty-Second Airborne. Got shot in the foot and played dead after his chute caught on the bell tower. Germans pulled him in."

Noble studied the church tower. "Red Buttons played the guy in the movie, right?" "Yeah, that's him," Soleski answered, still craning his neck at the mannequin. After obligatory pictures with Peter's digital camera, the men left their guide behind and strolled across the square to tour the Airborne Troops Museum. They spent more than an hour inside marveling at exhibits of uniforms, weapons, a restored C-47 and a Waco glider. Emerging into sunshine and a crowd of tourists, the group circled the squat muscular body of a Sherman tank and posed for pictures with artillery pieces. Peter spotted their guide talking to the driver of the Mercedes.

Georges abruptly ended his conversation with the man behind the wheel and approached his clients. He began pointing out various plaques on nearby trees and walls dedicated to paratroopers who did not survive the predawn assault on the town.

"I will take you now to Carentan, yes?"

They obediently filed into the van and resumed their journey on the peninsula. Cohen spoke for the group when Georges asked if they wished to stop at the closest of the five German cemeteries in Normandy.

"Not worth our time," Cohen said curtly.

They spent less time at Carentan than Peter wanted but he was able to point out several landmarks in the town, and provided his companions with a well-read description of the 101st Airborne's battle. "This area was one of the invasion's keys," he lectured. "Paratroopers had to seize the exits from the beaches and capture lock gates and bridges. The Germans counter-attacked numerous times and Carentan didn't fall until June 12." Noble smiled proudly at his grandson's recitation of the fight. Even Georges Cabot seemed impressed with the younger Noble's narrative and let him do most of the talking as they drove around the city.

They stopped for a quick lunch at a small café where the owner fawned over the veterans and Peter practiced his French to Cabot's amusement. "I compliment you, monsieur. Not only do you know your history, but you speak an acceptable version of the mother tongue."

After their meal, Cabot drove to Les Forges and turned east along D70 to the sea. They stopped briefly at Pouppeville to visit the spot where probing airborne troops first made contact with forward elements of the Fourth Division which had fought its way inland after landing. Peter took a dozen pictures. Cabot turned the van north on route D241 and passed two lumbering tour buses jammed with elderly couples who were being lectured by on-board guides.

Shore and horizon were now on Peter's right. All along the beach he saw small groups of people strolling across the sand and small children wading at the water's edge. Considering the real estate's history, the image struck him as surreal. At La Madeleine, Cabot slowed and pulled to the side of the road, engine idling, allowing the tour buses to pass their vehicle.

He turned, gesturing dramatically at the ocean. "Perhaps you wish to start here with Utah Beach, yes?"

Peter focused on the choppy slate-colored sea. Like the others, he fell silent.

Their chauffeur had evidently seen this reaction before and did not expect an immediate answer to his question. He drove the van forward and found a parking spot not far from a massive series of cement bastions known as Strongpoint W5. Peter and the men exited the vehicle in awe of the blockhouse. It was now, explained the driver, a memorial crypt. There was a prominent pylon, a marker to the First U.S. Engineers, and another nearby monument, an upright granite slab etched with a dedication to the 90th Division. Outside a small museum the men gathered around various Allied craft, one an LCVP Higgins Boat with lowered ramp. Peter excused himself and wandered away to snap pictures of rusting "porcupine" beach obstacles scattered like monstrous jacks across fenced-off sections of grass and sand.

"I will wait here," said the driver, slightly bowing as he shook a cigarette from a pack and lighted it. He had followed this routine many times and would tarry patiently while his passengers tried to absorb what they were seeing and feeling. The men moved off. Across the parking lot, Peter used his camera's zoom lens to follow Cabot as the driver finished his cigarette and strolled toward a dark blue Mercedes.

# CHAPTER THIRTY-SEVEN

## UTAH BEACH

"My God, we're on hallowed ground, Bill," whispered Samuel Cohen.

The four men walked toward the beach.

Soleski and the younger Noble followed slowly, passing a crude concrete obelisk emblazoned with a torch and a domed top wreathed in stars. It was painted with letters that read "Kilomètre 00 Voie de la Liberté."

Peter Noble paused by the marker. "It means Road of Liberty," he announced. "Like the marker we saw in front of the town hall back in Ste.-Mère-Eglise."

Peter kept pace with Soleski, the two of them following his grandfather and Cohen down a pathway in the grassy dunes where the sand was held back by heavy timbers. Emerging onto a stretch of shore, Peter and Soleski stood there, speechless. To Peter's left, surrounded by a dozen old men in caps covered with Army patches, a battlefield guide was using a laminated diagram to paint pictures of the June 6 landing for his ancient audience. Peter and Soleski traded knowing looks with each other, smiling as they passed the veterans. Peter, mesmerized by the history of the sand beneath his feet, stopped to take pictures of the shore. He trotted after Soleski and caught up with him.

Cohen and Noble watched them go.

"How you holding up, Bill?" asked Cohen.

"So far, so good. If I pace myself, I'm okay," replied Noble. "I'll let you know if I get out of sorts. Good enough?"

Cohen nodded and the two moved off in the wake of the nearby veterans, close enough to hear the guide's presentation about the role of Utah Beach. When they reached a fragment of concrete wall, Cohen and Noble sat down to watch the parade of visitors. As far as they could see the shore was dotted with locals or clusters of veterans and spouses, the former GIs easily recognizable in their embroidered jackets and hats. Some walked with difficulty across the sand and stones, canes poking at the beach, arms linked with sturdier comrades.

Noble sighed, resting his weakened heart, and spoke without looking at Cohen.

"You still disappointed more of the guys didn't come, Sam?"

Cohen gazed at the horizon several minutes before answering. "Of course. I know they had the right to walk away," sighed Cohen, "but for some reason I thought . . . the idea of finally settling accounts with Von Wurtz would appeal to them." He looked down. " I was wrong."

Noble looked up as a trio of American veterans shuffled by in the sand. Their eyes met and one of the trio snapped a salute with a crippled hand. Noble grinned and returned the greeting.

"Maybe it's for the best, Sam." He shifted his weight on the cement. "Clearly, Dawson would have been a loose cannon, unpredictable. We used to be so close. It's really sad, but he's turned into a drunk, Sam." Cohen didn't reply, just nodded at the truth of Noble's comment. "And Ole . . . well, I thought he'd come for sure after Sollie said yes.

"So there's Dawson, Ole and Ken Wolf. Actually, I understand Ken's reasons better than anyone's. He's high profile at home and he'd be risking a lot, with all those grandchildren."

"You think they'd risk more than us?" said Cohen. "What about your health?"

"Well, yeah, but you're risking the most, Sam."

"Not so, Bill." He nodded up the beach where Peter was talking with Soleski. He pointed at the young man. "His is the biggest gamble of all."

"You're right. But Peter's going into this with his eyes open." Noble nodded at his grandson. "Have you watched his reactions since we got here? The closer we got to Normandy the more intense he became. When we made our first stop, back at St.-Mère-Eglise, he seemed like a different person." Noble smiled. "Reminds me of us when we first came over."

Soleski and Peter spotted Cohen and Noble and headed their way, passing a menacing-looking gun emplacement, its long barrel still pointed out to sea.

"Yeah, you're right, Bill," said Cohen grinning as he watched the pair approach. "I know the expression. I saw it on your face when you started picking off the Germans that morning."

Soleski planted his feet in the sand in front of them, looking around him. "If I didn't know better, I'd say we were on Long Island, Sam."

"It does have a similar look," said Noble, "the grass, the sand, the water."

"Except for the ghosts," said Soleski softly as he sat beside Cohen.

Behind them, Cabot approached slowly, respectfully.

"What's next?" asked Noble spotting him.

The Frenchman made a chopping motion with his right hand, east along the beach. "Of course you must see Pont du Hoc, gentlemen."

The men rose to their feet and followed their driver to the parking lot.

Cabot drove along the coast to the chiseled cliffs of Pont du Hoc, where they parked and walked silently toward the battle site. Left much as it was after the assault, the knife-edged point had a grim, sepulchral appearance. Below them the sea smashed against the thin strip of rocky beach where the Second Rangers had begun their heroic climb.

Vegetation covered the headland like a threadbare quilt thrown over bones and the land was crisscrossed with footpaths, white scars on green. Everywhere were bomb craters and shell holes softened by decades of rain and wind. Pont du Hoc was honeycombed with ugly bunkers pocked with holes from naval shell fire and machine gun bullets. Barbed wire fencing kept visitors from the sheer precipice, while in other spots it marked paths or twisted back on itself, tangled in vegetation.

Great concrete remnants were upended at odd angles as though a malevolent child had scattered his blocks across a narrow triangle of emerald carpet. At the tip of the point, on the roof of an observation bunker, stood a concrete dagger memorial to U.S. Rangers who had stormed ashore one hundred feet below. In the crypt beneath the monument, a list of fallen Rangers was being read by visitors who reached reverently to touch the names.

Peter Noble moved among the bunkers snapping pictures of scarred ruins.

A gust of wind swept the lonely high ground, rippling through vegetation, shaking the barbed wire, snapping at summer jackets worn by tearful old soldiers. At the parking lot, more veterans arrived, elderly men tentatively picking their way across the cliff top toward the Ranger memorial. Here and there small knots of these graying warriors exchanged stories, talking with bony hands, correcting each other's version of events.

The group worked their way back toward Cabot, who took one last drag on his cigarette then crushed it underfoot. He went to the driver's side of the van and climbed in behind the wheel.

The men, sobered by the cliff top tableau they had just visited, were quiet as they filled the van.

Cabot started the engine and turned to Cohen who was studying his watch. "Omaha Beach?" he asked.

"Tomorrow," answered Cohen. "Take us to our hotel, please."

The driver shrugged and turned south, away from the shore, toward Bayeux.

# CHAPTER THIRTY-EIGHT

## NORTH OF BAYEUX, FRANCE

Once again Samuel Cohen had outdone himself with the accommodations.

The eighteenth-century château was situated in the middle of its own park. Each room's veranda opened on an immaculate lawn and flowering garden. Swan pairs glided across a picturesque pond and the grounds were lined with stately trees shading the huge mansion. Their driver deposited them with a promise to return in the morning for the final leg of their Normandy visit.

After the group had been shown to their rooms, Cohen convened the group in the château's lounge where they shared two bottles of wine before dinner. William Noble was showing the wear of travel and even irrepressible Myron Soleski was beginning to tire. They traded impressions of their day on the beaches and Cohen went over the next day's agenda.

"After breakfast, Georges will take us to Arromanches for a look at what's left of the Mulberry Harbor." The lawyer was referring to the giant concrete caissons that had been towed from England and sunk offshore to create an artificial harbor for the allied forces.

"That should please you, Peter," smiled Cohen. "Plus, it makes us less chauvinistic if we acknowledge British efforts as well."

"To the Brits," proposed William Noble, as he lifted his wine.

The quartet raised their goblets.

"I assume we'll stop at Omaha Beach, Sam," said Soleski.

"Wouldn't miss it, Sollie. It's our next-to-last stop. We'll go from there to the American cemetery overlooking Omaha Beach."

Cohen took a long sip of his wine, then squinted at his Palm Pilot. "We'll leave the cemetery at fifteen-thirty hours and come back to Bayeux. We have a sixteen-forty train to catch for Caen and one transfer to Paris." He looked up, searching for comments.

"What time do we get into Paris, Sam?" asked Peter.

"About nineteen hundred hours."

Soleski eyed the younger man. "That's seven o'clock for you civilians."

The group laughed.

Cohen put away his Palm Pilot and finished his wine.

"Shall we dine, gentlemen?" he asked.

They rose to their feet and adjourned to the restaurant for dinner.

After the meal, while the others lingered in the château's dining room, Cohen returned to his suite to call home. He asked his wife's sister to put the receiver up to his wife's ear so he could speak to her. When his sister-in-law came back on the line he sketched out travel plans for the following day, then said goodbye.

That night, a Channel storm moved onshore, lashing the landing beaches and drenching the countryside. Cohen heard only the initial drumming of rain on the terrace.

The constant walking across the landing sites had exhausted him and he slept without waking.

# CHAPTER THIRTY-NINE

### NORMANDY, MAY 30

In the morning they ate a leisurely breakfast while waiting for their driver. When Cabot showed, they checked out of the château and traveled freshly washed roads to the coast where they paid their respects at the Canadian and British invasion sites of Gold and Juno Beaches. Cabot parked the van at Arromanches, where they marveled at the remains of the Mulberry Harbors offshore.

The others elected to wait in the van as Peter made several forays among ruined German defenses. For nearly an hour Noble shadowed his grandson from the vehicle as he walked the shore, filling his camera. When Peter finally returned to the van, they drove west to Omaha Beach and everyone dismounted to join the ranks of visitors who seemed to be everywhere.

A stiff onshore breeze combed sea grass on the dunes behind Omaha Beach, where a massive concrete bunker squatted on a hillside. One cement wall sloped off to the right, drawing attention to a dark, gaping orifice where a large coastal gun had been sited. Naval gunfire had eaten away large chunks of concrete at the mouth and roof of the gun position.

A large bronze plaque commemorating the landing was fixed over the horizontal opening.

Peter Noble stepped reverently across the concrete apron and peered inside the cavernous opening, his voice echoing from the walls and ceiling. "This gun probably did some serious damage during the landing."

Myron Soleski approached the old bunker cautiously, as if he expected German troops to burst from its darkened interior. "Damn, those guys had balls to face this," he said softly.

"Couldn't have been much fun for the Krauts either," said William Noble, shuffling up beside the smaller man, and pointing at the punishment from shelling.

Samuel Cohen studied the fortification and turned, his gaze sweeping Dog Green Beach behind them.

The tide was out, leaving isolated pools behind. In the distance, remains of another Mulberry Harbor tilted like a marooned concrete barge, a casualty of the storm of June 19th, 1944. Small knots of visitors, mostly American, judging from their dress, wandered over the sands, probing hillocks and their ugly bunkers or stood around ever-present guides who recited details of the Battle of Normandy.

Several picnicking families had set up wicker baskets at the base of a long cement seawall and were sharing treats. Small children played tag or splashed in tidal puddles.

The sight irritated Myron Soleski. "Look at them. Don't they know this is sacred soil?"

Cohen placed a hand on the man's shoulder. "Don't be so hard on them, Sollie. They've reclaimed the beach and made it peaceful again."

"Don't seem right, that's all," huffed the little man.

He went down a flight of steps in the seawall to the beach, giving the picnickers wide berth. Peter Noble stayed with his grandfather and snapped several shots of the German bunker before trailing after Soleski.

Cohen and Noble leaned against the seawall, gazing at the ocean.

"Still want to go ahead with the Project, Sam?"

He nodded. "I've been struggling over whether or not I've done the right thing in bringing you over here in pursuit of what might be my own need for retribution. I've tried to brush away my own doubts about what we're planning to do, Bill."

"Have you decided what you want to do?"

Cohen's jaw tightened in flinty concentration. "My conclusion is that this is no time for second thoughts. Something tells me that with Ari's expertise we should be okay."

Ten minutes of silence grew into twenty. Cohen tugged at Noble's sleeve. "If you're up to it, Bill, let's walk to the water. Where our boys came ashore."

The two friends hobbled off across the stones toward a wide margin of wet sand still glistening in the mid-morning light. When the beach ended and the water began, they turned their backs to the sea and gazed past the seawall and dunes to the tree-lined bluff where the American cemetery was located.

Noble tried to imagine the June landings on this stretch of sand where they stood. He fought back tears as he thought of this same shore carpeted with dead and wounded, burning landing craft and discarded equipment. He dared not look at Samuel Cohen, afraid his emotions would betray him to the lawyer.

Noble knew Cohen was struggling, but he had no idea what demons his friend might be wrestling with as they stood on the shore. He left Cohen alone and moved slowly back up the beach incline, retracing his steps, pretending to study distant fortifications scattered among the dunes. He went back to the seawall, the effort taxing his heart. When he reached the cement barrier he sat on the steps to catch his breath, hoping Cohen would not notice that his weakened heart had betrayed him again.

He sat for an hour as his companions took their own tours of sacred ground. William Noble spent his time imagining that distant June morning of 1944.

# CHAPTER FORTY

### OMAHA BEACH, AMERICAN MILITARY CEMETERY

Their last stop in their Normandy itinerary was going to be the hardest one.

Samuel Cohen was counting on just that effect. He wanted to harden the group's collective conscience for what they were going to do.

After leaving the shoreline the white van wound its way along the beach road and joined a line of cars and tour buses heading to the American cemetery perched high atop the bluff overlooking Omaha Beach.

In the parking lot Cabot turned off the engine and his passengers eased slowly, almost reluctantly, from the van and walked past the visitor's center on the tree-lined path. Their driver stayed behind in the parking lot. Cohen guessed that he'd made the trip hundreds of times and had seen enough of the place to last him a lifetime. Besides, he probably wanted another cigarette.

Without speaking, the quartet moved down the shaded walkway which formed a margin alongside thousands of perfectly aligned grave markers of white Italian marble. At the middle of the cemetery they passed tours clustered around a small chapel set in the manicured lawn. William Noble led the way to the eastern end of the cemetery where twin pavilions joined by a curving portico were reflected in a still rectangular pool set in a flawless emerald lawn.

In the middle of the memorial, a large bronze sculpture of a stylized male nude, the *Spirit of American Youth*, rose from a base of metal waves. Behind the columns, down a short flight of steps, sat a well-tended garden and a low wall with the names of those dead whose bodies were never found. On the crowded terrace between the pavilions the men mingled for a few minutes with people of all ages, everyone moving in reverent silence with only clicking camera shutters or muted voices. There was no crying child or laughter to break the stillness..

The impact overwhelmed Cohen, and he knew it was affecting his friends.

The price paid on the beaches below suddenly hits all visitors, even those without husbands, fathers or grandfathers interred there.

In the midst of these orderly rows of more than ninety-three hundred markers, Samuel Cohen and the others were struck by the enormity of D-Day's cost. The enormous sacrifice weighed on him, weighed on them all. They grappled with it, each man trying to come to terms with it in his own way.

William Noble moved off by himself, unashamed of his sudden tears.

"Thank God . . . for these men," whispered Soleski, roving among the crosses.

"It's so peaceful . . . but so lonely in a way," murmured Samuel Cohen softly.

Peter reached down and gently touched one of the three hundred seven markers with "Unknown" carved in the marble. He moved slowly through the lines of stone crosses, passing the occasional Star of David, reading names and ranks of men buried beneath the tended lawn.

All around them now a steady stream of visitors shuffled along the path to the vast graveyard. Every so often a wheelchair, pushed by an aged spouse or adult child, stopped along the edge of the shaded path, its frail occupant offering a quiet salute.

"So many heroes in one place," wept Noble, sweeping his arm across the graves as his grandson joined him. He wanted to say something profound but failed. "Oh, God, kiddo," sobbed Noble, "I'm such a mess."

All the younger man could do was to reach out and put an arm around his grandfather as the old man wept. American volunteers, helping visitors search for particular graves, passed respectfully past the Nobles.

In the distance, among the long straight rows, Myron Soleski reached out to caress a cross and began crying like a lost child, rubbing his eyes with his sleeve, vainly trying to stop his tears. By now the sun was directly overhead and the men were exhausted emotionally. The men slowly drifted together without being called, gathering in the shaded corridor of trees along the cemetery's path. They paused briefly to take in the serenity of the view of Omaha Beach's Easy Red sector below.

# CHAPTER FORTY-ONE
WEISMANN ESTATE, ALSACE-LORRAINE, FRANCE, MAY 30

The elderly bespectacled German sat in a high-backed leather chair, making precise notes in a small black leather notebook, his pale blue eyes darting from a wide flat screen to the lined pages filled with tidy script.

Kurt Weismann made a final entry, then closed the little book. He put away his gold pen, shut down his computer and leaned back, glancing at the doorway.

A small bird-like woman with a pale, expressionless face, gray hair tied back in a bun, tiptoed to the edge of the study. A tall, dark-haired, coarse-looking man with long, ape-like arms stood behind her in the doorway, towering over the tiny woman. A thin white scar ran from his right temple through the corner of his thick lips and terminated in a hollow spot near the jaw-bone. Clearly a tough man even without the scars to prove it.

"Shall Karl bring the car around, Monsieur Weismann?"

Weismann slipped the notebook into the inside pocket of his tan linen jacket and nodded.

The hulking man immediately vanished from the doorway and the German heard him go out the side door. The house-keeper crept into the room and quietly removed a cup and saucer from the desk, bowing as she retreated. In the large book-lined office an ornate clock struck the half hour. Out of habit Weismann looked at his wristwatch to verify the time.

Rising, he pushed back from the huge antique oak secretary that served him as a working space. He straightened a stack of folders with a steel ruler and arranged three pens in perfect alignment to the left of the files. Pushing in his chair, he centered it precisely against the desk. He paused by a gilded, full-length mirror and ran his hand through thinning white hair, framing a lined, handsome face. Weismann was a diminutive man but lifts in his hand-made Italian shoes were not his only concession to vanity.

To forestall his dread of aging he had had his sagging neck and eyes done by one of Italy's best plastic surgeons three years prior. He had dabbled in Europe's flesh pots in his younger years, but had given up women ten years ago to avoid the risks that members of the opposite sex represented to men with his kind of wealth.

Now, women of any age bored him and his iron will conquered whatever lust remained, channeling his passion into making money instead. Money was power to Weismann and his energy went into adding to his millions.

The German checked the knot in his pale blue silk tie, smoothed his coat's lapels, then toyed with his gold cufflinks. He heard the car come up from the carriage house and walked to the covered side entrance.

A polished black Mercedes sedan pulled under the overhang and stopped on the shaded driveway. The driver came around the other side and opened the rear passenger door open for his employer.

"Thank you, Karl," said the older man as he settled into the soft leather.

The big car pulled away from the house and sped down the drive.

Two large Dobermans suddenly bolted from a stand of trees and sprinted alongside the vehicle, barking loudly. The driver punched the car's horn twice and the canines obediently ended their pursuit. As the sedan approached a wrought iron gate set in a high stone wall, the chauffeur reached up and tapped a button on the sun visor. The metal barricade opened rapidly and the car shot through.

Immediately the gate reversed its motion and began to close under a cyclops camera eye atop the gate. The lens housing rotated in a steady sweeping motion, feeding black and white images of his vehicle to one of the château's six security monitors in Weismann's private office. The guard dogs stood at the edge of the driveway and then loped back across the estate's wide manicured lawn to resume their vigil from the shade.

# CHAPTER FORTY-TWO

## BOIS-LES-BAINS, FRANCE

At Bois-les-Bains' only café, a bartender wiped down a small round metal table in the corner of an L-shaped terrace. A low stone wall, bearded with thick ivy, enclosed the flagstone veranda, providing privacy of sorts for the dozen small tables. The café sat at the far end of the village on a paved road that ran almost straight east to the German border barely five kilometers distant.

Bois-les-Bains and its single tavern, along with other towns of Alsace-Lorraine, had survived forty-three years under the German fist after the Franco-Prussian War, a quarter century of freedom, then five years of Nazi control before rejoining France at the end of the war. Nestled in a gentle forested valley on the south bank of the Moselle River, the village was home to residents who valued their independence and privacy.

A recent invasion by adventuresome tourists who discovered the area's provincial charm because of traveler's blogs was a welcomed impact on local pockets. Steady streams of bicyclists still flooded village streets and the surrounding countryside before and after the Tour de France's July madness. To the west was Thionville, with its tourism, industry, growing population and strangling highways. To the east was Germany's Saar valley.

Bois-les-Bains' main avenue ran past the village café's front door, just beyond a margin of struggling grass. On the cabaret's east side was a small rectangular gravel lot for cars, on the other end, a legal office and apartments in a two-level nineteenth-century building rebuilt no less than six times in the last century. Across the street sat a string of small shops, a busy bakery, a fruit stand and a popular bookstore, all on the ground floor, with housing above.

The bartender stood in the shade of the archway and checked on his patrons. Two of the tables were filled with customers.

At one table three out-of-work local tradesmen sat complaining about price supports; at the other, a quartet of young, backpacking Italian girls flirted with two male companions. For such a bucolic village it was not usual to have this many people to fuss over at this time of day. The proprietor was pleased.

His guests seemed content to chat over several bottles of wine and were satisfied with an occasional resupply of bread. The bar's carved antique clock just inside the café's entry showed five minutes to four.

As expected, an old German named Felix appeared at the café's small iron gate.

A short man with a scowling, weathered face, he was dressed in his usual well-worn black suit, white shirt, no tie and tweed cap. He shuffled with a slight limp, depending on a wooden cane to steady himself.

The octogenarian entered, waved a gnarled hand at the bartender and headed to the familiar table prepared for him in the corner of the courtyard.

The bartender poured two Heinekens and went out to the corner table, setting down the glasses.

"Good afternoon, Monsieur Ullrich."

"Good afternoon, Maurice," replied the old soldier. He sipped from the glass of beer and smiled, nodded. "Perfect," he said.

Two of the Italians beckoned to the tavern keeper.

"Excuse me, Monsieur Ullrich."

The old man waved him away. "Yes, yes, see to your guests."

Former SS Sergeant Major Felix Ullrich sipped his beer and eyed his fellow patrons. The French trio was engaged in the usual war of words, always something negative about the European Union and price supports. He looked past the men to the table with the Italians. The girls were delicious, long-legged, tanned treats wearing shorts with trendy sunglasses perched in their stylish sun-bleached hair. Two handsome male companions, both muscular youths, wore serious striped cycling jerseys plastered with brand names. Judging from the accumulated bottles crowding their table, the Italians were enjoying their wine.

The old Nazi looked at his watch and as he did so, a long black, polished car eased to a stop outside the café gate. The driver hurried to the Mercedes's rear door and opened it. Kurt Weismann got out and walked briskly through the low iron gate and crossed the flagstones to Ullrich's table.

It was precisely four o'clock.

Punctuality was a virtue in Weismann's world.

The old soldier watched his comrade's arrival and he raised his glass in salute.

"I see you've started without me," grumped Weismann good naturedly.

"I was hoping that maybe today would finally be the day when I would catch you being late, Hauptmann Weismann. But I am to be disappointed once again."

"Even an Englishman could set his watch by me, Felix. It is my curse."

"Or could it perhaps be that you are early?"

The familiar banter continued as Ullrich sipped his beer. They toasted dead comrades, the Fatherland and each other in turn. Weismann glanced around at the other guests.

Past the ivy covered wall, Weismann watched the big Mercedes make a U-turn and pull into the gravel lot. His chauffeur got out and walked to the terrace where he took up vigil at a small table in the opposite corner of the enclosure. The proprietor came over to him with a glass of beer and a newspaper.

The large man, Karl, was a toughened sixty-year old Corsican whose build belied his age. He was a former Foreign Legionnaire now doubling as driver and security guard for Weismann. For the last fifteen years he had been well paid to make sure his employer did not have to worry about prying eyes or potential kidnappers looking for vulnerable marks.

When Weismann traveled for business, so did his driver.

Eight years ago, in one of Moscow's finer hotels to meet with potential Russian partners in a joint venture, Karl had thwarted a slipshod robbery attempt by a inept gangster. Misjudging the elderly German and his escort for two Western businessmen promising a quick source of easy cash, the mobster's poorly planned ambush in a hallway went awry. The Russian was either dim-witted or incompetent, perhaps both. When the gangster cornered the pair by flashing a pistol, the Corsican feigned fear and fumbled a thick roll of bills onto the carpet, distracting the Russian.

When the thug reached for the cash, Karl delivered a savage kick to the man's testicles and seized the pistol. With the mobster momentarily disabled, the bodyguard produced a knife in his right hand and drove the blade upward into the man's throat and jaw. Eight inches of steel rammed deep into the man's skull, killing him instantly. Karl grasped the man's suit collar and used the knife's hilt to muscle the mugger's body into the maid's closet, where he propped the man into a sitting position among the mops. He pushed back the gangster's head and pulled the knife from under the jaw, then wiped the blade on the dead man's shirt. The big man cleaned his hands at the janitor's sink and put away his knife. Karl's conclusion was that a hotel maid had marked them for her bumbling underworld lover.

He and Weismann took a taxi to their hotel as though nothing had happened. The idea of the woman finding the carnage in her linen closet the next morning had amused Weismann to no end.

With such a man nearby Weismann could relax with an old comrade.

"I suppose some day we should make arrangements to close the terrace to everyone but ourselves at our usual hour, Felix." He sipped his Heineken and smiled at his table mate.

"And you would be one who could certainly afford to do that, Hauptmann." Ullrich needled his friend further. "Perhaps you should purchase this establishment so we can meet without sharing such a pleasant setting with just anyone who comes by."

"Ah, as usual, you exaggerate my resources, my friend," retorted Weismann.

"Speaking of resources, Hauptmann, how goes your latest project?"

Weismann grinned conspiratorially. "Felix, believe me when I say I am finally on the verge of assembling what may prove to be my last business deal. Within three months, if all falls into place as I think it will, I shall have no worlds left to conquer."

"That big, eh?"

Weismann stretched his arms apart. "Nothing I've ever done compares to this. You will read about it soon enough."

"Shall we toast your accomplishment, Hauptmann?"

"Ah, not quite yet," smiled Weismann. "Might be bad luck to do that, Felix. But soon I hope we will toast my success."

They laughed together and talked guardedly of old times, old soldiers, the war. The Frenchmen ignored the Germans at the nearby table and eventually left, still bickering. Then the Italians departed, walking their bikes and newfound female friends toward the center of town. The German pair watched them go.

They talked for another hour and at six o'clock, Kurt Weismann read his watch, drained the last of his beer and rose from the table.

His friend grinned and shook his head from side to side.

Weismann ignored the expected ribbing.

Across the veranda, Karl pinned several Euros under his empty beer glass and watched his employer head for the café's toilet. He nodded to Felix Ullrich and strolled out the gate to the parked Mercedes. He gave his boss exactly ten minutes and then started the engine. He set the sedan's A/C at the required sixty-five degrees and pulled slowly out of the lot to the café's gate where the car idled.

The dashboard clock read six-fifteen.

Kurt Weismann emerged from the café's arched doorway, waved farewell to Ullrich and strolled to the car. The big man opened the door for Weismann and glanced around out of habit. He shut the door, got behind the wheel and pulled away from the curb, doubling back through town by a side street, another precaution.

In the rear view mirror he saw Weismann sink back in the leather seat, humming a martial air to himself.

Though he dared not reveal his thoughts, the Corsican was always mystified, amused really, that his employer ran like some fine Swiss watch.

In summer his boss met Felix Ullrich every weekday at the same time, four o'clock. They sat at the same table, in this same café, and drank two glasses of beer. Precisely at six o'clock, the businessman would consume what remained in his glass and go directly to the café's water closet. He would emerge fifteen minutes later.

No sooner, no later. Always fifteen minutes.

The thought of this immensely wealthy man relieving himself to the very second in some established ritual was a wonder to the former Legionnaire.

In the winter, the setting changed to either the German's villa on the Italian Riviera or Weismann's home in Aruba, but the man's body clock was so tied to his bladder that the rite was faithfully followed regardless of the setting.

*When I need to piss*, smiled the Corsican, *I just piss*. The whole thing amused him to no end but since the German had amassed such immense wealth, the former soldier always wondered if there might be wisdom in bending one's life to a clock.

The Mercedes turned off the main road and wound its way through the tunnel of trees lining the gravel approach to Weismann's chateau. The car slowed slightly to allow the iron gates to yawn wide. Again the Dobermans arrived to provide noisy escort as the big sedan curved along the drive that once served elegant carriages.

The automobile stopped under the canopy at the side entrance and Karl leaped from the car to open Weismann's door.

The German went up the steps where his housekeeper waited, holding open a leaded glass door.

"Good evening, Monsieur Weismann."

"Good evening, Madame Cheroux."

Weismann went directly to his study and powered up the computers, simultaneously picking up a TV remote and calling up a financial news cable station. Leaning back in his leather recliner, he watched the top stories as European stock quotes crawled across the bottom of the screen. He tapped a button, splitting the screen so he could read what the American market was doing. He split the screen yet again to study Asian business news and then got up to go behind the large desk to review files on his computer.

He scanned his emails, replying to some and dumping others. He wrote coded notes to his fund managers in Geneva, New York and Tokyo and when he was done, his housekeeper appeared and announced dinner. He shut down his electronics.

In the large dark-paneled dining room, a single setting was placed at the end of an antique, twenty-foot oak table. Three candles had been set near his plate and as he ate, he read two French papers and a German finance magazine. He ate quickly, and in silence, and then declined dessert, opting instead for a brandy in the library, where, despite the warm night, his housekeeper had laid a small wood fire. He put on a set of classical music CDs and stared at the flames for two hours until they died. Weismann shut off the music, armed the château's security system and went upstairs.

From his room he saw the Corsican across the courtyard, silhouetted in his carriage house apartment's door as he played with the prancing Dobermans. His bodyguard had just finished his nightly walk about the grounds and was now showering affection on the canine sentinels.

Weismann turned off his lights and slipped into bed.

A small security monitor mounted high on the opposite wall cycled through different images from remote cameras around the property. Weismann aimed a remote control at the screen and killed the pictures.

## CHAPTER FORTY-THREE

### PARIS, HÔTEL DU CHARDIN, MAY 30

The taxi's meter read fifteen euros and Peter Noble considered the cost minimal considering their safe delivery from the St.-Lazare train station. He thrust a crisp twenty Euro bill at the man and thanked him in French. The driver acknowledged the payment with a huff and flashed his cab's light back to yellow. When the old men unfolded themselves from the back seat the Peugeot taxi pulled away from the sidewalk, leaving his four riders joking about their harrowing introduction to Paris traffic. They shouldered their bags and entered the Hôtel du Chardin's ornate, carved doorway.

Despite its ten-foot high decorative plaster ceiling, the hotel's lobby was intimate. Walls, covered with a pale floral fabric, were lighted by bronze wall sconces and a single crystal chandelier. On the left, a small kiosk stuffed with well-thumbed tour pamphlets shared a corner with a tall, parched palm. To the right, a small room, set off by two marbled columns, was crowded with plush red sofas and three pairs of armchairs. Gilded mirrors flanked a classical bust of Voltaire set in a shallow niche and two ceiling fans turned slowly, stirring the air. A couple talked quietly on one sofa, opposite a slouching man whose face was buried in the *International Herald Tribune*. Just beyond this lounge, a larger modernized space was jammed with a dozen tiny tables and chairs and serving counter for the hotel's breakfast service. A wide marble staircase with decorative iron railings rose to the upper floors in a series of sensuous curves. A small desk, piled with paperwork, was shoe-horned into the space under the stairs.

A slight, effeminate male with dark, oiled hair sat talking on a phone next to a flat blank computer monitor. Beyond the desk and its chattering receptionist, a narrow hallway lined with leaded glass doors led to a courtyard terrace.

Cohen approached the clerk who reluctantly ended his phone call.

"Bonsoir, Monsieur," offered Cohen. "Parlez-vous anglais?"

The youth smiled. "But of course. How may I be of service?" he cooed.

Samuel gestured to the men lined up behind him. "I believe you have rooms reserved for Cohen and party."

The pale little man swiveled the monitor and the screen came to life. He busied himself at a keyboard. In minutes he signed in the quartet and handed out room keys. "One of your group arrived yesterday, Monsieur."

"Excuse me," puzzled Cohen. "Did you say one of my party has arrived?"

The man behind the counter nodded toward the front room. "Yes, he is there in our lobby."

Cohen and the others turned to look at the occupants of the sitting room.

As if cued, the couple rose from the plush sofa and brushed past the men on their way out the door. Noble walked into the small sitting room, and stood in front of the wall of newspaper. He cleared his throat.

The newspaper dropped away revealing a grinning Burt Swanson. "Doctor Noble, I presume?"

The little lobby erupted in astonished roars as the men crowded around Swanson, pumping his hand and slapping his back.

Cohen was speechless.

"How in the world did you . . ." began Noble.

The Arkansan held up his hand. "I'll tell you all about it but first let's get you fellas settled. Then we'll grab dinner at this great little sidewalk café I found at the end of the block."

He continued grinning, pleased at the surprise his appearance had caused.

Swanson saluted the young desk clerk who shyly waved back. "I told Jean-Louis there to give me the high sign when you guys showed up."

"They put us all on the second floor, Sam. You'll have the suite of course and Sollie . . ." he turned to the little man from Michigan, "you're bunking with me." He clamped a big hand on the smaller Soleski. "And you'd better not snore."

Noble and Cohen rode the balky lift to the second floor while the others climbed the curving marble staircase. After a quick inspection of their respective rooms the new arrivals stowed their luggage. Samuel Cohen excused himself, saying he would be down shortly.

Upstairs, Samuel Cohen fished in his bag for the tiny cell phone Ari had given him in London. He opened a pair of tall windows and stepped out onto his suite's narrow balcony, then turned on the phone. He pulled a card from his wallet and tapped in the scribbled numbers. After six rings a voice on the other end answered and Samuel Cohen spoke a single prearranged sentence of just nine words.

"We have arrived and have checked into our hotel."

"Good," replied the voice. "Listen carefully. On Monday, you will be picked up in front of your hotel at five o'clock."

"How will we know you?" asked Cohen.

"Don't worry about that," assured the male voice. "Just have everyone there."

"There's been a change," volunteered Cohen.

"A change in plans?"

Cohen looked the stream of cars passing below. "Not exactly."

"What then?"

"Another member of our team has arrived."

There was a pause on the other end. "Does this complicate things for you?" asked the voice.

"Not at all. I believe this will actually help."

"Very well. Five o'clock, Monday. Don't call again. Goodbye."

Cohen switched off the phone and pocketed it.

He stepped from the balcony and shut the tall windows to help the room's feeble air conditioner. He set the dial to cool his suite and locked his door before joining the others. On the way down, he passed two male guests struggling up the marble stairs with bulging suitcases. The women who owned the luggage were slowly ascending to the fourth floor in the ancient lift, passing their sweating husbands who were laboring to keep up. Samuel Cohen smiled, feeling smug about insisting that his team travel light.

Outside, on the sultry street, Burt Swanson was the center of attention as the five strolled to the end of the block where Café Maréchal Ney occupied the entire corner. The owners had staked out a claim to the pavement with boxed hedges, and the

Americans sat at a table away from other patrons. Burt Swanson took charge. He waved over a reluctant waiter and ordered the café's signature scallops appetizer, followed by a halibut entree. The server suffered Swanson's French, then disappeared inside.

"I'm impressed, Burt, your language skill is pretty good," complimented Noble.

"It's a bit different but I picked it up from working the river in Louisiana, Bill."

Cohen propped bony elbows on the table and peered at the sergeant. "You're the last person I expected to find in Paris. Tell us, how in the hell did you end up here?"

Swanson looked apologetic. "Well, to be honest Sam, in Chicago I told you I wasn't planning on coming. But a couple of months went by and then I kept thinking about what you and the guys had decided to do. It just kinda ate at me."

He paused and leaned back. "So, first I called Ken Wolf and talked to him about it. Wanted to find out what he was thinking. You know . . . if he was having second thoughts like me."

"Was he?" asked Noble.

"Hell, yes." Swanson lowered his voice. "He said he and Ole Johnson had been in touch and both of 'em were wrestling with the whole thing."

"What about O'Reilly?" Noble asked.

Swanson snorted in derision at the cop's name. "He's worthless, Bill. We tried to talk to him but his mind was made up. At least when he was sober and talked to Ken Wolf about it."

Swanson chuckled and continued. "Turns out Ken called him a couple more times to make sure he hadn't changed his mind and both times he was so shit-faced he couldn't talk straight." He held up his hands in resignation and sighed. "He wanted no part of it so Ken and Ole gave up on him."

Swanson turned serious. "He would have been a liability if he had come along."

The waiter finally arrived with their wine and silverware. Cohen began pouring wine into the glasses. "Go on, Burt," urged Cohen.

"Well, the three of us came up with this idea to run our own little lottery. You know, sorta draw straws to decide who was going to come over and represent us. We pooled our money for one airline ticket and hotel room and I won."

"Or maybe you got the short straw," laughed Soleski.

"Yeah, there is that," smiled Swanson.

"How'd you find us?" asked Cohen.

Their old sergeant raised an eyebrow. "Boy, you didn't make it easy, Sam. Your She-Dog-From-Hell gatekeeper at the law firm wouldn't tell me a goddamn thing."

Cohen smiled at the idea of Swanson's tortured entreaties to his notoriously tight-lipped secretary.

"Finally she agreed to at least call your sister-in-law and tell her what I wanted."

"She eventually called me back. Once she told me where you might be, I had to scramble to get over here and sweet talk Jean-Louis into giving me one of your rooms. I think he kinda likes me." Swanson glanced around the café's crowded tables and the flow of evening foot traffic passing the corner bistro. He looked back at Cohen.

"Wasn't easy, Sam. Paris is hot and lousy with tourists this time of year."

Cohen raised his glass and toasted the new addition to the team.

"The important thing is that you're here. To Sergeant Burt Swanson."

Everyone thrust their wine glasses toward the center of their small circle.

Noble took a quick swallow then raised his goblet. "And here's to Ken and Ole. For sending us reinforcements . . . even if they couldn't come themselves."

The five gently tapped each other's glasses again.

Soleski stood up and leaned over at Swanson with one more salute.

"To the new guy!" The men around the table laughed and drank again. They set their glasses down as their server arrived, his arms balanced with plates of food.

They began to eat. Between mouthfuls Swanson nodded at Cohen. "Okay, Sam, bring me up to speed on what we're going to do next."

Cohen dropped his voice. "We're to meet with some people Monday and talk over some of the details for The Project. They've offered to help us."

"So, tomorrow is open for sightseeing. The next two days after that are free until five o'clock each evening. That's when we have our planning sessions for The Project."

"Sorry, Peter, looks like no night life for you," laughed Soleski.

"You've got tomorrow off," countered Cohen. "Stay out if you want, Peter."

"Yeah," said Swanson, "you can take Sollie to the Crazy Horse."

The younger Noble raised his glass. "As long as I get a chance to see the city during the day, I'm a happy camper."

Soleski put an arm around the young man. "Maybe I'll tag along and troll for some of them mademoiselles."

"You're in the wrong city if you're looking to find some dumpling who's three-foot six and two hundred pounds, Sollie," drawled Swanson.

As their dishes were being cleared, Cohen insisted on ordering chocolate truffles for dessert. He wouldn't take no for an answer. "We can't pass it up. Remember, we're in Paris!"

Peter held up a city map. "If you guys want to see the Eiffel Tower, the Arc de Triomphe and the Champs Elysées, meet me downstairs for breakfast by eight."

"Geez, I'm glad you brought him, Bill," kidded Swanson. "It's good to have someone so sophisticated along on this trip."

"Eight o'clock," reminded Peter.

# CHAPTER FORTY-FOUR

## LE BOURGET, JUNE 1

Northeast of Paris, a Renault van turned off the Rue Verdun onto Rue Marcel Bourgogne and dropped its speed. The van's driver glanced in the rear-view mirror to make sure the second car, a dark blue Mercedes, had made the turn. The two vehicles took the next right, paralleling a high, chain-link security fence. A hundred meters more and the Renault van pulled into a driveway, flashing its headlights as the car approached the picket shack. At the signal, the guard stepped out of the hut and swung open the gate. The driver lowered his window to wave at the sentinel, then headed for a three-story warehouse on the far side of a weed-choked asphalt lot.

The building's tall doors were rolled back as instructed. Once inside, the van pulled to one side and parked. The Mercedes came to a stop next to it.

Ari got out of the van and walked to the doors resting on rollers set in a channel in the concrete floor. A large, muscular man in short-sleeved gray coveralls jumped from the Mercedes and jogged to the other side.

Cohen and the others sat in the van, watching the two men push the huge doors shut. Near the doors, Ari punched a button in a row of switches.

At the far end of the building, large overhead lights crackled into life and the space was suddenly bathed in fluorescent light. The warehouse, two hundred meters long and thirty meters wide, rose twenty meters to a cap of broken skylights.

Ari and his companion got back in their vehicles and drove to the lighted end of the building. They parked next to a small office with broken windows. Cohen, followed by Noble and the others, left the van and found themselves in front of a wide wooden frame covered with cardboard. Empty cartons had been stacked to replicate a wall, and a row of smaller boxes were lined up in an L-shape to mimic a terrace. A dozen card tables, each with four chairs, sat in the open. A crude arch had been cut from flattened, corrugated cartons to replicate an entryway. Lines of tape had been laid down, simulating a flagstone walk. A second-hand bicycle leaned against one wall.

The cardboard facade was instantly familiar to Noble. "You know what this is, don't you, Sam?" he whispered.

Cohen smiled, impressed by the work put into creating the setup.

Peter gestured to the make-believe architecture. "It's the café," he explained to Soleski and Swanson who crowded around.

Just past the cardboard set, a large bulletin board sat next to a white, erasable board. Ari, ignoring the men, began pinning surveillance photos to the display board. A half-dozen chairs, obviously scavenged from the deserted warehouse office, were arranged in a semicircle in front of the board. The large, silent man in gray coveralls unloaded a large thermos, water bottles and sandwiches at a card table.

Ari finished with his photos. "Please take a seat, gentlemen. We must begin."

Noble and Samuel Cohen took two seats near the board and studied the pictures. Soleski and Swanson pulled up broken swivel-chairs and sat down. Peter straddled a wooden packing crate.

"We have the use of this space for the next two days, but only for four hours at the end of each day." He pointed to Cohen and smiled as he paced in front of the seated men. "You can see that this is where some of your money has gone."

"You should've insisted on better seating, Sam," chuckled Soleski as he twisted on his rusted chair. The men laughed, their voices echoing in the cavernous space.

"We won't be here that long," said Ari, unsmiling. "I promise you that." He waved at the large man. "Gentlemen, this is my associate, Ehud." The big man nodded impassively.

"He completes our team. Without his help we cannot accomplish what you want to do."

Ari continued. "We have a limited amount of time to perfect our plan, so let us begin. Pay very close attention, gentlemen. Because of the schedule you have set, these two days will be your only chance to rehearse The Project." He waved at the pinned photos. "These are recent pictures of Weismann, both at his château and at the café in Bois-les-Bains. They were taken by Ehud five days ago. The target's routine has not varied." He gave a brief summary of each photo, then moved to the white board.

Fishing a black marker from his pocket, Ari drew a large precise overhead layout of the village café with quick strokes. He sketched the surrounding roads and buildings and labeled them. When he was done he tapped the board several times for emphasis. "Every day Weismann shares two glasses of beer with an old SS comrade and then always visits the café's water closet at exactly the same time, six o'clock."

There were low chuckles from the attentive group.

"It is not glamorous I grant you, but during those ten minutes he is vulnerable. That is exactly when you must make your move."

He nodded to Ehud, and the big man rolled away the boards, revealing the cardboard setup behind him. Ari stepped over to the mock-up. "You can see, Mr. Cohen, once again we have spared no expense in materials to create an exact duplicate of the village café."

The men chuckled.

Ari turned to his audience. "We are going to rehearse this operation until I am satisfied each of you knows exactly what he is supposed to do. Each man must become familiar with his role—where he is supposed to be, how he is supposed to move and when he is supposed to move. You must also know what the others are to do. You must memorize their roles as well."

He glanced at his watch. "I will now explain this operation on the board several times and then we will rehearse your actions on our little movie set. Agreed?"

The men nodded.

Ari stepped in front of Samuel Cohen. "I assume that you are to be the shooter."

Cohen's expression revealed his dislike of the label. "That is correct."

"You all consent to this?"

The others nodded.

"Any questions before we start?

"Why the bicycle?" Peter asked.

"I was told you are an experienced rider, no?"

"Well, yes, I do bike a lot, but not competitively."

"Very good, Peter. You will see what your role is during our rehearsals."

There were no other questions from the group.

Ari rubbed his hands together. "Very well, we begin."

On the left of the drawing he wrote a time line listing, in turn, Felix Ullrich's arrival, Weismann's appearance and the habits of Karl, the bodyguard, pinpointing where the Corsican parked and where he sat. For the next sixty minutes, Ari drilled them using only the board's diagram.

At the end of the hour, the plan was set, and Ari ordered the men to take a break to eat before they rehearsed on the cardboard set. Ehud moved the easels and parked the van and the sedan on one side of the mock café. He chalked exact dimensions of the parking area to add more realism. As the men drank coffee and devoured sandwiches, they studied the boards. Ehud and Ari backed the cars to the far end of the warehouse in order to rehearse the mission from the beginning. Peter played his role with the second-hand bike as his prop.

With Ari as choreographer, they began rehearsing.

# CHAPTER FORTY-FIVE

At the end of the third hour, the men took another break among the tables of the mock café. Ehud went to the Mercedes and lifted a small metal suitcase from the trunk and placed it in front of Ari. The big man next went to the Renault van and began carrying filled sandbags to a corner of the warehouse where a sturdy wooden table sat against one wall. Ehud packed the sandbags into a pyramid until he was satisfied with his handiwork. Next, he went into the abandoned office and emerged with a dress dummy and a bulging plastic sack. He carried both to the wooden bench.

As Ehud worked, Ari beckoned from his table. "Mr. Cohen, if you would."

Cohen drained the last of his coffee and sat next to the seated man. The swarthy man pulled a pair of thin white gloves from his pocket and slipped them on. He tossed two white lab gloves to Cohen. "Put these on," he ordered. Ari released two clasps on the small metal suitcase and opened the lid.

Noble, Swanson and the others drifted toward the seated pair. Ari lifted a sleek, dark handgun from a cavity in the black foam cushion. He held the pistol for Samuel's inspection. "This is a Ruger MkII, do you know it?"

"No," Cohen answered, as he tugged on the gloves.

Ari handed him the weapon.

He talked as Cohen turned the pistol in his hand. "It is a semi-automatic with a nine-round magazine and is more accurate than most handguns." He smiled paternally at the large man standing behind the curious Americans. "It is one of Ehud's favorite tools." The hulking man barely smiled in acknowledgement.

"You will be using these," said Ari, plucking a single cartridge from a wooden block in the case. He held a tiny .22 round between thumb and forefinger. The small lead slug had a concave tip. "Do not underestimate the Ruger's ability to do the job. You will be firing hollow-point ammunition from perhaps three meters or less."

As Cohen studied the weapon in his hand, Ari pushed the tiny cartridge back into the wood block, then removed a dark, six-inch cylinder from the black foam. He held out his gloved hand for the Ruger and Cohen surrendered it. With several quick twists, Ari screwed the long black silencer onto the pistol's barrel, doubling its size. He handed the weapon to Cohen, then plucked an empty magazine from the foam pillow and began loading cartridges into the slender bar of black metal. When he finished, he put the loaded magazine into his pocket and took the pistol from Cohen.

The group's attention now shifted to Ehud's primitive shooting gallery. The big man waved them over to the bench stacked with sandbags. He balanced a melon on the dummy's shoulders and stepped behind Cohen as Ari slapped the loaded magazine into the Ruger.

He held the pistol in his left hand and stepped in front of the American. "You will be working in a confined space and have only one chance to hit your target." He held up two fingers and looked into Cohen's eyes. "You must take two shots without hesitation. You understand? Twice."

The taller American nodded solemnly.

Ari handed him the Ruger, pointing at the primitive target. "Walk to within three meters of the target and take two shots, then lower the weapon to your side and do not move, understand?"

"Yes," whispered Cohen.

His friends stood completely still, watching him hold the silenced pistol.

"Now," commanded Ari.

Cohen took three steps to close with the target, raised the gun in a slow arc and fired two quick, muffled shots. The weapon kicked slightly in his hand as the bullets created small holes in the lower portion of the melon. He lowered the gun as instructed. "Try again," commanded Ari. This time, Cohen took a more deliberate aim and placed two rounds higher in the melon. He lowered the gun.

Ari took the Ruger, flipped the safety on and inspected the hits. "Wiesmann is not dead. He falls to the floor, shrieking in extreme pain at the wounds in his throat."

Cohen shook his head, disappointed with his shooting.

Ari lectured the fascinated onlookers. "By now the German's companion, Felix Ullrich, alerts the bodyguard who rushes to his employer's aid." He bent down, plucked empty casings from the concrete and pocketed the brass. "Samuel will now confront an armed man who is considerably younger, faster and stronger."

The Americans shifted uncomfortably as Ari continued his scenario, pacing in front of Cohen. "The Corsican is trained for such a situation. He will corner you in the water closet or in the narrow corridor which leads to the bar and the small dining room. You will have nowhere to go, Samuel."

Ari stopped in front of the tall lawyer and placed the weapon in Cohen's hand. He reached up and tapped the American's high, domed forehead twice. "Two quick, aimed shots here and he will go down quietly. Try again."

Cohen fired twice. Both holes were higher, but not quite centered in the melon. They repeated the procedure with similar results. Cohen cursed his effort.

Ehud walked past the lawyer and whispered to Ari who nodded. "My learned friend suggests you steady the pistol like this." Ari took the handgun and released the Ruger's safety.

He gripped the weapon in both hands and fired a single, hushed shot. The .22 hollow-point bullet made a tiny hole in the center of the melon and disappeared in the pyramid of sandbags.

Ehud applauded his friend's shot. Then the big man set another melon on the dummy as Ari loaded the pistol with another eight-round magazine and handed Cohen the Ruger.

"Go!" barked his instructor.

Cohen stepped quickly toward the target and raised the weapon, steadying it with both gloved hands. He fired twice. The rounds drilled the melon in a perfect, tight pattern. Cohen stepped back, lowered the handgun and allowed himself a smile. Ari and Ehud clapped and the line of Americans joined in.

"Again!" ordered Ari. Two shots pierced the melon's top center near the previous hits. Cohen grinned and repeated the exercise twice.

"Very good," commented his instructor. "Enough for now."

Ehud took the Ruger in gloved hands and released the magazine. He unscrewed the suppressor and placed the handgun and cylinder in the metal suitcase. He closed and locked the case, then carried it to the Mercedes. Ari collected the pinned photos and stuffed the pictures into a briefcase. He wiped the board clean of his scrawled notes.

Noble patted Cohen on the back. Swanson and Soleski shook the lawyer's hand as Peter beamed at the old man's prowess with the pistol.

Ari ended the session by warning about conversations in public and then ordered them into the Renault for the return to Paris.

# CHAPTER FORTY-SIX
### PARIS, HÔTEL DU CHARDIN, JUNE 2

"I think our two guys are Israelis." Peter sat back and watched his grandfather's face.

The old man paled, and set down a full cup of morning coffee. He looked around the hotel's serving room. Only two other guests were busy loading their breakfast plates at the counter. Noble squinted at his grandson, lowered his voice. "What makes you say that, kiddo?"

"Their names, for one thing," said Peter. The younger man recited softly, "Ari, Ehud. Ari looks Mideastern doesn't he?"

The old man allowed the comment to stand.

"And Ehud," said Peter. "The left-handed man, Gramps."

Noble was genuinely puzzled. "I didn't notice," he replied.

"From the Bible. The Old Testament."

Noble's face was a blank.

"He was one of the judges in early Israel. An assassin. Killed one of the Chosen People's enemies with a sword. Ironic, huh?"

"And you're making the leap that these guys are Israelis?"

Peter leaned across the table as the two guests finished piling their plates with food and took seats across the room. "They're probably former Mossad or Shin Bet."

"You're talking to the wrong guy, kiddo."

"Those are Israeli security organizations, Gramps," explained Peter. "Bad dudes. They do a lot of dirty work around the world. When we were touring Normandy, I saw our driver, Cabot, always talking to some guy in a blue Mercedes. The car was definitely following us. Did you know that? It was probably Ehud, and I've got pictures to prove it." He sat back, satisfied. To his disappointment, the old man went back to his coffee without comment. "So, what do you think?" asked Peter.

"I think," said Noble, "that Ari and Ehud might not be their real names. Have you thought of that?" Peter put his elbows on the table. He conceded his grandfather's point, but was still convinced the two men helping them track Weismann were probably Israelis.

Cohen came into the room. "Good morning," he said, pouring himself a large coffee and orange juice. He pulled up a chair next to Noble.

"Peter's got an interesting angle, Samuel." Noble smiled at his grandson. "He thinks our guardian angels are Israeli security types."

"Maybe former security, Gramps. There is a difference."

Cohen sipped his juice. His eyes betrayed nothing. "Interesting theory. I've thought that myself."

Noble looked over at his friend. "Really? You never mentioned it."

Cohen shrugged. "What does it matter? They've been solid all through this entire exercise." He left the table to fix himself a plate of food. "You want anything, Bill?" he said from the counter. The old man shook his head.

"Why don't you ask them, Peter?"

His grandson folded his arms and slumped in his chair. "Maybe I should."

Cohen returned, heard the last comment. "And what would be the point of that?"

"Don't you want to know who we're working with, Sam?"

"Not particularly." He took a forkful of eggs and began eating.

"You have anything against my asking Ari if I'm right?"

Cohen stopping chewing and looked across the table. "Yes, I do. I'm not sure what good it would do to find out who they work for." He corrected himself, "Or did work for, Peter."

He resumed eating. "Right now they work for us. They're doing great so far and I don't want anything to jeopardize The Project. You might spook these guys. What if they are what you say they are?" He put down his fork and raised his coffee cup. "If they feel their cover is blown, they might back out and leave us on our own. Then what?"

Peter shifted uncomfortably in his chair. He looked at his grandfather but the old man's expression seemed in accord with Cohen's.

"If they were working against us in some bizarre way I'd obviously have a problem with it, Peter." Cohen's eyes narrowed. "I've made it a lifetime practice to read people. I've been told I'm good at it, and I don't see anything funny going on."

Peter started to speak but Cohen held up his hand. "Can you work with this situation, Peter? Put your assumptions aside?"

The younger Noble shrugged. "Sure. I'd never compromise the operation, Sam. I just thought it might be part of this puzzle to know just who these guys really are."

"When it's done, over, and you want to pin them down, go for it. Agreed?"

"Okay, I can live with that."

Swanson and Soleski sauntered into the serving area and nodded to the trio at the table before heading to the breakfast counter.

Cohen stared across the table at Peter. "Everyone on the same page?"

"I'm good here," said the young man.

Noble raised his coffee in a salute and emptied the cup.

Soleski and Swanson dragged chairs to the table and the mood changed.

"Where are we going today, Peter?"

# CHAPTER FORTY-SEVEN

That morning Peter Noble led his elders on a second day of exploring Paris.

They took a taxi to Notre-Dame and followed a throng of tourists into the cathedral's dark, cool interior. They were awed by slender, soaring Gothic arches and spectacular rose windows. Peter, on a dare from Soleski, climbed two hundred feet to photograph grotesque stone gargoyles made famous by Victor Hugo, then descended on rubbery legs, cursing himself for accepting the challenge. The men strolled to the Pont Neuf where they caught a sightseeing riverboat. There they ate a leisurely lunch on a shaded deck as the craft gracefully plied the river through the heart of Paris, gawking like ordinary tourists. The boat passed under slender stone bridges and glided past the fabled Quai d'Orsay, crowded with a parade of tourists. Back on shore, Peter took the men on a prearranged group tour of the Louvre which devoured ninety minutes of their afternoon. Their docent left the Americans enlightened but exhausted.

Outside the galleries, the men stood beside pools reflecting I.M. Pei's famous glass pyramid. The men succumbed to fatigue and voted to risk another wild taxi ride back to the hotel. Peter opted to stay behind and let the warriors go.

He studied the Louvre's crowds for a while and then continued on alone, walking through Paris as he had London.

At a romantic outdoor café he fell in with a group of young American coeds and flirted, paying for espressos and trading travel stories. A charming blonde from California caught his eye, and he lingered in her company. He wanted to stay, but was wary enough to give a false name and hometown when they exchanged addresses, promising to write when summer was over.

He said goodbye, wandered again and stopped at a small street market. He bought three ripe pears and devoured one as he headed to a nearby Métro stop. After navigating the lines without help, he surfaced near the Gare du Nord station and finished his excursion on foot, arriving back at the Hôtel du Chardin with an hour to spare.

In his room, he found the drapes pulled tight and his grandfather asleep in the cool air, his chest rising and falling in ragged breathing. Peter let him sleep. He showered and changed clothes. Before going downstairs, he awakened his grandfather, then roused the others. He went downstairs and took up a post in the front sitting room to wait. At five o'clock the men gathered outside to wait for the white van that would take them to their final rehearsal.

# CHAPTER FORTY-EIGHT

## LE BOURGET, JUNE 2

The team went through their paces flawlessly. Even Cohen's second day of shooting satisfied his coach. The men gathered around a visibly pleased Ari.

"Not one mistake, gentlemen," he crowed. "If you perform as you have this evening, you will do well when the time comes."

Cohen asked, "Should I do more target practice?"

Ari smiled at Cohen and put a hand on his shoulder. "Sometimes people get killed by thinking too much about a simple thing like shooting a man, Samuel. No, I think you are ready. I do not want to complicate your task. Besides, you will have a great advantage over Weismann."

"What's that?"

"He has no idea you are coming for him."

Ari gave the men permission to break for a snack. As the Americans ate, their tutors began dismantling the mock-up of the tavern. Ehud stripped cardboard from the wooden frames and sliced the sheets into two foot squares. Ari methodically broke each piece of lumber into shorter lengths of kindling. When they had finished, the set had been reduced to a pile of cardboard scraps and broken wood.

Ehud cut open the sandbags and scattered the contents. He piled the empty bags into the Mercedes's trunk along with the dress dummy. The big man stomped back and forth on the shattered targets, reducing them to pulp. Ari dismantled the bulletin boards and broke apart the easel.

When he was finished, he addressed them. "We will not meet again until Bastogne, gentlemen. Samuel, the cell phone I gave you, please."

The lawyer handed it over. Ari produced another one and gave it Cohen. "In three days, I will call you after your visit to the Ardennes." Cohen nodded.

"From Bastogne, we will take two vehicles to Thionville. From there, east to Bois-les-Bains, where we will prepare the next phase of The Project. Any questions?"

There were none. Ari rose, and motioned to the van. "Then I will now return you to your hotel in Paris." The men climbed into the white Renault van and left the warehouse. Ehud followed in the Mercedes.

The Algerian watchman waited for thirty minutes. When he was satisfied they were not coming back, he crossed the weedy lot and inspected the far end of the warehouse where the mysterious guests had met. Apart from some scattered chairs and battered folding tables, the building seemed undisturbed.

A towering pile of discarded cardboard and broken wood was piled in a corner. Sand had been strewn across the huge shed's floor and bits of melon rind were tossed about, brazen rats already nibbling at the scraps. The Algerian's fee of four hundred Euros was tucked safely in his pocket. He returned to his shack, locked the gate behind him and mounted his rusting Vespa scooter for the long drive home.

# CHAPTER FORTY-NINE

### PARIS, GARE DU NORD, JUNE 3

After breakfast, the men took a taxi to the train station. Cohen had purchased first-class tickets for a noon departure to Belgium. They sat together in comfortable, high-backed seats in the third car of a Thalys train. After leaving Paris, the sleek, serpent-shaped engine accelerated across the countryside at close to two hundred miles per hour.

"Damn, now this is what I call a real train ride, Bill," Soleski crowed. "Say what you want about the Frogs, they got it down right when it comes to wine and trains as far as I'm concerned." He turned and gazed at fields flashing past his window.

Bill Noble was unable to appreciate the scenery. For him, the rail journey was one of silent agony. He grimaced in pain, trying to hide the telltale signs from the others. In the seat next to him, Peter flipped on his iPod and recognized the familiar signs of a laboring heart.

Cohen studied Noble and read the same undeniable signals. He knew he would have to face the problem of Noble's participation in The Project, but for now, he was content to sit back and enjoy the ride. The tracks went east, and France's landscape blurred as the train accelerated, fields and forests merging under a perfect blue sky all the way to Belgium's border. They arrived in Liège in two hours and fifteen minutes as promised.

Myron Soleski craned his neck to take in the soaring steel and glass of Liège's Guillemins railway station. The great arching vault seemed to float above the tracks and platforms, giving a futuristic feel to the space. "I can't believe this place," he said. "They do know how to do stations, too."

Cohen hustled the men down several levels on escalators. Peter went ahead to pick up their rental car. In thirty minutes, he appeared behind the wheel of a tan Volkswagen Caravelle. Swanson was designated navigator and took a seat beside Peter. The former sergeant immediately got them lost in Liège traffic, but eventually redeemed himself. After negotiating a series of roundabouts they left the city behind and headed south on highway E25 for the next fifty miles. Swanson turned to look over his shoulder. Cohen was nodding, struggling to stay awake. Soleski and Noble were already asleep. Swanson nudged Peter, who glanced back at his passengers. "Get some shut-eye, Burt. When we get to Bastogne, I'll wake you."

The tall man folded the map and leaned back in his seat. "It's a deal."

The ride lasted over an hour and Peter found their hotel without a wrong turn.

## CHAPTER FIFTY

"Welcome to Belgium, gentlemen."

Retired U.S. Army Major Kent Bryan stood ramrod stiff outside Bastogne's Hôtel Melba. He flashed a wide smile as he greeted the men. Cohen, the first one out of the van, grasped the major's hand. He stepped aside and introduced each man as they exited the Caravelle.

Bryan, a trim man in his middle sixties had a square face and clipped, gray mustache that gave him a slightly British look. He wore a short-sleeved military-style khaki shirt with a red, white and blue "Bryan Battlefield Tours" logo emblazoned above his right breast pocket.

"As your letter requested, Mr. Cohen, I took the liberty of booking your group here because it's near the center of town. I think you'll find it quite acceptable." He smiled. "Let's get your party registered, shall we?" They walked to the front desk. "Am I correct that you'll be staying on after our two days together?"

"Yes. We thought we might do a little exploration on our own after you've familiarized us with the area."

"Well, by the close of tomorrow, if I've done my job right, you fellows should have a good grasp of the terrain and the order of battle."

"Thanks, Major. That will help. We only saw our own little corner of the action."

"Please, call me Kent for the duration."

"All right, Kent it is," answered Cohen.

"This ought to be an interesting two days," said Soleski.

"How so?" asked the former major.

"Well, it's just that Sam always had a thing about officers," said Soleski smiling. Bryan looked at the little Michigan man, unsure whether he was joking or not.

"Don't mind Sollie; he's our comic relief," said Noble.

"Every platoon needs one," said the major. The group laughed together.

They signed in and took their luggage to their rooms. Major Bryan waited patiently until the group reconvened in the lobby.

"What's on our schedule for today?" asked Cohen.

Bryan put away his map and flipped open a small notebook. "I thought we'd tour Bastogne and see some of the battlefield's immediate perimeter. Tomorrow we'll find that spot you want to see." He looked at the five men. "I've done some preliminary scouting for you and I think we'll be able to locate the general area, although I have to warn you, I don't think there's much there now."

"We've waited a long time," said Cohen, looking out a lobby window. "We'd be most grateful if you can take us there."

"Of course," said Bryan, "but you have to realize it's changed a lot. Most of the roads have disappeared and now it's either tangled forest or cultivated farmland."

"Just get us close and we'll know it," said Swanson.

Noble spoke up. "Burt's right, we'll probably feel it before we see it."

"I'll do my best, gentlemen." He smiled confidently at the five men. "If it's out there, we'll find it for you."

Samuel Cohen smiled back. "Oh, it's out there," he said softly.


Bryan led his tour group to a dark green Land Rover. "We'll take my four wheel drive just in case we meet up with General Mud."

Cohen tugged at their guide's arm. "I've got a quick phone call to make, Kent. Can you give me a few minutes while I take care of some minor business?"

"Of course."

Cohen walked away, pulling out the cell phone Ari had given him. He keyed in the number written on the back of a business card and waited.

After the tenth ring he heard Ari's voice. "You have arrived." It was a declaration, not a question.

"Yes, we've just checked in."

"What are your plans?"

"We'll use what's left of today to tour the town, see some things."

"And tomorrow?"

"We're going out to find the exact location where our story began."

"Good. Did you reserve your rooms for the entire week?"

"Yes. And we'll leave our rental here, as you suggested."

"Excellent."

"When shall I call again?" asked Cohen.

There was a brief pause. "Tomorrow evening at eight o'clock. I'll have further instructions." The call died.

Cohen put the tiny phone back in his pocket.

Kent Bryan was leaning over a large map spread on the hood of the green Land Rover.

"I suggest we start at the Bastogne Historical Center." He glanced at his watch. "We don't have much time, but you really should see the museum. Good collections of weapons, uniforms, vehicles, the works. And the Mardasson Monument, of course.

"From there we'll go to the center of town, McAuliffe Square. It'll give you a sense of the scale of Bastogne. Then we'll stop at some of the monuments, markers and the like. If we have some daylight left we'll work our way outward along some of the roads that figured in the various retrograde movements."

"That's a twenty-dollar word for retreat, ain't it?" said Soleski.

Their guide was not the least offended by the characterization.

"You could call it part retreat, part fighting withdrawal, Myron."

"Call me Sollie," said the little man.

"Okay, Sollie," replied the major. "This wasn't a mass panic situation where GIs somehow ended up in Bastogne. General McAuliffe said he had a 'feeling' that this was the right spot. Just like the Union cavalry brigadier at Gettysburg when he saw the ground."

"General John Buford, sir," blurted Peter.

"Very good, young Mr. Noble. You know your history."

Bryan put away the map and opened the doors for his passengers. As the men loaded, the ex-officer continued his impromptu strategy lesson for Soleski. "GIs like yourselves fought tooth and nail and were loathe to yield an inch."

Bryan wheeled the vehicle from the hotel's lot and toward the museum.

Soleski liked the sound of the phrase. "Loathe to yield . . ." he repeated the words aloud several times. "You're all right, Major . . . for an officer."

Swanson clamped a big hand on the little man's neck. "Give it a rest, Sollie."

The Land Rover headed along the town's narrow streets as Bryan continued his tactics lesson. "Every foot of ground the Germans captured was paid for with tremendous losses by their forces. Ultimately, it was your tenacity that won the battle. After we're done," he said, "you'll probably agree that Americans can be justifiably proud of how well you guys did under such lousy conditions." He ended his monologue as they parked near a hulking Sherman tank.

"About forty-five minutes 'til closing. Let's do some sightseeing, gentlemen."

# CHAPTER FIFTY-ONE

## BASTOGNE, HÔTEL MELBA, JUNE 4

Samuel Cohen looked up to see Burt Swanson looming over him. "What are you going to do about Bill?"

Cohen was finishing his second cup of morning coffee at a corner table in the hotel's restaurant. Across the room stragglers lingered over breakfast meals.

"Sit down, Burt," invited Cohen. "What's on your mind?"

The lanky southerner pulled out a chair and slumped into it opposite Cohen. "You know what I'm talking about, Sam. Bill Noble's about to fall over."

"That's a bit dramatic, isn't it?"

"Hell, no, and you know it, Sam."

Cohen stared at his half-empty cup, trying to shape an answer. "I admit he's been pushing himself pretty hard on this trip."

Swanson leaned back, threw an arm over the chair's back. "He's about to become a liability for the The Project. You know I'm right."

Cohen in fact, did know it, but he wanted to block out the thought. "Let me be the judge of that, Burt."

Swanson stared back. "You've got a conflict of interest. Admit it."

"All right, guilty as charged. But Bill's part of the heart and soul of this thing. I'm not going to let him miss out." He tapped the tablecloth with his long fingers for emphasis. "Not when we're this close to finishing it."

Swanson shifted uncomfortably, tried another approach. "Look, I'm as willing as anyone on this team to give Bill some sort of role in what we're doing, Sam, but just keep him out of harm's way for God's sake."

"What do you have in mind?"

"I don't know exactly. It's your show. But keep him out of the action. He'll only end up being in the way . . . and with his heart and all."

"Okay, so he's not well. Hell, none of us are running sprints on this trip."

Swanson hunched his shoulders forward at the man across the small table. "Sam, there's more at stake here than just wanting to make sure Bill gets to be part of this thing when it goes down."

Cohen raised a hand, a signal somewhere between compromise and surrender. "I hear exactly what you're saying, Burt. And I don't disagree with you. I'll deal with it, talk to him."

"I'm going to hold you to that, Sam. We're running out of time for you to make some sort of decision about this."

"I'll talk to him, I promise."

"I'll take you at your word." Swanson turned on his heel and headed for the restaurant's doorway.

Cohen sipped his coffee. It was cold. He held up his cup and signaled his server for more.

He swallowed fresh coffee and closed his eyes. He tried to imagine a lake to center his mind but his thoughts stalled. Across the room Peter Noble and Soleski were heading his way.

Peter did not sit down. "Bryan's Battlefield Express is here, Sam. Time to go."

Cohen signed for his meal and followed the men out to the major's car.

# CHAPTER FIFTY-TWO

## NORTHEAST OF BASTOGNE, JUNE 4

Belgium, like most European battlefields, remains pockmarked with scars. One- and two-man foxholes have been transformed into shallow trenches by decades of spring rains. Fighting positions more than a half-century old are now shallow crumbling holes, regardless of which soldiers dug the works.

The men traveled northeast from Bastogne, along N30, a road leading to the small town of Foy. When he approached the hamlet, Bryan turned right at a sign pointing the way to Bizory and headed southeast. The Land Rover rumbled to a stop on the side of the road where the road bisected thick forest.

Bryan killed the engine. "This is the Bois Jacques. Let's get out and take a look. It'll be worth it."

Dismounting from the vehicle, the men followed their guide into a stand of dark pine. Noble walked slowly to a straight, towering fir and rested against it. He looked down at the line of shallow depressions in the tree line.

Kent Bryan's booming voice echoed in the forest. "Easy Company fought here, gentlemen." He paused at a line of rough holes and held out his arms. "Second Battalion, Five-O-Sixth Parachute Infantry dug in here."

Peter stepped over to a shallow depression with exposed roots along its edges. "Band of Brothers," he whispered. "These are actually their foxholes?"

Kent Bryan crossed his arms and nodded. Peter began snapping pictures.

Bryan stepped down into one of the holes alongside Soleski. "I'll bet you had to dig plenty of these in your day."

The Michigander crouched in the dirt. "Yes, sir. It looks very familiar."

"And that's about as deep as he would go," snorted Burt Swanson. The old platoon sergeant circled the foxhole. "I never could get you to dig as deep as you should have, Sollie. Never." The two old soldiers laughed and the Arkansan hauled Soleski from the hole.

Cohen and Noble peered into the woods where trees stood in gloomy, claustrophobic rows. Their eyes met and Noble looked away.

"It feels haunted," said Cohen, "just like Omaha Beach."

"I'd like to get a couple of group shots, Gramps," pleaded Peter, herding the old men together for photographs.

With a minimum of grumbling the men formed a line, foxholes at their feet.

"I think we've seen enough," said Cohen after several posed pictures.

"All right then, back in the car," said Bryan. "We'll keep heading northeast."

The Land Rover passed through a quilt of farm fields on the way to Noville, like Foy, a town with a storied battlefield pedigree. But they didn't stop, and the town dropped behind away to the southwest. They drove by prosperous farms and more thick stands of wood. Bryan took them north and west through a series of hairpin turns. He raced through Houffalize and went underneath the E25/A26 autobahn to pick up route N827. It was a winding road that took them past solitary whitewashed stone houses, farms and thick, shadowy woods.

"I'm impressed, Kent," said Cohen. "You really know your way around this countryside."

"Thanks. It's a lot easier without tanks in the way and no one shooting at you."

Signs for Vaux, Cherain and Beho flashed by as they pushed east. They came to a T-junction and Bryan turned left, north along N62/E421.

"How much longer?" asked Noble.

"Another ten minutes and and we'll get on E42, a good north-south highway that will take us west and north of St.-Vith."

At Bryan's mention of the city, the old warrior sat up straight. "I remember being dug in somewhere north of there."

Bryan kept his eyes on the road and fished in a canvas bag on the floor. He pulled out a topographic map and passed it over his shoulder. "See if you can locate St.-Vith for us, Bill." Noble and his grandson unfolded the map and pored over it.

Ahead of them, the road ran between several large buildings, and Cohen glimpsed a stream of traffic on a highway ahead. They crossed an overpass and turned onto an access road behind a large Mercedes cargo truck. The Land Rover merged into traffic headed north.

Again, they exited and went southwest, passing through the first of three roundabouts. On the major's map the two-lane road was labeled N675, and it hugged a large tract of forest just above the town of Rodt. To the south were open, cultivated fields with isolated islands of trees and winding lanes with modest homes and thriving farms.

After the final traffic circle, Bryan drove another five hundred meters and turned onto a narrow gravel ending in a T-junction at a wall of trees. A low stone farmhouse squatted on the northeast corner where the roads met. Bryan pulled to one side of a weedy path serving as a driveway and parked.

"Where the hell are we?" asked Soleski.

Bryan opened his door and got out. "I hope we're not far from the area you're looking for, gentlemen. I'll just be a minute." He walked to the home and knocked.

"He's probably lost and stopped to ask for directions," chuckled Swanson.

The heavy wooden door creaked open and a stocky, white-bearded man in a pale shirt and dark brown trousers held up with bright red suspenders smiled and shook hands with Kent Bryan.

Noble handed the topographic map to Cohen. "Maybe you can figure out where we are."

Swanson opened his door and slipped out to stretch his cramped legs. Peter and Soleski followed and began pacing beside the Land Rover.

The man in the farmhouse disappeared inside and reappeared with a bottle of wine and a fistful of glasses. He went to a small patio at the end of the house and set the bottle and the glasses on a giant wooden spool serving as a table. A lattice frame arbor, covered in climbing vines, shaded the space. The home's owner pried apart a stack of cheap, white plastic chairs and began dragging them across the flagstones to the table.

Bryan waved at his passengers. "Over here, gentlemen." The men walked to the shaded veranda where Bryan introduced the Americans to the bewhiskered man. "This is my good friend, André Godin."

The Belgian went down the line of veterans, vigorously shaking each man's hand. He motioned for the group to join him at the upended spool where he had been filling glasses with wine. Godin and Bryan chattered in rapid French, the American trying to translate the Belgian's words as quickly as he could. The old man wiped tears from his eyes as he held his wine aloft. He was obviously proposing a toast.

Bryan smiled and nodded at the Belgian. "He salutes you as liberators, as heroes and as friends."

More rapid-fire words tumbled from Godin's lips. Bryan tried to stay with him. "He and his family have never forgotten what you did here. He considers all Americans his brothers, his family . . . he blesses you."

André Godin hoisted his glass and drained it in one swallow.

The Americans followed his example. Godin refilled their glasses and repeated the toasts until the bottle was empty. The farmer collected the bottles and glasses to give Bryan a place to lay out his maps. The men gathered around their guide, and Bryan posed a long series of questions about the terrain laid out before them. Godin responded with lengthy answers. He kept stabbing his stubby fingers at points in the green shaded areas and roads on the map.

The Americans listened in rapt attention as though they could discern what Godin was saying. Bryan occasionally looked up and gestured toward the north, to the wall of trees facing the farmhouse. Finally, the two men seemed to reach an agreement. Godin beamed at the old warriors, thumping Soleski and Noble on their backs, his head bobbing as he directed a steam of quick, unintelligible French at the men around him.

Bryan cradled his chin in one hand. "According to André, there are two strong possibilities that might be your spot." The former officer frowned. "Problem is . . . we think your German column was a straggler group from the Sixth Panzer Army and not where they should have been."

"We could tell they seemed lost," volunteered Swanson.

"Yeah, but then . . . so were you fellows," countered Bryan pensively. "It's a toss up as to which group was the more disoriented those first two days. And that complicates things a bit,

Burt." He bit his lip, placed his hands on the map, as though he could divine the answer by touching the contour lines on paper.

The Belgian busied himself with setting two wooden saw-horses in the shade as the Americans studied the map. Godin wrestled a large piece of plywood on top of the braces and beckoned for Peter to follow him into his house, He emerged holding a stack of plates. Godin followed with a roll of linen and baskets of bread. Their host set about transforming the plywood sheet into a luncheon table under the arbor. He directed Peter to lay out the china.

Cohen grew impatient at what he knew was to be a delay in their search. "Does he expect us to stay for lunch?"

Bryan raised his gaze from the map. "My wife knows André well. She packed a cooler for us, just in case."

"This is going to cost us valuable time, Kent."

Bryan shrugged. "It would be an insult to refuse his hospitality, Sam. Besides, we'll need André's help leading us to these two sites after lunch."

Cohen fumed over the delay but Bryan ignored him.

Peter retrieved a large cooler from the Land Rover and brought it to the veranda. More wine appeared, as did bottles of mineral water. Cohen eventually surrendered and pulled a chair to the makeshift table.

While luncheon preparations were underway, Bryan folded his map into a manageable two-foot square and studied probable routes which would take them north into the forest.

After a short blessing from Godin, the cooler was emptied and its contents shared. Wine flowed freely and, with Bryan's help at translating, the Belgian told the harrowing story of his family's flight from St.-Vith to Stavelot just ahead of the Germans. He was the only survivor of the wartime exodus.

After an appropriate pause, Bryan explained the purpose of the Americans' visit. Between mouthfuls of food, Godin peppered Bryan with questions.

The major turned to Cohen for help. "According to my notes and the information you sent me, Sam, your captors were likely shunted off to the south because of tremendous traffic jams that morning."

"Too many tanks, too few good roads," said Cohen.

There were nods of agreement around the table.

"The order of battle for the Sixth Panzer Army shows your man as part of the First SS Panzer Regiment, Peiper's outfit."

"That would explain the indiscriminate killing," said Noble.

Swanson glowered, wishing they could share about the coming retribution. "Von Wurtz was his own bastard, Bill."

There were murmurs of agreement. Even André Godin, deciphering the thrust of the conversation, nodded this time at the sound of the German's name.

"The problem," said Bryan, "is the total lack of after-action reports."

Soleski quickly interrupted. "We reported everything to headquarters."

"I'm sure you did, Sollie. But one of the complications was the chaotic situation up and down the line. There were just seven of you who made it back . . ."

"Eight," interjected Noble. "Don't forget Ted Mitchell."

"Sorry, I meant the remaining survivors, Bill. " He continued. "Who knows what happened to your report? It was probably one of dozens about shootings going on with the SS columns. Remember, Malmédy grabbed the headlines, but civilians suffered too. Stavelot was a terrible killing ground."

At the mention of the town's name Godin visibly sagged and shook his head.

"Who knows how many Germans came back from Von Wurtz's column? They didn't even rate a footnote in overall First Panzer Division losses." Bryan continued the battle's history. "The Germans had over one hundred-thousand casualties and over twenty-seven thousand of those were captured or missing."

Swanson glowered. "We lost almost ninety thousand ourselves, don't forget."

Bryan did not challenge the figures. "Yes, but with all due respect to your collective experience, it's understandable how a rogue officer like Von Wurtz escaped accountability."

"Some day he'll be brought to account for what he did," predicted Cohen.

Their guide shrugged. "Even if he survived the Bulge . . . and that's a big IF . . . he likely died in action."

Soleski ended the conversation. "Well, either way, he'll burn in Hell."

"On that note," said Bryan, "let's get back on the road and try to find your site."

The men rose and helped Godin clear the terrace. The veterans queued up to take turns in the home's tiny bathroom and then got back in the car.

Godin took Cohen's place in the front passenger seat, the map on his knees.

He rattled on in French and Bryan translated. "This forest is known as the 'Grand, or Large, Woods.' It's been worked since the thirteenth century by the locals. Firewood, fuel for forges. It's state land now."

They drove for twenty minutes along the edge of the pines, Godin directing.

# CHAPTER FIFTY-THREE

Bryan followed a gravel access road until Godin waved him onto an overgrown logging road that narrowed as it wound through the trees. Several times, the Belgian signaled for a halt and consulted the map before resuming the search. Twice, the Land Rover burst into a sunlit meadow, only to be swallowed up again by curtains of pine and birch on the far side.

The Belgian babbled excitedly at Bryan. "He thinks it might be just up ahead, gentlemen."

The vehicle slowed as they drove through a marshy area fringed with willows. Soon, they were in a wild, tangled section, and Bryan put the car into four-wheel drive to negotiate the soft ground. They emerged at a copse of dying trees and stopped. Godin slipped out of the vehicle and walked forward twenty meters.

He waved them ahead without looking back, scanning both sides of a heavily obscured track which wound up a slight rise. The farmer did an about-face and held up his hand to halt the Land Rover. He signaled for the veterans to inspect the ground where he stood. They scrambled out of the vehicle in anticipation. Cohen and the others did a three-hundred-and-sixty-degree inspection of the site. They seemed unsure.

"Well," asked Bryan, "what do you think?"

Cohen closed his eyes, tried to conjure up a battlefield memory. "Doesn't feel like it," he said quietly.

Noble frowned at the trees surrounding them. "There should be at least some sign of the farm. Stone walls or something."

"Yeah, there was a large manor house with a wall," murmured Swanson.

Peter did not speak. He snapped pictures as a precaution.

"Okay. Should we keep looking?" asked their driver.

They men agreed and climbed back into the Land Rover.

"Sorry," said Noble.

"Nothing to apologize for, Bill," said Bryan. "We have to be sure." He and Godin jabbered in the front seat as the vehicle began to move again.

With the Belgian directing, they found their way back onto a well-used dirt road. After twenty minutes, Bryan pulled to the shoulder and got out of the car to consult with Godin who had asked him to stop to study the map. The two men spread the sheet over the Land Rover's hood and asked William Noble to join them. Cohen tagged along to look over their shoulders. Kent Bryan was comparing a wartime map with the newer one.

Inside the car Burt Swanson propped an elbow against the glass and watched the gathering at the vehicle's front end. He stifled a yawn. "I'll give the Major an 'A' for trying but this is going to be a miracle if we do actually find the spot."

"Sam says we'll feel it, but I didn't feel nothing back there."

"Me neither, Sollie. But what I do feel is the sudden urge to take a leak." The Southerner climbed out of car and stepped behind a thick birch. "Don't leave without me!" he yelled to the dismounted group.

At the front of the vehicle, Bryan waved and propped a boot on the bumper. "One of our problems is that there are now trees where there used to be fields and fields where there used to be trees."

Cohen stared at the map again. "The house, or what's left of it, is the key. Won't we find some stones?"

Bryan nodded, "Maybe. If they weren't hauled away for use elsewhere. You said you remember a hill the artillery spotters used before the assault."

Noble grew animated. "Yes, that's right. The road skirted it, then dropped away behind it. We walked west on that road . . . walked out after the shooting stopped."

Bryan drummed his fingers on the topographic lines of hills and gullies. His eyes darted back and forth from the old combat chart to the modern map. Godin pulled at his white beard and peered at the grid lines. His eyes followed Bryan's index finger as he backtracked across the paper. Bryan's hand moved north along a stream bed and came to a stop on a hill indicated by a ring of tight lines. He asked the Belgian a few short questions. The bearded man pondered the remarks, shrugged and seemed to agree with Bryan's suggestion.

"Okay," Bryan announced, "we'll try a spot about two kilometers east."

The map now proved to be a marginal help on the forest tracks and this second site proved a false hope as well. Expectations rose again when Peter discovered a series of old trenches, but the find was an isolated one and their excitement was short-lived. Cohen began to despair. They filed into the car and backtracked to an intersection in the forest.

Bryan turned northeast, and within minutes they overtook a lone walker chaperoned by a dog trotting at his side. The car slowed in the tight corridor of trees and stopped.

André Godin leaned out the window and exchanged pleasantries with the trekker, a lean, wrinkled man with an enormous white mustache and reddish face. Tufts of white hair curled from under a tweed cap. The man recognized Bryan's passengers as American veterans, and he politely tipped his wool hat and smiled. He gestured in response to Godin's questions. The hiker used precise hand signals and seemed to understand exactly what his countryman was asking. His answers were emphatic, confident.

Bryan leaned across the steering wheel and listened to the conversation. "I think we may have found your miracle, Sam." He turned and looked over his shoulder at Cohen. "This gentleman says he knows of such a place . . . it's worth a try, anyway."

Godin was doing most of the talking, his voice a torrent of rapid questions. The hiker listened courteously and was unhurried in his responses. He raised his walking stick to emphasize each reply.

Godin offered the man a bottle of water and a lift, but the man politely declined both. Bryan thanked him profusely, adding his gratitude to Godin's.

The solitary trekker bowed and doffed his hat as they drove away.

# CHAPTER FIFTY-FOUR

## NORTHWEST OF ST.-VITH, JUNE 4

For twenty minutes, they followed this new lead northeast along a soggy trace through a leafy corridor. The muddy road led them to higher ground where the forest floor was scarred by well-worn furrows. Bryan nursed the Land Rover along in low gear as they bumped over the uneven track. They came up a rise and rounded a lightly forested hill.

Samuel Cohen's heart suddenly began to race. He reached forward and dug his fingers into Godin's shoulders. The Belgian turned, took one look at Cohen's face and ordered a halt.

Through the windshield, the men saw an overgrown road running straight before them across a fallow meadow toward a distant stand of birch and hardwood. On their right, a tangled wall of dead and dying sorbs and bilberries hemmed in the clearing. They had stopped just beyond a hill with a crown of stunted trees. But what had caught their eyes was a pile of stone and the crumbling outline of a chimney, remains of what once had been a grand house.

Kent Bryan drove forward another ten feet to level ground and turned off the engine. Only the ticking of the Land Rover's cooling motor broke the quiet.

A pair of curious birds swooped low and alighted on branches above the car. The men sat in complete silence for several minutes.

Cohen released his grip on Godin's shoulders and got out of the car. Everyone exited the vehicle without a word. They stood together in the clearing.

Finally Noble spoke. "Could you feel it, Sam?"

The old soldier simply nodded, eyes filling with tears, though he tried to blink them away. It was useless. He reached out and grasped Noble's thin arm.

Burt Swanson put his arm around Cohen's shoulders. "Me too, Sam," he said. "I felt it."

Soleski walked slowly, reverently, to his old comrades and stood next to them.

Peter moved off to one side to stand with Bryan and Godin. The trio of witnesses watched the four old men survey the clearing.

After what seemed an eternity the quartet made their way to the ruins. When they reached the stones Soleski spontaneously knelt by the fragments.

Swanson picked his way through the briars and saplings to circle behind what had been a large fireplace. He tested what remained of a wall and corner with his boot. A stone tumbled into the scattered blocks with a dull sound.

"Best be careful, gentlemen," warned Byran. "There could still be unexploded ordnance all around here."

Waist-high weeds and young trees grew in the midst of the remaining walls. Swanson poked his way past the stubby remnants of the chimney and threaded his way among skinny birch trees behind the ruins. "I hid my carbine right around here that morning!"

Noble shuffled along a line of broken, moss-covered stone. "And this is what's left of the courtyard wall."

Peter hurried to Soleski and helped the little man to his feet. "This is . . . just unbelievable . . . unbelievable . . ." the little man mumbled over and over.

Cohen turned and asked Peter to take plenty of pictures. "For the other guys, who couldn't come," he explained.

Swanson made a complete circuit of the crumbling foundation, steadying himself by grasping saplings as he made his way to the others in the clearing. He walked over to Bryan and Godin and grasped their hands. "This was worth it all. Thank you, thank you."

The former major smiled, as did the bearded Belgian.

Cohen added his gratitude to Swanson's. "This is fantastic, Kent. You did it. You and André. I can't tell you how pleased I am with what you've done for us." He beamed at both men.

"I'll get the box, Sam," said Bryan quietly. He went back to the Land Rover and opened the vehicle's back door. He pulled a long white box from the storage area and carried it gently to Cohen.

"Good idea, Sam," said Noble.

Cohen removed the lid. He lifted out two dozen, long-stemmed red roses tied with a silk ribbon and handed them to Noble. "You should do the honors, Bill."

"But this was your idea, Sam."

"Partly. But I'd like you to do this for . . . the boys we left here."

Noble forced a smile and took the flowers. He walked slowly to the ruins. His friends gathered behind him.

Peter crouched off to the side and began taking pictures as his grandfather tenderly placed red roses among the jumble of stones. Noble stepped back and folded his hands in front of him, bowed his head. Cohen and the other veterans did the same. They saluted and held the pose. Five minutes of silence seemed an eternity in the clearing. More birds gathered in the branches above to watch the strangers.

Finally, Noble let out a deep sigh and shuffled back to the group. "This is something I thought I'd never see in my life-time." The men nodded in agreement.

Soleski pointed east, down the weedy road. "We came down that road a couple of hours before the Germans, remember?"

Swanson turned in the direction they had come. "And we walked out that way when it was over."

Soleski stepped beside his old sergeant. "You led us out, Burt. You kept us together and brought us home."

"Sollie's right," said Noble. "You found a way to get us back in one piece."

"We lost Mitchell," whispered the former non-com.

Cohen reassured him. "Not your fault, Burt. He was hurt too badly."

Bryan read his watch and craned his head at the sky. Light was beginning to fade. "We should be getting you gentlemen back to your hotel in time for dinner. And I need to return An-dré to his home." The Belgian understood and began shaking each man's hand.

"Ah, almost forgot," said Cohen, "one last thing. Major, if you would . . ."

Bryan smiled and went back to the car. He reached into the cooler and came back with a bottle of champagne and a stack of plastic cups. Cohen took the bottle and stripped the foil from the neck. Godin smiled when the familiar popping sound echoed in the woods. There was a faint cheer, and Bryan distributed the cups.

A grinning Samuel Cohen poured bubbling wine for each man, then hoisted his cup aloft. He looked around the circle of men. "To the Fortunate Orphans!"

They roared in unison. "To the Fortunate Orphans!"

After a few sips Noble proposed another toast. "To Major Kent Bryan!"

Another round of cheers and drinking. Cohen shared the bottle's remaining contents among the men. He sang out. "To André Godin and our Belgian allies!"

Their cheers rang out, startling the watching birds into flight.

The stocky Belgian was visibly touched by these old warriors. He lifted his cup and bellowed into the surrounding forest. "Vive l'Amérique!"

The veterans responded. "Vive l'Amérique!"

They drained their cups and took a few last looks around the clearing and the manor house ruins on the edge of the forest. Bryan collected the cups and bottle, climbed into the Land Rover and started the engine. Peter took a series of panoramic shots, then helped his grandfather into the car.

They continued east along the overgrown route, looking for their original bivouac, but could not find it. Eventually they discovered a well-used secondary road which took them back to pavement and, eventually, the main highway. They raced the setting sun to André Godin's farmhouse on the edge of the state forest. It was an emotional farewell for everyone.

They were soon back on winding roads, passing farms, villages and forests until they reached Bastogne. Bryan got them back to their hotel as the light died.

Cohen was the last to exit the vehicle. He handed the former major a pair of envelopes.

"A little something extra for today, Kent." He tapped the smaller of the two envelopes.

"And please pass this one along to André with our best wishes."

"Thank you, Samuel, but you know it's not necessary."

"I know, I know. But you have to realize what this meant to us today . . . after all the false starts and wrong turns, you were able to literally take us back in time."

"Sam, it sounds trite, but there are a lot of stories worth telling still out there."

Cohen flashed a quick, rueful smile. "Most of them will remain untold. Not enough seasons left to share them."

The retired officer shook Cohen's hand and opened the driver's door. "I'm just glad we were in time to help you write the ending for yours." He came to attention and saluted.

Cohen returned the gesture. "Never had a major salute me before," he said, smiling.

"People of your generation who served are due a salute from everyone, Sam."

"Goodnight, Kent. Thank your wife for including the roses and champagne."

"All part of the service. I'll give your regards to her. I'm glad we met."

The Land Rover wheeled away from the hotel's entrance and Cohen stood there for five long minutes without saying a word. Then he looked up and counted the evening's first stars.

# CHAPTER FIFTY-FIVE
### OUTSKIRTS OF BOIS-LES-BAINS, FRANCE, JUNE 5

Two vehicles, an hour apart, drove southeast to Thionville and crossed to the south bank of the Moselle River. Their destination was a small stone farmhouse set in a copse of woods near the outskirts of Bois-les-Bains. The small village straddled a road leading to the German border less than five kilometers distant.

The first automobile to arrive, an old Peugeot van driven by Ari, was directed into a rotting cavernous barn by a short, mustachioed man in coveralls and knee-high rubber boots. He guided the vehicle next to a large flatbed truck. Ari pulled alongside the truck and stopped at the far end of the barn's dim interior. A silent youth, standing watch in the courtyard, hurried to shut the doors.

Cohen studied the farm hands from the van's front seat. "I suppose they're both on the payroll too, Ari?"

"Of course. Don't worry, they'll be useful." He gestured to the older of the two. "He is the owner. Opens his farm to cyclists during the season. Family's been here for centuries. His son over there guides bike tours."

Ari killed the engine. "They hate the Germans. The father blames them for all three wars. His father was Resistance so he and his son can be trusted . . . for a price."

"No surprise there," said Noble, exiting the van.

The occupants spilled out into warm air heavy with the scent of manure and decaying straw. When the barn doors were latched shut, Ari and the strangers shook hands. The Frenchmen led everyone across a large square courtyard enclosed by high rock walls connected to a two-level stone house. A shiny black BMW K1200 LT motorcycle, casually draped with a canvas tarp, was parked near the barn's door, a row of chained touring bicycles next to it.

They entered a large kitchen dominated by an open hearth and a long, weathered oak table with benches opposite a yawning fireplace. A deep porcelain sink and pump were set in tile next to a wheezing refrigerator. A pile of unwashed dishes was stacked in the basin. The room's peeling plaster walls were lined with shelves filled with mismatched crockery.

Burt Swanson surveyed the kitchen. "Julia Child would turn over in her grave if she could see this," he said. "They must be bachelors."

"Yes, how did you know?" answered Ari, not understanding the joke. He gestured to their silent hosts. "With the exception of our friend and his son we will be alone for the next forty-eight hours. They will not ask your names, nor will you know theirs. It's better that way."

He continued. "Ah, a reminder. I regret this precaution, and I know it will be inconvenient, perhaps even impractical for you, but try to touch as little as possible. If we leave no traces, we do not exist. So you will please observe this discipline." There was low grumbling but no dissent.

Peter and Soleski returned to the barn and began helping the farm owner's son ferry the men's luggage to the house.

"I grant you the accommodations are rather spartan, gentlemen," said Ari, "but they will do for the time we shall be here. Our host tells me that in a few weeks this countryside will be filled with groups of Tour de France aficionados riding vicariously in their own little versions of the grand race."

The farmer's son, understanding none of the interchange between Ari and the Americans, set the suitcases on the threshold.

He peeled off his muddied boots and left them by the doorway. He motioned for the guests to follow him down the house's central corridor.

At the end of the hallway, a large room the width of the house had been set up with a dozen sturdy canvas cots. A light blanket, sheet and pillow was laid out on each bed. Two large floor fans with corroded blades turned slowly, barely pushing the room's humid air toward two partly opened windows. From the high, beamed ceiling a naked bulb hung at the end of a frayed cord. After their previous lodgings, the room was primitive.

The French youth pantomimed the use of the home's single bathroom just down the hall and then spoke rapidly to Ari before retreating to help with the evening meal.

Cohen tossed his bag on a bunk next to Ari. "Judging from our accommodations, I've apparently run out of money." Laughter echoed in the room.

Ari stuffed his small bag under the cots and sat down. "As I told you, normally this is a way-station for riders who play out their Tour fantasies on the local roads during the summer. We'll be safe here, Samuel," he said, dismissing Cohen's comment. "We are, as you might say, off the radar right now."

"Under the radar," corrected Swanson wryly as he reclined on a cot.

The others drifted around the room and claimed their bunks.

Ari waved his hand around the room. "Think of this as a welcomed blank page in your journey, Samuel. No clues here. If the authorities are able to locate any witnesses at all, they will only remember you and the others visiting Normandy, Bastogne and Paris. I think that will be a good thing."

Noble sank onto a cot and gripped his knees. "You're right, Ari. It's a good thing we're out of sight for now, but I confess Samuel spoiled us on the trip . . . up until now."

Everyone but Ari laughed. "Consider this. We are now positioned unseen, close to your target."

"Okay, Ari, we concede the point," said Cohen wearily. "What's the agenda now?"

Their escort glanced at his watch. "When Ehud arrives, we will finalize the plan and recite it once, perhaps twice. Then we will eat a wonderful meal. Appearances to the contrary, you will find our host to be an excellent chef." He stood by his cot. "If you must move around, stay within the farm's walled courtyard as a precaution, agreed? Ehud should be here within the hour. We'll dine when he gets here."

The men nodded. Noble lay back on his cot and closed his eyes, fighting heavy fatigue. Cohen noticed his friend's exhaustion. Swanson fiddled with the controls on the fans, and the room's air began to stir. Cohen opened the windows wide and retreated to his bunk where he lay staring at the ceiling. He drifted asleep in minutes. Soleski and Peter went out into the walled courtyard to explore a corner of the farmyard where swine were penned.

Within the half hour Ehud arrived in the dark blue Mercedes. He unloaded two pieces of luggage from the car's trunk. One was an ordinary black nylon bag with the Ruger and its accessories, the other a large suitcase filled with theatrical props.

## CHAPTER FIFTY-SIX

### COURBET'S FARM, NEAR BOIS-LES-BAINS, JUNE 5

"Sam, Sam!" Noble leaned over the sleeping form, tugging at Cohen's sleeve. "Soup's on, Sam. Everybody's down in the kitchen."

Cohen swung his legs over the edge of his cot and sat up, rubbing his eyes. "What time is it, Bill?"

"A bit past seven. You hungry?"

Cohen stood up and stretched his thin frame. "Famished."

When they entered the kitchen, they were assaulted by delicious aromas from the crowded stove top where their nameless host was stirring several steaming pots. The large oak table was set for dinner and several bottles of wine and mineral water stood among the dishes and baskets of fresh baguettes. At a card table in the room's corner, Swanson examined a large map with Ehud and Ari. They paused as Noble and Cohen entered.

"Evening, Sam," said Swanson. "We're looking over post-operation routes."

Ehud stood and offered his chair, but Cohen waved him off.

"Where are Sollie and Peter?" asked Noble.

"Outside, test-riding Peter's bike."

Noble poked his head out the doorway and caught sight of his grandson pedaling circles around Soleski in the walled courtyard. The farmer's son was encouraging him from his perch on a wooden fence near the barn. Peter waved and Noble returned the salute.

He went back into the kitchen as the impromptu conference ended and sat down at the end of the table. Cohen was nibbling a piece of bread he had torn from a fresh loaf.

Ari folded the large map and joined the men at the table. "And how are you feeling, Samuel?"

Cohen looked across the table at the dark-haired man. "I'm okay. Anxious, I guess. I'd like to get this over with."

Ari touched Cohen's arm. "I understand completely. All in good time. You will do fine."

"I hope so. All this traveling and waiting is beginning to wear."

Ari reassured him. "Think of this as the end. Once this is finished, you will be free of your enemy."

Soleski and Peter, trailed by the young Frenchman, came in from the courtyard and sat down on either side of Cohen. Ehud and Swanson perched at opposite ends of the long benches and watched their chef carry a large porcelain bowl to the table. He set it in front of Swanson and returned to the stove to fill another bowl with something magical, aromatic.

"What are we eating?" queried Soleski warily. He poked a long wooden spoon at the contents of the steaming dish. "No offense to Chef Boyardee there, but I ain't eating no snails."

Ari laughed and opened two bottles of wine. He poured for the men. "Do not worry. No escargot for you, Sollie. But taste everything. That will gratify our host, and you will be pleasantly surprised. We have fish, cheese, fruit, bread and crème brulée for dessert."

Noble grinned at Soleski and raised his glass. "To our chef."

The stocky man turned from his duties at the stove and bowed, smiling at the raised glasses of wine. The group spontaneously applauded him, then began eating.

At the end of the two-hour meal, over dessert, Ari startled the men around the table by proposing an impromptu reconnaissance to the village café.

"You think that's wise? Won't it tip our hand?" asked Noble.

"By this time your target has gone. We will not linger. Just one glass of beer, but it will be well worth it to see the ground, even in the evening. Agreed?"

They pushed back from the table and carried their platters to the sink where Ehud had volunteered as dishwasher alongside the chef's son. Ari spoke briefly to the big man, then led the others out into the night.

# CHAPTER FIFTY-SEVEN

## BOIS-LES-BAINS

The van slowed a hundred meters from a small lighted café. Ari disabled the dome light and let Peter and Soleski out along the paved road.

He continued on and parked in the small lot adjacent to the veranda. The trio slipped from the van and sauntered to the café's courtyard. The Americans shot discreet glances around the setting. Several obvious tourist couples and a few locals were scattered among the softly lighted tables. No one looked in their direction as they took a corner table. Ari beckoned to the proprietor and ordered three beers.

"Is that the table where . . . he sits?" asked Cohen in a low voice. He nodded over Ari's shoulder at a table in the far corner of the paved terrace, where a middle-aged couple huddled over a half-finished meal. The diners were unaware of Cohen's stare.

"Yes, it is his table," whispered Ari. "Try not to be so obvious, Samuel."

Cohen touched Noble's arm. "Bill, can you believe this?"

His old friend forced a grim smile. "We're close, Samuel. So very close . . . to finishing this."

Swanson looked up as Soleski and Peter entered the veranda and settled at a table near their friends. He and Soleski ignored their nearby accomplices and chatted in barely audible tones. Peter ordered two espressos in perfect French. The server arrived with their tiny cups on a tray. After a few minutes, Peter excused himself and asked the location of the toilet.

The waiter pointed down a short hallway past a polished wooden bar where an overweight blonde woman and a bearded man in a beret sat drinking. Peter strolled past the two, glanced into the kitchen on his left and followed a short hall that ended at a dark, lacquered, wooden door.

He entered, shut the door behind him and leaned back against it.

Peter tried to slow his breathing.

Sounds from the café's kitchen came through the wall to his left and he detected strong traces of disinfectant and other pungent scents. There was no lock on the door to prevent others from entering. The door was the only exit from the small room and might prove a problem.

The room was approximately three meters wide, four deep. Bare, ceiling-mounted fluorescent bulbs washed pale green walls with harsh light. High in the wall opposite the lavatory's door, an opaque horizontal window had been nailed shut and caulked in its frame.

A single sink sat under a metal towel dispenser with a long loop of soiled cloth hanging from it. On its right was a narrow door, which Peter opened to an array of damp mops and cleaning supplies. He quietly closed the closet and then pushed open the door to a single stall with its one toilet.

The stool's water tank was mounted above, on a tiled, rust-streaked wall, and there was a cheap sliding bolt on the door. He backed out and let the door swing shut. In the corner of the lavatory, a chest-high urinal was anchored in grimy white floor tiles. Anyone relieving themselves would have his back to the room, his body half-hidden by a short wall providing minimum privacy.

There would be no escape.

Peter backed into the center of the room and extended his right arm, holding an imaginary weapon. There would be just enough room for Cohen to take his shot, but this is where he would have to surprise his quarry.

At this range an assassin could not miss.

He took a last look around the room, then left.

Brushing past Cohen's table, Peter whispered, "Your turn."

Ari nodded at Cohen, who left the table minutes later to retrace Peter's steps. He passed the counter where the couple sat at the rail, arguing.

Cohen entered the toilet and surveyed his killing ground. He memorized the layout and relieved himself at the tall urinal where Weismann would be. He turned to judge the distance where he would stand. It would be very tight, maybe a meter at the most. Cohen knew he could not miss his target this close.

On his way out, he brushed past the male barfly who was obviously in a hurry to use the toilet.

"Pardon, Monsieur," Cohen said.

The Frenchman grunted in reply and disappeared behind the varnished door.

The American returned to his companions.

"So, what do you think, Sam?" asked Noble.

He leaned forward. "I think we're in business."

He lifted his cup and tilted it toward Ari. "Here's to your suggestion that we look over the site this evening."

Across from them, Soleski and Peter rose from their table, left Euros under their saucers, and waved at the server. They strolled onto the the main road and disappeared into the dark.

After a reasonable interval Ari announced their exit. "We need to go, gentlemen."

He drained his beer and scattered some bills on the table. He stood, and the others followed suit. They went back along the low wall bordering the veranda and got into the van. The Peugeot pulled onto the darkened road and slowed after a hundred meters to pick up two silhouettes waiting patiently in the shadows of a shuttered shop. Peter and Soleski climbed into the van and took their places in front of Cohen, who sat staring at the lighted café as they left town. He tried to imagine his enemy on the terrace but the image would not come.

## CHAPTER FIFTY-EIGHT

### COURBET'S FARM, JUNE 6

Noble slept late, ignoring an irritating rooster just outside his window. Sounds from the kitchen finally forced him awake. His body felt like a metal folding chair that had been left out in the rain. Pain racked his joints, and his breathing was labored. He ran a hand across his face and rubbed tired eyes. He struggled into a sitting position on his cot and sat there, listening to Myron Soleski's snores echoing off plastered walls.

The room's two fans slowly rotated, already falling behind in the battle with the humid air. Noble perched on the edge of his bed and caught his breath. The flesh on his legs hung from scarred knees like wrinkled silk. He arched his back and stretched thin arms over his head.

Across from him Peter's bunk was empty. Probably down the hall in the kitchen making coffee. *How like his grandson*, Noble thought, smiling.

Samuel Cohen stirred, raised himself on a bony elbow and threw off his sheet. "Morning, Bill."

Noble nodded. "Sleep well, counselor?"

Cohen shook his head. "No. Kept thinking about today."

"You weren't alone," mumbled Swanson, now awake. He picked up his pillow and threw it at Soleski's sleeping form but the little man shrugged off the hit and slept on. "Sleeping on duty," Swanson said, grinning. "Some things never change."

The three chuckled. Swanson unfolded his frame from the cot and flexed. "You guys want to use the latrine first?" They declined, and the Arkansan sauntered down the hallway on his bird legs. Across the room, Soleski finally stirred and pulled himself into a sitting position.

"Morning, Sollie," said Cohen.

Soleski rubbed his eyes and grunted. He braced himself at the edge of the cot and fumbled for his dentures. Fresh coffee aroma drifted in from the kitchen and Soleski stood, scratching himself, loosening his bones and yawning. Cohen and Noble smiled at the clicking Soleski's teeth made as he walked from the room.

"I hope those belonged to him," chuckled Noble.

With Soleski gone, Cohen turned to his friend. "How you doing, Bill?"

"All right, I guess. I've been better."

There was a pause and Cohen continued. "You don't look so good, old friend."

"Just a little tired, Sam."

His eyes bored into Noble's. "It's more than just being tired, Bill. You're hurting."

There it was, out in the open. What both of them had been avoiding.

"I'll be okay. Just a rough night, that's all."

Cohen held on the sides of his cot and leaned toward Noble. "Every night's been rough for you. Remember our conversation back in Chicago? When I said I wouldn't let the mission be jeopardized by anyone?"

Noble nodded reluctantly. "Sam . . ."

Cohen held up his hand as if to catch Noble's answer in midair. "I want you to stay behind today, Bill."

Noble's face reddened at the words even though he knew what Cohen was telling him was true. He lowered his head and let out a sigh.

"I can't take a chance, Bill. I'd be worrying about you all during the operation. I wouldn't want anything to happen to you if . . . if something were to go wrong. You understand?"

"I don't have to be at the café if that's what you mean, Sam. I can stay in the van with Burt while you make the shot."

Cohen shook his head. "Too risky, Bill. I want you to stay behind with Ehud. Get things ready."

"What will the others think, Sam? What will Peter think?"

"They'll understand. And for the record, Peter's concerned about you too. He'd never forgive himself if it went wrong, and you got caught in the middle."

"Yeah, okay. Let me think about it."

"No need to, Bill. It's done. I've decided. You'll stay behind with Ehud."

Cohen avoided looking at Noble. He pulled on his pants and slipped into his shoes. He got up from his cot and put his hand on his friend's shoulder. Noble didn't respond, shrugged off the gesture.

Cohen left Noble with his disappointment and went down the hall.

When he had gone, Noble turned to see Swanson in the doorway. "I overheard. Bad break, Bill. Sorry about that, but Sam's probably right."

"Yeah," croaked Noble. "I know it on a practical level but. . . ." He didn't finish his thoughts. Noble lay back on his cot and felt his weakened heart laboring in his chest.

*Maybe it was too much to think I'd be allowed to be there*, he thought.

It wasn't fair but he knew it made sense. Still, the decision hurt.

## CHAPTER FIFTY-NINE

### BOIS-LES-BAINS, JUNE 6

The Peugeot van pulled to the side of the road and eased behind a parked truck. They were in sight of the café. Burt Swanson let the engine idle.

In his side mirror he watched a pack of approaching bicyclists. The helmeted leader, his head down, legs pumping, was setting a punishing tempo through town. His companions were strung out behind him in twos and threes. Swanson watched them race by in a blur of colorful jerseys. Somewhere back along that route, Peter was pacing himself to arrive at the café at exactly five-thirty.

Swanson glanced at his watch. The hands crawled toward ten minutes after five. In the front passenger seat, Ari raised a pair of black compact binoculars and scanned the road. His lenses swept the parking lot and the terrace. He focused first on the shiny black Mercedes sedan parked in its usual spot. The glasses moved slowly back to the low, ivy-covered stone wall.

"Is he there?" whispered Soleski from the van's middle seat.

"Yes, gentlemen. Your target is at his table with his friend as usual."

"The bodyguard?" asked Cohen.

"He, too, is there."

Ari pocketed the glasses and addressed the nervous men. "Remember, I will be across the road in the bookseller's shop if needed." He opened the passenger side door and stared at the Americans. "Mr. Soleski . . . Sollie. Are you prepared?"

The wiry little man held up the slender ice pick in his gloved hand and smiled. "It's as good as done, Ari." He lowered the sharpened steel to his side.

"Samuel," said Ari, "are you ready?"

Their eyes met and Cohen nodded solemnly.

"Very well. I leave you now." He donned a pair of fake glasses and a cap and slipped calmly from the van. He shut the door behind him and began a measured stroll to the bookstore which would put him opposite the café's terrace when the van arrived.

"Showtime," mumbled Burt Swanson to himself. The former sergeant pressed the phony beard and mustache against his flesh one more time. He shifted into gear and pulled into the road. He drove slowly to the café and turned into the small gravel lot. Swanson pulled the vehicle between the black Mercedes and the café, blocking the Corsican's view of Weismann's sedan.

The Corsican glanced up briefly as the Peugeot rolled to a stop. He saw two elderly men exit the vehicle. One steadied himself on a cane; the other, a bearded, stooped man, cradled a plaster cast on his left arm. Weismann's bodyguard saw no threat and returned to his beer and newspaper.

"Now, Sollie! Go!" hissed Swanson as he shut the driver's door behind him.

The little man, ice pick hidden in his right sleeve, slipped from the van and crouched between the two vehicles. He used the Peugeot's shape to cover his move to the left rear of the Mercedes and knelt as if to tighten a shoelace. When he was certain he was not being watched he let the ice pick drop from his right sleeve into his gloved hand and braced himself. He drove the pick into the tread and wiggled the blade to deepen the puncture.

When he wrenched the pick free, he heard a soft hiss of escaping air and the left rear tire began to slowly sag. Satisfied with his handiwork, Soleski slipped the steel pick back into his sleeve, and still in a crouch, retreated, keeping the van's profile between himself and patrons at the café. He backed toward a stand of trees defining the rear of the parking lot and turned sideways behind a gnarled trunk to avoid discovery.

His part done, Soleski walked unhurriedly around the rear of an adjacent brick building and headed back to the village's main road. He was to walk east until picked up by his co-conspirators. Sollie felt his heart racing and he talked softly to calm himself as he approached the eastern limits of Bois-les-Bains. He willed himself not to look back.

While Soleski had been at work, Swanson and Cohen nonchalantly skirted the low hedge along the parking lot's border and pushed open the café's iron gate. They took a shaded corner table where they had stopped two nights ago.

The proprietor approached them and Swanson ordered two beers. Cohen, tinted glasses in place, one hand on his cane prop, tried not to look at the corner table where Ullrich and Wiesmann sat. Swanson, his back to the Germans, leaned forward to warn Cohen to avert his eyes, but Cohen felt compelled to study his target.

"You're gonna blow this, Sam, goddamnit," sputtered Swanson.

When their server appeared with their drinks, Cohen lowered his head.

When the waiter left, Cohen focused on the Arkansan's face. "What time is it, Burt?"

"Five-twenty, Sam. Relax."

"Where the hell is Peter," groused Cohen. "He should be here by now."

"He's right behind you, but don't even think of turning around."

Peter Noble had slipped behind a trio of riders on the outskirts of town and now dropped off as they pedaled past the café. He wore black spandex shorts and a loud, yellow-and-white-striped polyester shirt. Stylish, wrap-around sunglasses hid his eyes, his costume a duplicate of the other riders who had been passing through the village since mid-morning. Peter walked his bike to the iron gate and propped it outside along the hedge, then strolled to an empty table and wriggled free of a small, dark blue backpack. He casually slipped the bag over one shoulder. Though he had ridden less than two hundred yards, he feigned exhaustion and stripped off his bike helmet to douse himself with the contents of a water bottle. He kept his mirrored sunglasses in place.

None of the patrons gave the exhausted cyclist a second glance. Even Weismann's bodyguard, normally supicious of all strangers, ignored the rider.

Peter shook the water from his auburn locks and sank into a chair across from Cohen and Swanson. He ignored them and began to knead his calves as though he were simply a biker relieving cramped muscles.

Cohen noted with satisfaction that Peter had not removed his biking gloves. A server approached and the younger Noble ordered a Schweppes.

When the man returned with the bottle and a glass, Peter dropped a ten Euro note on the tray and told him to keep the remainder. Before his waiter turned away, he made a point of asking where the café's toilet was located. The man pointed down the hallway and the cyclist, bag over one shoulder, rose from his chair, leaving his drink untouched next to his bike helmet. He passed under the stone archway with its clock and went down the short corridor to the varnished door. He stepped inside the lavatory and shut the door.

He was alone.

Peter stripped off his sunglasses and glanced at his watch. Five-thirty. His eyes adjusted to the light. He slipped inside the single stall and locked the door. He worked rapidly, but calmly. Sitting on the stool's wooden rim, he pulled the nylon bag from his shoulder, then quickly zipped open the pouch and gripped the silenced Ruger, which was bundled in a dark rag.

Noble unwrapped the weapon and dipped the rag into the bowl. He drew it out and twisted the rag to wring out excess water.

He carefully rewrapped the loaded pistol in the rag and placed it on the floor behind the bowl. The dark cloth completely covered the weapon and Peter smiled, confident no one would investigate the foul-looking cloth. He zipped the nylon bag shut and put it back on his shoulder, then quickly exited the stall.

Peter looked back to make sure the wrapped pistol could not be easily seen. Satisfied, he went through the door, past the bar, and took his seat at the table with his drink.

He waited five agonizing minutes, then drank half the bottle's contents. Peter read his watch, then replaced his biking helmet and nodded at Swanson.

He retrieved his bike from the hedge and walked it through the café's iron gate. He pointed the bicycle east along the main road and was overjoyed to see a single file of five riders heading in the same direction. The cover would be perfect. He hailed the passing riders, and they returned his wave.

He slipped his feet into the stirrups and began pumping furiously to catch them. He closed the distance to the riders, but deliberately trailed them out of town. When he passed the last building in the village, Peter slowed to let the distance grow between himself and the other cyclists.

At a stretch in the road, Peter whistled as he glided past Soleski, but he did not stop or look back. In less than a halfkilometer, he left the road to the border and turned north on a hard gravel spur to double back to the farm where Ehud and his grandfather waited.

He set a torrid pace and reached the farm ahead of schedule.

# CHAPTER SIXTY

## BOIS-LES-BAINS CAFÉ

"It's time, Sam." Burt Swanson stared across the small table at Samuel Cohen.

It was ten minutes to six. Cohen took several deep breaths and nodded.

"Take your time," whispered the former sergeant. "Don't miss."

Cohen rose slowly from the table. "I won't."

"Remember to walk straight to the van across the street, Sam. We'll be there for you."

Cohen grasped his cane and hobbled convincingly toward the café's toilet.

Swanson pulled a twenty Euro bill from his breast pocket and quickly slipped it under the stem of his empty beer glass. His right hand moved too fast for anyone to see the thin, flesh-colored latex glove he wore. He waited two minutes, then left the table.

Weismann's Corsican bodyguard folded his newspaper and finished his beer. When the man set down his empty glass, Swanson was already approaching the parked van. He climbed in and started the engine.

As he backed out and turned to leave, Swanson saw the Corsican crossing the terrace toward the gate. Swanson was sweating, worried his disguise would peel away at any moment.

He backed up and drove slowly from the lot. Swanson turned onto the village's main road and then right, onto the first side street past the café. He circled the block and brought the van back to the main road.

He parked, pointed west along the road. Swanson sat in the idling van, across from the bookstore where Ari continued to browse among stacks of old books lining the shop's window. Ari looked toward the van and nodded once to let Swanson know he was aware of his presence.

The old sergeant gripped the wheel tightly, his heart pounding. Perspiration dripped into his eyes and he blinked to focus on the café. He dared a glance at the parking lot.

The bodyguard had discovered the flat and was circling the sedan, checking the other tires, and cursing. The big man went over to the hedge and called to the Germans, gesturing at the disabled Mercedes. Weismann blithely waved to his bodyguard, acknowledging the problem, and resumed his conversation with the old SS veteran.

The Corsican bodyguard went back to the Mercedes and opened the car's trunk to get tools and a spare tire. He laid aside his jacket and began jacking up the car to change the flat.

Swanson cranked up the van's air conditioning and looked at his watch.

Five minutes to go.

## CHAPTER SIXTY-ONE

In the lavatory, Cohen locked himself in the single stall and straddled the wooden toilet seat. He hung his cane on the door hook and leaned over to tug at the filthy-looking rag stuffed behind the porcelain stool.

Cohen grasped the Ruger and put it in his lap. He listened for footfalls. Nothing.

Cohen gripped the pistol in his right hand and flipped off the safety. His watch showed one minute to six. Sweat began beading on his forehead.

Someone approached. He breathed slowly to ready himself.

The lavatory door opened. A shadow hesitated on the threshold.

Cohen coughed loudly, then reached behind him to pull the chain. A growl of rushing water from the mounted tank echoed off the tiled walls. The flushing sound drowned out the stranger's footsteps and a man's shadow passed in front of the stall's locked door.

Cohen imagined Weismann stepping to the urinal, steadying himself at the receptacle.

One last deep breath and Cohen was on his feet.

He raised the Ruger, unlocked the wooden door with his left hand and stepped out into the small room.

The German was in the corner, his feet apart, his back to the American.

Cohen raised the pistol in both hands and steadied his aim. "Von Wurtz," he hissed.

The smaller man turned slightly as if he had not understood the question. He saw the outstretched arms and the pistol steadied in both hands. The Ruger was less than a foot from the German's face and his expression was suddenly one of fear, which pleased Cohen.

"For Lieutenant Pressman and the others."

"Pardon?" The German saw the silencer and opened his mouth to scream.

Cohen fired two quick shots.

The first round hit Weismann in his forehead, the second, at the bridge of his nose. The German folded against the plaster wall. His back arched, then he slid down into a crumpled shape, his sightless eyes wide in terror, his gold wire spectacles bent and bloodied. One hand dropped into the urinal's drain, the other flopped lifelessly on the dirty tiles. The back of Weismann's head was a shattered egg, the wall behind him smeared with blood and brain.

Cohen stood transfixed at what he had done.

The acrid smell of cordite burned his nostrils and his knees felt unsteady.

He was jolted into action by noises in the kitchen beyond the door. Had someone heard?

Cohen robotically set the weapon's safety and tucked the Ruger in his belt, under his jacket.. He hurried to leave. He briefly looked in the oval mirror over the small sink.

Specks of dark red dotted his face. He ran the faucet to rinse off Weismann's blood, then used a towel to daub at drops on his jacket and shirt. He wiped the faucets, countertop and the stall's door handle and lock before tossing the towel.

Cohen was halfway out the door when he remembered his cane, left behind in the stall. He lost a precious minute retrieving it and nervously emerged from the lavatory as a hobbling old man. Cohen moved steadily past the bar and empty dining room.

From the corner of his eye, Cohen saw Weissmann's bodyguard stowing tools in the Mercedes. Felix Ullrich was standing at the terrace's hedge, heckling the big Corsican's efforts. Both men were laughing as the bodyguard slipped behind the sedan's steering wheel and started the engine. He wheeled the big sedan from the lot as Cohen passed under the arched doorway, the front gate now just a few feet away.

Across the street, in the book shop, Ari observed Cohen leaving the café. He put down the volume he had been reading and started across the road. As expected, the Corsican parked the Mercedes at the café's gate to wait for Weismann. So far, the plan had worked perfectly.

Ari had just reached the Peugeot when the scheme collapsed.

As Cohen reached the gate, Swanson watched in alarm as a patron headed for the toilet.

Seconds later, the man burst from the latrine screaming. "Murder! Help! Police!"

The old SS sergeant-major sprinted toward the lavoratory. On the café's terrace, patrons rose from their chairs in confusion. Cohen reached the van and scrambled into a seat as Ullrich exited the café's arch, shrieking.

"Assassins! They've killed Hauptmann Weismann!"

The old warrior frantically waved his bloodied hands and stumbled toward the idling Mercedes. The Corsican saw Ullrich's crimson palms and instantly knew the reason. He flung open his door and looked around frantically as Ullrich grabbed at him, babbling loudly.

Karl questioned the dazed soldier for details.

Ari ordered Swanson to drive away.

"GO! GO! Now, Swanson!" he barked, drawing a pistol from his waistband. "Drive normally, don't attract attention!"

On the terrace, stunned witnesses looked on in panic at Ullrich and the bodyguard. Even as the big man yelled questions at the grizzled SS veteran, the Corsican scanned the scene. The Peugeot van pulling from the curb immediately drew his eye. The bodyguard wrenched himself from Ullrich's grasp and stepped into the road, holding up his hands, signaling the vehicle to stop.

"HALT!" The big man blocked the road. The Corsican approached the van warily.

"GET DOWN!" yelled Swanson. "EVERYONE DOWN!" He floored the accelerator and headed directly at the bodyguard.

"Halt!" bellowed the Corsican.

Swanson pulled the steering wheel to the left and roared past. The van's mirror caught the bodyguard's shoulder and shattered as the big man threw himself to one side. He hit the ground hard and instinctively rolled to avoid the van's wheels. Swanson ducked below the dashboard, steering by feel as the car clipped the bodyguard.

The Peugeot skidded down the street and glanced off a parked car in a crunching blow. The impact dented the door but did not slow Swanson's panicked flight. He bolted upright in the driver's seat and fought to regain control.

"GET UP! We're safe, we're safe!" He brushed splinters of broken mirror from his lap. The Peugeot van hurtled down the roadway, tires squealing, and cleared the village. Ari let out his breath and put away his pistol. Cohen looked back. People were moving toward the café where the Mercedes idled at the gate, the enraged Corsican on his hands and knees in the dust.

## CHAPTER SIXTY-TWO

With Weismann dead, the clock became the enemy.

At a bend in the road to Thionville, Swanson took a hard right and careened along a gravel track toward the river. At Ari's direction, Swanson turned again along a secondary road and accelerated. They skirted the north limits of the village and headed east, the opposite direction of their initial flight.

Once past the town limits, Swanson turned south on Ari's command and picked up the main route leading to the German border. There was no traffic on the paved road and they raced unseen for a kilometer, slowing only at the sight of a lone figure walking by the side of the road. It was Soleski. The van stopped and the little man climbed aboard. They sped away, following the same gravel road Peter had biked twenty minutes earlier.

"What happened?!" yelled Soleski.

"Some problems on the way out," answered Swanson curtly.

"How'd it go, Sam?" Soleski asked as the van accelerated.

Cohen smiled weakly and looked out the window without answering. He tugged the Ruger from his belt and gave the pistol to Ari.

"He did the job," said Ari, glancing at the brooding Cohen.

"Well, that's it then!" said Soleski. "We're done!"

Ari turned grim. "Ah, not quite. Now comes another hard stage, gentlemen. We haven't much time to ensure your escape before the net closes."

In the courtyard, Ehud paced nervously, glancing occasionally at his watch. Noble stood by the blue Mercedes, its four doors open, waiting.

The large black BMW motorcycle was poised like a sculpture without riders. Two gray helmets sat atop the touring bike's seat, a tan jacket draped from the handlebars.

Ehud planted himself in front of Noble. The big man put his hands on his hips. "You have checked the sleeping rooms as I asked you?"

"Yes. I told you, I've been over the space with a fine-tooth comb."

"We must have no traces to show we were here, Mr. Noble."

"Of course. I understand completely. I wiped down every inch of the place."

"They should be here by now," groused the large man. He went to the farmhouse doorway and talked to the owner, who had emerged with a large plastic bag. Ehud followed the man to a newly dug rectangular ditch in the swine corral. The pit was eight feet deep with a towering pile of soil and manure ringing the hole. Clouds of flies hovered above the offal. The farmer pitched the bag into the deep hole and mounted a tractor sitting on the edge of the cavity. He fired up the engine, ready to back-fill on a moment's notice.

The owner's son, dressed in cycling gear, emerged from the weathered barn and nonchalantly walked across the yard to the high wall where he relieved himself against the stones. He tightened the chin strap of his bike helmet and waited.

"Rider coming in!" the farmer yelled from his perch.

Peter sprinted up the gravel driveway and jumped off his bike.

Ehud rushed to meet him. "Quick, make the change!" ordered Ari's partner.

"Peter, thank God you're here." Noble reached to touch his grandson. "How did everything . . ."

Peter interrupted. "Okay, I think. But I heard a crash. Don't know what that was all about." He stripped off his clothing and tossed his things into the pit. Ehud stood to one side, passing clean clothing to Peter who dressed quickly. He tossed the biking helmet into the hole with his clothes. Ehud grabbed the tan coat from the BMW's handlebars and threw it to Peter.

He slipped into the jacket and embraced his grandfather. "See you in Bastogne, Gramps."

"We'll be there, kiddo."

Ehud jammed a visored helmet on his head and handed the other one to Peter. The large man threw his right leg over the seat and cranked the motorcycle into life. The powerful engine purred. Peter, helmet in place, climbed behind Ehud. Both men dropped their visors, and Ehud slipped the touring bike into gear. The pair went down the gravel driveway and headed east.

Peter's arrival and flight aboard the motorcycle had taken only four minutes.

The farmer yelled a warning. "Van arriving!"

The motorcycle's riders waved as they passed the inbound Peugeot. Noble went to the blue Mercedes and crawled into the middle of the back seat. The battered beige van roared into the courtyard. It skidded to a stop in a shower of gravel and the passengers scrambled out.

Swanson went to the rear of the vehicle where Ari was already opening the cargo door. The men folded down the rear seats. The farmer's son pushed Peter's bike inside, then jogged to the driver's seat. He pulled out of the courtyard without a word being spoken and headed east.

Ari carried the stage props to the pit and tossed them into the hole. Glasses, cane, wigs, linens, things the visitors had touched or thought they had touched. Everything tumbled into the bottom of the hole next to Peter's biking gear and the black plastic bags. Ari embraced their host as Soleski and Cohen joined Noble in the big car's back seat.

Adrenaline was coursing through Swanson's body. "Let's go, let's go!" he bellowed from the sedan's front passenger seat.

Ari climbed behind the wheel of the blue Mercedes and accelerated out of the farmyard. The farm's owner immediately began pushing piles of dirt and manure into the gaping hole. He raked the dirt into a low mound. When he finished, he cut the tractor's engine and climbed down to reposition fencing, allowing his pigs to roam freely in their enclosure. He hauled a load of slop for the pigs now happily rooting in their restored pen.

# CHAPTER SIXTY-THREE

### MOSELLE RIVER, GERMAN BORDER, JUNE 6

Eight minutes ahead of Ari and the men in the Mercedes, Ehud and Peter followed the Moselle River east through a last picturesque French border village, Apach.

The BMW bike cruised north along the Route de Trèves, the French road marked as N153 on Ehud's map. The motorcycle paralleled railroad tracks curving along the river. Their route took them past several barges, leisurely churning their way west into France, and smaller boats headed downstream into Germany. It seemed more of a pleasurable road trip than an escape.

Ehud turned, raised his dark visor and shouted over his shoulder. "Deutschland now for a short time!"

Peter nodded. He trusted Ehud. He had to. The landscape gave no hint of borders to him. Peter thought the belt of trees lining the sinuous river beautiful, reminiscent of the St. Croix back home along the Minnesota-Wisconsin border. A lifetime ago.

Not much farther and the road's name changed to Am Dreilandereck. Ehud leaned left through a deserted intersection to pick up an elevated span that crossed the rail lines. Two minutes later, they rode over the Moselle River into Luxembourg. They pushed on, the touring bike purring effortlessly.

A half-kilometer behind them, the van—with its cargo of a single bike—was passing through Apach. Just after leaving the French border village, however, the driver took a right-hand fork and continued toward the larger town of Perl, just inside Germany's border.

He had been paid to take the van all the way to Saarbrucken where the chances of its being stolen were almost guaranteed. The farmer's son decided a quiet street in Perl would serve the purpose just as well. Besides, a description of the van with its shattered mirror and damaged door would likely be broadcast soon and the less time spent in the suspect vehicle the better. Abandoning the vehicle in Perl also meant a shorter ride home.

The driver slowed as he entered the town, looking for suitable places to ditch the Peugeot. On the north side of the town, he found what he was looking for.

A quiet neighborhood with cars and similar vans lined a shaded street. He stopped behind a parked delivery van and waited for a few minutes. He turned off the engine, left the keys in the ignition and walked to the back of the vehicle. He lifted the bike from the van and closed the door, then mounted the bicycle and rode toward the Moselle River.

The plan was for someone to find the van with its keys and steal the Peugeot.

At least, that was the plan. But the good inhabitants of Perl had been misjudged. That they would be adverse to such thievery had not occurred to the farmer's son.

It was to be a costly miscalculation.

He picked up his pace and peddled to Bois-les-Bains without seeing any riders. By the time the lone cyclist had returned to France, the blue Mercedes sedan and its five passengers were already entering Luxembourg.

## CHAPTER SIXTY-FOUR

In Bois-les-Bains, the Corsican rose from the pavement, holding his bruised side. He grimaced in pain, certain one or more of his ribs might be broken.

The small crowd parted for him as he limped toward the cafe. Ullrich was talking to someone as the bodyguard approached.

"Felix," rasped the big man, "we need to look after Herr Weismann."

The shaken SS man broke off his conversation with the bystander. "Of course."

He followed the bodyguard into the café where a knot of people stood looking into the lavatory, gaping at the murdered man. The Corsican glowered at the onlookers, pushed them aside and entered.

"You should wait for the police," warned the café's owner.

"Get out of his way," growled Ullrich.

The proprietor threw up his hands and yelled for someone to call the police. "It's been done," replied one of his staff. "Then where are they?" screamed the owner. "Call them again!"

Ullrich shut the door behind the Corsican and stood guard in the corridor.

In the lavatory, the bodyguard squatted next to Weismann's crumpled form. He grimaced in pain as he reached inside the breast pocket of the dead man's coat and withdrew a small green notebook and gold key. He stood and pocketed the items.

"He never had a chance," said the Corsican softly. He opened the door.

"What do you think?" asked Ullrich.

The big man lowered his voice. "It has the look of a professional job, Felix."

They looked back at the small room, down at Weismann's body. Outside, the high-pitched warble of police sirens grew louder.

"Keep your thoughts to yourself, Felix," whispered the big man.

"Ya, and look after yourself, Karl," said the old soldier, calling the bodyguard by name.

The Corsican leaned close to the old soldier's ear, his voice low. "Do you still have friends about?"

The grizzled veteran nodded.

"Good," said the bodyguard. "Find out who sheltered these men. It had to be somewhere close. Can you do that for me . . . for Herr Weismann?"

"Of course. I'll start immediately."

"Thank you, Felix. We cannot let this go unpunished. You understand?"

"On my honor."

The Corsican and the SS man walked out onto the terrace and sat down.

Four uniformed gendarmes jumped from a pair of police cars. A larger car with plainclothesmen pulled into the parking lot and two grim-faced detectives got out. One of the men hustled to open the rear door for the third passenger, a tall somber-looking gentleman with a shock of gray hair and a neatly trimmed mustache. From the deference paid him it was obvious he was senior. The tall policeman immediately took charge and began barking rapid orders. The policemen started herding witnesses onto the terrace.

The commanding officer walked briskly past gawkers being held back by two officers. As he passed by the outdoor tables, he glanced quickly at Ullrich and the seated Corsican. He summoned one of the plainclothesmen, and the two men disappeared into the lavatory.

Ten minutes passed, and when he emerged he began asking questions. The café's owner prattled on, gesturing with his hands, pointing again and again at Ullrich and Karl. The commander waved away the proprietor and whispered to one of his men.

The officer came over to the seated bodyguard. "Which of you was security to the victim?" The Corsican nodded, raised his hand.

"Name?"

"Rocca. Karl Rocca." The bodyguard flinched and pressed his hand against his side.

The policeman looked down. "Were you hurt, monsieur?"

Ullrich answered for him. "He tried to stop the assassins. They ran him down."

The detective pursed his lips, unmoved. He turned to the German. "And you are?"

The old soldier nodded in the direction of the lavatory. "A friend of the victim."

"Name, please."

"Felix Ullrich."

"And did you see everything, Monsieur Ullrich?" The old soldier nodded and sank into a chair. The cop looked over his shoulder at his superior. "Please do not leave the premises. Commandant Dupré will want to talk to you." He saw the Corsican wince in pain again.

"Do you require medical attention?"

Karl looked up, dismissed the comment with a shake of his bowed head.

"The bastards tried to kill him with their van," snarled Ullrich.

The policeman returned to Dupré's side to read his notes to the senior officer.

An ambulance arrived and parked, blocking the road. A stream of cyclists slowed, stared at the crowds and peddled slowly away, weaving among the pedestrians. More residents drifted toward the small café, drawn by word of the killing.

Another police van arrived and a half dozen gendarmes in military uniforms spilled out, armed with FAMAS automatic rifles. Dupré's deputy began assigning the newcomers in pairs to secure the scene. A pair of motorcycle police glided to a stop outside the café's iron gate and began directing traffic.

A forensics photographer arrived to take pictures of the crime scene. Flashes from his strobes lighted the hallway and lavatory. More crime lab people arrived. They combed the water closet and café for clues. Police personnel filled the small, plastered room, stepping carefully over and around Weismann's corpse.

Police Commandant Henri Dupré remained an unruffled, methodical presence. He took a table inside the café and was served an espresso while he listened to his staff report their findings. With a heavy gold pen, he took notes in a small, black leather book. Occasionally, he looked up to ask a question. He answered several calls on his cell phone, talking respectfully to his questioners on the other end. The queries were obviously from someone much higher in the police hierarchy.

Dupré delegated preliminary interviewing to his second-in-command. The detective, a dapper, handsome man with a long face and dark eyes, affected a brisk, perfunctory manner, deciding whom to send to his senior for further questioning. One of the gendarmes brought Dupré's chief deputy a pair of witnesses, nervous visitors from Brittany, who volunteered cell phone photos taken of the killers' van. The license tab numbers were relayed to headquarters immediately.

With each statement taken, phone numbers and addresses noted and IDs checked, the pool of actual witnesses began to thin. All were eventually released with warnings of being called back for further meetings if needed. Dusk was just beginning to fall when the senior man finally called Ullrich and the Corsican for separate interrogations in the café's dining room.

The old soldier went first. After a battery of questions, Ullrich was cautioned to remain available, then driven home by a policeman. As the bodyguard was being escorted to his interview with Dupré, the gurney with Weismann's draped corpse was wheeled past him to the waiting ambulance. The big man paused to watch the loading of his employer's body, and then told his story of the shooting and his attempt to stop the killers.

Dupré was intrigued by the bodyguard's story. "The proprietor says you went into the lavatory before the police arrived. Why did you do that?"

"I had to see Herr Weismann one last time. He was like family to me."

The policeman accepted the comment, frowned and made a note on his pad.

Dupré's senior aide stood off to one side, scribbling as the Corsican talked. The bodyguard went over his recollections twice, patiently narrating the day's events, correcting small details that contradicted what others had said about his actions. Dupré interrupted only once to have a member of the medical team examine the Corsican's battered torso to make sure he could be released without seeing a doctor.

It was dark when the bodyguard was finally allowed to leave in his Mercedes. He was told to appear Monday morning in Thionville for more questions. Dupré's team was also investigating a counterfeiting ring in the city and would be there most of the day. The Corsican promised them everything just to get away.

It was dark when the bodyguard arrived at the château and he cursed the police for costing him valuable time better spent running down the assassins. He dialed Ullrich's number and left a message for the German to call him.

Madame Cheroux listened ashen-faced as the bodyguard, Karl, told her of the shooting. They were now effectively both without jobs. The Frenchwoman knew she would likely have to leave the estate once Weismann's business associates got wind of his death.

This was not something she had foreseen. "Mon Dieu, Karl, who would do such a thing?"

He could only shrug, shake his head. At first he said nothing, kept his thoughts to himself, fuming at his negligence. "I should have been more alert. Should have watched more closely. I should have been armed."

"Perhaps, Karl. But who could know such things would happen? Do you think it was God's will?"

He stared at the little woman, incredulous at her remark. "What rubbish!" he roared. "Don't think such foolish things, madame!"

The woman bowed her head at his scolding. "But what are we to do now? Where should we go?"

His head hurt and the woman's whining wasn't helping. He had to get away. "We continue as before until we are told otherwise, Madame Cheroux."

"But what about you, Karl? What will you do?"

The Corsican shrugged, drew in a sharp painful breath. His entire body ached. He stood, towering over the housekeeper. "The police will want to talk with me Monday. I will have to go to Thionville." He looked at her. "They may want to ask you some questions as well. Routine."

She began to sob softly and Karl steadied himself on the chair. A new mission was already forming in his thoughts. "I'm going to wash up. Can you fix me something light to eat?"

The housekeeper was glad to be given a task.

"Nothing fancy, madame. I'll take it in the kitchen when it's ready." He limped out the side door and crossed the courtyard to his apartment.

# CHAPTER SIXTY-FIVE

## WEISMANN ESTATE

Karl stripped off his clothes and stepped under the shower. He let the hot water run over him for long minutes, then toweled himself dry. In the mirror, he gingerly ran his hand down a large dark bruise the length of his side, then dressed in clean clothes. He crossed to the main house, accompanied by the estate's watchdogs. Both animals followed him into the kitchen where his supper waited. For once, Madame Cheroux suffered the dogs in her domain, letting them curl at Karl's feet as she hovered over him during his meal.

When he was finished he stood and faced the small woman. "Thank you. I was famished, more than I thought, considering the day's events."

"Yes, I can understand the shock, Karl."

"I intend to use Herr Weismann's office for the rest of this evening, madame."

He paused at the kitchen door to caution her against interruptions. "I wish not to be disturbed," he said.

The gray-haired woman had barely heard him. She was nodding through tears.

The former legionnaire, trailed by the dogs, crossed the front hall to the château's study. He locked the oak door behind him and drew the drapes across the tall windows. The Dobermans settled into a corner to watch as Karl eased himself down into the soft leather chair at Weismann's desk and fished the gold key from his shirt pocket along with the small green leather notebook. He reached for a hidden button underneath the desk corner and pushed it.

A click sounded and a set of drawers unlocked. He drew open the second drawer and removed a black metal box. Inserting the gold key, Karl opened the lid to reveal pairs of colored notebooks, identical in size to the one on the desk. Choosing the lone green one, he placed it on the desk beside its twin and flipped them both open to the last page in each book. Columns of numbers in Weismann's tight, familiar script covered the lined paper.

A knock came at the study door. Both dogs raised their heads and growled.

The bodyguard froze. The police? He covered the books with a laptop computer and swiveled toward the door. "Yes, what is it?"

Madame Cheroux's reedy voice pierced the oak. "Karl, I have something for you."

He eased himself from the chair and hobbled to the door. He cracked it open. The woman held a tray with a glass of water, a bottle of cognac and a bottle of pills. He swung open the door.

"I thought you might need something to ease your pain," she said. She set the lacquered oriental tray on the desk and faced him, hands folded.

"I told you I was not to be disturbed, Madame Cheroux."

"Yes, but you should rest, Karl. You're hurt."

He nodded, forced a smile. "I've known pain before, madame. This is quite bearable."

She looked around the room, noticed the computer. "What are you doing, Karl?"

He went back to the desk and sat down wearily. "I'm trying to get things in order as he would have wanted."

"But . . . this is the master's office, Karl."

"Herr Weismann and I had certain arrangements. Contingencies, if you will." He stopped talking, watched her studying him.

"I never heard the master mention things of this sort, Karl."

The big man got up again and came around the desk. He put his arm around the housekeeper's shoulders, her tiny frame lost in his embrace. "He provided for you, for us, madame, for such an emergency. Trust me."

She looked into his broad face with its scarred nose and hard eyes. "What are we to do?" she whispered.

Karl ushered her to the door. "You will see. You will not be forgotten. Now, you must excuse me, I have a lot of work to do yet tonight before I can rest."

She stood on the threshold, her eyes pleading. "Tomorrow I will fix your favorite breakfast, Karl. Everything you like."

He smiled at her attempt to soothe him. "Thank you, Madame Cheroux. I would enjoy that. But for now, goodnight."

"Goodnight, Karl."

When she was gone, he locked the door.

The Corsican sat at the desk and compared the pages in the books. As a precaution, Weismann had tutored him annually about these codes. He held both books in one hand and walked over to an ornate gilded mirror set at eye level on the opposite wall above a small antique writing desk. Karl tugged at the mirror's frame and it came away from the wall, revealing a steel safe set into the oak paneling. He rotated the dial according to the numbers. It took three attempts but eventually the vault yielded, and he yanked it open. The safe's door, thirteen inches square, hid a metal box two feet deep.

Karl stepped back and stared at Weismann's treasury. Though he had been privy to the security codes, he had never seen the safe's interior. The hidden bank was completely stuffed with wrapped blocks of currency. He wrestled a thick stack of money from the safe and thumbed its corners. All the bills were one hundred Euro notes. Two hundred bills to a stack. He leaned against the rich oak paneling and caught his breath.

At the desk, Karl poured himself three fingers worth of cognac into a tumbler. He drained the glass and poured another. He shook two pain pills from the pharmacy bottle and swallowed them. A glass of water, followed by more cognac. His pain began to ease. *Perhaps his imagination? Maybe it was the money.*

He cleared Weismann's desk, and began stacking bricks of currency. The surface was soon covered with neatly aligned rows of money. When the safe was empty, he began counting. Forty wrapped stacks of crisp one hundred Euro notes. Eight hundred thousand in new bills. Karl teased one bill from a brick and held it up to the light. It was genuine. He softly repeated the sum. Eight hundred thousand.

The bodyguard rose and steadied himself against the desk. He raised his glass. "To you, Herr Weismann! To your memory! To your revenge!"

The phone rang. He recoiled at the ringing. Recovering, he sat down and pulled the phone to him. "Yes, who is calling?"

"It's Felix. Are you alone?"

"Of course, go ahead."

"I've found some news that will interest you. Two things."

Karl thumbed the edges on a stack of bills in front of him. "I'm listening."

"The first concerns a certain party you asked about earlier."

"I'm impressed, Felix. That was quick."

"In a town this size, it's not hard to find out who visitors are, where they stay."

Karl leaned back in the big chair and drummed his fingers on bundled currency.

Ullrich's thick voice rasped in the receiver. "People buy provisions, you know. Grocers like to gossip as well as anyone."

Karl sat upright in the big chair. "You have a name, a location?"

"Yes, it's not far from here. A father and son. Can you make a note?"

The Corsican found a pen and a sheet of writing paper in the middle drawer He wrote the directions quickly and read them back to Ullrich. "I'll stop to see them first thing tomorrow."

"Be careful, Karl. The police will be back in the morning for more interviews."

"I'm expected in Thionville Monday morning," replied the Corsican. " Perhaps these people might tell me something before the authorities have a chance to talk to them."

"Exactly. You do realize the police will eventually want to interview them."

"Well, then, I'll just have to call on them first, won't I?"

The German's voice abruptly took on a menacing tone. "Will you need help? I have old friends here. Men such as myself."

Karl thought about the offer for a minute. *Not a bad idea as a precaution.* "Very well, Felix, but I think perhaps just you and I should make this particular call. Can you be ready in three hours?" he asked the German.

"You can count on me, I'll be waiting."

"You mentioned two things. What is the other?"

"Yes, of course. I apologize. I must be getting old. Have you watched the news?"

"No, what's happened?"

"They found the assassin's van just across the border."

The bodyguard sat up straight at the news. "Where? How far?"

The German warmed to his tale. "In Perl. Do you know it?" Karl did not.

"Just inside the border. Maybe two kilometers. It was on a residential street."

"Who found it?"

"The police. A hausfrau saw a man leave it there. He was a cyclist. Just left it there in the open. It had a shattered mirror but, of course, you knew that." Ullrich continued. "She told the police the man rode off. You know, the farmer's son is a cyclist."

The link was too obvious to ignore. "You have good sources, Felix."

"Everyone likes to talk, Karl. Even lowly policemen like to feel important."

"You have done well." The bodyguard stroked a block of money. *Why not draw in the old soldier?* "You should know Hauptmann Weismann provided for you."

There was a pause. "Bless his soul, Karl. He was a good friend."

"Now we must try to avenge him, yes, Felix?"

"Without pity," said the German.

Karl glanced at the ornate clock. "We've already lost too much precious time."

"Very well, Karl. I'll ask around some more. See what else I dig up."

"No, no, you've done enough for a dozen men, Felix. Don't tip our hand further."

"Of course. Until tomorrow?"

"Yes. And from now on, Felix, let's talk only on the mobile phones, yes?"

"Goodnight then, Karl."

Karl rang off and ran his hands over the fortune in front of him. Even at this late hour his mind was racing, putting pieces together in his puzzle. *Madame Cheroux's silence could be bought with a decent sum of Weismann's money. Say, twenty thousand. That was a sizable sum and would ensure the French housekeeper's loyalty. What about the old SS sergeant-major?* wondered Karl.

He could afford to be generous to the veteran. Seventy-five thousand. Even that amount would not be missed from the treasure in front of him. *Yes*, he decided. *The sum sounded right.* The German could be a valuable asset. He would know how to extract information from the father and son. If they learned something of the killers, it would make sense to turn the old soldier loose. The SS man would track without stopping if there was a scent to uncover.

Karl smiled at the thought of sending the German on his way. He would draw the authorities away from the Corsican. Then, when the investigation went away, the bodyguard could realize his dream of returning to his island home. Back to the coast town of Bonaficio with its bay full of fishing boats and the villas on the hills above the historic town. A man could disappear on Corsica. It had been done before. His fortune would go a long way on the island. He smiled at the thought of hiring his own bodyguard.

He set aside the housekeeper's money and bundled Ullrich's seventy-five thousand into a black nylon bag. They would be given their share in the morning. Karl tossed one brick of currency back into the safe and closed the door, leaving it unlocked. The police would find it if they looked hard enough. That would throw them off temporarily and he would not miss the decoy. The rest of the money went into a worn leather briefcase. In the morning he would toss it into the trunk of the Mercedes, along with his mechanic's overalls and a set of tools.

Hiding such a treasure in plain sight appealed to him.

## CHAPTER SIXTY-SIX

### COURBET FARM, BOIS-LES-BAINS, JUNE 7

The driver of the black sedan killed the headlights and coasted to a stop.

Two figures dressed in dark clothing got out of the car and crept forward to a clump of trees at the corner of a high stone wall surrounding a farmyard. The first man carried a silenced 9mm Beretta with a fifteen-round magazine. The second man moved in the footsteps of his companion and held a much smaller Soviet PSM pistol. Neither of them anticipated having to use their weapons. Surprise and fear would be their tactic.

The men reached the farm's wall and hugged the rough stones. A dog barked twice. The two halted. They heard the canine sentinel padding toward them. The lead man raised his weapon and pointed it where the dog's head would appear. The animal came around the corner and Karl Rocca fired a single muffled shot that dropped the dog. He and Ullrich moved forward, stepping over the bundle of bloodied fur. The pair squeezed past the chained gate and moved quickly into the barn's deep shadows.

No lights appeared in the windows of the two-story stone house. The men crept to the large wooden door with its ancient lock. It did not open. Ullrich pocketed his pistol and pulled a leather pouch of metal tools from his jacket. He worked on the lock until it yielded. They entered the darkened house.

Motionless, they stood in a large kitchen. The Corsican signaled to his companion that he was going to check the first-floor rooms. He moved down the narrow corridor, his weapon held in front of him. The rooms were vacant. At the end of the hall, a large dormitory space also proved empty, a room with a dozen iron cots, each with its rolled mattress and pillow. He retreated down the hallway and pointed at the stairs.

Ullrich went up first, his pistol held high, close to his body. The Corsican followed slowly, hoping the ancient stairs would not give them away. They reached the landing. The German went to the right. The Corsican moved straight ahead to a large bedroom.

A naked man lay sprawled across an iron bed. The Corsican pulled a small penlight from his pocket and held it high, snapping on the beam. He aimed it at the sleeping man's eyes. Suddenly, he heard Ullrich bellowing at someone in one of the rooms across the hall. Probably the farmer's son, he thought.

The naked man stirred and Karl kicked the bed frame hard. The sleeper opened his eyes, squinting in the harsh light. He raised his right arm to shield his eyes. He saw only a man's silhouette and a silenced weapon pointed directly at him.

"Get up!" barked the Corsican. "We're going downstairs!"

"Mon Dieu, who are you?!" yelled the man. He reached for the sheet but the Corsican tore it from him and ordered him out of the room.

The farmer backed out of the room, his hands held above his head. Ullrich was already prodding the son down the stairs, his pistol at the frightened boy's neck. The barefoot youth wore only briefs and was shaking in fear. Ullrich told the son to put his face against the wall.

The Corsican ordered the father alongside the son. "Don't move!" he yelled.

He went to the dining room table and dragged two of its heavy chairs to the center of the kitchen. When the father glanced over his shoulder, the Corsican fired a shot into the plaster between the two men. "Keep your faces to the wall!"

The youth's tremors increased. The father was made of sterner stuff. Ullrich suggested they work on the boy first.

Karl grabbed the son by the hair and pulled him backwards into a chair. He took over guard duties while Ullrich taped the boy's arms and legs, wrapping the frightened youth until he was completely immobilized. Next, Karl pushed the naked man into a chair and guarded him as Ullrich wound tape around the farmer's limbs.

Ullrich tested the restraints. "He's not going anywhere."

Karl dragged the father's chair against the wall. The prisoners now faced each other. Karl tore off two lengths of tape and slapped them across each man's mouth. He took a pen from his pocket and stabbed small holes in the center of the tape covering each man's mouth. Immediately, the boy's breaths produced panicked, whistling sounds.

Ullrich filled a large copper tea kettle with water, carried it to the stove and took a wooden match from a ceramic holder. He spun one of the stove's dials and struck the match against the iron surface. A circle of blue flames danced softly in the dark kitchen. Ullrich set the copper vessel over the fire and sat down.

"We want some information from you," said Karl. "We don't have time to play games." He paced between the two prisoners. The son's terrified eyes followed him. "This week you had several guests in your home." He stopped in front of the boy and cupped the youth's chin in his hand. "We need to know how many they were, who they were, where they came from and where they went."

Steam curled from the kettle. Karl placed his silenced pistol on the counter. "If you understand me, nod your head." He caught the boy's pleading look at his father. The farmer's eyes were filled with rage. Silence. No movement from either man. A slow, faint whistle began leaking from the kettle.

Karl walked up to the youth and slapped him. Hard. "Did you hear me?!" Both heads bobbed. "Good, we understand each other."

Steam shrieked from the kettle and Ullrich rose to set the vessel aside.

"Keep in mind that my friend here is not as reasonable as I am," said Karl. "Did you harbor these men?"

Again, there was no response from the two.

Ullrich lifted the steaming kettle, walked to the naked man and poured a stream of boiling water into his lap.

A muffled scream erupted behind the father's taped mouth. His body snapped back and forth against his bonds. Cords on his neck bulged and his eyes closed in agony. His chair rocked violently, then went over on its side. The son witnessed his father's suffering and began crying.

Ullrich smiled and put the kettle back onto the stove.

Karl stepped to the youth and ripped the tape from his face.

"Yes, yes, yes, they were here!" babbled the youth. "They stayed here! Yes!"

They had been right to start with the boy. "How many?" growled the bodyguard.

"Seven. Yes, seven all together." He was shaking uncontrollably now.

"Where did they come from?"

"I don't know! Really! They contacted my father months ago!"

Karl yanked the boy's head back and yelled at him. "Names, did you hear names?! How did they address each other?!"

"One was called Ari. There was a Samuel and . . . and someone named Peter." The boy screamed his answers at his torturer between sobs. "Those are the only ones I heard! Believe me!"

The Corsican looked at Ullrich. "Did you hear him?"

The German nodded. The kettle began whistling from the stove. Ullrich turned down the flames.

Karl paced again. "Where did they go?"

"Something about Bastogne. Yes, Bastogne."

Something didn't fit. "Why Belgium?" the bodyguard asked Ullrich.

The German shrugged. "It's a small town. Shouldn't be hard to trace them."

"If they're still there," mused Karl. "Could it be a ruse?" Ullrich shrugged again.

The father regained consciousness and began to moan. Karl returned to the boy. "Were they English, American, German?"

The youth shook his head. "I don't know. Maybe American, maybe British."

"Ask him if they spoke English," said Ullrich.

The youth heard the question and nodded his head up and down.

"No German?" asked Karl. The head went back and forth.

"Anything else you can remember about these men?"

"When did they leave?" barked Ullrich.

"Right after they . . ." the youth hesitated.

"Right after they murdered Hauptmann Weismann!" spat the German.

The Corsican thought about what they had just heard. "Felix, you'll need to start immediately for Bastogne. Find them!"

"Will you be coming with me?"

"I cannot. Remember, I have an interview with the police in Thionville tomorrow." He glanced at his watch. "I have a friend who owns a small hotel there. It's better I go there today and stay the night. Go to Bastogne, Felix. See what you can find. We will stay in touch."

"What about these two?"

The Corsican tore off a new strip of tape and fastened it on the boy's mouth. "We're finished with them."

Ullrich picked up the kettle and poured its boiling contents over the father. A high-pitched animal squeal escaped from the hole in the tape across the man's mouth. He writhed in new pain, his torso straining involuntarily against the tape. The man's limbs jerked and his head struck the kitchen floor repeatedly until the spasms lessened. He lay there, gasping for air. Ullrich grinned at the boy and tossed the empty kettle across the room.

Ullrich took two large candles from a shelf and lit them from the stove. He turned off the gas burner and knelt to drip pools of wax on the wooden floor. He mounted the candles, one at each end of the kitchen. Karl undid the stove's gas coupling, pulled the copper tubing free and bent the line low to the floor. Propane from the tank outside the farmhouse wall began leaking onto the wide planks.

As they fled, Karl stopped to kick the youth's chair out from under him, sending the boy onto his back. They left him struggling against his bonds, next to the scalded body of his unconscious father.

The Mercedes was a quarter mile away when they heard the explosion.

Karl took Ullrich back to his house on the outskirts of the village.

Felix Ullrich lived alone in a low house covered in vines that climbed every square foot of plaster and exposed timbers. A picket fence badly in need of paint defined a weedy yard. It was run down, but quite comfortable for an old soldier.

Karl went to the rear of the sedan. He reached in, pulled out a bulging bag and handed it to the SS man.

"From Herr Weismann, Felix."

Ullrich took the bag, felt its weight. The old Nazi was visibly moved. "We must stay in touch, correct?"

Karl nodded. He shook the German's hand. "I wish you success in Bastogne, Felix. If anything turns up, call me." He scribbled a phone number on a card and handed it over. "You can reach me at this hotel in Thionville, if you need me. Mention my name."

They shook hands again and the Corsican got back in his car.

Former SS-Hauptscharführer Felix Ullrich held the small bag tight against his chest and watched the Mercedes until the car disappeared. Inside his house, he placed the bag on a table without opening it. He began throwing toiletries and clothing into a small valise.

Next, he phoned his brother-in-law and asked to borrow the man's ancient Renault. After enduring his relative's whining protest, Ullrich said he would pay cash. His promise of money solved the problem.

Felix Ullrich wanted to be in Bastogne before noon.

# CHAPTER SIXTY-SEVEN

## THIONVILLE, JUNE 7

The Corsican drove along the south bank of the Moselle River to Thionville.

He guided the Mercedes through a roundabout at Boulevard Robert Schumann and crossed a set of tracks before crossing the Pont des Allies into the city. Fighting traffic to the Rue de Strasbourg, he made his way down crowded side streets to a modest hotel and pulled to the curb outside the stuccoed building. A metal sign painted with the image of a graceful swan hung above a set of heavy wooden doors: Hôtel le Cygne. Karl grabbed the leather briefcase from the sedan's trunk and went inside. It took a minute for his eyes to adjust to the dark interior.

Behind the reception counter a beefy, bald man with a pockmarked face was smoking a cigarette. The man ignored the new arrival and blew smoke rings into the air above him. Karl set the case on the small counter and tapped a bell.

The heavyset man glanced up at the new arrival. "Look what the Furies of Hell have driven out into the world. On a Sunday no less!"

Karl leaned across the counter and grasped the man's sloping shoulders. "Auguste, how goes your career as the most reluctant hôtelier in all France? Have you mastered the trade of hospitality after all these years?"

The large man slapped the Corsican's chin in a gentle, playful gesture. "Karl Rocca. Come to make your yearly appearance at my humble inn?"

Karl pushed the briefcase across the counter. "A room for one night, Auguste. And put this in a safe place for me, will you?"

The man buried his cigarette into a large, overflowing ashtray and grinned as he lifted the leather case. His thick eyebrows rose and fell. "Feels like dirty laundry or a load of cash. Which is it, Karl?"

The Corsican ignored the comment and scrawled his signature on the registry page. He smiled. "Just put it somewhere safe for me, old friend. I'll be back for it tomorrow afternoon."

The man carried the leather case into a cramped office behind the front desk and squeezed the briefcase into a slot in a row of narrow lockers with wire screens. He shut the door, turned a key in the lock and returned to the desk.

He gave the Corsican two keys, one with with a cardboard tag attached to it. "There," he said, "secure as a bank. You can count on it. Your room is the second left, top of the stairs."

Karl smiled and tugged three fifty-Euro bills from his wallet. He tossed them on the counter. "I suppose you'd prefer francs like the old days, eh?"

The man snatched up the currency and pocketed it, laughing. "Euros will do just as well. You have business in Thionville, Karl?"

The Corsican nodded.

"Still with that German fellow, Weismann?"

"Not anymore, Auguste. Haven't you been watching the news?"

"What for? It's always bad. What of it?"

"Weismann was murdered yesterday. Assassinated would be more like it."

The man leaned across the counter, suddenly curious. "Sounds vaguely familiar. I'm sorry. Was that your man, Karl?"

"Yes. I'm here to meet with the police. They have more questions for me."

The man behind the counter snorted. "They always have questions. Nothing but questions. You know who did it?"

"No, but it had the look of a professional. A policeman, Dupré, wants to talk to me."

The man behind the counter furrowed his brow. "Ah, I know Dupré only by reputation and it's not good. He's National Police. Won't take money. You must be important to draw him in on this. Watch yourself, Karl. He's a real bastard. And be careful with your answers. He won't stop digging until he gets the truth." The hotel owner shrugged. "Can't be bribed. What kind of cop is that, eh?"

Karl shifted his weight and leaned against the counter. "I'll remember that. Good to see you, Auguste. You're looking very prosperous these days."

The man slapped his ample belly and laughed. "You're still the same, Karl. Full of it and always spreading it around."

"Would I lie to you, Auguste? After all our years together in the Legion?"

"You'd take the habit from a cloistered nun if you had the chance, Karl."

Karl pocketed the keys. "Let's have a drink together when you're off duty."

"You're on. Let me call my wife to cover for me. I'll show you a good restaurant and we can share a bottle or two. And when you get back from your dance lesson with Inspector Dupré, we can do it again, eh?"

Karl went out to the Mercedes to wait for his old comrade. When Auguste appeared, he slipped behind the wheel and followed his friend's directions to a local bistro.

# CHAPTER SIXTY-EIGHT

### BASTOGNE, BELGIUM

In Bastogne, Felix Ullrich tried again to raise Karl on his mobile phone. "Answer, Karl! Damnit!" The call did not go through and the old soldier scowled at the phone in his gnarled hand.

"Stupid machine! What use is it if he doesn't answer?!"

He sat in his brother-in-law's rusting Renault on a narrow side street in the Belgian town and tried to focus. Ullrich had followed the trail to the Hôtel Melba, only to learn the men he sought had left hours before. A helpful hotel clerk remembered loading luggage for their party. The men in question—Americans, said the bellman—had been driving a rental van. The clerk was certain of that. He had also overheard them talking about taking a train to Brussels.

As a precaution, Ullrich stopped at Bastogne's train station. A chatty rail agent snatched up the offered fifty-Euro note. The man confirmed that three Americans matching Ullrich's descriptions had purchased tickets for Paris that morning.

Paris or Brussels? Felix Ullrich faced two choices, both blind. He could alert Karl and follow the scent to Paris, or he could go to Brussels and see where that trail took him. The Corsican was complicating things by not answering his phone. Ullrich dialed the car's owner to let him know he might need the vehicle a bit longer than planned.

His relative answered in a state of panic. "Felix, what are you involved in?! Where are you?! What's happened?!"

Ullrich tried to calm the man. "Slow down. You're talking too fast. What the hell are you babbling on about?"

The answer came in a series of shrieks. "The police are looking for you! They came to your house this morning! They pulled me out of bed. Frightened my wife out of her wits. Is it true what they said?"

Ullrich grew cautious. He would have to make the call short. "What did they want?"

"They say you killed Christian Courbet and his son! That you burned down their farmhouse this morning! Felix, is this true?"

"Why do they say I was involved?"

"The boy was horribly burned. He lived just long enough to identify you and Weismann's chauffeur as his murderers." There was a pause as the man drew a breath. "Can this be true, Felix?"

Ullrich imagined his wife's younger brother wringing his soft hands, sobbing into his telephone near the kitchen table. Whining about his automobile. The man was spineless, but he had given the old soldier an invaluable head start. The hunter was about to become the hunted. But not just yet. Ullrich ended the call. They had not been connected long enough for a trace. He had to move. He also had to let Karl know before he walked into the arms of the police. He tried the phone again. No luck. He pulled the card the Corsican had given him and dialed the hotel in Thionville.

A woman's voice came on the line. " Hôtel le Cygne."

"Bonjour. My name is Felix and I'm looking for my friend, Karl Rocca." There was no response, so Ullrich continued. "Is he there by chance?"

"I'm afraid he's gone out. You might try him this evening."

"Very well. Tell him to call me when he returns."

"Very well . . . Monsieur . . ." The woman on the line paused, waited for a name.

"Just tell him to call Felix. He will know." Ullrich pocketed the cell phone and started for Brussels.

## CHAPTER SIXTY-NINE
### THIONVILLE, JUNE 8

In Thionville, the Corsican paced in a spartan third-floor office. At a tall open window, he looked down into the paved court-yard. Police cars were drawn up in perfect, military rows. Traffic flowed along the boulevard. Gendarmes came and went from the ornate entry directly below his window.

Footsteps drummed along the corridor outside the office. A single, uniformed policeman sat writing at a desk, oblivious to his visitor. A large oak table in the middle of the room was stacked with manila envelopes set on a large leather blotter. The phone on the policeman's desk rang. The officer nodded several times and hung up.

"Inspector Dupré has been slightly delayed," he said to the Corsican. "He will be with you shortly, sir."

Karl nodded and paced. His cell phone rang and he fished in his pocket. "Hello, Karl here." Ullrich's rasping voice came through the receiver. The old soldier was calling from Brussels with the chilling news about the discovery of their arson. Surely Dupré must know by now. Karl began to perspire. He propped a foot on a chair and retied his shoelaces to throw off the police-man at the desk, but the officer was busy with his paperwork.

Karl thrust one hand into his pocket and casually strolled toward the desk, talking, laughing to hide his panic. It worked. The man ignored him. Karl kept the phone to his ear and continued talking, though Ullrich had rung off.

The Corsican was trapped. The murder of the Courbets and the arson were no longer secret. He had to flee, get back to the hotel for his money and weapon and make a run for it. But he was trapped in this building.

Karl smiled at the officer. "Excuse me, is there a lavatory on this floor I might use?"

The policeman pointed to a door. "Through there, on the left, sir."

Karl bowed slightly, smiled again. "Thank you."

He closed the door behind him and followed the short hallway to the firedoor at the end. He tested the handle and the door opened. Quickly, he descended three levels of metal stairs to the ground level. The exit door was locked. He scrambled back to the first landing and emerged in a hallway lined with offices. Karl raced to the main entrance. As he reached the end of the corridor, an emergency bell sounded. Gendarmes and civilians began pouring out of the offices. He slipped through the crowd at the building's main doorway and jogged across the asphalt toward his car.

"Halt! Halt!"

Karl heard the distant commands behind him and to his left, but he ignored them and sprinted toward his Mercedes.

"KARL ROCCA! STOP!" It was Dupré's voice.

He jammed his keys into the car's lock and yanked the door open. A dozen men, some in uniforms, had spread out to flank his car. He cranked the engine into life and backed up in a squeal of rubber.

Dupré was in the lead, a pistol held away from his body.

A uniformed officer leapt for the driver's door, grabbed the handle with his free hand and pulled open the door. Yelling, his face inches from Karl's, the man grabbed a fistful of shirt. Karl drove his left elbow into the officer's face, but the man pushed himself into the driver's seat as Karl accelerated toward two policemen blocking his path. The Mercedes roared past the men who leapt away at the last second.

Karl whipped the car to his left to shake the policeman clinging to him. The officer screamed at him and hung on for dear life. The Mercedes skidded right in a second attempt to throw him and Karl hammered at the man with his fist. The car careened past parked vehicles. The gendarme wrestled his pistol free and jammed the gun's muzzle against the Corsican's ribs. He fired once.

The shot exploded against Karl's side as though someone had kicked him with a steel boot. Immediately, his hands dropped from the wheel. The Mercedes made a lazy circle before smashing against two parked cars in a crunching impact. The policeman was hurled to the pavement, his pistol still in hand. The sedan's hood tore loose and steam from the ruptured radiator shot up. The driver's door wrenched open in the collision and Karl felt himself leaning out, falling halfway to the ground, held in place only by his legs.

Sirens sounded. Shouts. Sounds of leather slapping as though an army were running toward him. Karl could not feel the lower half of his body. More shouts.

Someone lifted him from the blood-soaked driver's seat and lowered him to the pavement, but Karl only sensed it, could not really feel it. He tried to roll onto his side and rise but two officers pinned the big man's arms to the street. It made no difference. Karl's body was not responding and he flopped awkwardly onto his back. Someone patted him down for a weapon.

Dupré's angry face hovered above him. The detective was mouthing words at him but Karl barely heard him. An ambulance siren warbled in the distance.

Questions flew at him. "What did you do with the money?"

*What an odd thing to ask at a time like this,* Karl thought. "Money?" he babbled. Blood poured from his mouth and ears. He knew he was mortally wounded. *Wouldn't be long now.*

He heard his questioner again. "Your housekeeper said you gave her five thousand Euros to buy her silence!"

He heard the statement. *The bitch,* he thought. *She's going to come out all right.*

"She found the safe empty." Dupré leaned closer now for Karl's answers. "She said you and your friend Ullrich had Weismann killed for his money."

Karl tried to laugh, but the effort sent stabbing pain through his neck and jaw.

"Can you hear me, Karl?" It was Dupré again., his face inches from Karl. "Why did you kill the Courbets? Did you set fire to their house to cover the crime?

Karl thought he smiled and then felt himself pouring into the ground. He would not answer them now. *They could go to hell.* He would not answer. *Somewhere Felix was loose, on the hunt, and that was enough.*


Auguste Schell, the owner of Hôtel le Cygne, heard news of the shooting from his wife, who had returned from market with the day's provisions. Instinctively, the former legionnaire knew that his old comrade was involved. When his wife went upstairs to help with housekeeping, Schell unlocked the wire locker with Karl Rocca's briefcase and took it into his shed at the rear of the hotel. He opened the leather case and dumped the currency onto his work bench. Along with the cash was a 9mm Beretta with silencer. Without pausing to count the money, he shoved the bundled banknotes into a heavy plastic bag and put that bag inside a larger plastic sack. He moved the wooden bench from the wall and dropped to his knees to pry loose a board, exposing a narrow, meter-long trench.

Schell often used the primitive safe to store the occasional kilo of heroin for his dealer friends. He stuffed the plastic sack into the cavity and replaced the board. After testing the spot with his foot, he moved the heavy bench back into place. He scuffed dirt and sawdust over the planks. The innkeeper used a rag to handle the silenced pistol and returned the weapon to the briefcase. In the hotel's office, he added Karl's laundry and shaving kit to the leather satchel, shoved the case back into the wire locker and turned the key.

Schell lit a cigarette and went outside to exchange pleasantries with his neighbor, who was sweeping the sidewalk outside her small gift shop.

The police arrived at Hôtel le Cygne the next day. While two officers turned the Corsican's room upside down, another officer matched the key with one of the lockers behind the front desk. The alert detective inspected the registry and asked about Karl Rocca. The hotel owner cooperated and turned over Karl Rocca's briefcase. The officers made their notes and plied Auguste Schell with questions. The detective had no reason to search the small shed in the back, and eventually, the officers left.

# CHAPTER SEVENTY

## LONDON, JUNE 8

"What is the purpose of your visit?"

The old man cupped his ear and leaned forward, prompting the question again.

"What is the purpose of your visit to Great Britain, sir?"

A wide smile broke out on the man's wrinkled face. "A week of your magnificent architecture . . . and your wonderful museums."

The bored immigration man smiled like he had a thousands of times before. "Very well, Mr. Arneson, enjoy your stay."

He hammered his stamp of approval on the visitor's Danish passport and waved him on. Felix Ullrich retrieved his forged document and shuffled past the glass cage. He wormed his way through a queue of incoming passengers and moved along toward Customs.

A bored official patted UIlrich's sole piece of luggage—a worn, soft leather bag of clothes and toiletries—and waved him on without so much as a second glance. Ullrich bowed pleasantly and moved past the line of fellow passengers who had disembarked from the high-speed train from Brussels. He ran gnarled hands over the bulging money belt that girded his waist and smiled. He was inside the outer defenses and ready for the next step.

The old SS man found a phone and sank down on the metal stool to call his contact in London. He dialed, heard the ringing tones and listened to the suspicious voice that answered.

"Who's calling?" challenged an angry voice.

"A patriot. An old friend."

There was a cautious pause on the other end. Another voice came on the line. "This is a fellow patriot. Who's the old friend?"

"Ah, yes," soothed the German. "Call me Felix, an uncle from abroad."

Suddenly the person's voice changed from guarded to polite. "Isn't it wonderful to be in London this time of year?"

"Yes, it's so wonderful to be in London," growled Ullrich.

"And how was the trip?"

"Oh, quite ordinary."

"Do you have a piece of paper and a pen?"

Ullrich fumbled in his pocket and produced a small notebook and ballpoint pen. "Go ahead, I'm ready."

The voice recited an address and told him to take a taxi to the spot. "Be there within the half hour, Uncle. We'll find you."

Ullrich replaced the phone in its cradle and stepped into the pale light to hail a cab.

In thirty minutes, he was deposited on the curb outside a seedy-looking pub with several iron tables and chairs chained to sockets in the concrete. The ugly furniture was the bar's attempt at a sidewalk café. Row houses lined the littered streets in both directions and the sun barely shone through an overcast sky. It was a depressing working-class district where immigrants were already nibbling at the edges of the neighborhood's real estate.

Felix Ullrich took a seat and ordered a glass of dark ale from a scowling, flat-chested waitress with a tattooed neck and a tongue stud. When she reappeared with his drink, he paid for it and took a long sip.

Across the street, two jack-booted skinheads in torn army jackets, T-shirts and jeans arrived and began a reconnaissance of sorts. After a few minutes, the grim-looking pair was joined by a puffy-faced, older man who eyed the German. The newcomer cupped his hands to light a cigarette and studied the old man at the curbside table. The stranger said something to the punks and turned on his heel, disappearing into a recessed doorway in the shabby brick building on the corner. Whatever the man said sent the angry pair into the street. The two toughs dodged traffic and made straight for Ullrich. Wary of their approach, he stood and put his back against the wall. Both punks stopped on the edge of the pavement and circled.

"Uncle Felix, is it?"

"Yes," said Ullrich cautiously as he faced the two. "Who might you be?"

The taller one, an ugly, sallow-faced man in his twenties with bad teeth and a silver earring in one lobe, spoke for the pair. "A patriot, come to fetch you," he half-smiled, half-snarled. He nodded at his shorter version, a vermin-like nervous fellow with a facial tic.

"I'm Fletching and that's me mate, Mollerson. Molly for short if ya' like."

Ullrich sighed, resigned himself to the care of the two grinning misfits who were apparently going to guide him to his contact with London's neo-Nazi world.

*What has it come to*, thought the old SS sergeant-major, *when men like myself who knew discipline and order have to rely on garbage like this?* He thought it, but he did not voice it. Perhaps the commander of these two escorts would have his wits about him and could actually deliver on the promises given over the phone.

"Very well," sighed Ullrich. "Lead on, Fletching, Molly." He picked up his case and followed the two gargoyles toward the brick building.

Molly, the shorter, duller one, took up a lookout post in the archway and Ullrich followed the taller of the two up narrow wooden stairs to a second-floor landing with a scarred metal door. The entry was papered over with torn handbills announcing neo-Nazi rallies at various London parks. A peephole had been punched into the iron door, and Fletching put his eyeball against the tiny lens and rapped some sort of code loudly on the frame.

*How terribly original*, thought Ullrich.

Footsteps sounded behind the barrier and several door bolts were drawn back. The door opened and he entered the flat.

## CHAPTER SEVENTY-ONE

The man who had sent the two foot soldiers to fetch Ullrich retreated to the center of the flat's large, furnished room. The window frames were sealed with sheet metal, which allowed only the top third of the glass to let in light. The sandblasted brick walls were hung with rally posters and enormous portraits of a uniformed Adolf Hitler. Martial music played in the background from another room. Several computers and monitors, accompanied by the usual tangle of cables, covered a work table, made from a long door. Swastika screensavers glowed from the monitors. An enormous Nazi flag was draped on one wall, and the floor was polished concrete, covered with leftover squares of gray industrial carpet.

"Welcome to London, Uncle Felix," said the man, extending a hand.

"Thank you," said Ullrich. The two men shook hands.

Suddenly, the man raised his right arm in a stiff salute and barked, "Heil Hitler!"

Ullrich was taken aback at the sound of the old salute. The man stood there with his arm extended, waiting for his guest's response.

Ullrich raised his hand. "Heil Hitler."

The leader dropped his arm and stepped forward. He gestured to a large sofa. "Please, sit down, SS-Hauptscharführer Felix Ullrich."

Ullrich sat down and studied his host. The man was stolid-looking and his thinning brown hair was parted to affect an obvious imitation of the Fuhrer's hairstyle. Ullrich found himself oddly fascinated by the man sitting opposite him. The skinhead who had escorted Ullrich up the stairs stood respectfully to one side, trying to look soldierly. It was a wasted effort.

"That will be all, Fletching," waved the leader. "You may go."

The youth snapped his heels together and threw out his arm again. "Heil Hitler!" He dropped his arm and went out the steel door.

It was apparent to Ullrich that there were others somewhere in the flat. He heard voices, the sound of ringing phones, footsteps, doors being opened and shut. Music.

"Coffee, tea, mineral water?" asked his host.

"Ah, no, thank you . . ." Ullrich groped for a name.

"David will do, SS-Hauptscharführer Ullrich." The man flashed an oily smile. "Not my real name, but it will suffice. One has to be careful, you know." He continued, "Let me say it's an honor for us to have you here. May I call you Felix?"

Ullrich nodded. "Of course. My rank was gained a lifetime ago. Felix will do. I was told you could help me during my visit to London."

The man sat up straight. "Anything we can do to assist you is a privilege."

"My friends on the continent . . ." Ullrich smiled, ". . . old comrades, if you will, put me in touch with your people because you know this country and I do not."

"I understand, Felix. We are in this struggle together. We carry on where you left off . . . your traditions, your sacrifices are the stuff of legend and we honor you."

Ullrich smiled. "Yes, well, I thank you for that sentiment." He paused. "Just who exactly am I dealing with here, David?"

The younger man jumped to his feet and began pacing in front of the posters. "We are patriots. The last line of defense in a country in danger of becoming a mongrelized nation of the brown, the black and the Jew. We are a minority of iron trying to raise the alarm among fellow patriots who are committed, like you were in a earlier age, to preserving a noble heritage of racial purity."

"All very true, all very good," said Ullrich.

"I know I can speak candidly with someone such as yourself, Felix. Our group . . . my little troop, if you will allow me . . . was sired from the loins of the November Ninth Society. Have you heard of it?"

Ullrich confessed he did not know the group.

"We labor to turn back this tide of filth that spills from the edges of the globe."

"Forgive an old soldier's eye, David, but are your two stalwarts typical of the ranks?"

The man snorted and sank down opposite Ullrich, gesturing. "Ah, yes," he smiled and lowered his voice, "my good and willing lads. I regret that one has to make do with what is available at the time. Sometimes I feel as though I'm surrounded by cretins and imbeciles, but that will change. Even our beloved Führer had to begin his Reich with available resources, true?"

"Then I wish you well in your noble goals," said Ullrich. "My turn has passed. For me the mission at hand is much more simple, even modest." The old warrior sat back on the couch, gnarled hands in his lap. "My hope is that I am not too late."

"All I was told, my dear Felix, was that you seek men who murdered a comrade of yours, a fellow patriot. Is that correct?"

The German's face darkened. "Yes. They killed a dear friend, a fellow soldier who was about to fulfill a dream. They took all that from him, and I want to find them and repay them in kind."

"Am I to understand you think they might be British or American?"

"Possibly British, more likely American."

"Are you certain of that?"

Felix Ullrich smiled. "The information was solid, gained under some duress, but I have no reason to doubt the source of the intelligence."

"And you think they are here?"

"I hope they are still here, in London. I'm running out of time, however."

"How many traitors are we talking about?"

"Two, possibly three. Perhaps more."

"Very well. Do you have names?"

"Ari and Sam. And a younger man named Peter, possibly American."

The Briton arose and began to pace. "Those are terribly slim clues, but there are ways to check."

"They may have come over a day or two ahead of me," offered Ullrich. "From either Brussels by train or France on a ferry. To be frank, it's a gamble that they're still here."

"We'll have to move quickly then," said the man. "If your times are correct we have people in place who can tell us if they arrived. My dear Felix, such a task is not impossible. We cast a very wide net. There are many sympathizers who do not look like my two watchdogs outside. There are patriots who are quite ordinary in appearance. One would never suspect them of being anything other than law-abiding citizens."

The man warmed to his solitary audience. "We have friends everywhere. And forgive my boasting but we also have sources even within police ranks." He sat beside Ullrich. "We may even be able to find where they are staying . . . if indeed they are in London."

"I'll also need a small caliber pistol, easily concealable. Can you do that?"

The Fascist laced his fingers together under his chin and paused. "Yes, you will have it before the day is out."

Ullrich was pleased with the way the conversation had gone. He reached into his coat and drew out a letter-sized envelope which he handed to the man. "Excellent. I think you'll find enough there to reward your diligence, David."

The man felt the thick envelope and grinned. "This will certainly spur us on. Where are you staying?"

Ullrich told him and the meeting drew to a conclusion. They walked together to the heavy steel door and the Fascist pulled it open.

He bellowed down the stairs. "Fletching, go across to the pub and get Arthur off his fat arse. We need his cab for our guest!"

The youth bolted out the doorway and disappeared.

On the landing the two men shook hands. "Will your pursuit of enemies require assistance, SS-Hauptscharführer Ullrich? I can offer you some of my men if you wish."

Ullrich looked down the stairs where the skinhead named Molly loitered. "So kind of you to offer, but I think not. A single man stands a better chance."

"Heil Hitler!" The man clicked his polished heels together. "Heil Hitler."

## CHAPTER SEVENTY-TWO

### LONDON, HOTEL STAMFORD, JUNE 8

Ullrich's phone rang, awakening him. The neo-Nazi's voice was at the other end.

"The gentlemen are still here, Uncle. We think there are at least three. Two possibilities. Check the Hilton Paddington and Royal Lancaster hotels. Parties who fit your description may be staying at one of these locations."

The old warrior scribbled quickly. He repeated the message.

"That is correct."

"I must say David, I am truly impressed with your quick work."

"I told you we cast a wide net, uncle."

"Very well," said Ullrich. "I shall try both hotels and see if I am successful."

"Oh, and did my nephew arrive with your package?"

Ullrich slid his hand under his pillow to caress the Walther PPK. "Yes, tell your family I am quite pleased."

"May your mission end successfully, Uncle."

The old SS sergeant-major replaced the receiver. At least he had something to go on for now. He went to the cramped bathroom and washed his face. He put on his shirt, covering his money belt, slipped a well-worn leather holster over his left shoulder and donned his jacket.

Ullrich picked up the Walther PPK and slapped a six-round magazine into the butt of the handgun. He jacked a round into the chamber and flipped on the weapon's safety. Holstering the Walther, he slipped a silencer into his jacket's right-hand pocket and tucked a spare magazine in his belt. He made a last inspection of his room. It was time to go hunting.

Within fifteen minutes, Ullrich had paid his bill and was on the street hailing a cab. He directed the driver to the Royal Lancaster Hotel.

There, Ullrich wandered into the carpeted lobby and used a house phone to troll for his prey. Americans and Canadians had checked into the hotel according to the front desk, but nothing fit. No one with the names he sought had turned up, although he conceded to himself that they could have been aliases. He played the lapsed memory routine with a helpful switchboard operator until she eventually grew suspicious, forcing him to drop his ruse.

For a quarter-hour Ullrich watched the lobby from one of the two stuffed chairs flanking the white marble fireplace. He got up and went into the hotel's bar to sit at a two-person table with his back to a large picture window.

He nursed an ale, trying to spot someone matching descriptions the Corsican remembered from the shooting. The tactic proved fruitless and he gave up the chase. He had wasted a precious hour and began to doubt the information the Fascist had given him. Ullrich hurried outside and asked a gold-coated doorman for a cab.

A frustrated Felix Ullrich stepped from the cab near the Hilton Paddington as a swirl of commuters from the train station ebbed round him. A chattering tribe of rude Pakistanis pushed past him to claim the taxi he had just exited. Ullrich let them hustle him aside and fumed. In the old days, on the Russian Steppe, he had been famous for ordering people shot for much less. But he had more important things on his mind, so he ignored the noisy brown people. A steady line of black cabs rolled past the hotel's entrance to waiting queues at the train station.

Ullrich approached a uniformed hotel doorman. "Excuse me. I wonder if you might help me."

The pale young man was eager to please. "How may I assist you, sir?"

"I'm looking for some people I met on the train. Americans, I think. We agreed to meet here at their hotel for drink. Perhaps you might know of them."

The doorman excused himself to usher guests through the hotel's doors. When that was done, he came back to the waiting German. "Yes, you are looking for certain guests. I'm sure I'll be able to help you, sir."

Ullrich produced a fifty-Euro bill from his pocket and described his quarry.

## CHAPTER SEVENTY-THREE

### LONDON, HOTEL PADDINGTON

On the fourth floor, a soft knock sounded on Peter Noble's hotel room door.

"Yes, who is it?"

"Message from the front desk, sir."

Soleski, reclining on the sofa with a paperback, said, "Maybe it's from Sam."

Peter opened the door.

Ullrich bulled his way through and slammed the door shut behind him. He jammed the silenced pistol into Peter's chest, prodding him backwards.

"Over there, with him!" he barked.

Stunned, Peter retreated toward the couch where Soleski sat.

"Both of you, keep your hands where I can see them!" ordered the German.

"What do you want?" asked Peter, as he sat next to Soleski.

"Idiots! Shut up!" snarled Ullrich. He stood next to a chair and waved his weapon at them. "Where is the rest of your party?"

There was a moment of silence. Ullrich repeated the question. "You are not all here," he added. "Where are the others?"

"I don't know what you mean," replied Peter. He instinctively played for time despite the intruder's menacing behavior. Soleski sat paralyzed, his gaze fixed on the weapon pointed at them. Peter weighed his chances against the armed man and gambled on doing nothing to provoke him. He thought of his grandfather in the next room but kept silent.

Felix Ullrich sneered at the two men on the bed. "Oh, please, no games. I have no time for them."

"What do you want?" asked Peter again.

"I want to know where the others are!"

"I'm not sure . . ." The half-pleading words were barely out of Peter's mouth when, suddenly, Ullrich fired a single muffled shot into Soleski's right foot. The round ripped through the top of his foot and buried itself in the window frame. The older man cried out and doubled up in pain, clutching his foot.

Peter was petrified. Soleksi was wounded, and they were cornered.

Ullrich waved the handgun back and forth. "Don't fuck with me, boy. You will be next."

In the suite's adjacent bedroom, Noble heard the smothered gunshot. He eased from his bed in the darkened room. A sliver of light from the partly-opened bathroom doorway was the only illumination. He crept toward the door and listened to the exchange between the intruder and his grandson. He heard Soleski whimpering in pain.

Noble felt helpless, impotent.

But quickly rage rose in him and he scanned the room for a weapon of some sort. Nothing would do. He hobbled into the bathroom and glanced around the tiled space. He leaned against the doorway, peeled off one of his long black socks and stuffed a thick bar of wrapped soap into the bottom of his empty sock. He knotted the top of the stocking.

The impromptu weapon was his only hope. He slipped it into his robe's pocket, his right hand gripping the knotted end. He quietly filled a glass with water and held it in his left hand. There would be only one chance. It might end horribly but he had to try.

Noble slowly pushed open the door from the bedroom with an elbow and stepped into the suite's living room. Ullrich swung against the wall, his pistol aimed at Peter and a whimpering Soleski as Noble shuffled into the room.

Ullrich grinned. "Well, well, if one shakes the tree, one is rewarded with more fruit."

He threatened the new arrival with the handgun. "Over there with those two, old man!"

Noble shuffled, slowly turning his left side toward the gunman, his right hand knotted around the makeshift blackjack. He feigned befuddlement and stood transfixed in front of the others.

"Where is the rest of your party?" Ullrich hissed.

"Who . . . are you?" asked Noble, pretending confusion.

"A friend of Kurt Weismann's. You murdered a good man."

"We don't know what the hell you're talking about!" yelled Peter. He was cradling Soleski, who was rocking back and forth in pain.

Ullrich ignored the tottering old man and stepped closer to the sofa, thrusting the silenced Walther in Peter's face. "Assassins!" he growled. "You think that I don't know what you did?"

Noble tightened his grip on the sock, then suddenly whirled on Ullrich.

He threw the glass of water in the German's face and slammed his weapon down on Ullrich's gun hand. Ullrich dropped his pistol on the carpet and gripped his shattered hand. Instantly, Peter leapt from the couch, threw his body against Ullrich and drove him back into a chair, covering the German's mouth with his hand. Ullrich twisted but could not move, his body blocked by the much younger man. Ullrich clamped his good hand against Peter's windpipe and squeezed.

Noble raised his right arm and brought the heavy sock down on top of the German's skull. Ullrich collapsed with a moan, sagging in the upholstered chair as Noble scooped the pistol from the floor.

Noble staggered back, gun in hand, staring at the disarmed German. He swayed, then tottered toward the nearest wall, dropping the sock with its lethal load. He fell forward. Still catching his breath, Peter rushed forward and caught his grandfather before the old man collapsed. He lowered Noble onto the sofa next to Soleski, who was clutching his bloodied foot. Peter's grandfather sank down, eying the unconscious SS man who, only a moment before, had been in command of the situation.

Peter let out a long sigh. "That was . . . unbelievable, Gramps. How did you . . . ?"

William Noble leaned back against the headboard. "Don't ask," he wheezed, "I have no idea where the energy came from."

Soleski, despite his wound, smiled. "That was fantastic, Bill. I never seen anything like it. You saved our lives!"

Noble dropped his head on his heaving chest. "Never thought . . . I had a chance, Sollie. Had to . . . try something."

Peter kept one eye on the German's slumped body and put an arm around his grandfather. The young man's eyes filled with tears. "I thought we were dead men, Gramps, but you . . ." He could not finish the thought.

"What do . . . we do with him?" asked Noble between gasps.

"Kill him! The bastard was going to kill us," said Soleski.

"Don't you recognize him, Sollie?" asked Peter.

Soleski shook his head.

"Who is he?" asked Noble.

"The guy with Weismann at the café," explained Peter.

The two did not know the slumping figure. Peter released his grandfather and stood, hovering over the German.

"There may be others, Peter," said his grandfather.

"Geez, I hope not," said Soleski. "I was about done this time around. Won't this ever end? I just want to go home." Blood seeped through his fingers. Peter got a towel from the bathroom. It was an ugly flesh wound, but not life-threatening.

Peter wrapped Soleski's foot. "We need to call Sam and Swanson." He picked up the phone, dialed Cohen and was glad to hear the lawyer's voice. He explained their situation. Within minutes, Swanson and Cohen arrived. They examined Soleski's wound and determined they could doctor it with Cohen's first aid kit. No sense calling unneeded attention to the episode, Cohen said.

Soleski agreed. "But what about . . . him?" He nodded at Ullrich.

"Leave the sonofabitch to me," volunteered Burt Swanson as he stripped the comatose German of his passport and wallet. He emptied Ullrich's pockets. "Well, look at this!" he exclaimed, tugging at the man's money belt. "Our guy is loaded! He's wrapped in one-hundred Euro notes!"

"Don't touch them!" ordered Cohen. "We don't need to add robbery to murder."

"Murder, hell!" retorted Swanson, pulling bills from the German's belt. "It was self-defense, pure and simple. Besides, you really think anyone's going to compliment us for not robbing a guy we killed?"" He snorted, answering his own question. "I don't think so, Sam."

Noble's strained voice came from the bed. "He's not dead, Burt. He's hurt bad, but he's not dead."

The former sergeant stopped and peeled back one of the German's eyelids. "Hell, he's pretty much a goner, Bill. You gave it a good start and I say we oughta finish the job.

"Plus, he owes us," said Swanson as he continued rifling the money belt.

Cohen ignored Swanson. "Peter, we've got to clean up this place the best we can. Check the halls for cleaning closets or maids' carts. See if you can get us something to take care of this."

Peter left the room.

After Peter had gone, Cohen, visibly shaken, sat on the couch opposite Ullrich. "Question is, was he acting alone? Weismann's bodyguard must be nearby. Dammit, it's all my fault. We shouldn't have stopped in Bastogne."

Swanson put a hand on Cohen's shoulder. "Hey, cut yourself some slack. Bill needed a rest, Sam. We all did. The important thing was to get out of France and get back here. We can deal with this. Besides, if Weismann's man was in town, he woulda hit us, instead of Old Leadfoot here."

Noble and Cohen were not reassured.

Soleski gestured at Ullrich. "If he found us, so could the bodyguard."

The thought was suddenly a weight in the room.

"Doesn't makes sense, Sollie," reasoned Swanson. "If Weismann's goon is out there, why wouldn't he come at us instead of sending some old Nazi?"

Noble spoke from the sofa. "Maybe you're right, Burt."

"I know I am, Bill, but Sollie's right, too. We should stay alert anyway. Could be Sam's correct, that the bodyguard is still out there, even though my gut tells me this guy was acting alone."

Cohen and Soleski remained unconvinced. "Our flight doesn't leave until morning," said Soleski, watching the figure in the chair. "What are we supposed to do with him in the meantime?"

Noble spoke up. "We could let the hotel staff find him."

"And have him tie us into the Weismann thing? No way, Bill." Swanson stood over their assailant. "Anyway, like you said, he's hurt bad. Leave him to me."

There was a rap on the door, then Peter's voice. He came into the room with a collection of cleaning supplies, holding them up like trophies.

"Good job, Sport." His grandfather smiled from the bed.

Peter went to work immediately, wiping down the walls behind the German, then working his way across the woodwork and carpet.

Cohen stood next to Swanson and nodded at Ullrich. "What'd you have in mind for him, Burt?"

Swanson cupped his chin in one hand and flashed a grim smile. "Peter, when it gets dark, I want you to go downstairs and get a wheelchair from the bell captain."

Peter nodded. Dusk was two hours away.

"Okay," said Cohen, "but just what are you proposing, Burt?"

Swanson folded his lanky frame into the suite's couch, his big hands gripping his knees.

"Old Felix here has to disappear . . . permanently."

Cohen sagged. "I knew you'd say something like that. I don't like it."

"Got a better idea?"

Cohen paused and leaned against a wall, silent.

"I didn't think so," said Swanson. "Sam, I don't mean to take over your show, but we need to move fast. And until Peter gets the wheelchair, you can make yourself useful by doctoring Sollie's foot."

"I'll get my kit," said Cohen wearily. He crept back to his room and returned with the first aid pack. He cleaned and bandaged the jagged wound while Swanson explained his plan.

## CHAPTER SEVENTY-FOUR

### LONDON, HOTEL PADDINGTON

Peter and Swanson wrestled Ullrich into a hotel wheelchair and folded his arms as if the German were asleep. Cohen propped a cap on Ullrich's head, then waited while Swanson checked to see if the hallway was deserted. When he gave the all-clear sign, Peter wheeled his unconscious passenger out to the elevator.

"I'm going to follow you, Peter," explained Swanson,"but don't look back. Keep moving until I get outside to join you."

On the ground floor, foot traffic was light, and Peter and his unconscious passenger were ignored. Swanson distracted the solitary clerk on duty with small talk about an excursion to the Tower, while Peter steered the German out the door.

"Needs a little air. Too much ale," he whispered to a smiling bell captain. Swanson eventually wandered from the front desk, then slipped outside when the bellman was summoned by the night clerk.

Peter pushed his cargo for fifty yards along Eastbourne Terrace until Swanson caught up with him. Swanson directed Peter to Bishops Bridge Road, a concrete span arching over tracks leading into Paddington Station. Headlights from two speeding cars washed the scene, but the automobiles continued without stopping. Peter turned onto the bridge and covered a third of the span before Swanson whistled for him to halt. Checking to see that no one was nearby, Peter stopped.

Ullrich's breathing was shallow, ragged. Peter lifted the German's cap. A bloody, dark bruise had formed where Noble's makeshift blackjack had crushed the top of his skull.

"You gonna have a problem with this?" asked Swanson.

Peter replayed the earlier scene in the hotel room. "No," he said, without remorse. "Good," huffed Swanson as he lifted one of the German's arms. "Then let's give our Nazi friend a little help."

Peter stood behind the wheelchair and slipped his hands under the man's shoulders. They wrestled the body up and over the bridge's parapet, then let him fall. Ullrich dropped to the tracks below and landed with a sickening, meaty thud across a pair of rails.

"Okay, my turn," wheezed Swanson as he sat in the wheel-chair.

"What now?"

"Keep going. There's a canal up ahead. We'll toss the gun and head back."

Swanson settled in the chair, jammed the cap low over his eyes and rode in silence until they reached the canal. Withdrawing the German's gun from his jacket, he wiped it with a handkerchief and pitched it over the railing. A splash echoed back.

"About face," he barked. Peter hesitated. "That means, turn me around, soldier. Let's get the hell out of here before something else happens."

The night clerk nodded politely at the pair he'd seen wheeling past his post twenty minutes before. He barely looked up from his paperwork as they rolled to the lift.

They rode to their floor and Peter wheeled Swanson to the room where Soleski lay, his doctored foot now propped on a pillow. An exhausted William Noble sat beside the wounded man.

"My God, I hope this is the end of it," said Cohen. "I won't breathe easier until we're out of England and back home."

Cohen and Swanson went over plans for the early morning trip to Heathrow and then returned to their rooms at the end of the hall. Peter locked the door behind them and wedged a chair under the door knob. Once Soleski was comfortable, Peter escorted his grandfather into the second bedroom and eased the old man onto the mattress.

He leaned over the bed. "Try and get some sleep, Gramps."

"I wish I had never brought you along, kiddo. This was not your fight."

Peter sat on the edge of the bed and looked at the frail man. "It was my choice. No one forced me to come with you."

"Just get us home, Peter," he sighed. "We're done. Finished."

He took his grandfather's hand. "All we have to do is get through tomorrow morning and we'll be okay."

Peter left one light burning in the bathroom and stripped off his shirt. He settled into an armchair at the foot of the sofa, facing the door. For the rest of the night, he kept watch while Noble and Soleski slept.

# CHAPTER SEVENTY-FIVE

## LONDON, PADDINGTON HOTEL, JUNE 9

Peter Noble was jolted awake by an image of Ullrich waving a gun. He sat up and shook the memory free. He rubbed the sleep from his eyes, went into the bathroom and shaved. He finished dressing, roused his grandfather, then gently shook Soleski awake.

Soleski sat up and gingerly held his bandaged foot. "Don't feel too bad, considering."

Peter unwound tape and gauze and examined the wound. The bleeding had stopped. Cohen had done a good job. "We'll get a fresh bandage on that before we leave, Sollie."

The little man smiled. "At this point, I'd crawl to the airport, Peter."

"No need to, old friend," rasped Noble from the bedroom doorway. He inspected his friend's foot and shuffled to the bathroom. "You're made of pretty rugged stuff, Sollie."

Soleski lay back on the pillows, arms behind his head.

"I'll call Sam and we'll get you fixed up again," said Peter.

He got Cohen on the line. "All right. I understand. We'll be here." Peter nodded at the two men. "They'll be by for us in about fifteen minutes."'"

Soleski asked for Peter's help and limped to the bathroom with difficulty.

"We'll borrow the wheelchair to get you to the train, Sollie."

"I hate those things," he said looking at the chair. "Never thought I'd use one."

"Might as well get used to it, Sollie," kidded Noble.

"Hell, Bill, I walked out of the Bulge with a piece of me missing, so don't think this little inconvenience is gonna hold me back for long."

Peter smiled at the old soldier's bravado. With Soleski busy, Peter packed his small bag and his grandfather's suitcase and put them by the door. Soleski limped from the bathroom and Peter steered him to the couch.

The effort taxed the older man. "Geez, Bill, I'm sure glad you brought this young fella with us."

"No one else would go exploring with me, Sollie. I'm the one who should be grateful." The men laughed.

A knock sounded at the door.

"Don't be in such a hurry to open it this time, Peter," cautioned Soleski.

"Who is it?" Peter asked.

Cohen's voice came from the other side. "Burt and Sam."

Peter opened the door to the men and their luggage.

Cohen immediately moved to assess the raw wound on Soleski's foot. "Let me fix that for you." He dumped the contents of his carry-on bag on the bed. "I'll need a new towel, Peter."

While Cohen worked on Soleski, Swanson opened an ivory-handled penknife and went to the window frame. He began digging in the wood.

"What are you doing, Burt?" asked Noble.

"Seeing if I can get this slug out of here. Just a precaution."

Meanwhile, Cohen daubed disinfectant on Soleski's wound, cleaned dried blood from the skin, put antibiotic cream on the injury and taped a thick pad in place.

Soleski admired his friend's handiwork. "I suppose if this were being done in your fancy office, I'd have to pay two hundred dollars an hour, Sam."

Cohen wrapped the foot in gauze and taped it. "Who told you I worked that cheap, Sollie?"

The laughter helped defuse the tension in the room.

Cohen gathered the bloodied bandages and towels and stuffed them into a small plastic bag with those they had used the night before. "We'll toss these in a garbage can at the station."

At the window Swanson let out an exclamation. "Got it!" He held a misshapen lead slug. He told Peter to get a bar of soap from the bathroom. Swanson shaved curls of soap and packed them into the hole. When he finished, he stood back to admire his work. He drew the curtains across the disguised hole. "Well, it'll pass inspection at a distance."

"Good idea," said Noble. "I plan to be home by the time the maids find that."

"If our rooms are any indication," said Cohen, "they won't be looking for it."

A few more chuckles. The mood was lifting by degrees.

Cohen put away his kit. Swanson gently stretched a white sock over Soleski's wrapped foot and slipped the wounded man's feet into shoes.

"You're good to go, Sollie," Swanson said, "but you oughta ride to the station."

"Let's get him in the wheelchair," said Peter.

"Okay, gentlemen," sighed Cohen," let's get the hell out of here."

# CHAPTER SEVENTY-SIX

## LONDON, PADDINGTON STATION

The men rolled their luggage to the Heathrow Express platform while Cohen went to the ticket kiosk and bought five passes to the airport.

Noble strolled to the piled luggage and offered Soleski his metal cane. The little man protested, but Noble insisted. "Take it," he ordered.

"We just missed the seven o'clock," groused Swanson, looking at his watch.

"Fifteen minutes isn't going to make much difference, Burt," said Cohen.

The Arkansan scanned the massed travelers. "It's just that I don't want any more surprises at this point."

"If we stick together we'll have a better chance," said Noble.

"Oh, sure, we'll make a better target all bunched up like this," replied Swanson, searching the crowd.

Cohen laughed. "Still trying to get us to keep our intervals, huh, Burt?"

The passing minutes added to the stress everyone felt.

"Oh, geez, not now," whispered Cohen.

Three pairs of policemen suddenly appeared on the footbridge above the train platforms. A knot of uniformed officers in body armor, carrying submachine guns, was coming from the opposite direction. Senior officers directed armed policemen down the escalator to the train platforms. Suddenly, yellow police vests were everywhere.

Cohen was worried. "I hope this doesn't mean what I think it means."

Swanson moved close to Cohen. "Steady, Sam. Everyone just stay calm."

An express train entered the train shed and was sliding toward them.

"Hallelujah," said Noble. "Here comes our Get-Out-of-Jail-Free card."

"Our ticket out of Hell would be more like it," whispered Soleski.

The policemen moved among the waiting commuters, worked their way to the end of the concrete piers, then came back again. The train eased to a stop and the car doors hissed open. When the opening nearest them was clear of incoming passengers, the men boarded. Soleski leaned on the metal cane and limped to a seat, masking his discomfort.

Two policemen strolled by the open doors, eyeing the shuttle's passengers. Peter sat with his grandfather and watched the old man. Noble was utterly calm, smiling and nodding at those around him. Cohen pulled out his airline tickets and buried his nose in them. The doors closed and the train began to move, the platform and strolling policemen growing smaller.

"What was that all about?" wondered Cohen.

As they rolled through the first turn Noble pointed at the far tracks. "There's your answer, Sam." He nudged his grandson. "Look at that, Peter."

A cluster of police huddled over a crumpled, white shroud draped across a set of rails.

A pair of shoes poked from under the sheet. On the roadway above, four police cars and an ambulance were lined up, their strobes blinking in the morning sun. A wire basket was being lowered on ropes to the tracks below. Swanson gazed over his shoulder to study Peter's reaction.

"You okay, Sport?" asked his grandfather.

"Not really." Peter looked away and bowed his head. The sight of Ullrich's crumpled body in the early morning light drove home what he had done. He felt hollow and slightly ashamed.

At Heathrow, the men got a wheelchair for Soleski and Noble reclaimed his cane. They checked their baggage and went through the airport's rigorous security.

Once past the barriers with their screening machinery, the men followed Soleski's wheelchair to their concourse. They had a little more than two hours until their flight.

Peter bought his grandfather a bottle of juice and went in search of newspapers. He bought two British tabloids and a copy of *USA Today*. The London papers, *The Daily Star* and *The Sun*, both carried long stories about the Weismann killing on inside pages. Peter bought a hot chocolate and tucked two of the papers under his arm.

He read the *Sun*'s version on his way to the gate. "You ought to read this, Sam," he said when he sat down next to Cohen. He passed the tabloid to him. Peter gave the American paper to Soleski and resumed reading *The Daily Star*'s story. Weismann's death was big news and the writer was predicting a major impact on the European business community.

"Not one word about his Nazi past," scowled Cohen. "What a whitewash."

Peter got to the end of *The Daily Star*'s account, then passed the paper to Cohen. "There was one lousy line about him serving in the German Army, Sam."

Cohen traded tabloids with Peter. "Really? Well, read this version. The writer gives him a pass on that as well."

Peter scanned the copy surrounding a gallery of Weismann photos. Cohen was correct. Not one word of the German's wartime service. "You're right. It's not exactly great journalism."

Noble's voice got their attention. "Check out the TV, boys."

The four of them looked up at the wall-mounted monitor. Weismann's picture stared at them from the flat panel. A press conference with a small crowd of reporters was thrusting microphones at French police officials in a marble hall somewhere. The closed captioned words ran across the bottom of the screen. Peter and Cohen walked over to an aisle and stood beneath the monitor.

Cohen read the screen's scrawling words to himself. "They think it's possibly a professional hit for business reasons? Where in the hell did they get that theory?"

Peter turned to the lawyer. "Doesn't matter, does it?"

"I suppose not," answered Cohen. "Only, how do they figure that?"

"Did you both read the whole article?" asked Swanson. "Our guy was quite the mover and shaker. Big-time financier in Europe."

"But they're ignoring his Nazi war record," snapped Cohen.

"Big deal, Sam," said Swanson. "Even the Pope served the Fatherland."

"Maybe Burt's right," said Peter. "People just don't care about that stuff."

Cohen grunted in disgust. "That was the whole point of our trip,'" he hissed. His face flushed and he stomped back to his seat. On the TV, images of flooding in Italy flashed on the screen. Peter and Swanson watched for a while and then rejoined the others. Cohen sat with his arms folded. He was downcast.

Swanson tried to soothe him. "His war record has to come out eventually, Sam. He's too high profile now."

Cohen did not respond, so Swanson resumed reading. Noble hobbled off to find a bathroom. Soleski was lost in thought, the paper in his lap, unread. Peter pulled his iPod from his bag and shut out the terminal noise with music. Cohen got up to walk the busy concourse. The airport wait was testing his patience. They had left London but were not yet free.

Eventually, a subdued Cohen returned to his seat and read the news stories again. Peter went looking for his grandfather and found him heading the wrong way in a corridor filled with hurrying passengers and flight crews. He caught up with the old man and gently took him by the arm. "Where you going, Gramps? We're down that way." He pointed behind him.

Noble's face was drawn. "Got lost, Sport. Got turned around."

His grandson looked at him. "You okay?"

"Yeah, but I'm feeling my age," answered Noble. "I just want to go home."

Peter guided him back through the crowd. "We'll be boarding soon."

"What was that Sam was saying about Weismann?"

"He's upset because the news didn't mention Weismann's SS connection."

They came back to their seats and Peter eased into a chair next to his grandfather. "Eventually some reporter is bound to dig up that part of his past," he said. "Believe me, when that hits the fan, his big finance buddies will be scrambling to put a lot of distance between themselves and him."

"Ain't that the way it usually works," said Soleski.

In the background, an agent's voice calling their Chicago flight was competing with taped security warnings about strangers and unattended luggage.

"That's us, Gramps." Peter helped the old man to his feet and handed him his cane. Cohen told the men to take advantage of the early boarding process and they showed their tickets to the smiling gatekeepers. Swanson pushed Soleski down the jetway. The Nobles and Cohen followed. At the aircraft's hatch, Soleski left the wheelchair behind and limped to his assigned seat in first class.

All five had been grouped together at Cohen's insistence. Within minutes, other passengers holding tickets came aboard and began settling in the forward cabin.

A Nordic-looking flight attendant began taking drink orders while steerage filled. She smiled at Soleski as he ordered a white wine.

Cohen leaned forward, and tugged at Peter's sleeve, concerned. "How's he doing?"

"He's fading, but I think he'll make it home."

"Tell him to hold on until we reach Chicago. We can expedite him through Immigration and Customs if we have to. Once we're in Chicago, I can get him to the best doctors in town if need be."

Peter thanked Cohen and glanced at his grandfather.

Noble smiled. "Wake me when we land, kiddo." His grandson patted his arm. "Remember, Peter. None of that modern stuff. You have my music list."

"Hey, Gramps, don't talk like that. You're scaring Soleski and me."

Noble laughed and closed his eyes.

The cabin door shut and attendants went down the aisles checking seat belts. Screens lowered and the usual video about emergency procedures played. There was a gentle nudge against the fuselage as the 777 backed from the gate. The muted whine of the plane's engines rose and fell as the airliner taxied along the apron to its assigned spot in the takeoff queue.

Noble slept peacefully as the engines revved in power. He sensed the brakes release and felt the jet roll down the runway, gathering speed. When the big craft lifted from the earth, the old soldier relaxed for the first time in weeks and drifted into a wonderful, deep, serene sleep.

He dreamed of standing in deep snow on the edge of a familiar, deserted road. He stood there, head back in the cold air, smiling at his success in finding this road in the woods. He walked along a dark corridor of trees, west toward the sun. Noble finally felt safe, confident that the American lines were just ahead.

# CHAPTER SEVENTY-SEVEN

## CHICAGO, O'HARE AIRPORT

First class emptied quickly.

Cohen and his friends did not move to join the exodus. Peter reached up and tapped his call button. The Nordic-looking lead attendant left her post near the exit and came down the aisle. She reached over and extinguished the light. "Yes, sir, how may I help?" Cohen got out of his seat and stood in the aisle.

"There's a problem. It's my grandfather," said Peter. He nodded at Noble's slumped body in the seat next to him.

"Is he ill?" asked the attendant.

"I'm afraid he's dead," interjected Cohen.

The woman didn't appear shocked. Evidently, she'd witnessed such incidents on previous transatlantic flights. She placed a hand on Peter's shoulder. "I'm so sorry for your loss. Are you absolutely certain?"

"Yes, no question," replied Peter.

"I'll have to alert the captain," she said. "I think it would be best to wait until all the passengers have exited the aircraft."

She gave a wan smile and went across the cabin to her fellow attendants, who were herding the remaining travelers onto the jetway. The crew members glanced at the men in sympathy. The lead attendant went forward to the cockpit door and spoke to the pilot. Within minutes, the First Officer came back through the first-class cabin and stopped at Peter's seat. He offered his condolences and explained that he would summon paramedics to make an official diagnosis. Though it was obvious that Noble was dead, the co-pilot explained the airline's protocol for an in-flight death.

He went back to the cockpit and reported to the captain. The pilot called the tower with the news, then ordered the gate agent to alert airport security. The death of a passenger meant paperwork, and the pilot, although sympathetic to the man's family, knew his day had suddenly been complicated.

The crew would have to wait until EMT personnel took the body away. The pilot started his First Officer on post-flight paperwork and went into the cabin to talk to Peter. After gentle questioning to satisfy his curiosity, the pilot went away.

The plane was now deserted and a cleaning crew came aboard. A flight attendant sent them to the rear of the aircraft. A policeman and two paramedics with a narrow carrying board came into the first-class cabin. They gave their names, asked a few questions and then performed perfunctory tests on Noble's body. They lifted his body onto the stretcher and covered him with a sheet. Once the body was strapped with restraints, the pair lifted the board across the seats and left the airplane. They went down the jetway's outside stairway to a waiting ambulance with flashing lights.

The men loaded Noble's body into the emergency vehicle and shut the doors. Peter stood in the jetway and watched the van disappear behind a row of parked aircraft. The policeman pointed the men toward Immigration and Customs, while the gate agent requested a wheelchair for Soleski.

Cohen put an arm around Peter Noble's shoulders. "We can rearrange your flight. You can stay with me until we sort this out. When the medical examiner releases Bill's body I'll have him picked up by a friend's funeral home if you'd like. It's a family operation. I know them well."

Peter could only nod.

The four men moved down the sealed corridor to Immigration and went through the usual routine. The luggage carousel in Customs was nearly deserted by the time they arrived, and after they reclaimed their baggage, they were waved on through. In the terminal, they found a deserted gate and settled in the seats. Cohen asked the wheelchair attendant to leave them for a while.

An awkward silence surrounded the four of them. They made small talk, compared flight plans. Soleski's connecting flight was to leave in three hours, Swanson's in two. The pair opted to stay at O'Hare and have dinner together.

Cohen shook each man's hand. "I can't thank you enough," he said. "For more than sixty years, I never let go of the dream for justice. That someday we'd finish this." His eyes teared as he talked.

"I'm glad we did it, Sam," said Soleski from the wheelchair. "Too many years went by without Von Wurtz facing justice for what he did. We did good over there."

Cohen put a hand on the little man's shoulder. "Yeah, Sollie, you did. We had an obligation to . . . those who didn't come back."

Cohen looked at Swanson. "What can I say, Burt? If you hadn't come along I'm not so sure we would have pulled this off."

The lanky Arkansan smiled. "Sam, it was you who put this whole thing together. You made it happen. You deserve the credit for making it work."

"Burt's right," crowed Soleski. "It cost you plenty to give us quite a ride, Sam."

Swanson turned to Peter. "And son, I'll tell you what. You would've made one hell of a soldier. Just like your grandfather." He thrust his hand toward the young man. "I'm proud to have served with you . . . even if it was sixty-some years late."

Peter felt a lump in his throat. He took the outstretched hand. "My privilege, Sergeant Swanson . . . Burt. I'm only sorry that my grandfather didn't make it all the way home." His voice was flat, emotionless. He cleared his throat and looked away.

"It's okay, Peter. The tears will come later," said Swanson. "I know all about that."

"I suppose, but right now I'm kinda numb."

"Bill wanted to be with us," added Cohen. "He was the heart of the mission."

Noble's grandson stared at the three men. "I know he loved you guys. He talked about you a lot. He told me everything, about how you helped him survive the Battle of the Bulge and what that meant to him." He began to feel tears and stopped to catch his breath.

"The feeling was mutual," said Swanson. "I'm glad he got to come along."

"I hate to break this up, gentlemen," said Cohen, "but Peter and I have to make some arrangements for Bill, and you have flights to catch."

"So what do we do now, Sam?" asked Soleski.

"I don't know, Sollie. I'm going to tie up some details, go home, see Sondra and fold up my tent at the law office." He shrugged, looked around the bustling terminal. "I don't like ending like this . . . here, I mean. It just doesn't seem right."

Swanson waved at him. "Don't apologize, Sam. This was our last mission as a team. Let's just say goodbye and leave it at that. I know Bill would understand."

Soleski shook Peter's hand. "Thanks for the tours and all your help, kid."

"Like I said," replied Peter, "it was a privilege to be with you."

"If you do some sort of memorial . . ." began Swanson.

"Probably not going to be one, Burt."

"Well, okay, but if you change your mind, Peter . . ."

Peter waved at the old sergeant. "I'll let you know. Goodbye."

The men embraced and went their separate ways.

# CHAPTER SEVENTY-EIGHT

## MINNEAPOLIS, NOVEMBER 29

The autopsy report listed a clot, coupled with chronic heart failure and advanced age, as the probable cause of William Noble's death. His body was released to a funeral home Samuel Cohen recommended, and the old soldier was cremated as he had wished.

Peter stayed with Cohen for a week, then returned to Minneapolis with his grandfather's ashes. Two days later, he called Ken Wolf and Dawson O'Reilly after returning home. He met his grandfather's friends for dinner at some forgettable chain restaurant in the southern suburbs. They talked in generalities. O'Reilly got drunk halfway through the meal, and Peter had second thoughts about revealing too much about what had occurred in Europe. He discreetly promised Wolf he would follow up with another visit.

A month passed, and over dinner one evening, he swore Wolf to secrecy before telling him what had really happened during their European travels.

For Peter, the Minnehaha Avenue home became a tomb during what was left of summer. Burt Swanson had been right. The tears did finally come. There was a certain sadness that swept over Peter at unexpected times, and he would fight to keep his emotions in check without success. He reluctantly went back to his job at the county, but the days seemed hollow and he felt robotic. His doomed office romance with his girlfriend stalled, withered and finally died. In a way, he was relieved.

He sought counseling for help with the changes he had experienced, but the sessions sputtered and he ended them. Peter learned just enough to realize he might be suffering symptoms of post-traumatic stress disorder, but he also knew he was drifting and felt powerless to anchor himself. Before the month was out, Samuel Cohen called to tell him that his wife, Sondra, had finally died. The lawyer's voice seemed resigned as he shared the news. In the second half of the phone call, the two talked about The Project in guarded words. Cohen said he'd call again.

Peter started a four-day work week schedule. His grandfather's will had provided enough money for Peter to alter his weekly routine. The change allowed him to spend long weekends at the lake cottage.

Fall crept forward unseen, until late September when maples and oaks along Minnehaha Creek seemingly changed overnight. There was an early frost. Bursts of orange and scarlet among the trees reminded Peter of what was coming. He spent a solitary Thanksgiving week at the lake and then closed the cottage for winter. He returned to the Twin Cities along back roads, avoiding the holiday traffic. At home, he found a small mound of mail piled below the porch slot. There was a thick tan envelope from Samuel Cohen's law firm.

Peter set Cohen's package aside and sorted through the mail. He tossed most of it and made tea, dropped a lemon wedge into the steaming mug and went into the living room to start a fire. Flames crackled, licking at the dry wood, creating shadows on the walls. Peter turned on the tall brass reading lamp and sat in his grandfather's big leather recliner. He tore open the envelope.

A lengthy piece on Weismann's death from London's *Financial Times* unfolded in his lap, along with several magazine articles and a brief letter from Cohen. He set the clippings aside and read the letter first.

*Peter,*

*I trust this finds you well and happy. I still think often of your wonderful grandfather. I shall always miss him. Since my Sondra's death and my retirement from the law firm, I have been doing some rooting around about our little adventure in Europe. Lots of loose ends in ways that have bedeviled me ever since we concluded our business.*

*As you know, I had some serious misgivings about the way the media chose to handle the story. I turned up the enclosed articles within the last few weeks. I think you will find them very interesting. I've also uncovered new information.*

*We need to have a meeting when you have time. If your schedule permits, I would appreciate your coming here as I am not as spry as I used to be. Who among my contemporaries is? Please reply as soon as possible so that we can finish whatever details remain undone.*

*Sincerely, Sam*

Peter folded the letter and picked up the *Financial Times* clipping. Several pieces of newsprint were stapled together accordion-style. He read the article twice, put it aside and studied the magazine excerpts. When he was done, he put down the papers, threw two logs on the fire, then returned to go over the stories again. He got the portable phone from the kitchen, and dialed Cohen's Lake Michigan apartment.

He got him on the third ring. "Hello Sam, it's Peter. I just read your letter and the articles you sent with it."

The thin voice on the other end sounded relieved. "Peter, thanks for calling. What do you think? Can you come down to see me? Or should I come up to Minneapolis?"

"I suppose I could get down there in a week or so, Sam."

There was disappointment in Cohen's voice. "Oh, I was hoping to see you earlier than that, Peter. Can you get away and stay a day or so?"

"Is it that important? Couldn't it wait a week?"

"I don't think so. I'll explain when you come. Can you leave tomorrow?"

There was an urgency in the old man's voice. Peter thought of his schedule. "Possibly. I'd have to scramble a few things up here."

"Terrific," said Cohen. There was a pause. "I took the risk of booking you on a morning flight into Midway."

Peter shook his head, amazed that the man could still move mountains. "Sam, you're incorrigible," he said, surrendering. "Okay, give me the details."

Cohen read the flight and ticket numbers to the younger man. "I'll have my driver meet you in the morning, Peter."

"See you tomorrow, Sam."

Peter snapped off the light. Flames sent yellow light dancing on the hearth and ceiling. Peter watched the shadows and stared at the flames.

Samuel Cohen had his lake for contemplation; Peter Noble had fire.

# CHAPTER SEVENTY-NINE

### MINNEAPOLIS, NOVEMBER 30

The morning ran as if Samuel Cohen had preordained it.

Peter called his supervisor at the county and wheedled a few days off. He caught a morning commuter run to Chicago's Midway Airport and was met by Cohen's driver. The chauffeur drove him directly to the lawyer's lakeshore condo.

Cohen welcomed Peter in the marble foyer. It had been five months since the two men had seen one another. Cohen was much thinner than Peter remembered. He looked worn, frail. The familiar hatchet-faced profile was gaunt and there was a certain weariness.

"You've lost weight, Sam."

"I've got prostate cancer, Peter."

Peter felt shock, which must've showed on his face for Cohen tried to soften the news. "Hell, I've had it for years. It's just catching up with me now." He put an arm around his guest and steered him through the foyer. "Hey, don't be so glum. Most guys my age have it. If we live this long, we usually die of something else before the cancer gets us."

"Did the trip to Europe accelerate your . . ." Peter couldn't say the word.

Cohen finished the sentence for him. "Cancer? I went over there with it but it didn't slow me down." He ushered Peter into the spare bedroom. "Make yourself at home, then come down the hall to my study." Cohen padded down the corridor and disappeared into his book-lined office. Peter put away his things and followed his host.

Cohen sat behind his desk, fiddling with his open laptop computer. "Have a seat, Peter. I'll be right with you." Cohen was typing. "Just a few details for a trust I'm working on."

He closed down his computer and came from behind the desk. He sat in an armchair next to Peter and smiled. "Thanks for coming on such short notice."

"Sure, Sam. To tell you the truth, it's kinda nice to get away for a few days. I still haven't been able to focus on work. I'm sorry about the cancer."

Cohen waved away the comment. "Forget it, okay? We have other business." He nodded, then smiled again. "First I have to ask if you're hungry."

Peter shook his head. "I'm good for a couple of hours."

"Okay, then," said Cohen, "I'll have Gabriella fix us a light lunch for later." He rubbed his hands together and leaned forward. "Did you read all the stuff I sent you?"

"Yes, I did. Our late friend was quite the financier, wasn't he?"

"Absolutely. A big player by any standards. But a crooked one as well, right?"

"Well, yeah," agreed Peter. "I gathered that from the *Times* piece in particular. Weismann seemed to have left a lot of people holding the bag, didn't he?"

Cohen furrowed his thick brows. "High and dry, Peter. They're still sorting out the mess he left behind. Might take years before they pin it all down."

"I wasn't a business major in college, Sam, so a lot of it didn't make sense."

Cohen leaned back in his armchair. "It's pretty tangled, even for my head." He got up from his chair, thrust his hands deep in his pockets and slowly paced along a crowded bookshelf. "Okay, hold that thought about our friend's business shenanigans for a moment."

He stopped and faced his seated guest. "But there's something else that's come up in the last few weeks, Peter."

"Is this the reason for your urgency?"

"Yes, exactly." Cohen resumed pacing. "Remember how none of the media wanted to get into Weismann's Nazi past? His service with the SS? His involvement with atrocities during the war?"

"Sure, the first stories had virtually no mention of his wartime service at all."

Cohen stopped again. "Right. Even the muckraking tabloids didn't pick up on it right after he was killed. It infuriated me at the time."

Peter remembered Cohen's moodiness at the airport. "Yeah, I recall you being pretty bummed out about the news reports."

"You've got a good memory. I thought about making an anonymous phone call to CNN or the *Times* just to set the record straight."

"Did you?"

Cohen came back and sat down. "Never got around to it. With Bill's death on the way home, it got put on the back burner. I let it go for a while. Then the story got buried and I forgot about it." He stared at the carpet. "And, then, of course, my Sondra died and that overwhelmed me for a while . . . still does on occasion."

Peter Noble put an hand on Cohen's arm. "I was sorry to hear about that, Sam."

The old man sighed, recovered and went on. "Well, I did eventually get back on track and I looked into the whole thing." He looked at Peter. "Don't worry. I did everything very discreetly. Left no trails I'm aware of. I called Washington to talk to that fellow Banner at the Justice Department's Office of Special Investigations. Just to do some off-record follow-up, background checking on Von Wurtz . . . or Weismann as we knew him."

Peter leaned forward. "What did he tell you?"

Cohen sank back against his chair, did not look at Peter. "The number I used the first time was no longer in service so I called their main office. They had no such person on staff. Never heard of him. I called back the next day to check with a lawyer I know at Justice."

"And what did he tell you?" Peter knew the answer from Cohen's expression.

"He confirmed there had never been such a person on the payroll."

Peter insides began a slow turning. "But what about Carl Goldman, Sam?"

"Carl claims he was contacted by the guy at some Washington dinner eighteen months prior. Said the guy volunteered to help him find Von Wurtz through his job at Justice. Goldman says he's as mystified as I am about the guy."

"I'm getting a bad feeling, Sam."

"It gets worse, Peter. Remember that *Financial Times* piece?"

"Not every word. But yes, I read it two or three times. Why?"

Cohen got up again and went over to his desk. He fished among some papers and pulled out the newsprint he wanted. He came back to his chair and sat down. "Here, look at . . ." he scanned the article, ". . . look at this second page, fourth paragraph." He handed over the paper and pointed a bony finger at the section. He sat back and waited.

"Am I missing something, Sam?"

Cohen snatched back the newsprint and read it aloud. "Weismann's investment syndicate had been locked in this battle with the Anglo-American-Israeli group for several years . . ."

Cohen's eyebrows rose as he read a sentence with particular emphasis. "Responding to rumors of irregularities in his investment group's offer, a bank spokesman for Sir Hugh Symthson, president of the London-based association, denied the charges as a scurrilous attempt to derail his group's ongoing negotiations with officials in the Ruhr." Cohen sat back, raised the paper in his hand. "You see?!"

Peter remained perplexed. He did not see what Cohen was getting at. "Sorry to be so slow, Sam. But what exactly does all that mean?"

Cohen had to pace again. He strolled to one end of the room and came back to stand in front of Peter. He put a hand on the young man's shoulder. "It means that Sir Hugh Symthson was battling Weismann for one of Europe's biggest pies. Actually, more like the whole goddamn pastry shop.

"Sir Hugh was the gilt-edged, titled front man for investors who wanted to control Germany's New Century Project in the Ruhr region. Land reclamation, housing, new industry, parks, state of the art technology. The works. It was an ambitious, one-hundred-billion-dollar enterprise that was going to be a solid gold cash cow for the winners of the contracts." The explanation exhausted Cohen and he sank back into his chair. He reached for a bottle of water.

Peter asked, "So how does Weismann figure in this?"

Cohen put down his bottle. "He put the whole thing together eight years ago and got the ball rolling, looking for investors. According to the *Times* article, he secretly climbed in bed with one of the competitors, a French-German investment firm with deep pockets. Might have even been some Russian mob money in the pot."

Cohen took a long pull on the water bottle. "Anyway, they ended up bidding against others interested in the project and all but these two syndicates dropped out. Too rich for everyone's blood but these two well-heeled opponents."

"And Weismann was the middle man on this?"

"Bingo, Peter! He had his finger in all the pies. He was also working with the London group for a while until he was caught."

"Wow, Sam. Pretty ballsy thing for Weismann to do."

"You'd better believe it. He cleaned them out for huge fees before they got wind of his double-dealing on behalf of the French-German group."

"How much money are we talking about? I mean for Weismann?"

Cohen smiled sarcastically. "The figure, one hundred million, was mentioned but I'm not sure that's accurate. He took both groups for a sizable sum and then jumped ship to work exclusively with the French-German syndicate."

"Must have pissed off the London folks plenty."

Cohen nodded.

A light went on in Peter's head. "Geez, Sam, would somebody have actually wanted the guy dead over this?"

"Now you're thinking wise beyond your years, Peter."

Peter dropped back. "And we did the job for them . . . whoever they are."

"That's not the worst of it though."

Peter braced himself for more revelations. "You mean there's more, Sam?"

"I'm afraid so. And I have to bear the responsibility for this part." Cohen looked off toward the lake, paused, then turned to face his house guest.

"Weismann was not really Von Wurtz after all."

# CHAPTER EIGHTY

The news hit Peter hard. He felt his heart jump against his chest. "What are you saying, Sam? We killed the wrong man?"

Cohen's face took on a pained expression. He ran a bony hand over his wrinkled dome, covered his eyes and simply nodded. "Weismann served in the German Army, but he was strictly Wehrmacht, not SS as we were lead to believe."

"But all the information you had. The background. The photographs."

"All manufactured. Tailored for our consumption, Peter. The pictures were real. Our friend Ehud provided those from his surveillance."

"The wrong man," said Peter softly. "We murdered an innocent man."

Cohen heaved a deep sigh. "I doubt he was entirely innocent, Peter. Don't forget, the Wehrmacht had plenty of blood on its hands when the war ended. Even so, nothing ties Weismann to any of it and he wasn't SS. That I know for sure."

"What about Weissmann's friend, Ullrich, who came after us in London?"

"He was definitely SS. Schutzstaffeln. SS-Hauptscharführer Felix Ullrich. Hard core. Fanatical. They were friends. Old troops who happened to know each other."

"Sam, if we were used, then someone's bound to come looking for us."

"I don't know who that would be, Peter. Weismann's dead. His bank accounts are frozen and the two groups will now fight over the funds in the courts. I'm sure the Swiss bankers will be helpful . . . up to a point." He threw up his hands again. "You should know one last piece of the puzzle."

"I don't know if I can take much more of this all in one day."

"When your grandfather and I met with Carl Goldman in London to plan this whole thing, we were introduced to our professional contact, Ari."

Peter nodded. "Sounds more and more like those guys were ex-Mossad after all, Sam."

Cohen frowned. "Your instincts were probably right all along. It makes sense."

Peter spoke again. "Have you considered that they might have been on loan for just this mission?"

It had not occurred to Cohen. He could only shake his head. "The flat where we met Ari belonged to Sir Hugh Symthson."

Peter's face registered surprise. "The head of the London investors?"

"The same. He wasn't there, of course, but his good friend Proctor Johnson was on hand to meet with us before we were introduced to Ari."

"The former senator was actually there?"

"Oh, yes. And his right-hand man is the same Carl Goldman who passed me all the classified material on Von Wurtz, or Weismann."

"The sonofabitch set you . . ." Peter corrected himself, "set us up, Sam." He buried his head in his hands. "Thank God, my grandfather never knew."

"Small comfort, Peter," said Cohen. "But yeah, I'm glad Bill was spared this."

"What do you think happened to Von Wurtz, Sam?"

"Who knows? Probably died in the Bulge, or later. If there is a God it's in his hands now. In light of what's happened, does it even matter anymore?"

Peter stared at the floor. "Maybe you're right. Just curious, I guess." He suddenly looked up. "But then, what's Proctor Johnson's connection to Sir Hugh Symthson?"

"Sir Hugh is a former chancellor of the Exchequer," said Cohen. "He's prominent in Jewish circles. Oozes money. Big, big fundraiser for Israel."

"Is that the common thread between the two?"

"Part of it. Proctor Johnson's a well-known evangelical and also a high profile defender of Israel. One of their best lobbyists in America, a puppet, some say. Used to be one of their hand-picked voices in the Senate. Still raises tons of money for Israel every year on the talk circuit. There have been rumors for a long time that he was on their payroll, but I've never seen hard proof."

"Don't tell me," said Peter. "He lost money in this scheme too."

"Bingo, again, young man," said Cohen. "And he could ill afford his losses. Sir Hugh lost even more, but he also sold this dream to a lot of his wealthy friends on both continents. He was on the hook to them for huge sums and wanted revenge. Wanted Weismann to pay for it."

"So the circle's complete, right?" said Peter.

"What exactly do you mean?" asked Cohen.

"One, they get us to take out Weismann. Two, now they have a chance to get some of their money back. Three, we're supposed to think Von Wurtz was getting what he deserved after all these years. And four, the Fortunate Orphans get a sense of justice, and you're grateful to the good senator for leading you to the bad guy."

"Pretty good summation for an amateur counselor," said Cohen. "Is that it?"

"One more thing," said Peter. "Proctor Johnson's assured we'll keep our mouths shut because we killed someone, the wrong guy it turns out, and the senator comes out smelling like a rose." He looked at the lawyer. "I'm surprised the slimy bastard hasn't asked you for a campaign contribution."

Cohen leaned back and laughed. "He has!"

Peter shook his head and joined Cohen in the moment's twisted hilarity. When the laughter subsided, Peter saw tears in Samuel Cohen's pale eyes.

"What are you going to do, Sam?"

Cohen dabbed his eyelids with a tissue. "I've got an idea to run past you, but first, I think we should have lunch."

They rose and went down the hall to the dining room where the view of Lake Michigan was spectacular.

## CHAPTER EIGHTY-ONE

Cohen dismissed his housekeeper and sat down opposite Peter. They ate quietly.

Peter broke the silence. "Sam, there's something I've been wanting to ask you for a long time."

"I know what you're going to say," answered Cohen. "But go ahead, I can always take the Fifth if you put me in a corner."

The men smiled at each other.

"Maybe it's awkward to answer this, but what was going through your mind when you killed Weismann?"

Cohen put down his glass of wine and sat back. A deep vertical furrow appeared between his brows. He glanced once at the lake, then across the table. "It was all over much too quickly. I wanted him to know who I was, why I was there, why he had to die." His shoulders sagged against his chair. "I didn't have the chance to do that of course. Didn't have that luxury." He raised his head and caught Peter's stare. "You see, I never had the opportunity to process the whole episode, to think about it, to understand what I had done. I didn't talk about it to Bill, and I never said a word to Sollie or the others once we left the scene."

"We were too busy getting away at that point," said Peter.

"But it, the actual shooting, was oddly anti-climatic, Peter." Cohen pushed away from the table and went to stand in front of the picture window overlooking the lake. He turned back to his guest. "The planning and the journey we took together as a group was the high point of the whole thing actually. That's what really mattered when it was all done."

He came back to the table and stood there with a wineglass in his hand. "And now, the entire thing's gone upside down on me. I don't know what to think about my actions." He sighed and sank into his chair. "I served the law my whole life, and willingly gave it up for a chance at my own personal revenge dressed up as justice."

"Yes, but you can't blame yourself for being taken in by the senator, Sam."

Cohen flashed a rueful smile at the younger man and shook his head. "Oh, but I can, Peter. I was so eager to right a hideous wrong that I lost sight of my life's work, my long love affair with the law."

"Is that why you quit the law firm?"

"Yes, I knew I would before I left for Europe. I had to. I had deliberately stepped outside the law and I knew the consequences that came with that. So, it was that and Sondra's death that finished it for me." Cohen's face darkened in a meditative mask. "Then, when I found out we had been used, I got angry, lost it for a while. The anger helped focus me, brought me out of my depression."

"I've felt the same way for some time, Sam."

"You, too? Why you?"

"I felt disconnected when I got home. With Gramps' death and the end of the trip . . . plus, you know, the way it ended with Ullrich showing up in London." He paused. "I mean, I just wasn't prepared for the impact that being involved in the deaths of two men would have on me." He drained his wine and poured more for both of them. "I've been drifting for a while. Can't get a grip. Not sure what's really important anymore." He looked at Cohen. "Does that sound like someone who's depressed?"

His host raised his glass in a salute. "Sounds exactly like I was feeling until I got angry about this betrayal, Peter." Cohen leaned across the table. "Would you be interested in retrieving some of what you've lost?"

"What have I lost, Sam?"

"I hate to be dramatic, but maybe part of your soul, Peter."

"Okay. And how am I supposed to get that back?"

"Help me send a particular message to the good senator. You game?"

"If it gives me a little peace, then I'm all for it. What do you propose?"

The old man steadied himself against the table. "Let's go into the living room. Bring the wine, Peter. I'll light a fire and we can have the best of both worlds. A fire by the lake. Even if it is eighteen stories up."

Peter laughed, picked up the wine bottle and followed the lawyer into the larger room. Cohen tapped a button and a fire immediately appeared in the granite fireplace. They sat on a curving sofa, facing the hearth, Lake Michigan shimmering in the distance. "You'll have to make do with my gas logs, Peter. A poor imitation to your real thing, but my insurance company frowns on wood-burning fireplaces in high-rises. The lake, however, is real. I can vouch for that."

Cohen set his wine glass on the low, mahogany coffee table. "I want to set up a meeting with Carl Goldman and make him, as they say, 'an offer he can't refuse.' But I'll need you nearby to make this work."

"Won't he figure out what you're up to if he sees me?"

"Carl's never met you. He doesn't know what you look like."

Peter pondered the offer. "Okay. If it helps us salvage something out of all this, Sam, then count me in."

"Good. Here's what I want to do."

# CHAPTER EIGHTY-TWO

### CHICAGO, MARTIN'S GRILL, DECEMBER 4

Samuel Cohen settled back against the red leather seat and checked his watch.

The restaurant was filling with lunch patrons. He sipped his water. On his right, an elderly couple were halfway through their meal. To Cohen's immediate front, a group of advertising types were ordering their first round of drinks. On Cohen's left, Peter, dressed in a dark blue suit, was playing the part of a young business executive. An open laptop sat in front of him. He was killing time by scrolling through the online edition of the *Chicago Tribune*.

A small day-planner was perched on the edge of Peter's table with its hidden microphone aimed at the empty seat opposite Cohen. The lawyer spotted Carl Goldman talking to the restaurant's hostess. The woman came their way, Goldman in tow.

"Are you recording?" asked Cohen.

"Loud and clear, Sam," replied Peter. "Enjoy your lunch."

The restaurant's hostess pulled out Goldman's chair and handed him a menu as he sat. The two men shook hands across the table.

"Well, Sam, good to see you. How are you?"

"I could be a lot better, Carl. You look as though things are agreeing with you."

Goldman scanned the room, glancing at Peter and the other patrons. He pulled his chair closer to the table. "Have you ordered, Sam?"

"No, thought I'd wait for you."

On cue a waitress appeared. She recited the specials and waited for the men to decide. When they'd ordered, she took their menus and moved next door to Peter's table. She flirted with him as they bantered about the restaurant's reputation and its specialties. He chose a salad and the waitress left him. Peter resumed his role, drinking iced tea and stabbing at the keys, bringing up the *Tribune*'s sports page.

Cohen began with a few innocent questions to disarm Goldman. "How goes the senator's presidential campaign these days, Carl?"

Goldman laughed. "Oh, we're a long way from that, Sam. The senator's still putting his ducks in a row. Checking the public pulse, making a few calls."

"Checking which way the wind is blowing," said Cohen smiling.

"Did I leave out any clichés?" chuckled Goldman. Cohen had to admit that the man across from him was likable, despite his oily personality. Their server arrived with a basket of fresh bread and Cohen waited for her to leave.

"You know our little adventure turned out to be a disaster, Carl."

Goldman parried the comment. "I'm sorry about that, Sam. I told you how mystified I was about the false information this Banner fellow gave me. He seemed genuine from the get-go. We were all fooled."

Cohen tore open the loaf and began buttering the bread. His eyes avoided Goldman. "Let's treat each other like adults, Carl. You set me up with this Banner decoy to get me interested."

Goldman frowned at the statement. "I did no such thing, Samuel. I really thought I was helping you. How was I supposed to know the guy was being untruthful?"

Cohen felt his anger rising. "I won't dignify that excuse with a response. You should have been more up-front with me about the connection between the senator and Sir Hugh Symthson, Carl."

"No surprise there. They've known each other for years, Sam."

"We both know I'm talking about their business connection," said Cohen. "The partnership on Germany's New Century Project in the Ruhr." He braced for Goldman's reaction but the man was smooth.

"I'm not following," said Goldman. "What syndicate are you alluding to?"

Cohen paused while they were served their luncheon entrees. "Carl, I really do like you, but let's not play games. Between the published articles and what I've been able to learn on my own, it's pretty clear Proctor Johnson and Sir Hugh were on the hook for a lot of money."

Goldman suddenly began pushing food around on his plate.

Cohen scolded his lunch partner with a bony finger. "And a lot of that money was not theirs. Add it all up, Carl. We were given false information that resulted in the death of an innocent man, all because Weismann screwed your boss and his titled buddy out of a lot of money."

Cohen ignored his lunch and took a swallow of iced tea.

Goldman finally looked at him coyly. "That's a pretty far-fetched fantasy, Sam. You'd have a hard time proving your theory." He took a bite of roasted chicken.

"I don't think so, Carl. It was the senator who provided us with an introduction to Ari, or whatever his name is, and your man turned out to be a professional killer." Cohen's face reddened. "We thought you were interested in helping us, Carl."

"Lower your voice, Sam. Remember, Ari didn't do the actual killing, did he?" He tried to soothe Cohen. "None of us wants this to become public."

The lawyer fumed at Goldman. "We wouldn't be having this discussion if you hadn't delivered the wrong man. That's the crux of the problem, Carl. Weismann cheated your boss so he figured out a way to eliminate him by using a bunch of gullible veterans. Pretty slick of the senator."

Goldman was not yielding. He leaned toward Cohen. "Don't you stay up with the news, Sam? The French say the case is closed. My sources tell me they've pinned the murder on Weismann's bodyguard and that old Nazi thug. It sounds pretty reasonable to assume they've solved it."

"I've read about that Carl, but what's your point?"

"My point, counselor, is that there's no reason to rock the boat at this stage." He leaned back in his chair. "We're both getting a pass on this thing. Take advantage of it, for God's sake." The lawyer's face was unreadable so Goldman pursued his argument. "Sam, face it. You're in a bind here. If you go public with this, you're admitting to murder. You'd ruin your life and the lives of your fellow veterans. Think about it."

Goldman sat back, waiting for his words to sink in.

Cohen drummed his long fingers on the tablecloth before speaking. "Carl, you've been manipulated by your boss in this whole affair. Don't think for one moment that Proctor Johnson wouldn't cut you loose if this thing comes out." He pushed his argument. "You know how he operates, Carl. You've been at his elbow all these years. He'd profess no knowledge of this whole episode, say it was your show. Think about it, man. You're the one who introduced us to Ari. You're the one who gave us the bad information. Proctor Johnson's in the clear on all that."

Goldman's expression remained passive. He dabbed his napkin at the corners of his mouth and pushed his plate aside. "Still just an interesting theory, Sam. I'm not going to sit here and let you drive a wedge between the senator and me. Nice try, though." But he wasn't finished. "Tell you what, Sam. I admire your chutzpah but you're bound up in this thing as much as I am. If you go public, your life is finished. I'd think the prospect of spending what remaining years you have in a French jail would give you pause."

Now it was Cohen's turn. He laughed. "You've got to be kidding, Carl. How old are you? You're what, not even fifty? You've got your whole life ahead of you." He leaned across the table. "I'm eighty-two years old, Carl, and I've got inoperable cancer. Did you know that? The love of my life has died, and I have no family to go after. I've resigned from my law firm and I'm well along in the process of liquidating most of my assets. You think your threat frightens me?" He sneered. "I'd be dead even before the ink on an extradition request had the chance to dry." He sat back and gestured at Goldman. "On the other hand, you'd find yourself friendless and penniless in a week."

Carl Goldman kept his poker face. "You can't undo what's happened, Sam. So, what is it you want?"

Cohen laid out his request in blunt words. "I want you to tell Proctor Johnson that if he so much as thinks about running for President or the second slot I will go to the press with the story. I will absolve my friends of any responsibility in the German's slaying. I'll testify that I took a solo trip on the sly without them knowing what I was doing. I have hotel receipts, credit card bills and a detailed journal that recorded my every move. I'd have no trouble convincing a court here or abroad that Ari and Ehud helped me kill Weismann."

Goldman looked stunned at the audacity of Cohen's demand.

A minute passed. "You're crazy, Sam. Proctor Johnson would never agree to that."

"Well, that's your job then, Carl. Sell it to him. Make him face reality."

Carl Goldman sagged against his chair. He was cornered in the lawyer's bizarre mutual destruction pact and they both knew it.

Johnson's aide pleaded with Cohen. "You don't know the senator's limits, Sam. He won't take your threat lightly."

Cohen slowly folded his napkin and placed it by his plate. "There are threats and then there are promises. I hope he knows the difference. Now if you'll excuse me, Carl, I have work to do." He slid out from behind the table and towered over Goldman. "I've already paid the tab. We'll be in touch." The gaunt-faced lawyer walked from the restaurant.

Goldman stared at his half-finished meal for five agonizing minutes and then left.

Peter put down his tea and reached for the notebook on the edge of his table. He pushed a button on the tiny machine and pocketed the recorder. His server came over, and he stuffed two twenties inside the folder and told her to keep the change. He folded his laptop and exited the restaurant. One block away, a black town car pulled alongside the curb and Peter got into the back seat next to Cohen. The vehicle pulled away and headed for Lake Shore Drive.

There was fire in Cohen's eyes. "Well, I think that went rather well, don't you, Peter? Did you get everything?"

"Every word, Sam. I didn't know you kept a journal about our trip."

Cohen laughed. "I didn't, Peter. But Goldman doesn't know that. I think he swallowed that one whole. It'll give him pause. Especially the part about the paper trail, don't you think?"

"You had me convinced. I'll get to work on a transcript as soon as we get back to your place."

"We're not going back to my place. I'm taking you right to the airport."

"What about my things?"

Cohen patted Peter's arm. "I had your bag put in the trunk before we left."

Lake Michigan's surface shimmered in the tinted windows as they rode in silence for a few minutes. Finally, Cohen broke the spell. "I want you back home where you belong before all hell breaks loose."

Peter exhaled slowly. "I wouldn't want to be in Goldman's shoes about now."

Cohen allowed himself a broad smile. "Actually, I'd like to be the proverbial fly on the wall in Proctor Johnson's office. You'll probably be able to hear him all the way to Minnesota when Carl has his little chat with the good senator."

"You worried at all, Sam?"

"About those two? No, Johnson's basically a bully who delegates all his dirty work and Carl Goldman is a glorified office boy who's in way over his head on this.

"I'll be fine, Peter. I just want to live long enough to keep an eye on Proctor Johnson. I want to make sure he misses this election cycle. After that, it's up to you." He dismissed Peter's worry with a wave. "Don't worry, we'll stay in touch."

A week passed without further contact between Samuel Cohen and Carl Goldman.

Peter sent the lawyer an e-mail with a document attached, a transcript of the restaurant conversation with the senator's aide. Cohen read through it, then printed several copies. He put them into envelopes with the notation "*Upon my death, contact Peter Noble*" and sealed them. Each envelope went into a larger mailer with a card directing how to contact Peter.

One copy went to Cohen's executor at his old law firm and a second one to his sister-in-law. A third version, without Peter Noble's information, was sent that same day by messenger to Carl Goldman. Along with the verbatim transcript, Samuel Cohen penned a warning that any retribution against the Fortunate Orphans would prompt a release of multiple copies of the manuscript. It was a gamble, Cohen wrote, that he was willing to take.

It bore fruit before the week was out.

# CHAPTER EIGHTY-THREE

CHICAGO, SHERATON HOTEL BALLROOM, DECEMBER 15

"They're ready for the senator, Carl," Proctor Johnson's press secretary whispered to Goldman as he stood next to a bank of microphones. Camera lights ringed a podium set on a small, carpeted stage. A huge American flag stretched across a blue-curtained backdrop behind the stage. A scowling Proctor Johnson cast a murderous glance at Goldman and strode to the platform.

As soon as he entered the lighted arena, a wide smile appeared on his handsome, tanned face. There was a smattering of applause as the former politician moved athletically through a small knot of admirers who shook his hand as the cameras tracked his progress to the platform. Johnson turned at the last second and kissed his smiling wife.

"You'd think he's giving his goddamned state of the union address," sneered Goldman watching the entry.

Johnson's press secretary, a reed-thin, mannish woman in a pants suit, threw Goldman an angry look. She had been given the news of the former senator's withdrawal from presidential politics exactly one hour prior to the press conference. She was livid at the news. The only saving grace was that today's speech would dominate the evening news cycle. There would be some collateral exposure on CNN and other cable news programs. She had also managed to get Johnson onto the upcoming Sunday political talk shows.

It was small consolation to those in the former senator's office who had been riding high in the wake of his rising political fortunes. The press aide seethed at Carl Goldman because he was the closest person to the senator, yet had not shared this decision with the entire staff.

The small crowd of reporters settled into their seats as Johnson tapped at the microphones and did a quick sound check. "Seems these three guys walked into a bar . . ." he began. "No, wait, I don't think I want to tell that particular joke at this time."

His audience erupted in laughter, recalling his earlier gaffe in the last campaign. Reporters lapped up self-deprecating jokes and Goldman smiled at the Senator's disarming smoothness. Even the press secretary was smiling.

"As many of you know, my future political plans have often been the object of much speculation by the members of the Fourth Estate." There were polite chuckles. Proctor Johnson delivered another smooth line. "For the life of me, I can't imagine why." Sustained laughter and applause this time. A few youthful staffers hooted at the edge of the crowd.

The tall man behind the podium grinned. "But I have come to believe in these last few months that my best service to this great nation of ours would be to put aside my ambition and look to the greater good."

Goldman suppressed a gagging sound. The press secretary hissed at him, and he smiled back at her like a child caught mocking the teacher. Proctor Johnson had the crowd hanging on his every word.

"My vision is a Middle East where parties of all persuasion, from all involved nations, can sit down in an atmosphere of mutual trust and respect." More applause. The politician held up his hand. "Therefore, today I am asking that my friends, my supporters, not prolong their efforts to secure me consideration as my party's presidential nominee."

Sounds of surprise swept the crowd. Even jaded reporters turned to measure the crowd's reaction. The writers scribbled or tapped at their open laptops. The cameramen did slow zooms on Proctor Johnson or panned the room to film disappointed supporters.

"Please realize," intoned Johnson in his deepest, sincerest baritone, "that I came to this conclusion only after much soul searching and quiet reflection. I also sought counsel from my family." He swept his hand across the podium toward his wife, who flashed a wide smile at him. She gazed adoringly and blew a kiss at her husband, who responded in like fashion.

"My life's work, both in the Senate, an institution I passionately loved, and in the arena for peace in the Mideast, will always be close to my heart. I believe I can serve my fellow citizens best by continuing to speak out for rational dialogue in one of the most important areas of the world." Another ripple of applause.

"I will continue to write, think about and consult with others who value my efforts to effect a solution to conflict there. You know my work on behalf of Israel." He looked into the cameras with resolve. "That will continue, as will my search for a lasting peace." The silver-haired politician thanked the crowd, waved, then took ten minutes of questions. He sailed glibly through most of them under the watchful eyes of his press secretary, who moved to one side of the room and flashed prearranged signals to her boss during the session. Her planted softball question came from a local TV reporter. "Would you consider serving in the administration should the president ask you?" The woman sat down for his answer.

"I would certainly have to think seriously about such a request. To be asked to serve this great nation by one's president is hardly a summons one can ignore."

There was a jostling among the reporters and somehow a question about the failed project in Germany, and Johnson's involvement in it, slipped through the press secretary's net.

The questioner, a particularly disagreeable and slovenly newspaper political writer, interrupted to ask the one embarrassing question Johnson had feared.

"Senator, does your withdrawal from national politics at this time have anything at all to do with your role in the financial collapse of the New Century Project in Germany?"

Johnson tried to sidestep the question. "I'm familiar with the project but perhaps you could narrow your question."

The reporter wouldn't be diverted. "You had, did you not, Senator, a financial interest in a partnership with Sir Hugh Symthson? Now that the endeavor has collapsed with the death of German financier Kurt Weismann, there appears to be a growing problem with what some people are calling a gigantic scam."

Carl Goldman sucked in his breath and held it, waiting for the answer. He glanced to the edge of the crowd where the press secretary was panicking. Her signals to Johnson were going unnoticed. If the former senator saw her cues, he was unable to respond.

The reporter's question hung in the air.

Goldman was worried but he was betting on his employer's skills.

The former senator called the reporter by his name to regain the initiative. "Kevin, let me be clear about my interest in the New Century Project. I was persuaded by my good friend, Sir Hugh, to become a part of what we thought at the time was a tremendous opportunity to revitalize a neglected sector of one of our long time allies. Where others saw despair, poverty, joblessness and scorched earth, Sir Hugh Symthson saw opportunity and hope."

The questioner sat down for the finish. He had already lost the round to Johnson. He would record the politician's answer but he knew the man had slithered free.

Proctor Johnson finally read his press secretary's worried expression and wrapped up the answer with a polished flourish, warming to the sound of his own voice. "Our financial contribution, which was minuscule I might add, was made in the hope that we could be part of something noble, something good. Like the other, more senior participants, we were extremely disappointed to learn of the perfidy of some of those involved. The solid, hard-working people of the Ruhr are the losers here. We await an eventual outcome in the courts."

He held up a hand to signal his departure. "Thank you for coming. God bless you. And may God bless America!"

The man walked regally from the stage and grasped his wife's hand, the pair framed in a halo of camera lights. They made small talk with supporters and staff. Proctor Johnson signed autographs for adoring young fans, then was gone.

## CHAPTER EIGHTY-FOUR

### PARIS, MINISTRY OF INTERIOR, PLACE BEAUVAU

In Paris, Henri Dupré was growing impatient, irritated by the delay.

The policeman sat on an ornate but uncomfortable chair in an opulent anteroom in the Ministry of Interior. He was waiting to be interviewed by the Director-General of the National Police. On his lap rested months worth of work in a thin black folder—his notes and report on the Weismann murder. A bored young female receptionist sat at an oversized desk, methodically filing reports of some sort into three stacks of paperwork.

Her desk phone rang, startling Dupré. The woman listened, made a note and rang off. "The Director-General is ready for you, sir." She nodded at a tall door at the far end of the room.

Dupré stood and began walking toward the door. Halfway across the waiting room, the door opened, and an unsmiling, androgynous figure appeared in the framed opening. Dupré crossed the floor, his heels clicking on the polished parquet surface.

The diminutive man in the door bowed slightly. "Commandant Dupré, please come with me."

Dupré followed the slight figure through the doorway into a carpeted office with an enormous desk. Files, a bank of phones and two flat computer screens took up half of the surface. A large map of France covered most of one wall; a tapestry of a stag hunt with mounted riders hung opposite. A bank of windows framed in heavy gold brocade provided a dramatic backdrop to the official's desk.

The Director-General was a tall, austere-looking mustached man with dark, thinning hair combed over a bald pate, affecting a young de Gaulle likeness. He came from behind the desk and offered his hand to the policeman.

"May I present Commandant Henri Dupré," said the small man at his side.

"Ah, Dupré. I've been hearing excellent things about you from your peers."

"Thank you, sir," replied Dupré.

The Director-General pumped the officer's arm and guided him by the elbow to the armchairs. "That will be all, Louis. Leave us, please." The aide withdrew with a bow and closed the tall double doors.

The men settled into the chairs and Dupré offered his folder. "My report on the Weismann case, sir."

The official took the black binder and flipped it open. He scanned the notes. "Give me your thoughts as I read your findings, Dupré."

The policeman coughed nervously and began reciting. "My opinion, and that of my deputies as well, sir, is that the Corsican . . ."

"Karl Rocca, yes?" interjected the official.

"Yes, sir. We believe Rocca planned Kurt Weismann's murder with the help of a former German soldier who had befriended the financier."

"Is it true he was former SS?" The Director-General studied the briefing book. "This Felix Ullrich you mention here."

"Correct, sir. We theorize that he and Karl Rocca had help from a local farmer and his son, the Courbets. We're certain the son drove the getaway vehicle and abandoned it just inside the German border. Their police confirmed that the younger Courbet was probably the driver. A resident of Perl saw a cyclist leave the van behind. We think it was the young man. He is a well-known rider, even runs biking tours."

Dupré paused as the official continued reading. He did not look up. "Go on, officer."

"Monsieur Weismann's housekeeper, Madame Cheroux, was most cooperative. She summoned officers and surrendered five thousand euros Rocca had given her to buy her silence. A search of the deceased's home found an empty safe. It was Madame Cheroux's opinion that Karl Rocca had fled with the money."

"And what was your feeling, Commandant Dupré?"

The policeman shrugged. "We saw no reason to doubt her, sir."

"I don't suppose it occurred to you to shake her skirts for the missing money?" The official smiled. "Just a thought, Dupré. Continue, please."

"Yes, sir. Sometime the following morning, Rocca and Ullrich apparently killed their two accomplices, the Courbets. Both had been brutally beaten, and a fire set to cover the crime. The boy was horribly burned, but was able to crawl from the flames and survive long enough to positively identify Rocca and Ullrich as the killers.

"You know the rest, sir. We were interviewing Rocca in Thionville when we got word of the Courbet killings. He must have surmised as much and tried to escape."

At last the bureaucrat ended his reading and met Dupré's eyes. "Yes, most unfortunate," he sighed. "The suspect's death was regrettable. It leaves us with so many unanswered questions."

"Absolutely, sir."

"Are you aware the SS man was killed later in London?"

Dupré had been told the news prior to arriving in Paris. He was not given details, only that Scotland Yard had alerted the French National Police once they had identified the corpse as Felix Ullrich.

The Director-General closed the folder on his lap. "Seems your German was flying under false colors. He carried a Danish passport. Our friends say he had been in touch with British Nazis. He was thought to be carrying a large sum of money on him."

"Perhaps from the safe at Weismann's house, sir."

"It's possible, I suppose. The London police theorize that he died of a fall after a robbery attempt. The amount of cash on him may have tempted someone. They believe the old soldier was followed in order to rob him. What do you think, Dupré?"

"Sounds plausible, sir. But without being on the scene . . ."

The official smiled at the policeman. "A cautious answer, officer. Very correct."

Dupré pointed at the closed folder. "There is one more thing, sir."

"Yes?"

"We found a key on Rocca that matched a local hotel's luggage storage room. We recovered his belongings, which included a Beretta and suppressor."

"Hmmm, interesting. This Rocca was quite a dangerous man, wasn't he?"

"Yes, sir. I regret our failure to take extraordinary precautions with him."

"I'm sure, Dupré. But one cannot always predict how these things will go."

Dupré grasped at the rationale. "No, sir. I suppose not."

"Most regrettable and extremely embarrassing, however," added the official in a scolding tone. "The minister's interest in this case is somewhat delicate. The late Weismann was a man with many friends in this government. Certain national financial interests have been compromised with the gentleman's death. As the lead investigator, you are due the courtesy of knowing that much, Dupré. But only that. This is to be kept all very confidential of course."

"Absolutely, sir. I understand."

The Director-General stood and Dupré rose with him. The official flashed a polite smile and gripped the policeman's hand in farewell. "Good. We understand each other, Dupré. I will share your report with the minister this afternoon. Your government appreciates your work on this case."

He walked the officer to the tall doors and opened them. The aide was waiting. "Goodbye, Commandant Dupré."

The policeman bowed slightly and trailed his guide across the room.

The Director-General had already made up his mind that Dupré would suffer the consequences for the lapse in security at Thionville. It was messy business to have gendarmes kill a suspect in a public shoot-out. Too many prying journalists asking for details and too many questions to answer. The Weismann affair, as the episode was now being called in the cabinet, needed to be taken off the front pages and resolved quietly. Reputations were in the balance.

Part of the resolution would mean Dupré's resignation by year's end.

## CHAPTER EIGHTY-FIVE

Peter Noble knew Samuel Cohen did not have long to live. When he returned to Minneapolis and resumed his job, the nagging doubts about the trip to Europe began again.

He phoned Cohen weekly until the lawyer became too frail to talk.

The end came quickly. Cohen was dead by the end of the month from the ravages of his cancer.

He was mourned by Chicago's legal and political communities. A large crowd, including two former governors and the state's congressional delegation, attended synagogue services for the lawyer. When Cohen's will was read, his considerable fortune was divided among various Chicago charities, colleges and hospitals. His faithful housekeeper, Gabriella, inherited one hundred thousand dollars and planned her return to Mexico with family to begin a comfortable life. Anne Dailey, Cohen's devoted secretary of thirty-five years, received a like sum and immediately began retirement in Jacksonville, on Florida's east coast.

Peter was devastated at the news of Cohen's death. He went to Chicago for the funeral and stayed at the lawyer's apartment at the executor's request. The unit was to go on the market ten days after Cohen's death, but a codicil to the will specifically instructed that he be given access to the lakeshore apartment during that time. Cohen's sister-in-law insisted Peter honor those wishes, and now he sat at his friend's desk. Across from him, Cohen's lawyer was reading Samuel's bequest to Peter Noble.

Hank Moser was asked to repeat the figure. "Five million dollars, after taxes," recited the lawyer. "That was Sam's wish."

Peter sat in shock. Five million dollars. What had he done to deserve such an enormous amount? He repeated the figure aloud twice. Moser had him sign several forms and then it was done. "Oh, I almost forgot." He lifted two manila envelopes from his case and pushed them across the desk. "I was to give these to you. Sam said you'd know what to do with them."

Peter picked them up, recognizing Samuel's script. He knew instinctively what was inside the packages—transcripts of Carl Goldman's meeting with Cohen at the restaurant six months ago. Insurance.

Hank Moser stood and offered his hand to Peter Noble. "You're a lucky man, Peter. Samuel must have thought highly of you."

Peter smiled at the lawyer. "I had no idea . . ."

"Well, it's a lot of money. You have any plans?"

"Sam would tell me not to do anything rash."

Moser laughed. "Yes, he would. He'd be right too."

Peter smiled again as they walked to the entry. They paused at the door to shake hands. "Nice meeting you, Peter. Take care."

"I'll do that. Thanks for your help, Hank."

"My pleasure. Samuel Cohen was quite a man. A good partner. Goodnight, Peter."

"Goodnight."

He shut the oak door and went into the living room. A bottle of chilled wine and a single glass sat in the middle of the low coffee table. He poured the wine and flipped a switch to start a fire. Peter picked up a remote from the table and turned off the lights. Flames danced across the ceramic logs, outlining his face in yellow light. Far below him, the sunset washed faint rust and gold colors on glass and steel high-rises along Lake Shore Drive. Weaving strings of headlights wound their way along the lake's border.

Peter took his wineglass and went over to the large picture window overlooking Chicago and its lake. His heaviness suddenly lifted. Out beyond the lights, Lake Michigan was a vast, beguiling pool of dark blue. Samuel Cohen would have loved it.

"Here's to you, Gramps. And to you, Sam. I miss you both."

He lifted his glass. "And to the Fortunate Orphans."

# EPILOGUE

In Thionville, Auguste Schell sat on the Corsican's money for six months before he began tapping his windfall. Within a year, he sold his inn for a modest profit and moved to Saint Maarten. He was careful to stay on the Dutch half of the Caribbean island shared with France.

When Myron Soleski first returned to Marquette, Michigan, he regaled his wife with stories of his European travels, but left out important details. His uncanny skills with machinery were still intact, and those odd jobs provided him with spending money. He used some of his earnings to travel to Superior, Wisconsin, for a summer reunion with Ole Johnson. When the two old veterans sat in Johnson's rooftop garden they looked across the harbor at the lights of Duluth and relived their role in the Battle of the Bulge. After their wives went to bed, Myron Soleski swore the bar owner to secrecy and told Johnson the truth about his trip to the continent. Problems with his foot wound troubled Soleski until his death two years later. Ole Johnson attended Soleski's funeral and outlived his friend by four years.

As the result of a debilitating stroke, Dawson O'Reilly never spoke again to the members of the Fortunate Orphans. The damage was done during one of his more caustic arguments with his in-laws on Christmas Day. The injury to his heart and brain was compounded by cirrhosis of the liver. The old policeman now spends his days in a recliner in front of his television. He remains speechless.

Ken Wolf finally gave up his consulting business to spend long quiet evenings reading and working on challenging puzzles. He and his wife, Mary, take cruises to parts of the world they have always wanted to explore. His health remains good and he talks with William Noble's grandson at least once a year

Former First Sergeant Burt Swanson still keeps regular hours on the golf courses at Hot Springs Village in Arkansas. He never shared his role in The Project with his wife and, like the others, he remained ignorant of their mistake with Weismann.

Aside from Christmas cards, he does not stay in touch with his fellow veterans.

Peter Noble returned from Chicago and resigned from his job with the county. He sold the South Minneapolis bungalow and moved permanently to his newly-remodeled cabin in Wisconsin. There, on a frigid January morning, he scattered William Noble's ashes among a stand of bare trees, by a road deep with virgin snow.

He took Samuel Cohen's advice and banked his inheritance for a year without touching it. He eventually funded an annual fellowship for two public high school history teachers who show a particular interest in World War Two. The award is named for The Fortunate Orphans.